THE
OF POWER

※※※※

With the captive Seagryn in the center, the Arlian soldiers launched the boat into the river. Seagryn watched the riverbank recede as it was rowed away from Tunyian Falls. Then he turned instantly into a monstrous tugolith.

The soldiers had only time for brief screams of terror as the boat broke in half under the huge animal's weight. Half of them fell into the water, and the others clung vainly to pieces of the boat as the current began dragging them toward the falls.

Seagryn was also in the water, surprised by the buoyancy of his great body. Then, just before going over the falls, he discovered another fact about tugoliths.

Tugoliths couldn't swim!

By Robert Don Hughes
Published by Ballantine Books:

Pelmen the Powershaper

Book One
THE PROPHET OF LAMATH

Book Two
THE WIZARD IN WAITING

Book Three
THE POWER AND THE PROPHET

Wizard & Dragon

Book One
THE FORGING OF THE DRAGON

THE FORGING OF THE DRAGON

Book One of
Wizard & Dragon

Robert Don Hughes

A Del Rey Book
BALLANTINE BOOKS • NEW YORK

A Del Rey Book
Published by Ballantine Books

Copyright © 1989 by Robert Don Hughes

Library of Congress Catalog Card Number: 88-92845

ISBN 0-345-33744-1

Manufactured in the United States of America

First Edition: May 1989

Cover Art by Romas
Map by Shelly Shapiro

To our Bronwynn,
WHO LEARNED TO READ WHILE
IT WAS BEING WRITTEN—

AND ALSO PLAYED SOME OF THE PARTS.

TABLE OF CONTENTS

Chapter One

ALTERSHAPE

ON most days the people of Lamath worked hard at being prudish. But at weddings, especially occasions of this magnitude, the bonds that bound their passions seemed loosely tied indeed. The fragrance of a thousand freshly cut blossoms made a sweet-tasting syrup of the humid air. Shockingly bright garlands hung from every spire of the estate, and its walls echoed with nervous giggles. Today it would happen!

Lamathians thoroughly enjoyed seeing a good match being made, and this promised to be the stellar mating of the year—Elaryl, lovely blond daughter of a ruling elder, married to Seagryn, the rising star of the clergy. The matrons pouring the punch couldn't help but flush at the thought. But that didn't keep them from thinking . . .

They knew Elaryl, of course—had known her since her priestly father had placed her upon his lap as he sat in the nearby city of Valus and administered the laws of the region. Old Talarath had really been rather young then, but even as a young man he'd seemed old. By now he'd been their ruling elder so long he had to be old. And of course, the child upon his knee had been cute—*far* easier to look at than Talarath, even then.

Now . . . wonder upon wonders! She was a daughter any mother would cherish—a flawless face whose little nose was given dignity by eyes as piercing as her father's, large, frank lips that only stopped short of being pouty due to her resolute commitment to purity, and a chin as firm as her convictions. Elaryl was a good girl. Anyone could tell just by looking. Of course, tonight . . .

And then there was Seagryn, whom none of them knew at all, other than the fact that his mind sparkled like one of the gems embedded in the High Hall of City Lamath. They'd heard him speak, and his tongue thrilled them, for it could pry pieces of the tradition out of hidden places in their memories and fashion these bits together into ideas so artfully that even the densest among them could understand! Not to mention—the matrons mentioned to one another repeatedly with much gleeful cackling—the fact that he was built more like a warrior than a cleric. He had a jaw on him, too—and green eyes and thick bushy eyebrows that seemed especially designed to search out the faltering in the very back rows and demand that they listen to his lessons. He was a fine one, that Seagryn, destined to judge someday as a ruling elder. Perhaps when old Talarath departed? The matrons poured punch and planned the future, and a joyous time was had by all.

Seagryn stood at his window on the third floor of Talarath's mansion, and surveyed the festivities below. He was happy—and that worried him. He could not allow his emotions to dash wherever they chose. Those plump little ladies who cast admiring glances up at his window didn't really know him—they didn't know him at all. Throughout this week-long celebration, his sleep had been plagued by waking dreams, memories of the monster he'd once been . . .

None of his own people were here, of course. Bourne was far away in western Lamath, a poor region lightly regarded by those in the capital city on the flood plain. Seagryn had left it so long ago he no longer considered it his home anymore. He was an educated easterner, a top student, a man moving up—

"*Seagryn!* What in the Name of the Name we do not speak are you doing here!"

Gasping with surprise, Seagryn whirled around to face the lovely features of his betrothed. Elaryl had cocked an eyebrow so as to convey both shock and flirtation at the same time, and he was momentarily confused. "Why—I thought I was supposed to be here, that this was to be my room to—"

"Well of course it is!" Elaryl laughed, all pretense of surprise disappearing. Then her high forehead furrowed knowingly. "Did you forget? It's the custom!"

"Oh. Oh, yes. I remember." Lamathian custom dictated that, just prior to any wedding ceremony, the bride and groom were "accidentally" to encounter one another in a private place. In less pious settings, this often resulted in a delay of the proceedings—in fact, the old grandmothers liked to predict the longevity of a union based upon the length of this "chance" encounter.

If so, theirs would be a brief marriage indeed, for old Talarath would doubtless intervene soon. This was a formal ceremony in an elder's home, and events would begin on schedule and be done properly. To be honest, Seagryn felt a bit relieved at that. His courtship of Elaryl had been carefully supervised, with so few opportunities for passion in private that Seagryn had scarcely even touched her. She'd teased him about that, wondering aloud if he even knew how to demonstrate his affection. He let her mock. Seagryn kept his emotions tucked deep inside his broad chest, side by side with the memories that had driven him from Bourne. He valued this woman as he had no other person in his life, and that was the cause of his worry. If she should know— if she should learn—

"Seagryn, are you all right?"

"Hmm?" He saw the concern that had replaced her smile, and cursed himself for burdening her with his own worries on this most joyous of days. "I . . . believe I'm . . . nervous," Seagryn managed to mutter.

"Of course you are! Bridegrooms are *supposed* to be."

"Are they?" he murmured absently. This time Elaryl scowled.

"What *is* it?" she demanded.

"Nothing," he said, but the word soured on his lips, and he trembled with self-revulsion. The magnitude of the lie he'd lived so long suddenly crashed in upon him. He could no longer inflict it upon this precious lady! He turned his back to his bride. "My dear, there is something I must confess, something I cannot hide any longer—"

"Wait," Elaryl stopped him. "I know what you're about to say."

"You do?" Seagryn gasped, spinning to face her.

"I do." She nodded solemnly. "The other girls all told me. It's the true purpose of this meeting."

"What?" The cleric frowned.

"It's a . . . a thoughtful time for both groom and bride—and it tends to prompt premarital confessions. Am I right?"

"I . . . I—"

"You suddenly see me as your bride to be and feel unworthy and want to tell me about all the other women in your life."

"But it's not about—"

"Seagryn, don't you realize that I don't feel worthy of you, either?" Elaryl's eyes glistened with forming tears, but didn't blink. Her gaze never left his as she shook her head, and he saw light from the window dance across her golden curls. "If you confess, don't you see that I would have to confess, too? And my father will be coming through that door any moment to fetch us! I can't, Seagryn—and you don't need to." Despite the tears that still threatened to course her cheeks, Elaryl now wore an expression of stately serenity. "It doesn't matter what you've done, in any case. I'll love you forever."

Stunned, Seagryn could think of only one response. He lurched forward and clutched her to him, nearly smothering her against his barrel chest. So. The dreamlike memories of a monster in Bourne could be put to rest at last—for Elaryl loved him. Then he picked her up and kissed her.

She finally tore her face away from him, laughing once again. "So you *do* know how!" Elaryl threw both arms around his neck and squeezed. Perhaps, Seagryn thought, the ceremony would be delayed after all . . .

Then the door flew open. "Yes," Talarath said. The couple quickly parted.

It amazed Seagryn just how negative the old man could make such a positive word sound. "Finished?" Talarath asked. He didn't raise his voice. He didn't move his wrinkled forehead. Yet somehow he managed to express such deep suspicion that Seagryn felt slightly dizzy.

"Yes, Father," Elaryl answered dutifully.

"Good. Ranoth arrives at any moment. You'll both need to greet him."

"Sir—" Seagryn tried to interrupt, but without success as Talarath continued:

"The greeting must be stately but swift. There is danger in public appearances before crowds of this size. We're all aware these days of Marwandian marauders. They'll know, surely, that much of the Ruling Council will be present today. If they truly intend to make this region their own, they'd be fools not to attack us and, while these loathsome magic users are many things, unfortunately they are not fools. Come." Talarath started to turn away.

Magic users. The term struck at Seagryn's heart. "Sir—"

The old man turned around to face Seagryn squarely. "Yes?" he asked. Talarath spoke with great honesty and humility. He put no reproach into either his tone of voice or his expression. Yet somehow, as always, Talarath made Seagryn feel like a burdensome child whose words were to be tolerated, not heard. Seagryn hesitated—and lost the moment. "I understand how you feel, son," Talarath said brusquely—but of course, he didn't. The ruling elder of southern Lamath stalked out the door and down the hall.

Elaryl grabbed his arm. "Come on." Duty called, and dutifully Seagryn responded.

Guards waited at the palace door; when Talarath reached the bottom step, they formed a phalanx and pushed a pathway out through the crowd. The people cheered at the first sight of the couple and kept on cheering as if resolved to burst Seagryn's eardrums. He covered his ears, but Elaryl elbowed him in the ribs, and he turned to see her smiling at him ferociously. He smiled back—a grimace, really—then followed her lead and raised his hand to wave.

A troop of riders broke over a nearby hill. The assembled guests quickly disregarded the wedding party and turned their attention to the road. As these horsemen distributed themselves strategically around the palace grounds, a new set of warriors was sighted, and the cheering began again in earnest. This group moved at a stately pace, bearing among them an ornate litter completely enclosed by fish-satin curtains. Seagryn stood behind Talarath as he waited amid the crowd for the litter's arrival. When it reached him, he called out, "Silence!" The cheering abated.

Ranoth tossed aside the curtains that surrounded him and hopped nimbly from the litter. He was a spry little man with a firm grip—both in his wiry hand and in his equally wiry mind. Ranoth understood clearly his role in his world, and played it with satisfaction. The ruling elder of City Lamath and the Rivers regions that surrounded it, he was first among equals on the Ruling Council—and Seagryn's mentor. Now he raised his sinewy arm in greeting and called to Elaryl and Seagryn, "My children! Come! Come help an old man who needs assistance!"

Seagryn smiled at this ridiculous order, but didn't question it. He took Elaryl by the elbow and led her firmly toward the litter. Ranoth's very presence restored some of the confidence that days spent with Talarath had shorn from him. He felt much better already.

"Ah, children." Ranoth smiled with obvious pleasure. "What

a joy to see you two linked at last. You've had a few moments together, already?'' he asked, a naughty little twinkle in his eye.

Seagryn began, "We were—"

"You arrived precisely on schedule," Talarath interrupted. "No trouble?"

Ranoth's eyes lidded slightly—hiding something, Seagryn knew. He felt well acquainted with such behavior. "Shall we talk inside?"

Talarath swung around hard and gestured stiffly to his warriors. The path to the palace door reappeared immediately, as if by magic. The word sprang unbidden to Seagryn's mind. It nauseated him.

Moments later they were inside, and the heavy doors were bolted shut behind them.

"Now," Talarath muttered quietly. "What trouble? An ambush on the road?"

"Nothing today . . ." Ranoth muttered, leaving the truth dangling unspoken.

"But?"

"But they're clearly abroad. Reports of them everywhere." Ranoth's voice lowered another level. "Fearful reports."

"Quit that!" Elaryl snapped in Seagryn's ear, and the young man spun around to look at her. "You're crushing my hand!"

Seagryn relaxed his grip immediately, and Elaryl jerked her hand away and cradled it tenderly against her bosom. Her expression quickly softened—for Ranoth's benefit, Seagryn knew—and she explained, "He's acting a bit strangely today, my Father. He says he's nervous."

Ranoth's eyes danced merrily as he studied the woman's lovely face. "He's excited. I quite understand!"

"What reports?" Talarath demanded. The old man never allowed the free flow of conversation to interfere with important details. There was no distracting him.

"Odd things. Very odd."

"Magic?" Talarath snarled. "Was magic used?"

"One tale I heard held that a group of our people were attacked on a road very near here. You've not been told this?"

"Weddings have a way of obscuring the truly important," Talarath grunted, never noticing the impact his comment made upon his daughter's face. "Go on?"

"Out of nowhere, a gigantic *bear* appeared and proceeded to rend apart every Marwandian in sight." Seagryn noticed the strong emphasis Ranoth had placed on the word "bear" and it puzzled him. Talarath suddenly stepped backward and stiffened his shoulders.

"Perhaps these are things better discussed in private. Elaryl, have you no final preparations to make?"

"Of course, Father." Elaryl knew she was being dismissed.

"More preparations?" Ranoth asked, seizing her hand before she could walk away. "Is it possible that such a one could make herself even more beautiful?"

Elaryl smiled chastely and murmured, "Thank you."

"And you, Seagryn?" Talarath mumbled.

"Ah—yes." Seagryn nodded, and he reached out to take Elaryl's arm to lead her down the hall.

"Seagryn can stay," Ranoth said quietly; then he added with a cackle, "Afraid to let her go, lad? No wonder!"

Seagryn glanced at Elaryl, and she nodded briefly and glided quickly away. He turned back to the conversation, feeling heady at having been included. But then, that was always Ranoth's way—

"He attacked *Marwandians*, you say?" Talarath was asking.

Ranoth nodded, then he added, "And ate them."

Talarath trembled with disgust, then spat out, "Magic user!"

"Yes," Ranoth said thoughtfully. "What about you, Seagryn?" he suddenly asked. "Do you know anything about all this?"

Seagryn had been trying to make sense of the limited information while struggling with his own private terrors. The question took him completely by surprise. "What? Me?" He grunted too sharply. "Nothing."

His response puzzled Ranoth, who peered up at him with concern. "Son, are you all right?"

"Yes . . . yes, of course," Seagryn replied, forcing himself to slow down his rate of speech and to seek to turn the conversation elsewhere. "I . . . I guess I'm just . . . dismayed by this talk of . . . marauding magic users, that's all! I . . . I don't understand! Why would they invade us? What have we done to them?"

"We've done nothing to them," Talarath said. "It's Arl, far to the south, that's the cause of all this. The armies of Arl are putting pressure upon these disorganized savages who call themselves Marwandians, and driving them toward us."

Ranoth tilted his head back and seemed to study the frescoed ceiling, but Seagryn knew from experience the elder's eyes were turned inward, not outward. "It's all a part of the larger troubles, of course. Why we never see representatives of the Remnant about any longer—why the peasants of Pleclypsa keep drowning their masters—''

Seagryn relaxed inside. "The One we do not name is bringing judgment upon them for their unbelief," he said firmly. It was the proper answer—the one these very elders had themselves taught him—but this time, both men turned to look at him as if he'd uttered an obscenity.

Ranoth sniffed and glanced away, but Seagryn knew the old cleric had not taken his inward eyes off of him. "Ever notice, Seagryn, how judgment upon anyone leaves scorch marks on all those nearby?" Seagryn pondered that, but thought it wise not to try to reply. He was being instructed and he knew enough to recognize it. "I'm not really certain that the One we do not name is all that pleased that the old One Land is so divided up. After all, there were once believers in all the lands . . .''

Seagryn didn't allow his mouth to sag open in shock, but he felt it. What his mentor was saying bordered upon heresy! He glanced over at Talarath and saw his future father-in-law spearing Ranoth with a look of warning.

"The key issue here," Talarath snarled, "is Marwandians in the forests and magic users at our very door. Something must be done." Seagryn watched unspoken thoughts pass between them.

Relieved to have their eyes off him, Seagryn muttered "Dark knows, that's the truth." It was an offhanded comment, one designed to finish the matter and direct the conversation elsewhere. He regretted it immediately. Both Ranoth and Talarath stared at him.

"What do you know of Dark?" Talarath snapped.

The question shocked him. "Why . . . he's . . . he's a prophet, isn't he? People use his name all the time . . .''

"What people?" Ranoth asked, more kindly than Talarath but with no less intensity.

"Why . . . the . . . people in the villages." Seagryn shrugged. "You know how they are. Is he a real person, though? I thought he was a legend."

Ranoth peered at him for a moment, then abruptly turned to Talarath and smiled. "But why are we wasting such a marvelous occasion on such worthless chatter? Your daughter marries to-day—and to a wonderful boy!"

"Yes," Talarath agreed quietly. "Very promising."

Seagryn had been referred to as "promising" all his life. The term had long since lost any complimentary meaning and become a kind of reproach, as if those who used it were actually saying, "But what has he done with his gifts?"

"We should be celebrating!" Ranoth smiled, raising both his arms jubilantly. "Talarath, come! Give the signal to begin! Let's get these young people joined at the feet!"

Talarath turned his head to search for the chief of his household staff. "Find Elaryl. Bring the shoes," he commanded without enthusiasm.

The ceremony itself was to be held in the inner patio of the mansion. There they could be open to the sky, as custom demanded, yet still could be securely defended. This courtyard already teemed with dignitaries. Elaryl ignored them as she swept around the perimeter of the court toward her beloved. Behind her ran a servant carrying an ornate, oddly shaped trio of shoes. Elaryl reached out to grab Seagryn and bussed him on the cheek, then unceremoniously dropped to the floor and hiked up her skirt. "Come on, get these on. We haven't much time."

"Elaryl!" Talarath scolded. "A bit more modesty, please!"

"Let them work it out, Talarath," said Ranoth, grabbing his peer by the gown and pulling him toward the courtyard. "They're going to have to, soon enough. We'll be expected at the front." The crowd parted to let them pass through toward the altar.

Elaryl continued to lace feverishly. Seagryn knelt beside her, taking the shoe the servant offered. It had been tailored to fit his left foot. Except for its size, it was the twin of the shoe Elaryl laced up her right calf. He sat down, put the slipper on, and laced it up. Then he waited as Elaryl slipped her left foot into the joint shoe fashioned to hold both of their feet snugly together. She scooted over next to him, and he pushed his right foot in beside her left, their ankles rubbing together in the process. They then worked in concert to lace their calves together and to help one another to stand. Elaryl slipped her arm around his waist and leaned up to kiss his cheek. "Are you ready to be laced to me for life?" she asked sweetly.

"I'm ready," he answered. But was *she*? If it should ever be learned that—but this was Elaryl. She'd said she would forgive him anything. Perhaps one day he could even tell her—

The chief of the household staff had been searching for them frantically. Now he raced up to them and bent over to gasp for breath as he pleaded, "It's time!" Seagryn and Elaryl obediently hobbled out into the patio.

Those guests who stood between the pair and the altar stepped aside. A choir began chanting as they limped forward. The event of the year had begun.

Seagryn was only vaguely aware of the enraptured sighs and stifled sobs of those nearby who watched them struggle forward. He focused all his attention on staying in step with his grunting bride. It was considered bad form for a pair to fall flat on their faces on their wedding day. It revealed that they were not in rhythm with one another, and necessitated postmarital counseling. Halfway to the altar, Seagryn realized that their laces were far too tight. Before they reached Ranoth he'd had time to wonder if *all* brides and grooms laced themselves too tightly, since they'd never experienced this before? That could certainly account for the terrible expressions of pain he'd seen on the faces of certain wedding parties in the past. Then they arrived before Ranoth, each gasping with relief and hugging the other for support as the small elder began the ceremony:

"You have chosen to link your paths together in the bonds of wedlock, to knot your destinies from this day forward. Hobbling one another, walking on three legs instead of four, you are nevertheless also supporting one another, dependent *upon* one another. You are linked before the land and before the One we do not name. This is a holy moment, for lives so linked cannot be—"

He went on, but Seagryn suddenly couldn't listen. He'd heard a clashing begin outside, the noise of swords hammering upon shields. "Attack!" he told himself with great disbelief. "Marwandians—attacking here? *Now?*" He looked at Elaryl, but she appeared unaware of the commotion. The radiance in her eyes rivaled the glistening highlights of the afternoon sun on her hair, and suddenly black despair clutched again at his heart. "Hurry, Ranoth," he urged his mentor silently. "Hurry, before they spoil it!" The noises outside the mansion grew louder. The crowd began to buzz with anxiety.

"A momentary disturbance! We're safe within this house," Talarath announced with crisp authority. "Relax and enjoy the proceedings."

But Seagryn could not relax. He heard the clash of spears on armor, heard men screaming, and his memories of that incident in Bourne, so long ago yet made so fresh by a week of dreaming, could be restrained no longer. He dropped to his left knee and struggled urgently to untie the laces that bound him to his beloved.

"Seagryn." Elaryl smiled down anxiously. "Seagryn!" she

said again, her tone scolding but still hushed. "What are you
doing?"

"You said you'd forgive me anything—"

"But—but this is terrible luck! It's just not done! You're embarrassing me in front of—"

Seagryn spotted a dirk in Ranoth's belt. Without bothering to
ask for it, he jerked it out and cut the laces. "No time—" he
murmured. Then the doors at the back of the patio shattered
inward, and the crowd surged screaming toward the altar.

Seagryn felt the blood rushing to his brain as he scooped
Elaryl into his arms then hoisted her above his head. "Give me
room!" he roared—and he tossed his dumbstruck lady over the
altar. "You'll be crushed—" he warned again, but it was already too late for those nearest him. In that moment Seagryn
became a tugolith.

Before turning to race across the flagstones at the marauders
pouring in behind him, Seagryn took the time to watch Elaryl
bounce up to her feet. As he'd known they would, her shocked
eyes immediately sought him out—and that firm jaw gaped open
in horror. She was quick. It took only a moment for her to
recognize who—and what—he was and to understand what had
befallen. Then it came: revulsion, disgust, and repugnance.
Seagryn had been right. There was at least one thing a daughter
of old Talarath could *not* forgive—magic.

His mind didn't change. He remained Seagryn, up until this
moment a prominent cleric of Lamath, henceforth a hated out-
cast. In this land where the use of magic had long been regarded
as the most heinous of sins, Seagryn had revealed himself to be
a wizard. His dreams had shattered with those stained-glass
doors behind him. He was lost—set adrift by that very Power in
whom he had trusted.

He now wore the body of a two-ton beast with an armor-plated
hide and a single enormous horn. And one thing was certain—
if these Marwandian raiders had just ruined his life, he certainly
had the wherewithal to ruin theirs in vengeance. Bellowing in
rage, Seagryn whirled and charged.

One moment, Marwandians were pouring in the doorway.
The next, they were pouring back out of it, screaming just as
lustily as the guests. Many never made it out of the hall, being
squashed flat instead upon the flagstones. Those who did get out
of the palace fared no better; with room to swing his horn,
Seagryn was now spitting Maris upon it. Most of these he slung
aside, throwing the bodies forty feet at a heave. But two corpses

did not slip readily off. He dipped his head between his wrinkled forelegs and flung these skyward. Then—to his own horror—he opened his vast maw and swallowed them, much as a boy might eat peanuts by tossing them first into the air. He paused then and looked around. That's when he noticed that his great bulk had torn off the whole front wall of the mansion and that the roof was sagging dangerously close to collapse. He thundered back to it and wedged his body under the weakened structure. "Out!" he heard his tugolith voice rumble. It sounded nothing like his own. On the other hand, it did sound far more powerful . . . "Everyone leave this house!" he roared.

They did, apparently, but no one came past Seagryn. There were other exits, and these were evidently preferable to stepping anywhere near this Mari-eating monster.

Once he felt certain all were safe, Seagryn began to relax. As suddenly as he'd turned tugolith, he again became a human. He heard the rumble above him and sprinted toward the open air. The masonry collapsed behind him, and the impact threw him forward onto his belly. Dust rained down around him, and Seagryn covered the back of his head. He'd not noticed the noise—there'd been so much of that around him for the past few hours that he'd grown accustomed to it. He did notice the awful silence that followed that thunderous collapse. He lay facedown in the grass, unmoving, marveling at how quickly a palace—or a life—could crumble.

Eventually he had to get up. He coughed as he struggled to his knees, for dust still clogged the air. He shook his robes, then glanced around for the people. They had to be nearby, and he couldn't resist making some attempt to justify himself. After all, hadn't he routed the Marwandian invaders? He scanned the horizon until he spotted the crowd, clustered under a large tree near the road. He started for it.

A large portion of the throng departed as soon as he made a move toward them. Ranoth didn't, however, nor did Talarath. Elaryl, too, waited for him, although he'd never seen such an odd expression on her face. He knew what it meant—though he longed to believe otherwise. Ranoth waited until he got within thirty feet, then shouted:

"Stop right there, magic user!"

Seagryn stopped, and waited, but Ranoth said no more. When it became apparent that no one else intended to speak, Seagryn made his attempt. "I . . . I was only trying to help—"

"You destroyed the house of my ancestors!" Talarath croaked. "You call that help?"

"But I saved you from the Marwandians!"

"Now who will save us from you?" This came from Ranoth—his teacher!

"I swear I will do nothing to harm any Lamathian or—"

"Then prove it by leaving! Immediately!"

Seagryn paused, his mind racing. For years he'd dreamed of meeting exactly this reaction. He knew there was no hope. Yet now that he faced it, he found he couldn't give it up without at least trying to make them understand. "This isn't my fault!" he pleaded. "Do you think I want to be like this?"

"It makes no difference!" Ranoth responded, his voice quavering with passion. "Just go!" Seagryn was startled. He'd never seen the ruling elder this agitated.

"But—but I'm a Lamathian! I belong here!"

Ranoth drew himself up straight and squared his shoulders, then stretched a bony finger out at Seagryn and shook it accusingly. "Young man, the people of Lamath are people of faith! Two centuries ago we withdrew from the magic users and other heathens because we could not abide their presence among us! You suddenly reveal yourself to be one of these infidels, a spy, a mudgecurdle in our midst. And do you now expect us—the arbiters of Lamathian justice—to let you remain? Go, Seagryn—or whatever your true name is! Go swiftly, or we shall certainly send an army equipped to dispatch you! Go!" Ranoth now pointed that trembling finger westward toward the region of the hated Marwandians.

"But Ranoth, just *today* you spoke of—of drawing together with the neighboring lands, of joining together with those of the other fragments to—"

"I said nothing of the kind!" Ranoth screamed, his face turning a brilliant red. "You are a liar, a heathen, and a magic user! Begone!"

"But the Marwandians will not welcome one who routed them—"

"Who ate them whole?" Talarath added scornfully. "What they do with you is their affair. Depart, Seagryn. But know this—we'll have an army on your trail by the morning!"

Desperate now, Seagryn searched through the crowd for just one understanding pair of eyes. He saw only terror and hatred there—even in the gaze of Elaryl.

"You said you could forgive me anything," he murmured

flatly. "Can't you forgive me this?" She trembled at his question, then hid her face against her father's sleeve.

That was enough. A few more words passed between him and Ranoth, but he couldn't recall them later. Elaryl had cut him off, and he saw no use in further attempts to redeem himself. After a moment, he shuffled away, moving westward, not because he'd chosen that course, but because that way had been chosen for him by those who'd been his life's authority. After an unremembered time of walking, he was deep in an unknown forest. He walked on . . .

Several hours later he came to his senses and stopped beside a large clump of bushes. "I've got to make plans," he announced aloud. An anger he'd kept dammed up within himself for years suddenly exploded, and he raised a defiant fist to the sky. "Very well then! I'll *be* a wizard!" Energized by his commitment, he thrust off toward the west with thoughts of vengeance boiling through his mind. Now, at least, he had chosen his fate.

He stalked away so rapidly he didn't see the enormous bear rise up out of the clump of brush to watch him go. The bear's black lips curled away from its fangs, which gleamed pink in the light of the setting sun. A malevolent intelligence burned in the great beast's eyes, a human intelligence that was at the same time more than human—and utterly, irredeemably selfish.

When Seagryn disappeared over a tree-covered rise, the bear dropped to its forepaws and shuffled out of the underbrush. Then it sniffed the ground where Seagryn had stood. "Stinks of tugolith." The giant bear snorted. Then it lifted its huge head, eyes gleaming, and followed.

Chapter Two

※※※※

DARK TIDINGS

SEAGRYN sat alone beneath the blackest night he could remember and faced the sobering truth. "I can't become a wizard! I loathe wizardry!"

"You'll grow out of that," a voice above him said, and Seagryn grunted in shock and leaped blindly away from it. "A good thing, too," the voice continued, "since self-hatred can really cause you problems. Are you all right?"

Seagryn was not all right. He'd landed spread-eagled upon a pile of loose gravel and had slid several feet down it. He pushed himself up on his hands and peered into the darkness. "Who's there?" he demanded.

"Some consider me the voice of the Power."

Clearly it was a youth, Seagryn thought to himself, and an impudent one! "The One we do not name is ageless!" he barked. "Surely that One's voice has had time to change!"

The unseen stranger chuckled. "I bet you imagine the Power as an ancient grandfather with a floor-length beard."

"I do not discuss the One in such disrespectful terms," Seagryn answered self-righteously. "Nor do I appreciate talking to a person I cannot *see!*"

"You can't see the Power yet you talk to H—"

"Who are you?" Seagryn roared, leaping to his feet. That was a mistake. The gravel slid beneath him, and he wound up back on his face, this time a few feet further down the slope.

The youth cleared his throat, then announced, "I am Dark

15

the prophet. And I would be happy for you to see me, but you've neglected to start a fire. I wish you'd done so, since that would have made it a lot easier to find you."

Seagryn pushed himself onto his knees and began scraping bits of imbedded sand from his burning palms. "I had nothing with which to start a fire," he grumbled.

"There's wood—"

"But I have no flints!" Seagryn shouted. "I had no time to prepare for this journey," he added sourly.

"Oh, you had time," the boy chided. "You just chose not to face the fact you were leaving."

Seagryn carefully got to his feet and stared savagely toward the voice. Unfortunately, his fierce expression was quite lost in the darkness. "And what do you mean by that?"

"You know."

"I don't know, but I should like to know!" Seagryn challenged, sliding cautiously forward through the gravel as he balled up his fists. "Who are you? Why are you following me?"

"I didn't follow you; I met you here," the voice answered with youthful annoyance. "And I already told you who I am."

"You said you were Dark the prophet!"

"Then you did hear?" the boy asked sarcastically.

"Show yourself!" Seagryn demanded.

"You want me to pull the moon down through the clouds and hold it up to my face? You're the powershaper, not I."

"And you are an impudent boy!" Seagryn proclaimed. "Continue to taunt me and you'll suffer for it!"

"What'll you do?" the voice mocked. "Run your horn through me and eat me for supper?"

Seagryn's stomach knotted with self-revulsion, and he fought a sudden dizziness. The boy *knew*. Guilt gushed through him. After a silent moment, the youth asked:

"Are you still there?"

Seagryn didn't answer. Instead, he sat down in the gravel and put his head in his hands.

"You know, most powershapers can make fire, if they try . . ." the boy suggested.

"What's a powershaper?" Seagryn mumbled. He no longer looked toward the voice. His head ached.

"A powershaper shapes the powers. He—or she—is a wizard. Like you."

"You deny that you followed me here, yet you know that I'm . . . cursed . . . with wizardry. How is that?"

A pair of feet hit the ground next to him. The boy had evidently been on top of a large rock, or up a tree. "I really think I've answered that already," the lad groused. "I can't help it if you don't believe me."

"I've heard of Dark the prophet all my life," Seagryn muttered scornfully.

"Are you sure?" asked the boy. "Or does it just seem that you have? You'd be surprised how quickly people come to believe they've been doing something forever—"

"Does your mother know where you are?" Seagryn asked. When the reply didn't come immediately he enjoyed the silence, feeling smug.

"Yes, she did. Does," the boy said after a moment.

"What?"

"She told me—tells me—well, I guess I'd better say she will tell me that she did. Not that she has the gift; it's just that she has a sense about these things."

Seagryn frowned into the darkness. "I don't understand what you're—"

"Gets confusing, doesn't it? To me, too. I get ahead of myself, and it's hard sometimes to stay in the present."

"What are you talking about!" Seagryn barked.

"Oh." The boy sighed. "The future. What will be. That sort of thing."

Seagryn snorted. "No one can tell the future."

"Wrong!" the lad corrected. "There are plenty who tell the future. There are very few of us who actually know it." Seagryn groaned, and rubbed the knotted muscles in the back of his neck. "And those who actually do, if they have any sense, don't tell what they know. Otherwise, they might get themselves beaten!" Seagryn groaned again, but the lad seemed to be talking to himself now and took no notice. "Unfortunately, I tend to tell too much. A character flaw, I realize. My s'mother says I'll grow out of it, but who can believe her? She doesn't know the future." The boy sighed heavily, as if he bore the weight of fifty years upon his shoulders instead of a mere fifteen. "Why do I have to?"

Seagryn waited a moment. "Are you finished?"

"Am I boring you?"

"If you're finished, then please leave me in peace. You apparently know a great deal about me. Perhaps you know also that this has been the worst day of my life."

"Not quite," the boy muttered.

"What!" snarled Seagryn.

"Oh nothing . . . just that there might be worse still in store—"

"Leave me be!"

"I will," the lad mumbled, and Seagryn heard footsteps crunching away. Then they stopped. "One more thing before I go . . ."

"Yes," Seagryn sighed.

"When you hear somebody yelling tomorrow, would you mind responding quickly? It'll be me, and I'd appreciate suffering as little as possible."

Despite its dependence upon a foundation of faith, Seagryn's education had been hedged about by a rigid system of logic. He'd never heard such nonsense in all his life, and the boy's words made him wince up at the dark sky in protest. He said nothing, however, fearing that might encourage the lad to stay, dooming him to listen to this adolescent drivel all night. He waited in silence as the youth departed, reassured by the sound of receding footsteps. Then he got down on his knees to search with his hands for the grassy spot he'd originally occupied. When he found it, he lay down, rolled onto his back, and gazed upward. The sky had grown no brighter. "With my luck, it'll rain tonight," he grumbled. Then he slept.

It did not rain; but with the high humidity and the late summer heat, Seagryn might have been more comfortable if it had rained. He was no outdoorsman. Dreams of flies and snakes and unnamed crawling things plagued his sleep. But throughout the night's fitful naps he was at least oblivious to his tragic personal loss.

Not so in the morning. He awoke sitting straight up and shouting, "Elaryl!" He was at once fully conscious, feeling the burden of his grief settling down around his shoulders to be borne through yet another day. He had lost his love. He had lost his life.

He wasn't at all hungry, and he attributed that at first to his grief. Then he remembered with disgust his feast of the day before. He had consumed—how many fully armed Marwandians? His stomach boiled at the thought, and he wondered momentarily what had happened to all the bits of chain mail and shield. The explanation was both simple and horrible. Magic.

The very word caused a wave of nausea to sweep Seagryn's stomach. He realized again that his strong aversion to its presence in his life would not be easily overcome. While he did need to learn how to manage his curse as swiftly as possible, he decided he shouldn't think about it all that much. He got up, picked a direction, and shuffled forward.

He moved aimlessly—but how could it be otherwise? There were no congregations of the faithful out in these forests, waiting for a leader to come and guide them. Perhaps there would be homeless to care for, but he would have to count himself among them now, not as one who could lend aid. He was lost in this wilderness—a perfect metaphor, he thought grimly, of his own spiritual condition. For in a way he'd not been since he'd been forced to abandon his home so long ago, Seagryn was lost.

He raised his head, and his green eyes narrowed as he tried to peer into the northwest. Would *they* accept him in Bourne, once this was known? No. If anything, Bourne was more rigid than City Lamath itself. Besides, when they heard this news, the simple folk of the west country would be putting it together with the awful appearances years ago of a terrible beast who'd devoured one of their finest young lads. There *had* been a few who actually knew the truth. Did they live still? Would they still look at him with the same revulsion in their faces?

"Yes," he mumbled, tousling his brown hair. "I can't go back there."

He tried to feel grateful that the charade was over. He'd known, somehow, that discovery was inevitable. He was too well known, too closely watched to hide a secret this huge. "Huge," he muttered with bitter irony. Certainly an apt description. "Too huge to hide. Someone had to see me eventually. If—if I could only control it, as the magic users do—" But he could not control it. And to a man of faith that meant that the One who is not named had permitted this calamity to befall him. Seagryn felt betrayed by the very Power he'd led others to worship. He gazed imploringly skyward. "Why?" he begged. "Why would you allow such a horror?"

"Stop where you stand!"

Seagryn was surrounded by Marwandian warriors so quickly he hadn't time to be frightened, only astonished. "Where did you come from?" he asked the circle of faces.

"We live here," grunted one fighter. "The question should rather be where did you come from, although it's obvious from your gown that you're a Lamathian cleric." The man looked around at his raiders. "So the boy was right again."

"What boy?" Seagryn asked, but he closed his mouth when the tips of several lengthy swords danced before his nose. Assuming these instructed him to keep silent, he heeded their pointed urgings.

"What next?" someone asked the leader.

"We can't hunt the bear with a captive in tow—"

"Then let's kill him," another warrior suggested.

"The boy said we would take him back to camp when we found him . . ." the leader murmured to himself.

"Then let's kill him to prove the boy wrong." The same warrior shrugged, and Seagryn frowned at the bloodthirsty fellow. The man frowned back.

"No," the leader growled. "We'd better let Quirl make that decision . . ."

Seagryn noticed an exchange of looks that made him feel uncomfortable. These men knew more about him than they were saying. Did they know he was a wizard? Worse, did they suspect he was the magic user who had stomped or swallowed some of their friends? And was this boy— "He couldn't be Dark the prophet," Seagryn mumbled to himself.

The leader stepped closer and asked, "What did you say?"

"Why are you doing this?" Seagryn demanded. "You don't even belong here! These are Lamathian lands!"

"Silence, priest, or I'll slaughter you here!"

"You should have done that already," the bloodthirsty Marwandian grumbled, drawing the leader's eyes away from Seagryn.

"You shut up, too, mod Herjak," the man said wearily. Then he looked around the circle. "Let's take this priest to Quirl mod Kit so we can get back to hunting the bear. He's nearby today— I can *smell* him."

Someone behind Seagryn gave him a push, and he started walking. He wasn't afraid, which surprised him a little. What he felt most was weariness—he was just tired of the constant stress of the last few weeks and in despair at the sudden collapse of all he'd struggled to build. Was he now about to be butchered in the forest by a band of strangers, just for being a Lamathian priest? What bitter irony, considering his current feelings toward the One who is not named! What a fitting end for one so abandoned as he!

After a fast hike that left Seagryn sticky with sweat, the band stood upon a bluff overlooking a pleasant valley. Directly below them a semicircle of fish-satin tents faced a small stream. A larger semicircle of sharpened timbers formed a rough stockade which enclosed the camp. One of the warriors pushed past him toward a path and slid down it. Then he held his sword in readiness as Seagryn was forced to slide down. Soon the group clustered around him again, and he was escorted to a stile that crossed the stockade wall. Moments later he was being pushed into the tent of Quirl mod Kit, the yellow-mustached Marwandian who commanded this encampment.

"We found this one in the forest," the group leader explained apologetically in the face of Quirl's contemptuous smirk.

"He was waiting there for you, no doubt," Quirl snorted. "You did well in bringing him to me." Then Quirl looked at Seagryn. "I'll say this for the boy. He does a clever job of setting up support for his lies. But what I don't understand is what you Lamathians hope to accomplish by all of this? Are you in league with the bear? Is that it?"

"I don't know what you're talking about."

Quirl snorted again. "Yes, you do. But what do you gain? You hope to frighten us away. But why? This easternmost edge of the Marwilds has no value to you, while to us it is a last retreat from the bear and the armies of Arl! If you think a ruse will drive us from it, you are much mistaken. Nor will we be swayed by this morning's rumors of a horned monster." Quirl's golden mustache twitched as he grinned with half his mouth. "We of the Marwilds recognize the power of magic, but we have better sense than to believe such foolishness."

As he struggled to absorb Quirl's words and make sense of the man's strange conclusions, Seagryn heard the unmistakable crack of a strap hitting a back, and a strangled grunt in response. He jerked upright, his eyes wide. The boy?

"Oh, yes." Quirl smirked. "We caught your little friend, and now he's paying for his constant jokes. Can you tell me why you deserve any better treatment?"

The whip cracked again, somewhere outside the tent. "Seagryn!" he heard the boy cry out. "Seagryn, remember last night?"

Indeed he did, and the memory of that conversation and its implications jolted him into action. "Stop!" he commanded, and he ducked out of the tent. His response was so swift and unexpected that the two guards who had been holding him were left staring at one another. Quirl mod Kit flashed them both a look of incredulous disgust before darting between them and out after Seagryn.

"Stop!" Seagryn shouted at the man who held the strap, but not soon enough to prevent another lash.

"Oww!" Dark hollered. "Didn't you hear the man? He said *stop*! I'm not going to be responsible if he sticks a horn through you—"

Three pairs of hands grabbed Seagryn's arms and shoulders, and he heard Quirl shout "Keep flogging!" at the executioner. Something the lad had said the night before sprang to mind; as the whip was raised again, he wondered if this, too, might be so. "Powershapers can make flame if they try," the boy had said. Seagryn tried.

"Ahh!" shouted the executioner as he dropped his strap to the ground and stepped away to stare at it. "It's on fire!" he gasped. Indeed, it was, and Seagryn, who had willed it so, was as surprised as any of them.

Dark didn't seem surprised at all. "Better turn me and this wizard loose," the boy ordered his captors, "or the next thing to fry will be you."

Quirl looked at the boy, the burning strap, and Seagryn in quick succession, his astonishment evident. "Are—are you a powershaper?" he asked.

Seagryn didn't like the question. Given his loathing for magic, he didn't like it at all. But circumstances demanded that he not quibble with that description just now. He nodded.

Quirl jumped back. "Release him!" he shouted. "Release the boy, too!"

"Dark," the lad said wearily. "The name is Dark." The boy was quickly untied, and he immediately pulled down his brown tunic and turned to Seagryn. "Whew," he muttered, rolling his eyes. "I'm glad that's over." Then he sauntered past Quirl mod Kit and ducked into the leader's tent. Quirl followed him. Seagryn saw little alternative but to go back inside it himself.

"Hello, mod Kit!" Dark was saying cheerfully. The lad had stacked a tower of cushions in a corner of the tent and lay on his stomach across it. Seagryn found it a bit difficult to connect this slight figure to that strange voice that had visited him in the blackness the night before. He'd imagined the lad to be taller, somehow, and gangly and blond—as were most of these Marwandians. But Dark was—dark; he had brown eyes, dark brown hair that curled up at the back of his collar and hung in a straight fringe across his forehead, and deeply tanned skin. Dark winked at him, then went on to his captor, "Didn't I promise that you'd survive yesterday's attack by the bear?"

"You arranged it thus, traitor!" Quirl snarled—then he looked fearfully back at Seagryn. "Are you about to set this tent aflame?"

"No," the fledgling shaper mumbled.

"Then please take a seat and help me understand the purpose to all of this. As you see, your partner has already made himself comfortable."

"Not entirely," Dark grumbled, rubbing his back.

"You were lucky this time," Quirl threatened. "You'd better stay close to your powerful friend, or such misfortune might find you again."

"There's no question of that," Dark snorted. "I know precisely when and where it will. But that's *not* before it will find you, Quirl. Was there any more of this?" The boy gestured with a cup that had held some beverage. Quirl glowered at him, then grabbed the cup away and left the tent, snarling muffled curses. Dark looked knowingly at Seagryn. "They'll try to kill us tonight."

"Who are you, really?" Seagryn demanded.

The boy sighed heavily, then answered with exaggerated weariness, "I am Dark the prophet. I know that sounds incredible: 'He's just a boy; how can one know the name of a prophet who's just a boy; surely Dark the prophet is an old man,' and so on. That's what you've been thinking, right? But I can't help it. I'm Dark. And whatever you believe, I'd appreciate you using the name. You'll be convinced soon enough."

"I suppose you've reviewed our shared future and know the precise instant of that?" Seagryn mocked.

"I do. But we'll be discussing my gift of sight later. Here's Quirl." Dark fell silent as Quirl stepped back into the tent.

"Here," he said, thrusting filled cups toward them. "Please sit still, and I'll bring you some supper." He ducked back out.

Dark leaned toward Seagryn and whispered, "They're having a quick meeting to decide what to do with us. They'll agree to kill us, plan how to do it, then Quirl will return all smiles to convince us they've accepted us into the family."

"You're certain of all of this?" Seagryn wondered, amazed at the boy's self-confidence.

"I was certain of it last night! If you'd let me stay I could have told you this whole day's events. Of course, I knew in advance you wouldn't," Dark grumbled.

"Just as you knew of the beating," Seagryn murmured to himself.

"Oh," the boy moaned, "I've known about that for months."

Dark shivered. "I'm so relieved to have it over, at last. Can you imagine what it's like to know for months you're going to get a drubbing and not be able to do a thing to avoid it?"

"But that makes no sense," Seagryn said. "If you knew such and really wanted to prevent it, you'd simply be elsewhere! I think you planned last night to let yourself be caught, knowing that I'd—"

"For what!" Dark snapped, truly angry. "That's exactly what these forest fools thought, and why they were beating me! Just because I know something's coming does not give me any control over it! Why is it everyone thinks it should? I told Quirl and his people they would be ambushed. They were. Does that make me responsible? It does to them, even when I tried to warn them! You don't like the future? Punish the prophet. Happens all the time." Dark swirled the liquid in his cup and took a long, ferocious draught.

"Then—you actually know the future . . ."

"Anything I care to know. And a whole lot I don't care to know."

Seagryn nodded. "And you already know what will happen tonight—that these Marwandians will try to kill us but we'll manage to escape?"

"Close," Dark corrected. "They'll attempt to kill us and most of them will manage to escape—from you, anyway."

"Then—I'll turn tugolith again tonight," Seagryn said quietly. When Dark didn't reply, Seagryn asked, "How long have you known?"

Dark raised his eyebrows. "Known what? You have to be specific, Seagryn. I can read the future, but not minds."

"That I would become a tugolith."

"Oh, that. Long enough."

"Long enough for what?"

Dark sipped his drink and swallowed, his eyes not leaving Seagryn's. He seemed about to answer when the tent flaps opened.

"Ah, my friends!" Quirl smiled as he stepped inside, bearing two steaming bowls. "Marwandian stew! You'll enjoy it." As Quirl passed the bowls to his two guests, his smile seemed a bit too brilliant. Dark caught Seagryn's eye and nodded knowingly. Seagryn looked at his bowl with some worry, then back at Dark, but the boy was already eating. So . . . not poisoned. Seagryn tasted the stew and found it to be delicious, but he ate without appetite, due to Dark's revelations. That annoyed him. Why did this lad burden him with such disturbing predictions?

Quirl had fetched a bowl for himself and reentered the tent to sit cross-legged in front of Seagryn. "Now my friend," he began. "Just tell me straight. Weren't you really sent by the Conspiracy to destroy us?"

The question stunned Seagryn. "Sent by whom?"

"The Conspiracy!" Quirl smiled belligerently. Seagryn looked at Dark for support but found him studying his stew meat. "Oh." Quirl chuckled. "You're going to pretend you've never heard of it."

"Of course I've heard of it. Who hasn't? But it's really only a rumor—a theory people in distress rely on to rationalize their failure." As he listened to himself quote Ranoth, a dart of doubt stabbed at his heart. This is what he'd always been told, but then he'd always trusted his teachers. Why should he now, when they had so swiftly abandoned him in his need?

"I see." Quirl mod Kit smiled dangerously. "So you're saying that I lead a band of distressed failures?"

"Why—no, I mean that—"

"The Conspiracy's just a stupid myth," Dark muttered.

Quirl whirled on the boy. "A myth you are a part of!"

"Me? A lad?" Dark cackled. "If there were such an organization, do you think they'd allow a boy to be a member?"

"Do you actually know something of this Conspiracy?" Seagryn asked eagerly. "I've always wondered, but it's not a topic for polite conversation in Lamath."

Quirl mod Kit's expression mocked Seagryn's parochial culture, but he jumped at the invitation to share his collected lore. For, like many who hated the Conspiracy with a passion, he also loved nothing better than to whisper about it long into the night. He told of a treasonous alliance between leaders of every land—warriors and shapers, merchants and priests. Seagryn scoffed at the idea of Lamathian participation, but Quirl swore it was true, even though he admitted he could name no names. Much of it sounded ridiculous, but the new wizard listened in rapt attention, while Dark interjected annoying jests and generally made a nuisance of himself.

"But why?" Seagryn kept asking. "What's their purpose in these secret rituals?"

"The purpose of the powerful in every age!" Quirl shouted, his eyes ablaze. "To subjugate the poor! To keep us under their heel! To rob us of our land and gold and thus grow ever more wealthy themselves! To steal our freedom!''

The sun set and the tent's interior grew dark, but Quirl had still more to tell. When he finally finished his tale they could barely make out one another's faces.

"Well,'' Quirl rumbled, his throat grown raspy from so much talking, "there will be more time to discuss this tomorrow. It's night. Rest here, the two of you. I'll find a bed elsewhere." He ducked out of the tent, then put his head back inside to say, "I hope you sleep soundly." Then he was gone.

"He means that, too,'' Dark muttered, "and we know why."

"I find Quirl quite personable," Seagryn argued, "and his story fascinating. You really believe they would attack us after such warm conversation?''

"I don't believe, Seagryn. I know. They'll wait until the middle of the night when they're certain we're both asleep. But you won't be, and you'll turn into a person-consuming monster and chase them screaming from the camp."

He found the boy's authoritative tone highly irritating. "Suppose things do happen just so? How will I know that your suggestion didn't put my reactions into my mind?''

"Self-fulfilling prophecy," Dark muttered sourly. "Why can't anyone ever ask me a new question?''

"What if it does?" Seagryn demanded.

"Go to sleep. I intend to." Dark snuggled into his pile of pillows.

"You can sleep when you fear someone is about to take your life?''

"That's just it, Seagryn, I don't fear. The reason I'm so sleepy now is because I didn't sleep at all last night, knowing today I'd get a beating." The boy turned his face to the tent wall.

"And you're not afraid of a death threat?" Seagryn asked, incredulous.

"Of course not. It's a threat, not a thing that will be." Dark's voice already sounded groggy.

"Well, I can assure you that I won't sleep since you've told me this," Seagryn grumbled, and the boy gave a low, sleepy cackle.

"I know." Dark smiled. "That's why I can . . ." Moments later the disgruntled Seagryn heard the regular breathing of a deep sleep. He wished he could feel so drowsy . . .

It happened exactly as predicted. Seagryn suddenly came awake, gripped by an uncontrollable shaking. Then a sword slashed through the fish-satin tent wall, right above his head. He turned tugolith in an instant, exploding the tent around him, and both the sword and the one who wielded it bounced harmlessly off his thick scales. Seagryn trampled that horrified warrior, then roared with tugolith wrath and charged down the line of tents, flattening each one and, he hoped, their occupants as well. Screaming Marwandians ran everywhere, but he couldn't see them. Evidently tugoliths possessed poor night vision. He galloped toward the sounds of their howls and suddenly felt the stockade walls splintering around his forequarters. Then he stopped, listening as the screams of terror receded into the black woods beyond. Turning around and trotting back into the enclosure, he listened carefully and discovered that his huge tugolith ears possessed a sense of hearing that more than compensated for the poor eyesight. Someone nearby approached him—by the casual nature of the stride he knew it was Dark. "I didn't crush you?" he said, his voice sounding horribly deep.

"Not I. I had enough sense to sneak out of the tent before—"

"Hush!" Seagryn grunted, then he listened more intently. Far, far away there was still screaming, but he heard another sound, too. In eerie counterpoint to the shouts of terror he heard—music. Beautiful, incongruous music. He listened carefully until it faded. Then he turned his giant head in the direction of Dark's voice. "So," he muttered. "You were right. Again."

"Boring, isn't it," the boy answered glumly.

Seagryn recovered his human shape suddenly. "How could such a gift be boring?"

"Can you imagine living without any surprises?" Dark asked. "Believe me. It's boring."

"Very well then, Dark the prophet. What happens to us next?"

"We try to find a tent still standing and get some sleep. Then tomorrow we start toward the meeting-place of the Conspiracy."

Seagryn's jaw gaped. "You said there was no Conspiracy!"

"So?" Dark said. "I lied."

Chapter Three

✖✖✖✖

CONSPIRING VOICES

Paumer the merchant owned a hundred mansions, many of them splendid. But none could rival the grandeur of this house. It balanced upon the edge of a volcanic crater which cupped a bottomless blue lake. This lake was fed each summer by the melting snowcaps of the jagged peaks that ringed it. "The Hovel," as Uda's father liked to call the palace, nestled in a crack between two of the sharpest crags.

Had she been anxious for Paumer's return, the petite, black-haired girl might have waited on the Hovel's inner portico, watching for the barge to start across the lake. That's how her father would come, for the only road into the cone wound up the mountain to the landing on its far side. But Uda was in no hurry to see him, nor the special birthday surprise he had promised. It wouldn't be what she wanted. That he could grant with just a word—if he would . . .

Instead Uda passed the time on the Hovel's outer face, gazing down upon the green forests of northern Haranamous that ringed the volcano's base and making plans. On most days, clouds clustered just below this summit, obscuring the view. But on this, her thirteenth birthday, the sky was so clear she could see all the way to the ocean on the eastern horizon. She could almost make out tiny galleys, plowing the waters to north and south. Did they catch the winds in the red-and-blue sails of the House of Paumer? Probably. Her father owned everything. Everything of any importance, anyway.

And that should make her powerful, she argued with herself as she planned. Her brother would doubtless call it scheming. He often accused her of such. But as she perceived it, only those without power schemed. Those *with* power planned how their influence should be applied—and protected. And Uda liked to think of herself as powerful. Why shouldn't she? When Uda surveyed the world at her feet, she truly thought of it as her world.

Yet even as she thought it, Uda acknowledged her self-deceit. She was always scrupulously honest with herself, if with no one else. The power she longed for was still only potential power as long as her father continued to regard her as a little girl. How could she change his attitude? Her brother had managed to do so simply by acting boorish! How could she wring the same kind of respect out of him? As she listened to her own thoughts, Uda guessed she was scheming, after all . . .

"Got it all laid out, do you?" her brother said from right behind her, and she jumped, startled by his sudden presence. Regaining her composure, she swiveled her head to look back at him disdainfully, and the fine strands of her waist-length black hair parted like a heavy curtain on either side of her right shoulder.

"Whatever are you talking about?" she asked him, her blue eyes wide with pretended innocence.

"Oh, come now," he mocked. "We both know what you're after, don't we, Uda?" He exaggerated the guttural sound of her name to annoy her, and succeeded. Uda had always hated her name—it didn't fit her, for it wasn't the slightest bit pretty! But then, it wasn't hers by choice. Her naming had sealed a contract long ago. While she'd never learned all the details, she did know it was an acronym formed from the first letter of the names of some forgotten trading houses now totally absorbed by her father. It comforted her that her brother had suffered a similar misfortune—only in his case there'd been several more partners.

"Do we, Ognadzu?"

Her brother only smiled. In his blue eyes, so very much like those that gazed back from her own mirror, Uda saw only self-ishness. She wondered briefly if he saw the same in hers. "Admit it, child. You're after a chair on the Grand Council. Have been, ever since I got mine. For your birthday, perhaps?" He cackled in genuine pleasure at her answering scowl, then clucked with the bitterest of sarcasm. "Happy birthday, little Uda dear!"

Uda whirled away, the long train of her hair twirling out behind her. She could not imagine how people as fine—when they were apart from one another, anyway—as her parents could have given birth to such a repulsive ogre! How had this obnoxious, immature little toad managed to con Paumer into making him a member of the Conspiracy!

She wasn't allowed to call it that, of course. That term infuriated Paumer. He referred to it only as the Grand Council for Reunification and required his household to do the same. But everyone else in the world called it the Conspiracy and hated it—if they knew anything about it at all. For while the most influential wizards, warriors, and merchants in the world served as its members, they'd managed to keep its existence largely a secret. Rumors of its activities circulated constantly, and patriotic bands in each of the six fragments had sworn themselves to expose it. But Paumer wasn't worried. He boasted that his agents had infiltrated every little group sworn to bring it down. Uda felt certain her father could destroy them at will, but he never would. And though only thirteen today, she already understood why. "Political power rests upon perceptions, not facts," she'd heard her father explain. "Let people know enough to believe you can do them terrible injury, but never enough so that they could obstruct your goals." Those were words to live by, Uda believed, and she intended to do just that. But Ognadzu, who never listened to their father's wisdom, had been made the second representative from Pleclypsa instead of her. Why? Just because he was a few years older—and was male?

"Uda!" They both heard a voice calling—their father's voice, amplified by the surface of the lake.

Ognadzu languidly scratched his back. "There he is. Why not run around and see what toy Daddy's brought you *this* time?"

Uda shook her head. There was no question they were related. The eyes, the pointed chin, the black hair—they all matched. But could someone have made a mistake at his birth . . . ?

"Uda!" Paumer called again, more insistent this time. With a sneer calculated to show Ognadzu she didn't care what he thought, the girl raced off around the colonnaded portico that circled the mansion and down to the marble landing. Her father, beaming broadly, jumped onto the dock and loped toward her, his arms held wide.

Paumer had silver hair and large, friendly teeth. He also had a prominent nose, but that didn't matter to Uda as long as her own didn't start growing to match it. He was lean and a little bit short, but still tall enough to scoop his daughter off her feet and twirl her around twice before setting her down and kissing the top of her head. "Thirteen," he muttered in her ear. "Who could imagine?"

Uda smiled up at him sweetly, then leaned up to kiss his cheek. "What's that?" she asked, pointing to an enormous crate that two dozen servants and bodyguards were struggling to push onto the dock. Paumer broke free from her embrace and barked:

"Careful with it! Annoy him and he'll break right out!"

"Him? Who? What is it?" Uda shouted, all in one breath.

"You'll see," Paumer said, grinning like a schoolboy. Then he shouted, "All right! Open it up!" A pair of servants went to work on several latches, and soon the front of the wooden box fell open with a heavy clunk.

Uda caught her breath. Grabbing her father's arm with both hands she squeezed tightly against him. "What is *that*?"

Paumer's smile glistened in the setting sun. "That, dear daughter, is a tugolith. Happy birthday!"

A huge horned beast strolled out of the crate and regarded its new mistress. "Hello," it said.

Uda squeezed her father's arm tighter, her blue eyes quite round. "It talks," she whispered hoarsely.

"Of course he talks!" Paumer grinned, and he took a step toward the beast. "Massive, isn't he?"

Uda swallowed, still staring. The tugolith returned her stare without blinking.

"Isn't he marvelous?" Paumer said enthusiastically as he tried to pull his daughter closer to this most unusual gift. "Listen, here's a joke." He chuckled. "You know where a tugolith sits?" When Uda didn't respond he asked her again, more loudly: "You know where a tugolith sits?"

Uda at last took her eyes off the creature and looked up at her father. "No. Where?"

"Anywhere he likes!" Paumer shouted, then he hooted in self-appreciation. The guards and servants supported him with hearty—and thoroughly false—guffaws. Uda smiled brightly at her father, and Paumer relaxed at last. His daughter had let him off the hook.

But while Uda was willing to indulge Paumer by appearing to be pleased, she wasn't about to go near this awesome talking animal. Not yet. "Ah . . ."

"Yes?" Paumer asked.

"What's he . . . for?"

The question took the merchant by surprise. "For? Why . . . he's . . . for riding!"

"Riding?"

"Certainly! You can ride him all around the Hovel!"

"Inside?" Uda asked, teasing her father. As usual, he didn't catch the nuance and took her seriously.

"Of course not inside!" he blurted. "He'd wreck the antiques, spoil the rugs!"

"Not housebroken then," Uda observed wryly, and Paumer realized she'd been kidding.

"Ah—he's also for protection!"

"What?"

"To protect you! From kidnappers and such! Let them try to take my daughter and Vilanlitha will either stick 'em or squash 'em flat!"

"Vilanlitha?" Uda frowned.

Paumer nodded. "That's his name."

"How do you know?"

Paumer smiled his "how do you *think* I know, idiot" smile and said, "Because I asked him."

"Oh," Uda muttered. She looked back over her shoulder at the tugolith. "Where's my mother?" she asked.

He quickly looked away, false smile firmly in place. "She wanted to come, darling, but she had a meeting in Pleclypsa. Culture, you know. Where's Ognadzu?"

This quick change of subject sent Uda a clear signal; her parents were fighting again. She sighed, then turned her attention to his question. "He's up on the outer face. He's harassing me today."

"Good, good." Paumer smiled as he walked quickly up the dock toward the house. He hadn't heard her at all. Uda watched him fondly. For a man of his age, he still could move.

"You are my mistress?" a deep voice rumbled behind her, and Uda squealed and whirled around. There she froze in terror. The beast stood right in front of her! It gazed at her a moment, then said, "You seem frightened."

Uda swallowed. "Yes," she answered.

"Of what?" Vilanlitha asked. Was that a frown? Uda asked herself.

"Of—of you," she squeaked.

"Why are you afraid of me?" the tugolith asked her.

"Because you're huge! You could hurt me!"

Vilanlitha's eyes rolled. In anger? Uda quaked in dread. "I am a wise tugolith!" he announced.

Was that an explanation? "Yes?" Uda asked.

"You are my mistress!"

"Go on?"

"I won't hurt you!" the tugolith thundered.

Uda blinked several times. "That . . . that pleases me no end . . ."

"But—" the beast roared, and Uda stiffened again.

"Yes?" she asked, her throat dry.

The tugolith's eyes changed, narrowing in unconscious imitation of the human expression for cruelty, as it sneered, "I *do* like to hurt!"

Uda felt a chill seize her, but it disappeared as quickly as it came. Her cosmopolitan upbringing had prepared her to handle unusual situations, and this certainly qualified. More than that, it suddenly struck her how she must appear to the servants standing around. Her rôle required her to accept this gift with grace, recognize its value, and make full use of it. "Good," she grunted. Then, while the servants were busy marveling at her boldness, she said, "My father says I can ride you. How?"

Vilanlitha kneeled down, putting his gigantic chin on the dock as he instructed through clenched teeth, "Climb up behind my horn."

It seemed simple enough and it was. Soon Uda straddled the beast's horn, and primly arranged her birthday frock around her knees as she gave Vilanlitha the command to go.

The tugolith carried her up onto the terrace and around to the outer face of the Hovel. "Stop!" she commanded suddenly, and Vilanlitha obeyed as she slipped down off of his face and ran to join her father and brother and a most unexpected guest. The wizard Nebalath was here!

"Call it what it is!" aged Nebalath was shouting at her father. "It's a conspiracy, and you're the one who's made it so!"

Ognadzu saw her coming and stepped toward her. "Go away," he ordered sharply.

"How did he get here! Has he been hiding? Did he come up with—"

"He just suddenly appeared up here. Now get *away*!" Ognadzu snarled, displaying his teeth like a vicious guard dog.

"Why should I?" she snarled back, her expression the mirror image of his.

"This is Grand Council business," he said officiously—and

the way he said it, the glee with which he rubbed it in, made joining herself to this trio of men a cause for which Uda would risk her life!

"Who do you think you are?" She dodged around him.

"Stop!" Ognadzu shouted, and he grabbed her by the shoulders and pulled her back. That was a mistake.

"Is he hurting you?" Vilanlitha rumbled, stepping up behind Ognadzu to tower over him. It was the young man's first glimpse of the tugolith, and his feet took root in the tiles as he stared up in terror. Uda merely smiled and plucked her brother's hands off her shoulders.

Nebalath, too, gazed up at the beast, but he obviously didn't fear it. "So," he mumbled. "You've got yourself a tugolith."

Paumer seemed embarrassed. "It's—it's a gift. Today's my daughter's birthday . . ."

"Hello," Uda chirped at the wizard.

He evidently didn't consider her worthy of a response, for he immediately turned back to Paumer. "You do what you will with your little council, since you seem to think you own it. I'll no longer be a party to it."

"But without you we're lost!" Paumer pleaded. "You're the only wizard worth—"

"*Pah!*" Nebalath exploded. "You merchants are such potent liars you begin to believe yourselves. You have Sheth, don't you?"

"But the bear is—is uncontrollable!"

"Oh-ho! And I am controllable?"

"I didn't mean that," Paumer muttered, angry at himself for choosing words so poorly. "I only mean Sheth is a murderous recluse—"

"That's true enough."

"While you on the other hand are—"

"Leaving."

"Wait! What will we do for another wizard!"

Nebalath shrugged, then frowned. "Didn't young Dark say a new one was coming?"

"Oh," Paumer groaned. "Dark."

"He's a seer. He's always right. You should trust his word. I do." Nebalath rested his chin on his chest and tilted his head to one side. Paumer reached out to grab the wizard's arm, and Nebalath cursed in annoyance. "Why do you always do that when I'm trying to leave?" he demanded.

"If you resign, who'll be the second voice from Haranamous?" Paumer pleaded.

The wizard turned his head to scowl at Uda. "Child, we are in Haranamous here, are we not?"

Uda shrugged. "I guess so."

Nebalath looked back at Paumer. "Since you seem to want to keep it in the family, let her be it," he grunted. "I'm leaving." Then he vanished.

Paumer tottered a bit, as if dizzied by the wizard's departure. Then he looked at Uda, a perplexed expression twisting his face. "We—we meet in a matter of days. Would . . . would you like to—"

"Father don't!" Ognadzu shouted, but Uda was already rejoicing.

"Yes! Oh, Father, yes, of course!" Then she did a merry pirouette and kissed her giant present upon his armor-plated cheek. Now that she'd had some time to get used to him, she'd decided Vilanlitha was indeed cute—but he was nothing compared to a seat on the Grand Council. That was a present she could use!

The hideous pyralu terrified all people everywhere. A nightmarish beast with venomous fangs, barbed talons, and a vicious stinger-tipped tail, it kept to itself in dark forest glades, and everyone did their best to leave it alone. Fortunately for humankind, the dog-sized insect did not seek out trouble.

The black-clad Army of Arl followed a life-sized model of this beast into battle—but Arl did not share the pyralu's reclusive spirit. What the Arlian king did have in common with the beast was its paranoia . . . to the great misfortune of the lands that bordered his own. Today his minions attacked Haranamous. As the Arlian horde swept across the field, their standard—the image of the striking pyralu—performed its function once again. As in so many previous battles, the warriors of Haranamous broke ranks and fled. The Arlian general, watching from a nearby hillside, shook his head in dismay.

It wasn't that he had such an effective army, Jarnel reminded himself. He often worried how his force would fare against an enemy that dared to stand and fight. This was better, of course, far better—little loss of life on either side and a bit of unimportant territory gained. But he had advanced dangerously close to the heart of Haranamous this time. Within his ceremonial helmet, glossy black and barbed like a pyralu's mandibles, Jarnel frowned as he watched yet another rout unfold. Would Chaom *never* stiffen his weak-kneed army's resolve?

"Another victory!" Merritt shouted gleefully. Jarnel barely grunted. He felt his subordinate's nervous gaze, but didn't glance that way. Young Merritt was a venomous mudgecurdle who would work his treacheries no matter how Jarnel responded to him. The general had decided simply to ignore him. Merritt couldn't abide being ignored, however, and needlessly blurted out, "They're breaking!" Jarnel shot him a contemptuous glance, and the man seemed to fold in upon himself.

The Pyralu General looked back down at the field. A cluster of Chaom's warriors had managed to rally, and the two forces finally closed. It took several moments for the sound of the clash to reach them, here across the river, but they could survey the whole valley from this vantage point, and it kept them safe from any nonmagical attack. A powershaper could be lurking anywhere nearby, of course, cloaking himself from view, but Arlian spies had reported that old Nebalath no longer protected the warriors of Haranamous. Without magical aid, the purple-clad defenders of that unfortunate land were badly outmanned and collapsed quickly.

Merritt chanced another grin at him and chuckled nervously. "So we didn't need the bear after all!"

"A good thing," Jarnel growled from within his mask, "since Sheth felt no need to appear."

"Wizards know about wizards," Merritt explained grandly. "Sheth knew he wouldn't be needed."

"And what do you know about wizards that has provided you with this insight?" Jarnel asked. Merritt flushed, and stepped back a pace. Jarnel reached up under his chin to trip the latches that anchored his headdress to his breastplate. Then he lifted the thing off his head and dangled it beside him as he mopped the sweat from his high forehead and his thin, angular face. He felt Merritt's eyes upon him and glanced over at the younger man. "What?" he inquired, cocking a gray eyebrow.

"Nothing," Merritt answered quickly. "I just—it's amazing how much that helmet changes your appearance."

Jarnel held up the mask and examined it. "Repulsive, isn't it?"

"But so effective!" Merritt grinned broadly.

"And you'd like to wear it," Jarnel muttered, his thin lips unsmiling. This straightforward remark caught Merritt off guard. "Why—no! I mean, my Prince—"

"Don't lie, Merritt. You're no good at it. Few soldiers are."
Jarnel watched the rout below them. "Besides," he added after
a moment, "how could I trust a warrior without ambition? We
live to strive—to attain—to win." There was no accusation in
Jarnel's voice. He meant what he said.

"Very well," the emboldened Merritt responded. "May I
have permission to speak frankly?"

"So you can ask why I didn't send a contingent to ford the
river downstream and cut off their retreat?"

Merritt paused. "Well, it *would* have resulted in total victory," he muttered.

"Total victory." Jarnel smiled cynically. "Yes. And then
what?"

"What, my Prince?"

"What would happen if we totally destroyed old Chaom's
army?" the commander asked.

Merritt shrugged. "I suppose we would sail our war boats on
into Haranamous and claim that city for the king."

Jarnel snorted. "Then what?"

"We would row home and be hailed as heroes." Merritt spoke
harshly, piqued by Jarnel's mocking tone.

"Heroes!" the general said, hoisting a fist into the sky. Then
he turned to gaze soberly at Merritt. "For how long? Think,
man. When Haranamous falls, Pleclypsa falls too. Then it's easy
enough to tiptoe past the underground fragment of the Remnant
and invade Lamath. How exciting! Another war, this one even
further from our home!" Jarnel turned his weary eyes back to
the field of battle. It was littered now with corpses, and undisciplined Arlian warriors were busy stripping these of their purple garments—souvenirs of the victory. Jarnel shook his head,
then went on, "And when we conquer *that* distant land, what
then? Battling crazed bands of raiders in the Marwilds? Not for
me. No, I would then be remanded home—to be honored for
my splendid victories, of course—and then be quietly eliminated
by a king who would surely see me then as his foremost remaining threat." Jarnel shot Merritt a friendly grin, and the man
jerked, startled by it. "No, I'll leave total victory for you to
win, Merritt, when you wear this disgusting mask." The Prince
of the Army of Arl set the helmet on the ground behind him,
then walked a few feet eastward and pointed into the distance.
"Is that Chaom and his staff withdrawing?"

Although the afternoon sun was behind them, Merritt made

a needless show of shielding his eyes and peering in that direction. "It appears so."

"Good," Jarnel grunted. "Then I think we can safely count this a true victory and not one of Nebalath's magical traps." Jarnel pulled off his black gauntlets and tossed them to the ground beside the mask. "I need to be elsewhere. You're in command." He started down the hill, then stopped and looked back. "Try on the helmet if you like, but I warn you—it's hot in there." He turned away again.

"Is she pretty?" Merritt called out suddenly, and Jarnel froze, astonished by his subordinate's temerity. He looked back with an amused leer on his face.

"Haven't you guessed the truth yet? I'm off to a meeting of the Conspiracy!" He cackled derisively and walked down the hill toward his pavilion. As he threw his tent flap aside he heard Merritt laughing appreciatively.

Dusk had come by the time he'd bathed, anointed himself with a heavy perfume, and donned his finest gown. A bonfire burned upon the parade grounds as the warriors of Arl loudly celebrated their victory. He chose the finest horse in his cavalry and did not spare the animal. He had important business to discuss with his enemies.

These were dangerous times. The quirkiness of Nebalath had pushed Haranamous to the brink of collapse. He'd told Merritt the truth today. Victory in this war would only insure marching off to another. But he knew such arguments would never dissuade a younger commander from seizing that important first conquest. Chaom needed magical protection soon, and they all needed to find some means of restoring the balance of power between the fragments. Otherwise the old One Land could look forward to nothing but marching armies for at least another century. Jarnel hated that thought. He hoped just once in his lifetime to experience the sweet savor of peace.

He rode northeast through the night, skirting the edge of Haranamous. A few hours after dawn, he reached the forest inn that served as his cover. Everyone knew it was a brothel. Few knew for certain that it was owned by Paumer, but the reach of the merchant was so long most just naturally assumed some red-and-blue connection. Jarnel entrusted his mount to a stable lad with a coin and a lewd wink, then swaggered into the main house with the look of a man prepared to enjoy himself.

Less than an hour later an aging courier in Paumer's red-and-blue livery galloped out of an underground cavern several miles northeast of the inn. Jarnel despised these colors, but he had to admit that no one ever took note of him when he wore them.

The rendezvous point was a Paumer mansion at the foot of the South Gate—the narrow mouth that led up to the Central Pass from Haranamous. Jarnel left his borrowed steed at the front door and stalked inside unannounced. Chaom—similarly attired—waited for him in the entryway.

"You got here quickly," Jarnel murmured.

"I had the unfortunate advantage of a headstart," Chaom answered coolly. "You, after all, had to secure your victory. There was nothing left for me to secure."

Chaom was a huge man—beefy and powerful. A gifted warrior in individual combat, he had moved up through the ranks of Haranamous less on the strength of his strategic abilities than on the basis of his personal heroism. His face was large and round, and the relative smallness of his eyes and mouth made it appear even more so. Jarnel rarely thought of his rival's size until they were thrown together like this. He thought it ironic that if the fortunes of Arl and Haranamous were to be decided by a duel between their respective generals, the issue would be quickly resolved in Chaom's favor. "It could have been much worse," Jarnel mumbled. "Where was your wizard?"

"Where was yours?" Chaom snapped back. While coconspirators, the two men were far from friends. Neither felt any need to pretend they were.

"Absent—to your good fortune!" Jarnel snarled. "Had he been present there's no way the two of us could have spared you! My king does get his reports."

"Oh, yes." Chaom smiled grimly. "Your young Merritt."

"Correct." Jarnel nodded. "My ruler is too fearful of Sheth to criticize the shaper to his face. I, on the other hand, am constantly reminded that I can be replaced. And what happens then?"

"I assume Paumer would simply induct your successor into our circle." Chaom shrugged, his voice tinged with bitterness.

Jarnel stiffened. "Paumer is only a member of this council, Chaom. He is not its lord."

"Ah, but does he know that?" Chaom wondered, raising a meaningful eyebrow. "Look at your costume, Jarnel—and at mine."

"Subterfuge, that's all. An effective guise."

Chaom nodded. "So I'd thought, too, until Paumer managed to make his boy one of our number at the last meeting. The man is adept at making himself sole proprietor of other people's enterprises! You don't doubt he intends to rule our respective lands as well?''

Weary from his all-night ride, Jarnel had no patience for such talk. "For all I know, Paumer may already own half of Arl. But he's never dared to set his foot within our borders. And this is the most powerful man in the world? I think not.''

Chaom shrugged and yawned broadly. He, too, had ridden all night. Jarnel nodded and yawned back, and they moved together into the sitting room, each taking an empty couch.

"When is the merchant due to arrive?" Jarnel asked as he stretched himself out.

"These servants know nothing," Chaom gumbled, turning onto his side in quest of a comfortable position.

Jarnel was already drowsing off, but remembered a warning he'd intended to pass along, and forced himself to sit up. "By the way—next time guard the fords. Merritt wanted to cross the river behind you and cut off your retreat. I wouldn't let him.''

Still shifting, Chaom turned his back to Jarnel and snuggled his hips into the cushions. "You should have. We'd laid snares in all those fords, and you would have been *rid* of your troublesome Merritt.''

"Snares?" Jarnel frowned. "How?" But Chaom's only answer was a snore.

"I don't wish to be rid of Merritt—nor of any of my people,'' Jarnel growled to himself. "What I really wish is to spare them any more . . .'' Before he finished, sleep had claimed him.

The bear cracked a human skull between his teeth, enjoying the crisp crunch it made. He liked the taste, too. Marwandians had a delicate flavor—probably from all the wild forest herbs in their diet. He chewed slowly. There was no rush. He could watch from here upon the bluff, and there appeared to be no one stirring inside the single tent left standing in the ruined stockade.

Did the boy know of his presence? Probably. That mattered very little. Dark was a nuisance, but hardly a threat. He could only relate the future, and that future he told contained the results of all Dark's own best efforts to change it. Besides, he was a boy and subject still to all boyish insecurities. And fears . . .

This Seagryn, however, with his tugolith shape and lofty religious ideals, might prove to be a problem if not quickly mastered. The bear tore off another chunk of flesh and gnawed it thoughtfully. He could take Dark aside and force the boy to be precise about his predictions. But Sheth didn't like knowing the future. It seemed to tie the hands of the present.

No, he would simply wait. Perhaps circumstances would permit an early confrontation with this would-be wizard. Having finished the last of the Marwandians that this Seagryn had chased into his paws, he felt no need to linger. He had business to finish before the Conspiracy met. These two would be there. Dark had promised.

The twenty-foot-tall bear metamorphosed into a man—a caped patrician gazing arrogantly into a little valley. Then, just as suddenly, he was gone, and the humid air rushed to fill the void with a sharp snap.

Chapter Four

※※※※

PROPHECY'S BURDEN

SEAGRYN woke with a start. He sat trembling for a moment, remembering where he was. Dark still slept on a pile of cushions nearby. "Dark?" he whispered. The boy groaned, but never moved.

The heat within this tent felt stifling. Late morning . . . it had to be late morning! "Get up!" Seagryn whispered, sliding off his own pallet of cushions to crawl to the tent flap. He peered out.

The stream rolled through the ruined encampment, sloshing gently against the rocks that lined its banks. Insects buzzed over the few patches of grass that hadn't been tramped down by Marwandian boots. Seagryn listened—had they returned? Did warriors wait on either side of this tent to spear them as they stepped out? He crawled to Dark's side and shook the lad. "Wake up," he muttered. "Wake *up*!" he spat in the boy's ear, and Dark's eyes shot open.

The boy blinked a couple of times, then smacked his lips together and grumbled, "Give me one good reason why I should."

"There are enemies about!"

"Of course there are," the boy agreed, shifting his body away from Seagryn and snuggling into a cushion. "But not any right outside this tent."

"How do you know that?"

Dark yawned, and shrugged his shoulders in a clear signal that he intended to go back to sleep.

Seagryn stood. "If, as it seems, you know everything in advance, then you know I'm about to do this!" He grabbed Dark by the collar and belt and jerked the lad into the air. The boy struggled ineffectually as Seagryn turned him upright and set him on his feet.

"Oh, I knew you were going to do it," Dark growled, "but that doesn't mean I needed to help you."

"You actually knew I would jerk you out of the bed?"

"Of course. Just as I know that our friends have not returned to camp and that later on you're going to toss me into that river out there."

Seagryn leaned his head back disdainfully, then folded his arms on his chest. "I see. But that's where you're wrong."

Dark scowled, then rubbed the sleep from his eyes as he said, "And now you're going to prove to me that I don't control your future by vowing *not* to throw me into the river." Dark walked to the tent flap and casually tossed it aside, then ducked out and went straight to the stream. He knelt there and washed his face. Seagryn followed him, casting furtive glances to either side but seeing no one else around.

"Are you now going to throw yourself in and say I was responsible?" Seagryn challenged.

Dark stood up, drying his face with his sleeve. "No."

"Well?"

"Well what?" Dark asked, his brown eyes finally open and fixed upon Seagryn.

"How can you account for the fact that I won't throw you in?"

Dark gazed at him a moment, his eyes looking much older than the rest of his youthful frame. "How much of this do you actually want to know?"

"How much of what?"

"What's going to happen today."

Dark's blasé tone infuriated Seagryn, so he pretended not to understand. "What do you mean?"

"Just that." Dark shrugged. "How trivial do you want me to be? How much detail?"

Seagryn stared at the boy a moment, then shook his head in disgust and walked away, looking at the row of squashed tents and trying to judge which one might contain the food supplies.

"For example, right now you're going to find us something to eat—"

"Well, of course I'm going to find food!" Seagryn snarled, whirling around to look at Dark again. "It's almost noon! I'm hungry! Aren't you?"

"—and you'll find some dried meat in the third tent down." Seagryn put his hands on his hips and glared at the young prophet. "But now you'll try every way you can to find something to eat somewhere *else*, just to prove I'm wrong." Dark found a patch of grass and sat down on it. He picked up a rock and tossed it idly into the river. Seagryn did, indeed, search the other tents first. The boy waited, watching the water glide past. After a few minutes Seagryn rejoined him, frowning in frustration as he shoved some dried meat the boy's way. Dark took it, saying, "Just tell me when to shut up. My s'mother always does."

"Where is your mother?" Seagryn asked gruffly. "Does she know you're here?"

Dark took a bite and chewed reflectively before answering. "She knows I'm safe. I've told her that much. More than that she doesn't want to know. It's very tedious having someone around who knows everything you'll do before you do it. But you'll discover that soon enough."

Seagryn was thinking he already had learned that when it registered upon him that, if he felt that way, Dark had again predicted his reaction properly. "No!" he lied brightly. "I don't think it tedious. In fact, I find it fascinating!"

"Right," Dark muttered, lying back in the grass to gaze into the clear summer sky.

"I do! How do you do it?"

Dark turned his head to frown up at Seagryn, then closed his eyes and laced his fingers behind his head. "How do you become a tugolith?" he asked.

Seagryn thought. "I don't know."

"Nor do I understand my ability." Dark shrugged. "It's just the way I am. A part of me. My gift, or curse, or whatever you want to call it."

"It's a gift, certainly," Seagryn said. "Look how it's helped us already."

"How?" Dark frowned.

"Why, we can . . ."

"Don't say we can avoid trouble, because we can't. I have the welts on my back to prove that."

"But you could have avoided it!" Seagryn challenged. "You could have . . . been home with your mother!"

"Oh," Dark grunted. "Like you could have avoided turning into a tugolith last night?"

"I don't control that," Seagryn muttered.

"And I don't control the future. You think I didn't try to avoid these outlaws? I did. I wanted to stay with you! But—as I knew you would—you sent me away. So, I was trying to run home and ran right into three of them instead."

"But didn't you know you would?"

"Of course I knew. Don't you understand? Knowing just makes it worse! You can't avoid the future any more than you can avoid the past!"

Seagryn puzzled over this awhile. "Then everything in the future is fixed? Is it all preordained?"

Dark snarled in frustration. He'd obviously tried to explain this many times. "It's not like someone, the Power for example, orders the future to be such. It just is. Decisions now don't change the future, because the future isn't, yet. My problem is I know what it will be, what all the decisions will add up to. If I decide to do something to change an outcome, inevitably it's the very act that makes that outcome happen. Augh—" He broke off wearily. "Why do I even try to make people understand . . . ?"

"Then," Seagryn began in a philosophical tone, "you know the instant of your own death—"

"No!" Dark shouted, and he was suddenly onto his knees and had grabbed hold of Seagryn's robe. His words tumbled out. "Please don't ever say that, don't ever mention that again, Seagryn, in the name of friendship or the Power or whatever you want to say! Please don't! My sight of the future is like your memory of the past. Things are there; you could give attention to them if you wanted to, but some things are too painful, so you don't, you block out those memories by thinking of pleasant ones, right? Don't you?"

"Ah—I guess—"

"You do, everyone does, and so do I! I block that out, I talk about foolish things, I look at the future of others, I play games with their minds, and all of it is designed— Listen to me Seagryn! It's all designed to keep that one secret from me! Please! Change the subject!"

The boy's dark eyes implored him. Seagryn didn't know what to say.

"Something else! Anything else! Get my mind off of this before I—"

"So you remember the future?" Seagryn said quickly, unsure if that would help.

"Yes!" Dark smiled thankfully. "Yes, that's it! I remember the near future best, just as you recall events of the past two or three days better than you do what happened last month. Critical days, important days, they stand out in your memory regardless of how long ago—oh, the details get fuzzy, but you understand. And I know of critical days in the weeks and months ahead, many of them days we share . . ." Dark trailed off, and his young eyes grew distant as he looked inside himself at what was to be. "I know of events that will shake you to your core—and the world as well . . ." He said this so dramatically that Seagryn could not help but be drawn into the vision.

"Do—do I play a critical role in these—events?"

Dark came back into the present and stared Seagryn in the face. "Everyone wants to be important," he said, quietly. "Everyone is."

Seagryn flushed, embarrassed by his own ambition. "Of course," he muttered.

"However," Dark added with a hint of mystery, "by virtue of luck or providence or fate, some get close enough to the wheels of destiny to turn them by their own weight . . ." He paused, and it seemed he was holding this morsel out as a temptation for Seagryn to ask more.

The former cleric frowned. "And . . . I am . . . one of those?"

Dark nodded curtly. Seagryn felt a bit light-headed at the news. The thing he had always wanted most was to be important. Here was confirmation that his dreams would be realized. "And . . . you could tell me exactly how?"

"How much do you want to know, Seagryn?" Dark asked again, but now his voice could have been that of an ancient oracle. No wonder Dark's name had already moved into legend, Seagryn thought with a shiver. "Do you want to be made to feel powerless by knowing the outcome of your decisions in advance?"

Seagryn stared at the boy for a minute, then shook his head. "No. Occasional help maybe, but no."

"Good choice," Dark muttered. "I only wish I could make it."

The lad seemed older now—much older, almost a peer. And

Seagryn began to understand the weight of the boy's burden. He thought carefully before asking his next question, but decided to risk it. "Is there any other area you prefer not to think about?"

Dark met his eyes worriedly—then a slight smile turned up the corners of his lips. "One."

"And what's that?"

Dark blushed. "Ah . . . love." Seagryn raised an eyebrow, and the boy shrugged and continued. "I think whom you love and . . . and *how* you love . . . that kind of thing . . . ought to be a surprise. Don't you?"

Seagryn chuckled, but glumly. "I suppose." He thought of Elaryl, remembering how the sun glistened in her hair in that moment before the Marwandians broke in upon them. Where was she at this moment? Did she think of him? "Although," he murmured, "there are some things about my love I'd like to know." Seagryn wasn't really asking—or at least he told himself he wasn't. Nevertheless, Dark answered:

"You'll get her back."

Seagryn frowned slightly, fighting the impulse to grab the boy and shake him. "You're certain?"

"I'm certain," Dark replied firmly, and Seagryn nodded, not daring to ask more. "Of course," the boy continued offhandedly, "you'd better not treat her the way you did that girl back in Bourne—"

"How did you—!" Seagryn's reaction was swift and violent. Cursing in a most nonclerical manner, he grabbed Dark by the tunic and flung the lad mightily toward the river. The moment he let go he realized what he was doing; as the boy plunged into the water, Seagryn had to double over with laughter at his own lack of self-control. Dark came up gasping and spluttering and waded out immediately. He was grinning; when Seagryn couldn't stop cackling, Dark laughed along with him.

"How did you know?" Seagryn asked when he finally contained his mirth. "I've never told anyone that story, and she's the only other person who knew!"

Dark shrugged and wiped his face. "You're going to tell me. Sometime next week."

Seagryn shook his head in amazement, then sighed. "Very well then. I confess that I cannot alter the future. And since you've showed me abundantly that while you can't either, you do know it. Why don't you lead us to wherever we are about to travel next?"

Dark nodded thoughtfully as he wrung the water from his full sleeves. "These times always make me uncomfortable."

"What times?"

"When I make—suggestions. Well. Shall we pack up our tent and go join the Conspiracy?"

Seagryn's smile faded, then returned with a little less enthusiasm. "After hearing Quirl mod Kit's lengthy diatribe against it, I'm not sure that's a good idea."

"I understand." Dark nodded, peeling a wet curl from his forehead and squeezing the water out of it. "But you also learned you can't trust what a Marwandian tells you."

"Can I trust what *you* tell me?"

Dark focused his eyes past his forelock and on Seagryn. "I thought I'd already proved—"

"To be in my best interests?" Seagryn expanded.

"Oh. Well. Aren't you going to have to judge that for yourself? After the fact?"

"You can't judge it for me before it happens?" the new wizard asked.

Dark's brown eyes were large and liquid. He answered with utter sincerity, "I wouldn't dare."

Seagryn nodded and turned back to the tent to begin taking it down. "You can tell me one thing," he said as he knelt to pull up a peg.

"What's that?" Dark asked, scrambling around to the other side to help.

"Is the Conspiracy evil?"

Dark stopped and stood straight up. "It didn't start out to be."

"But it is now?"

"Not entirely. We have time to save it . . ."

"Is it worth saving?"

Dark's expression turned thoughtful. He blinked twice, then looked back at Seagryn. "I think it's the world's best hope."

Seagryn shrugged. "In any case, it's already fixed. You already know we join it."

The boy seemed saddened by this comment. "Only because we choose to—"

Seagryn finished bundling the tent, passing a few coins he'd found inside it to Dark. "Whatever." He brushed the dirt from his clerical garb and looked back up at the boy. "You do influence the future, you know. Your—gift. It does have an impact on events."

Dark swallowed. "That's a part of the burden . . ."

Seagryn nodded and looked at the bundle he held in his hand. He thought in quick succession of burdens, then packhorses, and then of what a tugolith might be able to carry. This led him to the realization that he knew now how to control his ability to take on that enormous shape. He held the bundle behind his back and—as he had the day before, in willing the fire to appear—visualized what he wanted to have happen. He thought of himself as a tugolith and he became one. "Care to ride?" his altervoice rumbled, and Dark grinned up at him with excitement.

"Of course!" he shouted, and he clambered up behind Seagryn's ears and sat astride the horn. While in some ways Dark seemed ancient, in others he was still just a boy. Then again, Seagryn reminded himself, weren't most men so? They set out, moving south at Dark's direction.

The first night they camped in a forest of lofty trees unlike any Seagryn had ever seen. The trunks were as big around as castle towers, and the branches made a gray-green canopy that blocked out the heat of the sun. Seagryn breathed air filtered by millions of pine needles and found it incredibly fresh. They moved on at dawn the next morning; by late afternoon, they had reached the outskirts of Ritaven, a free city on the northwest edge of the Middle Mountains, which sat near the center of the old One Land.

"Looks like a pleasant enough place," Seagryn said as he took his human-form before stepping out of the forest onto the main thoroughfare.

"It is." Dark nodded. "For the moment."

"For the moment?"

"Arl is coming." The lad shrugged, as if that explained everything. When he glanced up and saw the concern in Seagryn's face, he quickly added, "Not tonight! Next year!"

"Oh," a much relieved Seagryn said. They spent that night in a cozy Ritaven inn, paying for their lodging with the gold they'd scavenged from Quirl's camp. "Tomorrow," Dark said meaningfully as they lay down. He didn't elaborate, and Seagryn didn't ask.

The next morning they began climbing the mountain in Ritaven's backyard. An hour past noon they stood at the bottom of an enormous rockslide. Huge boulders perched precariously against one another, threatening to resume their ancient dash to the valley at the slightest provocation. Seagryn eyed this jumble of granite, then looked back down the mountain. The windmills of Ritaven looked like tiny blue flowers, and the rows of thatched houses like orderly lines of pebbles arranged by a child. Seagryn frowned.

"What's wrong?" Dark called down to him.

"Why do we come this way? I see no other members of your august Conspiracy scraping their fingers and knees to climb this hillside."

"Of course not. They all went in the main entrance."

"There's a main entrance? Then let's go find it!"

"Can't."

"And why not?"

"It's two days walk around the mountains, then another day's journey back underground. We'd miss the meeting. Besides, they wouldn't let us in."

"Wouldn't let— You led me to believe you were expected!"

"Expected, yes—but not welcomed," Dark said. When Seagryn stared, Dark seated himself on a rock to explain. "You see, they don't want me there. They say membership in the group is by invitation only, and I've never been invited. But they know they can't keep me away, since I always know in advance where they will have met. Never mind," he went on when Seagryn frowned. "Just trust me. At the top of this pile is an entrance." Dark hopped off his perch and started up again. Seagryn didn't move.

"If you're not welcome, I'll certainly not be, either."

"True," Dark called, "but you still need to come."

"Why?"

"To move away the stone!" Dark shouted, now high above. "Come on!"

Seagryn looked down again at Ritaven. A pleasant village, he thought. Might they welcome strangers? Perhaps he could—

But Dark's hints of some mysterious destiny had ensnared him, as had the lad's promise of a reunion with Elaryl. Besides, Arl was coming—whatever that meant. Seagryn looked up and saw the boy lounging on top of a house-sized boulder. He climbed up to him.

"How much further?"

"We're here. Ah—would you mind moving this rock?"

Chapter Five

※❀❀❀❀

INTO THE REMNANT

"**G**ET up!" a girlish voice screamed in Jarnel's ear. "Get up and get out of this room! Do you think this house is the servants' quarters?" The shrill noise set him onto his feet before he was fully awake. He blinked the sleep from his eyes and peered down at the tiny speaker, who kept up her verbal fusillade until Paumer burst into the room behind her.

"Uda!" the merchant bellowed. The brilliant red of his face matched that of his gown.

"What?" the girl snapped, spinning around to face her father. Jarnel realized quickly what had happened. He rubbed his eyes and forehead as he waited for this family disturbance to ease. When he pulled his hand away, he saw Chaom shoot him a knowing smile.

Paumer pushed Uda behind him as he bowed apologetically to his two guests. "My daughter," he murmured. "She—she saw your garments and—excuse me." With a final horrified grin, Paumer whirled around and catapulted his daughter across the entryway and into another room. He followed her quickly, and slammed the intervening door behind him.

Jarnel looked at Chaom and raised his eyebrow. "I like a man who knows how to handle his family."

"So do I," Chaom replied evenly. "Which is one more reason to despise Paumer."

Confused, Jarnel started to ask for an explanation. He didn't, for the son of Paumer, that smirking lad who'd been introduced

51

to them at the last meeting, had sidled into the room and was looking at them strangely. Jarnel met the boy's eyes. The lad quickly looked at the floor.

"You're—" Jarnel began, aware that he'd forgotten the name but pretending to search for it.

The boy's eyes stabbed back upward immediately, and his jaw tightened. "Ognadzu!" he snarled, obviously offended. "I'm as much a member of the Grand Council as you are!"

"Of course you are, Ognadzu," the Prince of the Army of Arl said, taking careful note of the lad's passion while pretending to ignore it. "Nominated as the second voice from Pleclypsa, by your—father? Wasn't it?" While he took no pleasure in further alienating the boy, this seemed a good opportunity to learn more about the merchant. Young Ognadzu's vehement response surprised him.

"I'm not my father's puppet, if that's what you imply! I'm my own man, and no one makes my decisions but me!"

Jarnel responded with an exaggerated widening of the eyes and looked over at Chaom as if for support.

Chaom still wore his knowing expression. "You see?" he asked.

"See what?" Ognadzu demanded, and Jarnel turned his gaze back to the boy. How very like the hideous pyralu this son of Paumer was—all fangs and stinger. It occurred to Jarnel that his own king had probably been a boy much like this one. He was saved from having to reply when Paumer bounced nimbly back into the room.

"I apologize for my children." The merchant smiled. "I've— I've taught them to speak their minds, and they do. Regularly!" He gave a nervous laugh and continued, "Of course, I'm proud of that, in a way. They'll be excellent leaders. Are excellent leaders already," he corrected himself, smiling brightly at his bristling son. "Now if you gentlemen are ready, we'll journey to the place of meeting."

"Where is that?" Chaom inquired pointedly. "Or are *servants* privileged to know such things?"

Jarnel picked up on Chaom's tone and amplified it. "You see, Paumer, Chaom and I are somewhat bothered by your proprietary air."

"Proprietary air?" Paumer grinned. "Toward what, may I ask?"

"Toward the Grand Council!" Chaom said. "You act as if it's just another arm of your trading house!"

Paumer's smile vanished, replaced by a chastened look of utter humility. "Oh. I feared as much. You *were* offended by Uda's outburst. I'm so sorry . . ."

"Your daughter has nothing to do with—"

"Oh but she does! Those colors. My fault. I'm so sorry . . ." Paumer repeated, shaking his head. "I thought we had simply agreed that, since my organization is the only link between all the fragments, I would have to serve as the message-bearer. But—" Here Paumer sighed sadly. "—I can see how the humiliation of wearing servants' tunics would prey upon the honor of such warriors as yourselves."

Jarnel looked to Chaom, but Chaom shook his head. They had heard this speech before and knew Paumer would now deliver all of it whether they interrupted him or not.

"Perhaps this is why the two wizards seem to have lost interest as well. And who could blame them," Paumer pleaded dramatically. "They, after all, are among the powers of this world and, like you, they're accustomed to honor and respect. Which is their due! Being nothing but a simple businessman myself, I cannot say I understand such feelings fully. It has ever been my lot to wear the simple tunic of the common trader I am, while—but enough of that. I do want you to know that I shall submit wholeheartedly to any decision of the Grand Council as to what my role within it is to be. I am unimportant. The goal of reunifying the One Land—that is all that's worthwhile!" Paumer ended his passionate appeal with a fist clenched over his heart.

What a performer, Jarnel thought to himself. Even so, he knew that Paumer believed every word of it—including the line about humility. Jarnel had long been a student of the art of self-deception, and Paumer practiced it well. As to the goal of reunification, the general would not allow his cynicism to dim his commitment to the ideal. He wanted peace. He, too, would willingly sacrifice himself to attain it. "I didn't mean to offend, Paumer," he soothed, playing the uncharacteristic role of diplomat. "Shall we get on our way?"

The merchant clucked his tongue in self-deprecation as he examined their livery and his own. "If you don't mind traveling a little further in these demeaning costumes . . ."

"We'll manage," Chaom grunted. "Where to?"

"Inside again. But don't worry," Paumer added quickly in the face of Chaom's groan. "I've given Garney special instructions not to admit the lad who plagues us."

"In that case, he'll have already arrived." Jarnel shrugged.

"Not this time." Paumer chuckled. "I have it on excellent authority that he's been seen very recently in the Marwilds on the far side of the mountains. Dark has no way to get inside!"

Jarnel nodded doubtfully. "We shall see."

"Indeed we shall," Paumer promised. "Let's be off." A few moments later they had become part of a Paumer House packtrain headed up into the South Gate.

They met much traffic—traders, mostly, coming from the west with pack animals of their own, carrying goods picked up in the vast Marwilds. Few of these deigned to greet them, since free traders not yet absorbed into Paumer's vast enterprise avoided all contact with his operations. None of these merchants had ever been close enough to Paumer to recognize his face and, since the man wore the tunic of a common servant, they all ignored his affable smile. This seemed to please Paumer enormously. "You see?" he gloated to Jarnel. "It's better than being cloaked by a wizard!"

The general nodded wordlessly and turned his head to look at the scenery. As they climbed higher into the pass, they saw more and more ruins of the old capital. By all accounts it had been a gorgeous place, a beautiful giantess astride the crossroad of the world. Jarnel wished he might have seen it in its glory. But internal strife had set it afire, and an epic siege had starved it into ruin. Built to embrace both people and ideas, it had none of the attributes of a good citadel. The royal family and those loyal to it had withdrawn into a vast system of tunnels carved into the northern face of the pass, and the rest of the population had fled—the religious folk to the northern farmlands, the magicminded to the tangled forests of the west, and the commerceoriented to the warm-water ports of the south. And what was left? Only these ruins and the few still loyal to the One Land concept who dwelt in the darkness of the tunnels—the Remnant.

"Tragic," Jarnel muttered.

"What's that?" Paumer asked, but Jarnel shook his head.

"Is Dark coming?" Uda called up from her palfrey near the end of the column.

Paumer scowled and turned around in his saddle. "I told you I don't want to hear any more talk about Dark!"

The girl ignored her father. "I hope he does come," she murmured with obvious excitement. "I want to see him."

"He's nothing special to look at, believe me," Ognadzu told his sister. "If he manages to get in, you'll see what I mean."

Jarnel frowned. Did the little girl expect to attend their meeting along with her brother? He avoided looking at Chaom. He didn't think he could tolerate yet another meaningfully arched eyebrow. Paumer was turning this grand Conspiracy into a family affair.

"Dark said he'd be with us," Chaom reminded them all, "and his words always prove true. He also promised to bring with him a new powershaper. In the absence of Nebalath, I count that a hopeful prospect."

"Nebalath is not coming?" Jarnel exploded, reining in his mount and turning to face his military rival. "But he's one of the founders of our effort!"

"He . . . he says he's getting old—" Paumer explained apologetically.

"He's no older than you or me!" Jarnel turned back to glare at Chaom. "Why do we even bother to meet! If Nebalath has withdrawn, we've no one to balance against Sheth!"

"My point exactly." Chaom nodded.

"Why wasn't I told Nebalath had withdrawn!"

"Please, Jarnel," Paumer soothed. "We're almost up to the Central Gate—"

"All our labors have failed! I'll never hold the bear in check now!" Jarnel gazed soberly at Chaom and shook his head. "The Pyralu will sting your capital within the week."

"Wait! Listen," Paumer pleaded in the same conciliatory tone. "There's no way of our knowing what Nebalath will do, nor Sheth either! They're *wizards*, Lord Jarnel, not people! At least not people like us. Why, Nebalath might suddenly appear among us right here! The old shaper can toss himself from place to place by a simple act of will—I've seen him! Certainly he's done stranger things. And if he doesn't show—well then, we must make some plan to deal with his absence. Am I not right?" the merchant appealed to Chaom, who shrugged and nodded in agreement. Paumer looked back at Jarnel and widened his eyes imploringly.

The Pyralu General studied the merchant's face. How could this sniveling coward have bent the efforts of so much of the world to his own ends? "Ahh," Jarnel muttered to himself as he discovered the answer to his own question.

Paumer looked puzzled. "What was that, my Lord Prince?"

Jarnel understood it now. Paumer trapped his opponents into underestimating him. Jarnel reminded himself once again never to trust this cringing merchant and always to keep a careful watch upon him. "I understand much more clearly now, Paumer,'' the general said at last. "You're absolutely correct. We must plan for every eventuality." He lightly spurred the flank of his horse, and the column started upward once again.

After all the years of burning and scavenging only one structure remained in the Central Gate. The Outer Portal of the One Land rose from the floor of the mile-wide pass to a height of two hundred feet. While its pillars and towers had not been painted in many years, it nevertheless made an impressive picture, squatting beside the sheer cliff of the Central Gate's northern face. Jarnel scanned the peeling battlements. He saw no guards, but he knew they were there. At least a dozen bowmen concealed themselves beneath those ramshackle shutters on the third tier. Garney wouldn't drop the staircase until he could see their faces clearly. They rode under the lip of the creaking facade and dismounted.

After a moment of silence they heard a metallic crunch somewhere above them, followed by the sounds of a turning wheel and huge links of chain clanking through a metal casing. The bottom dropped out of the Outer Portal. It took several minutes to crank it down, but soon they faced a wooden staircase a full forty feet wide.

"They've painted it," Jarnel muttered. "I wonder why?"

Paumer grunted as he led his mount to the rampway on the right side of the staircase. It was coated with pitch to give sure footing to pack animals as they ascended into the darkness. Once the column had climbed inside, the staircase cranked up behind them, closing out the outside world once again.

Garney, Doorkeeper of the Outer Portal and a member of the Grand Council, stared down at them from the top of the ramp, his eyes glowering. "You're late," the sharp-faced little man snapped. Garney took his council responsibility seriously, as seriously as he did keeping the door. Jarnel had never seen him smile.

"Terribly sorry," Paumer lied smoothly, "but we had an animal go lame on us and we were forced to destroy it. Are the others here?"

"The *king*," Garney said forcefully, "is waiting." It obviously miffed the little man that Paumer would place priority on a mere committee meeting.

"Ah, yes." Paumer sighed, smiling wanly. "Let's go greet the king." The entourage bowed its way into the dome-shaped throne room. The king of the One Land sat casually in his jewel-crusted throne atop a dais raised thirty feet into the air.

"You can rise," he called down, and they all craned their necks to look up at him. "Keeper of the Outer Portal, remind me of who these people are . . . ?"

Garney cleared his throat and spoke up loudly: "O Master of the One Vast Land, Ruler from Time unto Time, these are but a few of your humble subjects, members of the Ad Hoc Advisory Committee on Provincial Concerns. They've come to join with myself and Wilker to discuss external affairs."

"Ah." The king nodded and shifted position, tucking one leg beneath him. "Problems out there?"

"None, my gracious King," Garney answered quickly. Jarnel studied the ruler's dark eyes. Even as Garney spoke, the king shifted his gaze here and there around the huge room, evidently bored beyond measure. Oh, what the Pyralu of Arl would do to this man once these walls were penetrated— yet the king of the One Land knew nothing of the danger, nor would his counsellors tell him. That was the tradition within the Remnant—the royal family had never been informed that the One Land no longer existed.

"You're not coming to the play, then?" the king asked Garney, and the doorkeeper dropped humbly to his knees.

"No, your Majesty. These matters, while trivial, demand my attention."

The king nodded. "Pity. What a nuisance." Then he got to his feet and stalked down off the far side of the circular dais, followed by a dozen fawning servants. Once he was gone, Garney looked at the group.

"Now we can join the others," he muttered, and he started toward a hallway that branched off the throne room.

"Where are we meeting?" Paumer asked as they followed Garney out.

"A small room on the back side. We'll need to ride." He led them out of the throne room and down a long ramp, then around a corner into a stable carved out of the rock. There he provided them each with a horse, since their own animals had been confined to pens within the Outer Portal. After two hours of subterranean riding through the seemingly endless passageways, Garney reined his horse to a stop. A moment later he ushered them into a modest conference chamber.

"Welcome!" Wilker, the effusive fop who fancied himself the supervisor of this council, smiled. Like every other resident of the Remnant he conceived of the world outside as a small, uncultured village—this despite the fact that he had visited both

Arl and Haranamous. "We've been patiently awaiting your arrival."

The other members of the Conspiracy who were present snorted derisively. "*You* have, perhaps," the smaller of the two said.

"Greetings, Ranoth," Paumer said cordially. "And to you, Talarath. How are things in Lamath?"

"Not well," Ranoth answered gruffly. "Displaced Marwandians invade us. Our children turn into monsters. Who can predict what might happen next?"

As if in answer to his question, the back wall of the conference room suddenly crumbled away, and dust and the afternoon sun streamed in from the outside world. Uda screamed, several others gasped, and Jarnel grunted at the shock. Standing in the gap was the slim figure of Dark, and beside the boy loomed a beast Jarnel knew only from legends. "So this," he thought, "is a tugolith."

Chapter Six

✖✖✖✖

CRISIS IN THE COUNCIL

Dark shielded his eyes and peered in. Then he stepped through the gap and glanced around the meeting room. "Why is everyone staring?" The boy shrugged. "I told you we'd be here."

Like the sliding pebble that sets off an avalanche, Dark's words released a landslide of chaotic activity. "What have you done?" Garney screamed as he vaulted the table and shoved his pointed nose in Dark's face. "You've ruined the citadel! You've breached the palace!"

"Well I'm sorry, Garney, but we had to get here and this was the only way we could make it on time." Dark brushed the dust from his clothing. "Besides, I didn't breach it at all. He did." He jerked a thumb back over his shoulder as Seagryn, now once more in his human shape, stepped carefully over the rubble and looked around. Garney continued to rail as Dark turned to explain to Seagryn. "This man is the Doorkeeper of the One Land. His name is Garney, and he takes his job very seriously. Excuse us, please," Dark mumbled as he took Seagryn by the sleeve and led him past the infuriated official.

Garney vaulted the table again and began shaking a finger in Wilker's face. "That's Wilker," Dark advised quietly, "the other representative from the Remnant. Never mind," he added. "They're always fighting."

By now Seagryn's attention had shifted to another, larger argument at the far end of the table. Dark saw his glance and quickly pointed out the participants. "That's Jarnel, the Prince

59

of the Army of Arl. That huge, heavy-faced man with him is Chaom, who guides the armies of Haranamous. You recognize the colors of the House of Paumer? Well the silver-haired man wearing them is Paumer. As for the other two—I suppose you know them already? Rather well?''

Seagryn's jaw had sagged open. Long before Dark finished his commentary the almost-bridegroom had locked eyes with the familiar scowl of the father of the bride. "Talarath!"

Paumer had turned to glare at Dark and now stalked down the length of the table, his gray eyebrows abristle with rage. "What are you doing here, boy?'' he half whispered. "What do we need to do to rid ourselves of you? Kill you? Will that do it?'' The words and tone were menacing enough to draw Seagryn's eyes away from Talarath to watch Dark's reaction. The boy surprised him. He didn't flinch at this abuse; instead he came right back in Paumer's face.

"Threaten all you like, Paumer, but I know the date of your death! Do you know it? Would you like to?'' Dark stepped toward the merchant, but it wasn't necessary. The man had already thrown up his hands to cover his ears and was retreating. Seagryn happened to glance at the two warriors who wore Paumer's livery and observed their smiles of delight.

"So, Dark,'' Ranoth snorted, and Seagryn looked now at the man he'd honored as a leader all of his adult life. "This is the wizard you promised to bring us? I already know he can change into a tugolith and knock down walls. But can he do anything else?''

This was too much. "Hypocrite!'' Seagryn exploded. "You and Talarath both, you're hypocrites! The people of Lamath trust you, believe in you as representatives of the One who is never named, yet here you are consorting with merchants and magic users!''

"Careful, Seagryn,'' Ranoth muttered. "You're here, too, you realize.''

Seagryn stiffened to his full height and threw out his barrel chest. "I'm no part of this Conspiracy! I came here in the presence of an honest prophet, and I'll depart with a single goal in mind—'' He pointed a trembling finger at Ranoth. "—to expose your involvement in this scandalous enterprise to every believing Lamathian!''

"Umm,'' Ranoth grunted, nodding. "And . . . ah . . . those who don't swallow it I suppose you'll just turn into a monster again and swallow them?''

"Ranoth," Talarath warned his associate quietly.

"Let him eat me!" Ranoth shouted back at Talarath, then his sharp eyes sought out Dark. "Is today my day, boy? Is that why you've brought this heretic wizard among us, so he can gulp the conspiracy whole?"

"Gentlemen, please," Paumer broke in nervously, "let's have no more talk of death or swallowing today—"

"What are we to talk about, Paumer?" Jarnel snarled from the far end of the room. "When the wisdom of a Nebalath is replaced by children—"

"Please, Jarnel!" Paumer snapped with unaccustomed savagery. "You will—have—your—chance!" The Prince of Arl held his peace, but his eyes shared readily with everyone his contempt for this whole affair. "Now," the merchant said more calmly, "with one notable exception, we seem to be all present. Shall we take our seats at the table?"

"I will *not*!" Garney shouted, and everyone looked toward the door.

The man was not answering Paumer. Rather he struggled to get past Wilker, who held the Doorkeeper by the shoulders as he explained over the smaller man's head, "He says he's leaving—"

"Let him go!" Ranoth erupted. "We need him even less than we need the monster!" Seagryn's face burned, but he held his temper. He'd never seen Ranoth so out of control.

"It isn't quite that simple . . ." Wilker said, but he stepped aside, and Garney shot out of the room's only official door. The handsome Wilker shrugged apologetically to the group as he came to sit at the table.

Dark tugged Seagryn's sleeve and motioned toward the nearest chair. Seagryn ignored the grumbling around him as he moved to it; but once in place, he glanced up and down the table to see who might be staring at him. Someone was, and he bumped Dark's arm and indicated the sullen adolescent across from him. "Who's that?" he muttered.

"Hmm?" Dark grunted. "Oh. Ognadzu, son of Paumer." Dark shot his fellow teen a toothy grin. "How are you?" he asked brightly, but this only deepened Ognadzu's scowl.

"And who's the girl?" Seagryn whispered, nodding toward the only female present.

"She's . . ." Dark began, turning his head to look at Uda. Then he froze. Uda lounged sideways in her chair, both legs thrown over one armrest, her elbow and torso supported by the other. She chewed her thumbnail reflectively as she stared at Dark. Certain she'd at last caught his attention, she glanced down at the hem of her skirt and gave it a little flip. If this gesture was designed to cover a bit more of her legs, it failed miserably. Dark noticed that, then glanced nervously back up at her eyes to see if she'd noticed. She had. She definitely had . . .

Seagryn watched this exchange with embarrassment. No Lamathian girl would behave so disrespectfully in the presence of a group of elders. He tried to frown the girl down, but she ignored him completely. She had eyes for Dark alone, and Seagryn felt the lad sliding backward in his seat. The young prophet kept clearing his throat and swallowing.

"Uda, pull your skirt down," Paumer muttered. He didn't wait to see if she obeyed, but plunged into his agenda. "We're assembled to discuss the international pressures that trouble us all. Jarnel's king has made no secret of his intent to crush Haranamous; from there, it's only a swift bite for Arl to consume Pleclypsa as well. Ranoth, Talarath, I believe you're being bothered by roving Marwandians, forced out of the Marwilds by Arl's intrusion there. Once the Pyralu controls both the western and southern mouths of this pass he's certain to pincer the Remnant—"

"Oh he won't trouble us." Wilker chuckled, but Paumer cut him off immediately.

"He will bother you, and Lamath too, unless we find some way to halt his march!" The merchant wheeled around to look toward the end of the table. "Jarnel. Would you or Chaom apprise the rest of us of the military situation?"

Seagryn leaned forward to see the general's response. The man's expression hadn't changed. "The rest of whom?" Jarnel snarled. "What purpose could that possibly serve without Nebalath being present?"

"Jarnel," Paumer growled quietly, "this is still the Grand Council—"

"I see two ineffectual priests from the high holy north, one grasping money-handler and his two spoiled brats, one know-it-all child prophet, a destructive pseudowizard I've never heard of before, and my sworn enemy from the battlefield! *This* is a Grand Council?" The general's gaze blistered the whole assembly. "Oh," he added belatedly, "Pardon me Wilker, I do see you also."

Seagryn glanced at the Remnant's remaining representative and watched the man chew his lower lip in humiliation. He then looked back at the Prince of Arl with respect—he agreed with the man. This was the Conspiracy Quirl mod Kit so feared and hated? Seagryn was not impressed.

Jarnel continued. "I see not one person present who can actually do anything to change the situation—"

"I'm here."

This announcement was devastating, coming as it did from the empty space above the table. Even more so was Sheth's slow unveiling of himself. He said no more until he'd made himself fully visible. Then, with a smirk, he strolled to the far end of the table from Paumer and sat down upon it. The entire assembly was stunned. Uda finally stared somewhere other than at Dark, and the lad began to breathe again. This was impressive, Seagryn thought to himself—along with being loathsomely magical, of course.

"As I was saying," Jarnel picked up again, and it was apparent in his voice that Sheth did not impress him. "I saw no one here who could help. Now I see one who could, but won't."

Sheth chuckled, then smiled, his black mustache parting to reveal perfect teeth, but not extending out far enough to obscure his dimples. "Such integrity, Jarnel. I wonder, though, if the king would consider it integrity. You remember him, don't you? Our king?"

Jarnel slumped back in his chair and fingered his forehead as if it ached. Defeat? Or just loathing? Seagryn glanced back at the beaming wizard, his own sense of distaste growing. Although certain he already knew from Quirl's bitter account, he leaned toward Dark and muttered "Who is this man?"

Sheth heard the question, and scooted up the table on his knees to stare into Seagryn's face. "You don't know me?" he asked with mock incredulity. "Dark," he scolded. "I think you've been remiss in this prayer sayer's education."

Uda's stare had already driven Dark far down into his seat. Sheth's gaze nevertheless drove him deeper. "This is Sheth," he managed to strangle out.

Sheth beamed, and looked back at Seagryn. "Yes . . . I'm Sheth. You've heard of me, perhaps?"

While Uda's manners had embarrassed Seagryn, Sheth's left him appalled. The man sat and crossed his legs two feet in front of Seagryn, almost in his lap. "A bit," he managed to get past his gritted teeth.

Sheth laughed aloud. "A bit!" Then he leaned forward, his blue eyes turning icy. "I hear you've found your altershape, and the clerics have tossed you out. Well, if you want to be a wizard, then watch me. I'm the only powershaper worthy of the title—and I intend to remain so."

A ripple of terror jellied Seagryn's spine. This Sheth was threatening him! But threats had never had their intended effect upon Seagryn. He responded wisely to warnings, redemptively to confessions, thankfully to offers of advice. But threats just made Seagryn angry, and right now he felt nothing if not threatened. "Would it be possible for you to take a seat at the table as any other civilized person might do?" He spoke with great force, his green eyes locking hard into Sheth's penetrating gaze.

His words drew a surprised gasp from several members of the council, and Sheth himself leaned back on his hands.

"Better do as he says, Sheth," Ranoth piped up quickly. "If he turns into a tugolith and sits on you, you'll be the flattest powershaper worthy of the title."

The comment drew a nervous laugh—and successfully defused the tension. Sheth shot the bearded priest a wry grin, then casually swung his legs over the edge of the table and hopped off. He ambled around to a vacant chair and plopped into it.

Seagryn watched him go, feeling fierce with victory. He'd been challenged and had met the challenge squarely. Sheth glanced up and saw his look, and nodded affably. Respect? Had he won this wizard's respect so easily?

"Do you think it possible to return now to our business?" Paumer asked with saccharine sweetness. Feeling more a part of the proceedings now, Seagryn shifted in his seat to face the merchant. He noticed as he did that Uda had again directed her hungry gaze at Dark. The boy sat paralyzed, and the thought crossed Seagryn's mind: Was he remembering some future with this girl?

"Before we do," the warrior Chaom interrupted, "could I have some explanation as to who represents what lands? I'm afraid I'm a bit confused . . ." Seagryn could tell from the man's expression that Chaom was not confused at all. If the question had been designed to fluster Paumer, it obviously had succeeded.

"Ah—ah—certainly," the merchant mumbled, seeming to flutter in his chair like a trapped bird. "Wilker and Garney represent the Remnant—"

"The One Land," Wilker corrected in a manner both kind and firm.

"Ah, yes of course." Paumer nodded. "Jarnel and Sheth

represent Arl, Ranoth and Talarath keep us abreast of Lamathian concerns, Ognadzu and myself come from Pleclypsa. As for Dark and his guest, I can't imagine who they believe themselves to represent—''

''We're from Marwand!'' Dark said sharply, which surprised Seagryn. He'd thought the boy rendered senseless.

''That's ridiculous,'' Paumer snarled. ''The Marwilds aren't a land—''

''But they are counted as one of the fragments,'' Dark argued. ''In any case, the Marwandians are a people, and they deserve to be a part of our process as much as any other people.''

''You don't represent their interests!''

''Oh, but we do. Much more so than you do the interests of the people of Pleclypsa!''

Seagryn was watching Uda as she watched Dark debate her father. Her eyes smoldered. With anger or with desire?

''He has you there, Paumer,'' Sheth spoke up. His was a deep voice, rich and commanding.

''And I think you skipped a land, Paumer, to return to my question,'' Chaom reminded the merchant. ''Who represents Haranamous?''

''Why—you do, of course.'' Paumer shrugged weakly.

''That's correct. And who else?''

''I do,'' Uda announced, and she tossed a quick scowl at her father for being too cowardly to say so. ''I was appointed to the post by Nebalath himself,'' she finished, and she folded her hands primly in her lap.

Chaom rolled his head around to look at Jarnel. ''You see?''

The Prince of Arl sneered in disbelief. ''I see.'' He looked at Uda. ''And are you also replacing Nebalath as wizard to King Haran?''

''Of course not,'' the girl snapped.

''Uda,'' Paumer warned quietly.

She frowned. ''What's your problem?''

''Uda shut your mouth,'' her older brother whispered savagely.

Uda's hair whirled as she glared back at Ognadzu and snapped, ''You were there, too! You heard him!''

''Uda if you don't—'' Paumer began, but Ranoth cut him off.

''Let the girl alone, and Dark and Seagryn as well. They're here—and so what? Sheth, with Nebalath no longer protecting Haranamous, is that land doomed to fall to Jarnel's army?''

The wizard shrugged elaborately. ''Dark knows,'' he said,

but with no reference at all to the young prophet sitting in their presence. "I've been busy in the Marwilds, chasing the bear baiters our 'guests' claim to represent. Jarnel? Will it fall soon?"

The general's expression of disdain did not alter as he replied, "Its collapse is certain. For all I know my second-in-command is marching on the capital even now."

"Let him," Chaom grunted.

"With Sheth here you may feel secure," Ranoth grumbled, "but without a wizard to cloak your people, what hope do you have against him?"

Chaom studied his sword-callused hands. "Ask him yourself."

Ranoth looked at the wizard expectantly. "Can you continue your wilderness wanderings until winter forces Arl's army home?"

Sheth revealed his widest, toothiest smile yet.

"Ranoth!" he mocked. "Are you asking *me* to be disloyal to my king?"

Ranoth hesitated only a moment. "Yes," he grunted.

Sheth's response was just as blunt. "No."

The room fell silent. In the stillness, they all heard the unmistakable clatter of armed men in the corridor, a host of them, and Chaom jumped to his feet in alarm. "Who's that?" he demanded of Wilker, and the Remnant representative hung his head.

"It's Garney. I told you when you made me let him go that it wasn't that simple. He's so concerned about that gap in the wall that he's decided to drive you all out through it and seal this room up tonight."

"But our horses!" Paumer exclaimed. "You want us to walk down the mountain?"

"These two came on foot," Wilker hedged, pointing at Dark and Seagryn.

"They're not officially members!"

"I realize it's an imposition," Wilker continued, "but it's hardly our fault." He frowned at Seagryn as the door flew open behind him and two-score armed warriors burst into the room.

"But we weren't finished!" Paumer roared, his face red.

"Yes, we were," Jarnel said with finality as he skidded his chair backward and stood up. "The Grand Council is finished for good."

Sheth cackled loudly at that. "For good, maybe, Jarnel. But not yet finished for evil, right? Right, young Dark?" The wizard hopped blithely over the table and stalked out the gaping hole in the wall. His exit was every bit as dramatic as his appearance had been. Indeed, the meeting was over.

Chapter Seven

❈❈❈❈

BEAR HUNT

THE meeting didn't just break apart, it shattered. The shouting match between Paumer and Garney was only the loudest of the ensuing arguments. Jarnel and Chaom snarled quiet threats at one another, while Paumer's son tried to prevent his sister from going after Dark and got an earful of oaths for his trouble. Seagryn glanced at Dark and saw the young man's gaze still riveted upon the girl. Terror? Excitement? Both? It didn't matter. The sensual energy the two exchanged reminded him of his own feelings for his lost Elaryl. And there at the far end of the table stood her father.

"Talarath!" he called. When the elder refused to meet his eyes, Seagryn rounded the table to confront him face to face. "Elaryl," he demanded. "How is she?"

"How do you suppose?" The gaunt elder's words exploded out, powered by unrestrained bile. "How would any Lamathian woman react who discovered at her foot binding that her groom was a heretic wizard!"

"But it isn't my fault—"

"I don't care whose fault it is; I don't care anything about you, save only this!" Talarath made a fist and shook it in Seagryn's face. "Forget her! Forget she even lives!" The man straightened up then, his dignity restored, and his lips became a thin line as he finished, "As I've already forgotten you."

Seagryn had known Talarath a long time. The man's vehemence did not surprise him, nor would he try to fool himself into believing he could change this old cleric's resolve. Yet he found he still couldn't abandon the attempt completely. He turned to look imploringly at Ranoth, and was startled by the ruling elder's odd smile.

"Let me deal with this," Ranoth soothed Talarath. He slipped an arm around Seagryn's waist and walked the younger man toward the wound in the wall.

"You surely understand that there's no way we can restore you, Seagryn," he began quietly, glancing up at the hole. "You've generated quite a spectacular ability and you seem compelled to demonstrate it in the most public of places. Hundreds of witnesses at the wedding, a dozen of the most influential voices in the world here—Ungh!" Ranoth grunted sadly. "And you showed such promise, too. That's the tragedy of it all." He turned to gaze out at the blue sky.

Despair put a lump in Seagryn's throat that he couldn't swallow. There was nothing more to say—nothing more to hope. Seagryn, too, looked out at the world.

"And yet," Ranoth said with a practiced guile that seemed to grab Seagryn by the shoulders and wrench him around, "there does seem to be one possibility . . ."

"What?" Seagryn demanded, and when Ranoth hesitated he seized the man's sleeve and pleaded, "Tell me! What is it?"

Ranoth glanced down at his arm and waited until Seagryn released it. Then he smiled and leaned his head up to whisper, "Since you have these abilities, perhaps you should learn how to control them." Then he gave a knowing nod toward the hole in the wall and raised an eyebrow.

Seagryn frowned. "Are you suggesting I follow this Sheth and attempt to learn something from him?"

Ranoth nodded again, but now he refused to look his former student in the eye.

Seagryn reeled at the thought. "But—but that's using magic!"

"Did you seek these abilities, this shaping of odious powers?" Ranoth whispered.

"Of course not, they—"

"Then perhaps they're a gift from the One we do not name! How should I know? But what does it matter, boy? What other option do you have? Go and learn what you can! And remember—when a nation has need of your services, it can overlook a multitude of sins." As quickly as this was out of his mouth, Ranoth scooted back around the table. Seagryn watched him go, watched as he placated the still seething Talarath, and watched as both men made a point of turning their backs on him. But Ranoth had not left him hopeless. There was a chance. He stepped to the gaping hole his massive altershape had made and peered down the mountain. The tiny figure of Sheth was still visible far below.

"Don't go," a trembling voice pleaded behind him. He looked back over his shoulder at Dark.

"Why? Do you need my protection from that predatory miss?"

"I do," Dark acknowledged, "but that's not the reason for my warning."

"Warning?" Seagryn frowned. "What's going to happen?"

Dark raised an inquiring eyebrow. "You're certain you want to know?"

Seagryn hesitated only an instant. "No," he snarled, and he plunged out the breach and down the mountain. Sheth had disappeared into the timberline. Had he lost him? He scrambled downward, slipping on the gravel in his haste.

"Slow down! You'll catch up to him!" he heard Dark call. He did slow his pace, but did not look back. A moment later Dark shouted, "You're my friend, Seagryn! I only want to help you!" Seagryn descended in silence for several minutes more before Dark yelled again, and this time his voice seemed far removed. "It's going to hurt!" the boy called, but Seagryn closed his ears and kept on going. He thought of nothing but Elaryl.

Once into the woods, he looked for footprints. While he believed Dark's assurance that he would find the wizard, he had no idea when or under what conditions. If possible, he wanted to find Sheth and not the other way around. But Seagryn had spent his life searching out facts in old manuscripts, not hunting creatures in the wild. He found nothing that would give him any clue to the shaper's path, and soon abandoned this scientific approach for the intuitive method that had served him so well as a cleric.

This Sheth was said to be a recluse. He would therefore prefer to stay as hidden as possible. That trick of slowly revealing himself—could the wizard somehow work it in reverse! Seagryn had heard Dark talk of cloaking. Was this perhaps that ability? Seagryn stopped where he was and listened. His mind whirled on.

Despite his evident arrogance, Sheth had revealed great interest in the subject matter of the meeting. Did he really take it all so casually to dismiss those deliberations with a high-handed insult? Or was Sheth the type of person who used language more for its dramatic effect than for its ability to reveal truths? The wizard had heard with the rest of them the news that all would have to depart through Seagryn's ragged doorway. Was it possible that he'd hidden himself here in these woods and was waiting to follow one of the parties home?

Seagryn whirled around and stared hard at a spot ten feet behind him. Much as it had happened in the meeting room, Sheth slowly became visible.

"So." Once Seagryn's eyes locked onto his own, the wizard shrugged. "You found me." Sheth sauntered forward. "Did you know you could penetrate cloaks?"

"What?"

"I thought not." Sheth chuckled, and he shuffled past Seagryn to continue down the incline. He'd gone about a dozen paces when he stopped and looked back. "Well, aren't you coming? I assume you chased me down for some reason . . . ?"

Seagryn nodded self-consciously and joined the shaper. They walked together in silence for several minutes before Seagryn raised the courage to ask, "What does it mean to penetrate cloaks?"

Sheth snorted scornfully, then frowned as if deep in thought. "I'd cloaked myself," he finally grunted. "You saw me. That's shaping."

"How exactly did I do it?"

"How should I know—exactly?" Sheth sneered. "You did it. You figure it out."

"Can you penetrate cloaks?" Sheth's look of utter disdain made it clear that the question had been a stupid one. "What other feats can you perform?"

"I knew it," Sheth growled, and he smiled at Seagryn sarcastically. Never had Seagryn felt so humiliated by a set of dimples. "You want me to teach you to shape. Am I right? A warm mentor-disciple relationship, resulting in your becoming someone I can respect as a peer? One of the boys? That's the way you do it up in Lamath, right? Elders and initiates, cloistered away in some moldy monastery, exchanging lofty platitudes that maintain the spiritual status quo?" The wizard gave a derisive hoot. "Well I'm not much for teaching. If you want to follow along, fine. Apparently you have the power to pursue me. If you happen to see me do something spectacular—" here Sheth paused to cackle "—that's only to be expected. If you should want to try it yourself, just make sure you put some distance between us. I don't want to be caught in the backwash of your failed attempts. If I am—'' Sheth's expression turned forbidding ''—then that's trouble between us. Be forewarned.''

Seagryn refused to be intimidated by this wizard's melodramatic threats. He responded quickly and quietly. ''Fine. Shall we go?''

Sheth seemed a bit surprised by this, but he recovered easily, and his cheeks dimpled again. ''I forget myself. I'm dealing with a cleric, and who has more confidence than that fool who thinks he has the ear of some almighty power?''

Seagryn didn't respond, but he felt his initial dislike for this man growing in intensity. Another emotion swelled inside him, one he'd practically forgotten since his days of formal schooling. He'd gotten along well with his classmates as long as no one attempted to compete with him. Once a challenge was issued, however, Seagryn could never rest until he'd thoroughly outperformed his competitor. Sheth might not yet be aware of it, Seagryn thought, but his attitude had just created for himself a formidable rival.

''One other thing.'' Sheth smirked. ''I do have my enemies. Don't be surprised if you find yourself in the line of fire. And if you do, don't expect me to protect you.'' Sheth stalked off, leaving Seagryn to follow several paces behind.

''I should be able to protect myself,'' Seagryn mumbled to the wizard's back. ''I have a rather thick skin when I choose to wear it.''

''Oh, yes, the tugolith shape.'' Sheth nodded. ''I've never spent much time with other powershapers; but, on the few occasions when I have, we've invariably discussed altershapes. Everyone has the same theory—that the altershape one takes reflects some deep-seated aspect of the wizard's personality.'' Sheth stopped and looked back. ''Tugoliths are stupid and they stink. Which of those are you, Seagryn? Both, perhaps?''

Before he could react to the insult Seagryn saw Sheth's eyes cut to the left. Suddenly the shaper disappeared. War cries erupted all around him, and Marwandian raiders leaped out of the bushes. Arrows whizzed through the clearing, and Seagryn froze in his spot, wishing he could become invisible. Not until the warriors raced past him did he realize that indeed he had. ''Down the path!'' shouted someone very close by. ''Pursue them!''

The band turned to rush down the incline, and Seagryn found himself grinning at them in giddy excitement. But he soon found that being invisible had disadvantages as well as advantages. One burly warrior did not swerve to avoid him, and knocked him sprawling. The Marwandian evidently knew what had hit him, or rather what he had hit, for he quickly grabbed onto Seagryn's robes and began to shout "I've got one!" A moment later he was surely wishing he hadn't. He had a tugolith by the horn.

"Northbeast!" the Marwandian screeched as he let go. Then the glade emptied of Marwandians, and Seagryn was left alone. He stood in the silence a moment, rocking unsteadily on his feet. Things certainly happened quickly for powershapers . . .

It had been a very long day. The sun was setting, and he felt famished. Sheth had disappeared, and Seagryn doubted if he would find him anywhere near this time. Still, the brief encounter had been a great confidence builder. He could make himself disappear. He could also ferret out another shaper who knew the same trick. There seemed to be little learning involved in making use of these powers—whatever he wished to do, he did. Apparently he could do what other shapers could. He just didn't know enough about shaping yet to recognize the possibilities. That's where exposure to Sheth could help him most, he realized, and he decided he would chase the arrogant wizard down again tomorrow. Tonight, however, he wanted nothing more than a good meal and a roof over his head. Seagryn remembered gratefully that the lovely town of Ritaven was very near. He headed toward it.

He expected to find Dark waiting for him. He no longer had any doubts about the boy's ability—Dark could do what he said he could. Seagryn still found that a bit disconcerting, as if Dark wasn't quite playing by the rules. He was grateful for the boy's loyalty, however, and appreciated the warning Dark had tried to give. Obviously he'd been trying to prepare Seagryn for the Marwandian ambush, although when he was knocked to the ground he'd been more surprised than hurt.

Seagryn returned to the inn where he and Dark had spent the previous night. He hesitated at the doorway, however. The common room was filled with Marwandians. The same group who had attacked this afternoon? He couldn't be sure, but lingering on the threshold could only draw attention to himself; rather than stand and stare, he made his way through the crowd to find a small table in a dark corner and sit behind it. He didn't glance around immediately. When he did raise his eyes, he saw with relief that no one watched him. Too late, he recalled that he could have cloaked himself before entering the place. It would take time for him to learn how best to use his shaper powers. Even so, he had other abilities born from much longer training. While the people of Lamath were sincere believers, the presence of a clergyman always made them behave a bit more piously than necessary. He'd learned long ago to blend in with his surroundings, and he did so now.

He didn't recognize the meat in the stew, but at this point anything would taste wonderful. He ate it gratefully, then asked his host for a room with some privacy. A tiny closet in the loft cost an exorbitant sum, but since Quirl mod Kit was paying for it, Seagryn didn't argue. He wedged the door shut, and dropped into the straw.

Seagryn woke the next morning refreshed and excited, Ranoth's words of the day before very much in his mind. He again had hope, and his day had purpose. He bought a hunk of cheese and a loaf of bread for his breakfast and started westward into the Marwilds. He ate as he walked, knowing with some odd inner assurance that he headed directly for Sheth's lair. Once he'd finished his meal, it occurred to him that, since he no longer needed his hands, he could take his tugolith-form and make much better time. "And draw the amazed stares of everyone I pass," he reminded himself as he discarded the idea. He could, of course, cloak himself as he traveled, but could that possibly deplete his store of magical energy? He decided to rely upon his human legs to carry him and to hide behind his unremarkable appearance.

He made good time. By late afternoon he felt Sheth's presence very near, and corrected his course slightly. Walking through a tiny meadow, he glanced up and saw a round-topped hill just ahead. "There," he muttered to himself. A few minutes later he was climbing its blackened slopes. A recent fire had denuded it of brush, and Seagryn wondered at that. He did not ponder long, however, for his quarry waited at the summit, and Seagryn had spent the entire day rehearsing this confrontation.

The invisible Sheth sat on a clump of granite boulders a hundred feet above him. Seagryn stopped walking and looked up. "Show yourself, Sheth!" Seagryn commanded brightly.

"Why?" Sheth called back, his voice strangely subdued. "You can already see me."

"True." Seagryn chuckled. "So why maintain this pretense?"

"I prefer not to reveal myself just yet to the army that followed you here."

"What?" Seagryn frowned, and Sheth laughed harshly.

"Fool!" the experienced wizard snarled. "Look at the base of the hill! Just look!"

Seagryn whirled around and stared downward in amazement as fifty, seventy-five, a hundred armed Marwandians stepped warily from the forest and slipped around the perimeter of the scorched knoll. "I never—"

"Never realized they followed you? Of course not! Because you're a fool. And yet—I'm grateful," Sheth said with a cackle. "I really am." The wizard leaped to his feet atop the rock, and threw his arms wide. In that moment he revealed his presence, and the Marwandian raiders shouted with excitement and charged up the hill. It happened so quickly Seagryn panicked. Trapped between a grinning shaper and Marwandian spears, Seagryn could only drop to his face and cover his ears. He barely heard Sheth's last comment: "I do hope you like percussion . . ."

Thunderous music rained from the skies, so loud it penetrated his hands, so haunting it wrenched at his soul. At the first deafening blast, he squinted his eyes, but it didn't fade as most loud noises do. Instead it grew louder, broadening, deepening, swelling in an unending crescendo that seemed to lift his vibrating body off the ground. He forced his eyes open and stared upward in horror. Sheth gazed down at him, his lips curled up on one side in a handsome sneer. "How?" Seagryn howled into the crashing waves of chords, but he couldn't hear his own voice, nor would he have heard the shaper had Sheth deigned to answer. Writhing onto his back, Seagryn peered down the hill and saw rather than heard the screeches of the attacking raiders. Not a man among them was still on his feet. All wore the same twisted expression Seagryn knew contorted his own face—a mixture of pure pain and esthetic ecstasy.

He recognized it now—the music he'd heard in the forest the night he'd wrecked the Marwandian camp. But that had been at a distance; this time it surrounded him. This epic orchestral opus held a hook for every raw emotion, retelling every stirring story he'd ever heard. He wept as much from joy as from the pain. But it was killing him, he knew, and he struggled to rise. Survival demanded that he run.

It seemed he had no legs. The music had robbed him of them. He still saw a bit and watched as one Marwandian after another pitched forward onto the scorched grass, blood spurting from ravaged ears. He longed to uncover his own, to surrender to the sweet melody that spoke of heroic failure and the nobility of sacrifice. But he didn't. His heart had been too recently brutalized for Seagryn to remain a romantic. A burst of resurgent cynicism found him his feet.

He churned up the hill, hands still crushing his ears, his elbows angled out before him like the runners of a sled. The angle of the slope grew sharper, and he found he was able to bounce all the way up to his feet. Still he churned through the dust and ash, up to the rock where Sheth had stood and past it, on to the crest of the hill and over. Then he was tumbling into a chasm, one more object in an avalanche of gravel and sand. He clenched his eyes and tucked his head against his chest as he bounced, first on his backside, then on his hip, then on his shoulder. He was tumbling still as his mind went blank, but there was that one victorious last thought—he heard the music no more.

Chapter Eight

❈❈❈❈

OGNADZU GOES

U_{DA} didn't understand her brother. Long after the others in their party had grumbled their last, Ognadzu continued to rage at the injustice perpetrated upon them all by the self-important Garney. It had been an inconvenience, certainly, and Uda assumed there would be repercussions within the Conspiracy. Very important people had been driven out that hole and down the side of the mountain—influential people who could do Garney harm and doubtless would, once the opportunity arose. Uda would certainly remember Garney.

But why did Ognadzu keep going on about it? The incident had, after all, forced the greats of Lamath, Haranamous, and Arl to rely upon the hospitality of their father. With his limitless credit, Paumer had been able to purchase horses for all of them in some tiny town at the foot of the mountain. Guest lodgings for the night could easily be provided at a nearby family castle. Uda recognized in this little nuisance an excellent opportunity to build contacts for the future. Her brother was making a fool himself. Why couldn't he see that?

Uda had lived all her life knowing that no matter where she was, some Paumer palace was within only a few hours' ride. What her father called the Bush House sat at the edge of the Marwilds not far from where they'd been expelled. Uda had rarely been there, for she wasn't the rustic type, and while the palace itself was opulent, the servants couldn't control the insects. She rejoiced, however, when it came in sight. She needed a bath—but far more than that, she needed a respite from Ognadzu's boorish yammering.

Naturally, Paumer's arrival at the palace was totally unexpected, so—as usual—they had to wait at the gate until the house steward could be found to verify that this was, indeed, the master. Then they had to endure the stream of pitiful apologies for their not having been admitted immediately. It happened all the time. They had so many palaces the family couldn't get around to all of them every year. With the turnover in servants, they could hardly expect to be recognized at a moment's notice. Nevertheless, Ognadzu apparently looked upon this as the day's prime insult and slammed through the front doors, slashing at the maids with his riding whip. Uda lingered beside her father as their guests dismounted and the horses were led away. "I don't know what's gotten into the boy," Paumer muttered apologetically to Jarnel and the others. "He never acts like this."

Uda rolled her eyes at that comment. She'd not intended to be seen, but Ranoth, the bearded priest that she thought looked like a wizard, happened to catch her. He smiled slightly, and Uda first covered her mouth in embarrassment, then smiled back. What did it matter, she decided? They all knew her father was lying.

Paumer led the group into the entryway and instructed the steward where each was to stay. Then he explained where dinner would be served and invited his guests to rest in their apartments until then. The group dispersed, but again Uda waited with her father and walked with him to the family apartments.

"Why did he do that?" she muttered.

"Oh," Paumer said wearily, "you know your brother. He had no chance to speak in that ruin of a meeting. I suppose he felt the need to make his presence known."

"He succeeded," Uda huffed.

"Remember, young lady, it was just this morning that I caught you blistering the ears of the two most powerful generals in the world!"

"They were dressed like servants. How was I supposed to know?" she began, but Paumer was chuckling, so she relaxed and continued more quietly, "Besides, I think that I more than made up for that this afternoon."

"You did, indeed." Paumer smiled. "You were very much the proper hostess." Uda was about to be very pleased by that, but then her father spoiled it all by patting her on the head. She hated that!

"At least one good thing came out of the day," she announced as Paumer turned in at his doorway.

"And what was that?" he muttered as he unfastened his servant tunic. He wasn't listening, of course, and that infuriated Uda far worse than the head pat. But he was *about* to listen.

"I met Dark the prophet," she said theatrically, then she sashayed down the carpeted hall to her own room.

"What?" Paumer shouted as he bounded back out into the hallway behind her. "What was that?"

Uda arched both her shoulders and her eyebrows. "You heard me." She danced through her door. Inside her room, she found a maid feverishly sorting through gowns, trying to find one Uda's size. "Hello," she said. The woman whirled around and stared at her in terror. "She probably expects the same treatment from me she got from Ognadzu," Uda had time to think before her father burst into the room behind her and whirled her around to face him.

"I can guess what you meant by that, young lady, and I don't like it! That boy has caused nothing but confusion since he first appeared, and I'll not tolerate any romantic notions being directed toward him by my own daughter!"

"Romantic notions?" Uda frowned innocently. "Did I say anything about romantic notions?"

"Now listen, child, you may think your father notices nothing but business, but I can assure you I was well aware of your dewy-eyed staring this afternoon!"

Uda glanced over at the maid, who was so astonished by this heated exchange that she had quite forgotten herself and was staring. "He's jealous," Uda explained.

"Uda!" Paumer roared. Then he glared at the hapless servant. "Get out!" he bellowed, and the woman dashed between them and through the door. Uda giggled merrily. "Why are you laughing at me?" Paumer screeched, his composure totally fled.

"Because!" Uda kept giggling. "You're funny!" She covered her face with her hand and doubled over, then straightened up and peeked through her fingers, expecting him to be laughing too.

Paumer wasn't. Hurt spilled onto the merchant's face, not in tears, but in an odd caricature of his normal smile. Uda had often seen this look, but she'd never before put it there herself. She'd thought only her mother capable of hurting her father so. The sudden discovery that she could froze Uda's laughter in her throat.

"I'm sorry," she said immediately.

Paumer stiffened, then cleared his throat. "What for?" He shrugged. Then he quickly left her room.

All the spring seemed to drain from Uda's legs as she wobbled to her bed and sat down on it. "Maid!" she called. "Draw a bath!" She had much to ponder.

Ognadzu did not appear at the dinner table. No one took public notice of that, but everyone seemed more at ease. Uda said nothing, preferring to look demure and listen while the principal figures of the Conspiracy spoke of the crisis they faced.

"Is there no way you can contain him?" Paumer pleaded with Jarnel.

"I'm no wizard," the Pyralu General said. "It takes a shaper to counter a shaper; you know that."

"Which means?" General Chaom asked, arching an eyebrow knowingly.

"You know what it means. We all know what it means," Jarnel answered. "There will be an invasion of the capital city of Haranamous. I can no longer prevent it."

"How convenient for you," Chaom grunted as he took another bite.

"You think me insincere," Jarnel said quietly.

"Gentlemen—" Paumer cautioned.

"I think it convenient for you, that's all I said. You're trapped between your mad king and your vain wizard, with no honorable recourse but to cut my warriors to pieces."

"It will cut my warriors to pieces as well, Chaom! Or do you think I don't care about my people in the same way you care about yours?"

"My friends—"

Jarnel ignored Paumer's peacemaking as he continued, "Is it convenient for you that your aged powershaper has abandoned his friends in their time of need? Of course not, Chaom, and I do not accuse you of it. Nor will I allow you to accuse me of abandoning my friends. Yes, Paumer, my friends, for so I regard all of you." Jarnel looked straight at Chaom. "Yes . . . even you." The general stood up, folded his napkin beside his plate, and bowed deeply to his host. "I thank you for the meal, Paumer, and the offer of a bed. I fear I must decline the latter, for I left my army under the command of an underling impatient to make his reputation."

"But you've not rested in two days—"

"Ah, but I have napped," Jarnel said, firing such a bright

smile at Uda that the girl jumped in surprise. "Haven't I?" he asked.

Uda said nothing, but she felt her face flush. She wanted to race from the table in embarrassment. Fortunately Chaom stood up too, which drew everyone's attention from her face to his. Uda was able to breathe again.

"I travel with you," Chaom muttered to Jarnel.

"That may inconvenience you," the Pyralu General murmured. Uda cringed, expecting the argument to erupt anew.

It didn't. Instead, the general of Haranamous laughed aloud, and walked around to clap his rival on the shoulder. Uda didn't understand the exchange at all and would have dismissed it as simple masculine posturing. She couldn't help but notice, however, that the two men obviously understood one another, while her father appeared not to understand them at all. Uda had always regarded men as very much alike. Was it possible there were different types? If so, how many different types were there? She overheard the two religious leaders whispering to one another, so she took another bite and listened carefully.

"May the One we do not name preserve us from the laughter of warriors," Talarath muttered.

"Umm," Ranoth grunted. "Or send Lamath one who can make us laugh."

Uda studied the peas on her platter, but her mind was busy elsewhere. She had still more to ponder now and she worried that she wasn't learning fast enough.

The leaders of Lamath did not hurry at their supper, nor seem to feel any compulsion to rush away. Was this because they had no war to fight? Or was it true what she'd heard rumored, that religious leaders would go to great lengths to avoid being uncomfortable? The thought made Uda momentarily scornful, until she realized that she, too, had the good sense to avoid needless sacrifices. Was it possible that these religious folk simply had better sense than the two warriors? Perhaps that was the reason they had no war to rush off to fight! Uda felt certain that these men would not be sitting at her father's table if they did not possess great wisdom of some kind. The House of Paumer dealt only with the best. Since she knew so little about these oddly pompous Lamathians, she obviously had much to learn from them.

She had many questions she wanted to ask, but something in their tone of voice or the way they looked at her warned Uda against addressing them. She was either too young or too female to engage them in conversation.

Dinner ended, and the two guests disappeared down the corridor toward rooms Uda was certain she'd never been inside. She needed to tour this place in the morning, she thought to herself. For now, however, her main task was to comfort her father. She scurried down the family hallway after him; hooking her arm through his, she slowed to match his strolling pace.

"Are you all right?" she asked.

Paumer looked weary. "I don't know," he muttered. She waited for him to say more, but he didn't. She shifted strategies.

"Did you forbid Ognadzu to come to dinner?" she asked.

"I did not." Her father frowned. "That was his own choice. I don't know what's wrong with that boy . . ." Uda recognized that he said this more to himself than to her. She was losing him.

"He'll be fine," she comforted, just as she'd heard her mother comfort him many times before. "He just had a bad day. You'll see tomorrow."

Paumer faced his daughter, looking deeply into her eyes. "Will I?" he asked pointedly, and Uda blinked, startled by the intensity of his stare. Then he seemed to go limp, and his eyes flicked back to the tapestried wall behind her head. "Good night, child," he murmured. He gave her forehead a perfunctory kiss, then drifted into his own apartments and closed his door.

Uda frowned. That hadn't gone well. She reviewed her mistakes as she walked down the corridor and into her room. Then she cursed the maid. Her tapers had not been lit!

"She didn't do it," a voice said in the darkness, and Uda gasped and jumped back against her door. "It's just me."

"I know it's just you, but you still scared me," Uda snarled. "Why weren't you at dinner?"

Ognadzu sighed. "You sound just like mother when you scold. If I remember rightly."

Uda's eyes were adjusting, and she saw her brother clearly now. He sat in the window seat and had opened the shutters to the night air. The moon wasn't up, but there were many stars. They gave enough light for her to see the wetness glisten on his cheeks.

"She's not gone that much—"

"Come now, Uda," Ognadzu sneered. "You think you're talking to one of those priests?"

"You missed some good conversation. Some important conversation!"

"I heard every word."

"Oh?" Uda said with a quality of sarcasm possible only between siblings. "Were you under the table?"

"I had my ear to the talk-box."

"The what?"

It was Ognadzu's turn to be snide. "You don't know anything about this house, do you?"

"Why? What should I know?"

"There's a gilded box in the upper library that can listen in on any conversation that takes place inside this palace! Didn't you know that?"

"No! How did it get there?"

"One of our parents had some wizard put it there to spy on the other. And don't ask me which one did it, because I can't remember. Who knows, perhaps Paumer is listening to us this very moment."

"No," Uda said quickly. "He's gone to bed."

"Then maybe it was mother who had it put there. He may not even know it exists."

"And how do you know!"

"I've lived here, remember? I like the forest." Uda did remember now that Ognadzu had spent several summers here, as well as parts of the last two winters. He was really the only family member who had. Suddenly she understood a bit better his angry display at the gate.

"I—guess you probably feel this palace is—yours?"

"Astute, Uda," Ognadzu mumbled.

"And the rest of us are—"

"Invaders." Ognadzu bounced off the window seat and came toward her with frightening speed. "But then, you've made a lifetime of being that, haven't you?"

"What do you mean?" she asked, though she knew precisely what he meant. Suddenly she felt him grab her by the shoulders and whirl her around him. She could see his angry face clearly in the starlight.

"Why did you come? Being part of the Grand Council was my one chance to be with him alone! You've wedged between us on everything else, Uda; now you've wedged us apart in this, too!"

Uda said nothing for a moment. When she did speak, it was

in a monotone that proclaimed her lack of care. "Are you going to beat me up as you do the maids?"

Ognadzu grunted in shock. Then his rage took over. He picked her up and threw her across the room. Either by luck or because he couldn't bring himself really to hurt her, Uda landed on her own bed. Even before she quit bouncing, he was climbing out the window. "Where are you going?" she demanded.

He leaned back inside to answer her. "What do you care? Should anyone ask you about me tomorrow, just explain that it got to be too much and I had to go."

Uda had rolled to her feet and ran to the window herself. "But where?" she whispered loudly to his retreating back. "Father has very long arms! He'll not let you leave the family."

Ognadzu stopped and came back. "Leave the family? Did I say that?" Ognadzu took her hands in his and squeezed them, first gently, then with increasing brutality. "Oh, Uda. For such a bright little girl you can be truly naïve."

"Ow!" Uda cried as she jerked her hands away and scampered backward into the room. When she returned to the window a moment later, her brother was gone.

"Ognadzu?" she called quietly. "Ognadzu!" she repeated, a little louder this time but not strongly enough to wake her father. Only the crickets answered.

Dazed by the importance of this event, Uda wandered back toward the center of her room. Suddenly the tension and excitement of the day dropped upon her shoulders like a fallen boulder, and she pitched headlong across her bed, sobbing. She cried herself to sleep.

She woke to the bright sunshine of midday and realized immediately that she'd slept all morning. She sat up in bed, yawned, then saw with chagrin that someone had dressed her in her nightgown and put her under the covers. That bothered her. It was the kind of thing nannies did to little girls, and she was certainly no little girl! She kicked off the covers with a savage—and very adult—oath, then padded to her closet to see what the servants had been able to find in her size. She was fully prepared to fly into a rage, but was disappointed—she found there an excellent selection of attire. She gazed for a moment at the rack, then selected a riding costume and quickly changed into it. She had some thinking to do, and nothing aided the workings of her mind like a long ride.

As she glided out her door, a solicitous servant sprang to attention and asked if she was interested in food. She waved him off disdainfully, striding down the corridor and out the side door to the stables. Moments later she was mounted and riding through the front gate. She'd said nothing about it to the groom, but had noticed Ognadzu's horse was missing. As she cantered into the forest, she kept her eyes on the ground. She was looking for tracks.

Uda loved her brother. She hated him, too, of course—everyone did. But that didn't eclipse the deep bond of loyalty she felt toward him, forged through years of being privileged children together, left for the most part alone. Who would she talk to now? With whom would she fight?

Later, as her horse walked more sedately through the trees, other questions intruded upon her silence. Did their father know? Were the spies of Paumer even now pursuing the wayward son toward who knew where? Or—and this seemed somehow worse—had Ognadzu not even been missed yet? When she got back to the palace would her father grill her about last night's events? If so, what would she say?

"Stop!" she called sharply, and her mount obeyed. She'd heard something, something most strange. The rhythm of hoof-beats now silenced, she heard it more clearly—music! Beautiful music, the kind her mother commissioned, the kind rarely heard outside the refined art houses of Pleclypsa! Uda sat transfixed upon her disinterested pony, realizing for the first time a little of what her mother felt in the concert halls. But from where was it coming? She booted her horse in the flank and they took off at a gallop.

They plunged deeply into the Marwilds, far enough that even the fearless Uda began to question the wisdom of the search. It hardly mattered now, she supposed—the music had stopped. About the time she turned her horse around and started home, she realized she was lost. She didn't mean to, but for the second time in two days Uda cried.

"Can I help you?"

"What!" she shouted, terrified at the closeness of the voice. She threw her head around to look behind her and met the eyes of a face she recognized. Her heart skipped a beat. "You—you're the wizard . . . Sheth?"

"You haven't forgotten me so quickly, have you?" Sheth grinned, and there was no mistaking the menace in his smile. "It was, after all, only yesterday."

"You—you remember me?" Uda gulped.

"Of course. You're the daughter of Paumer. And crying, too. I wonder—are you lost?"

"I'm not lost!" Uda snarled quickly, then added, "I mean, not very lost. I was following some music," she explained matter-of-factly. "That may sound odd, to hear music in the midst of a forest, but I did. So there."

"Many odd things happen in the Marwilds." Sheth grinned again, in a manner Uda found far from comforting. "Would you like to come visit me and see more?"

Uda didn't hesitate. "I think at the moment I'd like to return to my father's house. Since you're his friend, would you be willing to guide me there?"

"Am I his friend?" Sheth smiled wickedly. "Has he ever told you so?"

Fear was just not a sensation Uda was accustomed to feeling. Thus, when it did come, it shattered her. She stared at the wizard, acknowledging for the first time how very deeply into danger she'd put herself. She gazed into the most menacing face she could recall and wondered what this man was about to do to her.

Abruptly, the powershaper's expression changed. "Come child," he said officiously. "I'll take you home."

Chapter Nine

※❂❂❂❂※

S'MOTHERED

"**M**y ears!" Seagryn thought immediately upon waking. Had he screamed that thought? He couldn't hear his own—

"Your friend is awake," said a pleasant voice nearby, and Seagryn moaned with relief. He could hear after all.

"I told you he would, didn't I?"

"Oh, I'm almost certain you did, yes."

"You never listen to me."

"That's not true, son," Dark's mother responded amiably. "I always listen to you. I just never pay any attention to what you say."

"And that's what I mean by not listening!" Dark sounded vexed.

After a brief pause, Seagryn heard the woman again. "Ehm? I'm sorry. What was that, son?"

"I give up!" Dark screamed, but it seemed to Seagryn a mocking scream, a loving, gentle, playful scream. The conversation continued, but he was floating away, buoyed by the warmth of those two voices . . .

He walked in a peaceful parkland, along the moss-covered bank of a brook. No, he didn't walk—he floated instead, and he thought that odd, but disregarded it as no more odd than many other things he'd seen and felt in these past days. None of the strangeness mattered any longer, for he was about to be wed, and his anticipated joy rinsed all his recent troubles from his mind. What troubles? It occurred to him that he needed to re-member them, that some critical things had happened, that a total loss of memory could be quite dangerous . . .

He realized he was lost. The woods had grown sullen, choked with weeds and thorny shrubs. There was a path, but he took it unwillingly, wishing for other options but finding none. As he followed it, the forest seamed itself shut behind him, impelling him forward. And there was something up ahead, he knew, something very fearful, something that both drew and repelled him. He stopped. He started backward, but bumped into the bole of a giant tree that had suddenly grown up behind him and which shoved him further down the path with its ever-widening girth.

Then he heard music—enchanting music, meat for the spirit, and he realized what awaited him and good-naturedly berated himself for being such a fool. His wedding, of course! Elaryl awaited! Now he sprinted down the path, which seemed to drop downward in a sharp incline. He burst out of the woods into a meadow aglow with every conceivable shade of yellow. There she stood, his bride, the sun behind her head, her golden hair a halo of high-minded promise, and the music swelled and swelled—and swelled still further—until he felt himself ready to burst with it, and he glanced down in horror to realize that his body had swelled along with the sound!

He'd grown scales, the scaly armor of a lizard or a snake! In the midst of his forehead an enormous horn sprouted and grew, and he crossed his eyes to stare at it in humiliation. He turned his enormous head to gaze downward, and saw that his expand-ing torso had ripped through his wedding garments. They lay in tatters on the ground between his massive hooves, and he was utterly naked! Mortified, he looked for Elaryl's reaction, certain of her rejection.

She wasn't even looking at him. She'd wrapped herself in the music, that gorgeous, haunting music, and now wore a beatific expression that focused upward upon the One they did not name, the One who had betrayed Seagryn to the—

Music! Too much music! Seagryn struggled to cover his ears but no longer had arms or hands. He bounded around the meadow, crashing through tables and chairs erected for the oc-casion, bellowing in pain and humiliation. Yet the music would not stop, the magic would not stop, and he found himself facing that new-grown tree and began to bang his mighty horn upon it in rhythm to the all-pervading melody.

Then it seemed the tree was a tree no more, but a man, a giant, a handsome giant with blue eyes and a mustache and dimples and a horrible, abusive laugh. When Seagryn realized that this man's laughter was the music, he wept in abject humiliation.

He rolled in the dirt at the giant wizard's feet, twisting from side to side, then opened his eyes pleadingly and found himself ringed now by giants—the wizard behind him, the glowering Ranoth on his right, the snarling Talarath on his left, and before him, garbed in the robes of a high prophetess and wearing the most scornful frown of all, stood the lady Elaryl. He gasped, then opened his mouth to plead for forgiveness, but before he could utter a word her visage changed—to that of Sheth. The sorcerer smirked down at the cringing Seagryn, then chuckled, and then he laughed—

"The music! Stop it! I can't bear—!"

"There, child. There, there, child. It's all right. You're all right. There, there."

Someone cradled Seagryn's head against her enormous bosom, and he let her do it, grateful for the touch, for the care, and for the warmth. He was awake, aware of his sobbing, and in the process of controlling it, but it was going to take him a moment to get beyond the nightmare's deafening chords.

What he needed most was a friend. He allowed the woman to rock him gently as he gasped for breath, listening to the pounding of his heart and doing all in his power to slow it. At last he sighed and rolled his head back off the woman's pillowy chest. His eyes met Dark's. They watched him with deep concern and affection. Seagryn managed a weak nod.

"Better?" Dark asked.

"Yes," Seagryn muttered.

"I told you there'd be pain—"

"Oh, hush!" the woman snorted, and she hugged Seagryn's head again, crushing his ears. He managed to struggle out of her embrace, then looked up at her face. It was round and red, creased into a permanent smile by a profusion of wrinkles. This woman loved life, and didn't care who knew it. Seagryn had to smile.

He glanced over at Dark, who had raised a meaningful eyebrow. "S'mother, this is Seagryn the powershaper. Seagryn, this is my s'mother."

"Your mother?"

"No," the woman sighed, then she laughed girlishly. "His s'mother!" And to prove it, she hugged Seagryn again, earnestly enough to choke the breath out of him.

"He's got it," Dark informed her wearily, and the woman released Seagryn with a hearty laugh.

Unfortunately, she then grabbed him by both cheeks to turn his face toward hers as she said, "He's called me that since he could talk—which sometimes seems like it's been forever!" Her smile softened. "You're welcome here, Seagryn. For just as long as you choose to stay, as well as whenever you choose to come back. Call this home. Call me Amyryth." Then she kissed him on the cheek and released him. "Stew's on the stove. Need some firewood." Then the woman was out the door and gone.

Seagryn blinked.

Dark sat on the edge of the bed. "You see why I'm gone so much?" he moaned.

"I see that you're very much loved," Seagryn mumbled. He rubbed his bruised cheeks and gazed around the cottage, now fully alert. "Where is this place?"

"In the Marwilds. Not far from where you had your last encounter with Sheth."

"You live in the Marwilds?" Seagryn wondered.

"Have for years. Why not?"

"I guess . . . I thought . . . because you're a prophet . . ."

"Not all believers inhabit your precious land of Lamath, Seagryn, despite what you may have been taught by the elders. Just as—I'm sure you know—not all who live in Lamath are really believers."

"True enough," Seagryn mumbled, rubbing a huge knot on the side of his head. "Still, it is the land committed to belief—"

"Come on, Seagryn. I may be just a boy, but even I know land doesn't believe anything. Only people believe. Some people."

Seagryn swung his head around to gaze at Dark soberly. "And you? Do you believe?"

Dark grinned. "How can I help it! I'm a prophet, right?"

"Are you a prophet? Or do you just possess a different type of magic from that of Sheth?"

Dark's good humor evaporated. "Why do you doubt what I say?" he asked sadly. "Because we live in the Marwilds instead of within your little corner of the old One Land? We once lived in Lamath, but we finally had to leave. The faithful like to talk a lot about prophets, but they don't like having one live nearby. As soon as my gift became apparent, they drove my family out. Doesn't that sound familiar? Didn't they do the same to you?''

"That was different," Seagryn grumbled, recalling the terrible events of his wedding day. "I deserved it."

"Why?" Dark demanded angrily. "What did you do!"

"I used magic!" Seagryn snarled back. "And mine *is* magic! Magic most foul! Whence it came I have no idea, I only know it's robbed me of my life and my love, and that I cannot ever use it again!"

Dark was gazing off into his own mind. "I knew that was coming," he muttered.

"What was coming?"

"This disavowal of your gift—"

"What gift!" Seagryn sneered bitterly.

"Oh, it's a gift. You may not like it much at the moment, but you can't deny it was given—"

"But by whom!" Seagryn demanded. Dark's answering smile infuriated him.

"Who else?" The boy prophet grinned. "Didn't Ranoth say something about that to you? If he hasn't, I know that he will the next time you—"

"He did," Seagryn grunted.

"Well, then." Dark chuckled. "You see?"

"I'm not using it." It didn't matter if the gift had come from the One they never named. That Power had betrayed him! As Elaryl had betrayed him . . .

Dark propped his chin on his hand and gazed quietly at Seagryn for a moment. Seagryn ignored him. Finally, the boy hopped down from the high bed.

"You're not going to listen to me anyway," Dark muttered. He left the cottage.

Seagryn peered around at the brightly painted walls and felt a disabling hopelessness creeping up from deep within himself. There was nothing he could do—or rather, nothing he could feel righteous in doing. As a person who had lived all his life seeking righteousness, he found that realization crippling.

"Here we go," Dark's mother said as she stepped back inside the cottage. She carried a bundle of firewood across the room and set it next to the stove. Then she straightened up and glanced around. "Disappeared again, has he?"

"He just stepped outside," Seagryn responded. The woman's answering giggle surprised him.

"Forgot you were a powershaper and might take me literally. That's what I meant—he's gone?"

"Ah—yes . . ."

"Good." She grinned as she reached out to lift the lid on the stew pot. "Not that I like him gone, you see, but you've traveled enough with him to realize that he can cause a throb in the forehead. You've not eaten any of this. I'll wager he didn't offer it?" Amyryth was already grabbing a bowl.

"No—"

"You need to eat. You look awful." She thrust the bowl of stew in front of him and held it in his face until he took it. "Not as bad as when we first dragged you out of that mud, mind, but still as wretched as a three-days'-dead cat. Can I get you some more?"

Seagryn had yet to take the first bite. "Ah—no . . ."

"You want me to feed it to you?" Amyryth said, nodding eagerly.

"No," Seagryn blurted and took a quick mouthful. He found the stew delightful, and that showed on his face.

"Thought it might taste good to you." She smiled, turning back to her stove. "Had to ask my boy what wizards eat, but he assured me simple fare was best."

"I'm not a wizard," Seagryn grunted. He took another bite.

Amyryth turned around to gaze at him. "Yes," she said after a moment, "Dark told me you'd say that."

Seagryn's only response was to raise his eyebrows and take another spoonful. The woman turned back to her chores, busying herself around her tiny kitchen area. She kept a close watch on him, however; as soon as he took the last mouthful, she was retrieving the bowl and refilling it.

"I was in the mud?" he asked when she brought it back to him.

"Head first. Up to your neck. We had an awful time cleaning it out of your ears and nose."

Seagryn covered his face, embarrassed that this stranger would be so familiar with his nostrils. "How long had I been there?"

"Not but a moment, or you would have drowned."

"Then you heard the music?" Seagryn frowned. "How did you avoid—"

"I heard very little of it." Amyryth smiled serenely. She pointed to her ears. "We plugged them."

Seagryn sat back in the bed and considered this. "Dark knew where it would happen . . ."

"An annoying trait sometimes—I've never been able to surprise him, neither for a gift nor for a tanning—but on occasion it has been a real life-saver. You going to eat that or stare it down?"

Seagryn took another bite, and she nodded and went on.

"It's been a hard gift to accept. Caused his father and me great grief, sometimes, because it's been such a burden for the boy to bear, but the Power does what the Power chooses and it's better to rejoice than to moan." Amyryth looked sideways at him, her expression sly.

Seagryn immediately understood where she was leading, and resented it. "I wish I'd been blessed with such a gift."

"No, you don't." The woman sighed as she took his bowl and carried it back to her tiny table.

"I do," Seagryn called to her back. "I've been cursed instead!"

"You think Dark's gift hasn't been called a curse many times? Right here in this cottage?" Dark's mother did not turn around to face him as she said this, nor did she speak with much passion. Her attitude made him angry.

"What difference does it make what I feel?" Seagryn demanded. "Why should it even concern you?"

Amyryth turned around slowly and gazed at him. "Because I like you. Because I care about your being happy. Because I love the Power and see you as the Power's handiwork. And not incidentally, because your gift and my son's are bound up together, and his joy and safety will depend largely on you." She dropped her eyes to the polished boards of the floor. "Even as yours will depend on him."

Seagryn could not mistake the woman's care for him, nor question the obvious logic of her last thought. But her unrestrained use of a common name for the One who was not named repelled him. Despite their warmth and love, how could these people say they shared his faith yet use such crass language? "Would you . . . would you mind not using that name for the One beyond naming?"

"Ehm?" Amyryth asked, glancing up.

"Perhaps that seems a petty request but—"

"But all your training's taught you to keep the Power at a holy stone's throw. That's all right. I'll say the Nameless, or whatever you choose, just so long as you don't prevent me from including Him in the conversation. He's my friend, you know."

Such intimacy with the One caused Seagryn to squirm with discomfort. It seemed so—coarse!

Dark's mother chuckled at him, and Seagryn looked around at her. "You're a spiritual, I can tell," she said.

"A what?"

"A spiritual. You know the Nameless One so well you're certain He could never make a move without you, and the very thought He might is obvious heresy."

"Now wait just a moment—" Seagryn bristled, but Amyryth wasn't in the mood for waiting.

"I've known plenty of you. You're the type that sent us scrambling, not long after Dark's gift became clear. But it's all right— I'm happy for you. Probably a lot happier than you are for yourself."

"And by that you mean—"

"Only that the toughest thing for a spiritual to handle is to be spit on by other spirituals. And I should know, since I was one." Amyryth suddenly found something in her kitchen that needed attention. Seagryn sat up, dropping his feet off the side of the bed.

"You say you were one once?"

Amyryth smiled. "Once. Yes. Once upon a time. Terribly worried about the intrusion of faithlessness into the land, adhering to the path, and remaining a spiritual cut above my neighbors. But the Power took care of that. Whoops, I mean the One we do not name. Gave my son a gift beyond measure and a purpose of true spiritual import—and knocked me on my material fanny in the process." The woman laughed again, then shook her head and gazed thoughtfully into a dark corner of the cottage. "And it made me wonder. If we don't even know ourselves, how in the world can we believe we know all of His secrets?" Then she shrugged, grinned a wrinkled grin at Seagryn, and went to stuff more firewood into her stove.

Seagryn looked down at the quilt that still covered his lap. "And you think I'm one of these spirituals?"

"Just exactly like the ones who drove you out," she replied without interrupting her work.

He meditated for a moment, listening to the irregular clunks as the wood dropped into the hole. "And you think this—magic—I do might be a gift and not a betrayal?"

"No," the woman grunted as she stood up and wiped her nose with her apron. Then she looked at him. "I don't think it. I know it."

"How?" Seagryn demanded. "How do you know it?"

"How do you think?" Amyryth chuckled again. "I've got a prophet in the family!"

"Has she convinced you yet?"

Seagryn craned his neck to see Dark peeking in the doorway. Then he looked back at his bare toes. "You can come on in."

"Does that mean she has?"

"You know already. Why ask."

Dark stepped into the cottage and walked toward the stove to fetch a bowl. "I try not to be rude. Did you eat all of it?" He frowned down into the stew pot.

"Supper's coming," his mother mumbled as she elbowed him aside and reached for a pan hanging on the wall. Dark raised his eyebrows and strolled back toward the bed.

"You're feeling better."

"I am."

"Ready for the next step."

"I'm ready." Seagryn nodded.

Dark sat beside him, sighing heavily. "I'm glad you are. I'm certainly not."

Seagryn felt the fear grab his gut again. Sheth! There'd be the music to face. "Will there be more pain?" he asked, and Dark frowned at him.

"What? For *you*? I—I don't guess I've thought about that much." He squinted his eyes and peered into the distance. "You'll be all right." He shrugged. "It's me I'm worried about . . ."

Seagryn tried to look properly concerned for the lad, but all he felt was relief. But for how long would he do all right? Did that include some renewed relationship with Elaryl? The urge to know more was too strong to resist. "I—I will? Even against Sheth?"

"Even facing Sheth. Of course you won't be facing him, exactly, just—stop me if I've gone too far . . ."

"No! No, I want to know! Some at least. What is this trouble that's ahead for you? Can I help?"

Dark shook his head glumly. "Not likely. I'm trying not to

think about it. It's as if I'm about to walk into a megasin's cave, and I don't relish the idea one bit!''

Seagryn frowned. ''What's a megasin?''

Dark seemed surprised, then raised a knowing eyebrow and sighed deeply. ''You'll see. Believe me—you'll see.''

Chapter Ten

✕✕✕✕

A MONSTROUS DESIGN

As they rode through thick forest, Uda regaled Sheth with an account of her mother's most recent public triumph. She laughed much too loud, giggled far too long, and flung her head from side to side, acting every inch the giddy teen. Her eyes, however, kept a vigilant watch on the road ahead. The wizard radiated menace as he brooded beside her upon his stallion. Any minute he might turn on her and—but she wouldn't waste precious moments enumerating the frightening possibilities. She spent her energies doing the smartest thing she could think of—she acted the fool. And for once, Uda took comfort in being ignored.

When at last the Bush House came into view, she sighed deeply and allowed herself a bit of a grin. Safe again in her father's house! The powershaper was honest after all—or at least he had been with her—and she could now afford to enjoy the stir their entry into her father's mansion would cause.

In fact, they found the place a clawsp castle of activity. Servants ran everywhere while being urged to redouble their efforts by more exalted servants, who were themselves hounded into still more intense activity by the steward himself. Chaos reigned—but evidently Uda was its queen, for as soon as she was spotted, the courtyard fell silent. The steward stared at her for a moment, as if trying to decide whether to reprove her or fawn upon her. He chose to do neither, instead darting inside the mansion door. A moment later a snarling, snapping Paumer launched himself out of it and off the porch, running toward her with violence in his eyes. When he recognized her riding companion, however, he stopped short and made an obvious effort to reassemble some dignity. Uda watched him with relief, knowing exactly what he would do—first came the deep breath, then Paumer unveiled the smile in all its dazzling glory.

"Sheth!" Paumer grinned radiantly. "Welcome to my home! What brings you here on this rather distracting afternoon?"

"I've come to return something that belongs to you," Sheth mumbled and he jerked his handsome head toward Uda. "You let your children wander in the woods?"

"I got lost," Uda blurted, jumping down from her horse. "It was quite by accident, Father, really, and I had no wish to cause you any alarm." She danced over and tried to kiss Paumer on the cheek, but her father stiff-armed her attempt as he continued beaming at the wizard.

"You mention my children." Paumer chuckled. "You didn't by chance come upon my boy also?"

Sheth frowned and made a great show of thinking deeply. Then his eyes lit up, and he raised his eyebrows as if with sudden insight. "You mean that surly young chap who sneers every time you say anything?"

Paumer winced. Uda saw, and with her seeing felt two complementary emotions erupt inside—pity for her father and hatred for this arrogant wizard who so obviously enjoyed skewering him. Never mind that Sheth was right—that only made his comment worse. "I know about Ognadzu, Father. If you'd like us to go inside I can—"

"The boy can wait," Sheth interrupted. "We have matters to discuss, I believe?"

Paumer hesitated, then his smile broadened. "Certainly, my friend!" He was torn—Uda could see that clearly, if no one else could. Paumer loved his children. But he loved his power and influence more, Uda thought to herself as she watched her father reach out his hand and say, "Come in! Come in!" He tried to put his arm around Sheth as she'd often seen him do when closing an agreement, but the wizard's eyes warned him off. Paumer said nothing more to Uda—didn't even look at her as he led his guest inside. The events of the morning were not forgotten. Her father would summon her later and lose his temper and get all red in the face. But she could handle Paumer. She'd been doing it all her life. She was more concerned now with whether her father could handle Sheth.

She glanced around and realized most of the servants were

staring at her. This was not the Hovel, where the help was accustomed to watching world-changing events unfold in their presence. Nor did these people seem to know how they should regard their master's daughter. She took this opportunity to set them straight. "Do you believe yourselves to be important or some equally ridiculous notion? Stop scowling at me and get back to work!" She spun around and stalked into the house, not watching to see if her order was obeyed. Whether it was this time or not didn't matter—only that they should know she felt in charge of both herself and them.

Now, how to help her father? She couldn't trust him to take care of things himself. Where were they talking? And where exactly was the magic talk-box Ognadzu had told her about? In the library, she remembered. But where was the library in this rambling palace? "You!" she shouted at the steward, who had followed her inside. The man's eyes flew wide, and he bowed officiously. "Where's the library?" she snapped.

"The—library?" he asked.

"Of course!" Uda barked. "Do you take me for a dunce who never reads? Show me to it this instant or I'll—" But she didn't need to finish the threat, for the startled servant was scuttling toward a hallway, smiling nervously as he waved his arm for her to follow.

He stopped at a pair of engraved doors, then bowed to her again and opened them. "The library," he said.

"Yes." Uda nodded. Then she frowned.

"A—problem, milady?"

"Yes. Is this the lower library, or the upper library?"

"Ahh. Once inside, you'll see a staircase which spirals upw—"

"Fine. Go away."

The man did so with haste, and Uda walked into the library. She didn't give a second glance at the volumes which lined its walls, but went straight for the staircase and up. It opened into a large room with two alcoves attached by narrow corridors. In one of these Uda found what she sought— a gilded box the size of a linen chest. There was no one else in the area, either downstairs or up. Nevertheless she glanced around to see if anyone hid behind the stacks and watched her. She saw no one and turned her attention back to the box.

How did it work? She knelt down and leaned her ear against it. Nothing. She searched around its back and found that it was lidded, and that the lid was held closed by a clasp. This was padlocked shut, and she slapped it in frustration, cursing her brother for not leaving the key. To her surprise, the lock dropped open, and her curse turned into praise for Ognadzu's thoughtfulness. The padlock was off in a moment, and the lid was up—

The box opened into a backed bench, the back and seat both being covered by thick cushions of green velvet. Uda put her ear to the seat, but still heard nothing. Then she turned around and plopped into it. Conversations suddenly erupted into her mind.

"Ohh," she yelped and jumped up. The talking stopped. "Any conversation in this palace," she muttered to herself, remembering Ognadzu's words. "But how do you settle on just one?" That he hadn't explained. She sat gingerly on the cushion and once more her mind filled with spoken words. This time, however, she was prepared. Using mental processes honed by years of tuning in private conversations in the midst of filled ballrooms, she began running through the different discussions, discarding those of no interest to her. She chanced upon one exchange that infuriated her. She couldn't tell from where it came, but it seemed to be between two maids and it centered on her multiple inadequacies, both as a guest and daughter. If Ognadzu had heard such discussions about himself, no wonder he'd torn a swathe through the servant population! "And no wonder they fear him so," Uda mumbled to herself. He had at his disposal a potent instrument for uncovering disloyalty!

"What was that?" she heard Sheth's voice say quite clearly, and she froze.

"What was what?" she heard her father answer.

"Are you certain we're alone?" the wizard growled. "I thought I heard someone."

"There's no one! We're perfectly safe within this chamber! The walls have been lined with lead—as I'm sure you've noticed by the stifling heat. Unless there's another wizard in here who's cloaked himself remarkably well, we can speak freely. And I venture to say Nebalath is miles away, playing with whatever pet project has taken his fancy this week."

"There is another powershaper who can cloak himself," Sheth murmured quietly.

"Oh?" came Paumer's worried response.

"But you needn't fear him today. I left him head first in a mud puddle."

"The—the—new shaper that abominable Dark boy brought with him? He can cloak himself?"

"He can."

"Did you—kill him?"

"Why?" Sheth chuckled. "What kind of alliance do you plan to offer him as soon as I'm out of your sight?"

"Oh! No deal, no. None at all. We have—or, I assume you and I have—a working relationship that is constant. Solid. Irrevocable, from my side." Uda heard Sheth's disbelieving snort, and began to relax. They were talking business now, no longer worrying about someone listening in. Uda was quick-witted, and it made good sense that, if she could hear them while she sat here, they could possibly hear her. She would take care never to speak or sneeze while she sat here.

"No," Sheth continued, "I did not kill him. I was just about to when I thought of a marvelous scheme. He can help us with it and we can dispose of him at the same time."

"Scheme?" Paumer chuckled, and Uda knew why. One of her father's chief joys in life was being privy to secret grabs for power. If Sheth was playing Paumer for a fool, he'd certainly chosen the right gambit. Oh, Uda thought to herself, if her father would only let *her* advise him!

"A monstrous design," Sheth said and now he chortled, too. Uda suddenly relaxed. With that one statement the wizard had revealed his own weakness. This was a man in love with his own ideas. Uda recognized the character flaw easily, for her mother shared it with Sheth.

"Monstrous in what way?" Paumer asked with calculated excitement. Good, Uda thought—he'd recognized it, too.

"I can make a dragon," Sheth whispered, and the chill in his voice set Uda shivering.

"A—dragon?" Paumer said. "I've heard of such—some that fly, some in the sea and so forth—but they're all elsewhere—aren't they?"

"I don't know," Sheth muttered. "I've never seen one either—except my own."

"You've made a dragon?"

"A tiny one. Formed from two mice. Counting wings and all, it's only as big as a rabbit, but it can fly, and it has a nasty temper." Sheth chuckled. "It likes to kill cats!"

"Oh?" Paumer asked, and Uda could hear her father's mind working diligently behind his words. "And how does it do that?"

"I don't exactly know. Its two heads just seem to—"

"It has two heads?"

"It does—they seem to mesmerize the cat and then it simply—sizzles away."

"I see. And you keep this dragon caged, I assume?"

"Of course."

"And what does all of this have to do with—"

"My dragon is tiny. Necessarily so, since I had only rodents to work with. Ah, but give me a pair of beasts of enormous size, and I could make a dragon huge enough to change the destinies of nations!"

"A pair of—tugoliths?"

"Precisely."

"This new wizard would be one of them?"

"No. This new wizard would lure a pair to us, then would help me shape the beast. It's terribly draining work, Paumer. It's the real reason I've not been much help lately to the Prince of the Army of Arl. I've been exhausted. But I know now how to do it and how to conserve my strength. We'll let this Seagryn believe himself to be my apprentice and use his energy to bind the two beasts together. Then," Sheth finished, "I'll dispose of him."

Uda listened to a lengthy pause. When her father then asked, "Have you checked all this with Dark?" Uda gaped in astonishment.

"I thought you loathed Dark," Sheth muttered.

"I do, but that doesn't change the fact that he knows the future. Have you checked any of this with him?"

"I'll not do it," Sheth snapped. "You may, if you choose."

"No, no, no . . ." Paumer trailed off. "Two tugoliths, you say?"

"Two. Perhaps three would make an even bigger dragon, but I know I can make one of two, and why take chances?"

"Wise thought. Ah—I have a tugolith—"

"You? You do?"

"It's a pet. My daughter's. But once she understands my need for it, she'd be happy to give it up—" Uda suddenly had an idea of her own as her father continued. "I *would* like to know a bit more about how we would control this beast that would, as you say, dominate the destinies of nations? And how will we convince this fellow Seagryn to fetch us what we need? Small matters, of course—'' Paumer added sardonically.

''He believes himself to be a member of the Grand Council. Why not use that in some way? Exactly how, I'll leave to you. I'll handle controlling the beast once it's made.''

''I see. And, of course, my interests will be served by the finished monster, as well as yours?''

''Of course,'' Sheth responded quietly. ''I understand we have a solid, irrevocable agreement.''

''Ah—yes. But—can you tell me why I should trust you? I mean, when I loan money I require collateral—''

''Be grateful I don't require collateral of you!'' Sheth roared, and there was a sudden jarring ''*snap!*'' that shook the whole box, knocking Uda off of it. Terrified of being discovered, she closed the lid quickly and replaced the clasp and lock, putting it back just as she'd found it. Then she fled down into the lower library, grabbed a book at random, and flung it open.

She sat at a table pretending to read for several minutes before she could convince herself all was well. When she left the library she had a fully developed scheme of her own in mind. She had something her father wanted. Well, there was something *she* wanted, and she was perfectly willing to trade her tugolith for him. She wondered briefly if the boy already knew . . .

Chapter Eleven

✖✖✖✖✖

SHAPER SKIRMISH

Seagryn shouldered his way through the forest, snapping off tree limbs as if they were twigs. They'd been moving southwest for three days. Dark refused to say any more than, "You'll see," whenever he was asked why, but Seagryn had decided it didn't matter. Never in his life had he felt so free!

Since the terrible revelation of his altershape had forced him to leave Bourne and seek his future in the capital, he'd been enslaved to a voracious ambition. When faced with the choice between powerlessness or submitting his destiny to the control of the Council of Elders, he'd easily submitted. He'd first been a dutiful acolyte, then a model student, then a promising leader on the rise. But as he'd reflected over it these past three days he had realized that it had never been any fun.

Being a tugolith was fun! A trunk rose before him and, rather than stepping aside and going around it, Seagryn rammed the bole with his horn. Another tree fell in the forest, and the sound it made was a pleasing crunch!

"Do you *have* to do that?" Dark complained, his arms wrapped tightly around a massive ear.

"No!" Seagryn laughed in a rumbling bass. "But I enjoy it."

"Well I don't!" the prophet grumbled. "Try being a bit more courteous toward the person riding on your forehead!"

Seagryn only laughed again. He didn't feel courteous today. Not that he felt discourteous; mostly he just wanted to play. Was that his tugolith nature coming out, he wondered?

The past few days had given him the opportunity to experiment with his altershape, and most of what he'd learned thrilled him. Oh, there were disadvantages. His enhanced sense of smell, for example, was hardly an advantage when one stunk like a tugolith. Perhaps his scent would be attractive to another of the species, but he'd found that, even when wearing his altershape, he maintained all his human sensibilities. The essence of tugolith took some getting used to.

But the advantages of this tugolith body! For the first time in his life he could do something about obstacles in his path! If a boulder blocked the way, he shoved it aside. Another tree? Instant firewood!

"Would you stop that!" Dark pleaded.

"Why?"

"Think how I must feel! All this—hammering terrifies me!"

"You could get down and—" Seagryn stopped himself. His much-improved hearing had picked up an unfamiliar sound. "What's that?" he asked.

"What's what?"

"It's—a roaring noise—"

"Oh, that." Dark nodded. "You'll see."

" 'You'll see, you'll see.' Is that all you know how to say?"

"I can't please you, can I?" the boy said bitterly. "You say you don't want to know the future and yet you do! So does everyone else—"

"Perhaps if you stopped feeling so sorry for yourself, you might see that I asked for simple information—the kind normal people exchange all the time."

"Then ask a normal person!" the boy growled. "Wait!" Dark added in horror. "What do you think you're doing?!"

"Running!" Seagryn rumbled, and indeed he was, leaving shattered branches in his wake. He really gambolled more than he ran, like some immense ballerina dancing through the woods. . . .

"Stop!" Dark screamed. "Wait! Quit! Cease! Whoa!" The boy kept on shouting for several minutes as he clung in terror to Seagryn's horn, for the transformed magician paid him no heed. When they broke into a clearing—literally, for two towering giants crashed in chorus as they entered it—Seagryn stopped and raised his head to peer forward. His tugolith eyes, however, were too small and too widely spaced to allow him to see very far into the distance.

With the quickness of a thought he changed back into human-form, and the boy who'd been on his back suddenly found himself dropping out of midair. "Ow!" Dark shouted as he hit the ground of the meadow. There was more disapproval than pain in his voice, so Seagryn ignored him.

"What's that?" he asked, pointing above the treetops to the south.

"What does it look like?" Dark grunted as he got to his feet and wiped the crushed grass from his backside.

"Smoke. Is it a fire?"

"No," the prophet muttered as he checked for broken bones, knowing in advance he would find none. "Somewhat the opposite."

"What does that mean?"

Dark glanced around until he spotted a tall deciduous tree that had escaped the tugolith's indiscriminate reaping. He walked to it and started climbing, then looked down at Seagryn. "Come on up and I'll show you." A hint of his boyish grin had returned.

It had been a long time, but Seagryn hadn't forgotten how to climb a tree. He shinnied up this one behind Dark, and soon they were high enough to see over most of the other vegetation. Seagryn looked southward, and shook his head. "Still looks like smoke to me."

"It's mist," Dark explained.

"Mist?"

"From Tunyial Falls. Come on!" the boy shouted, and now Seagryn saw real excitement in his eyes. They both scrambled down the tree and the powershaper once again assumed his lumbering shape. Within an hour they stood at the edge of a breathtaking cascade, and Seagryn's enormous mouth gaped open in wonder.

He'd spent many years living next to the large river that meandered placidly through Lamath. They called that 'the River' there, as if there were no other. But compared to this waterway, that was just a stream. He could barely see the other shore—in fact, from this vantage point he couldn't. It was hidden in the cool spray that billowed up from the vast gorge below. Torrents of water raced toward a cliff and leaped off it—and both cliff and river seemed to go on forever. Water droplets beaded on his back, reminding him just how hot it had been through these summer months, and how refreshing a cool dip in a stream could be. But here there was no need to jump in—the water came to him. If ever anyone could drown while standing on the riverbank, this would be the place. Dark let him enjoy it in silence a moment, then explained.

"This is the river that links the land of Arl to Haranamous and the sea. It starts far to the west in Arl Lake. It's the main highway between the two lands—the two warring lands," Dark added meaningfully; then he turned and started walking back toward the north.

"Where are you going?" Seagryn called.

Dark turned around, but kept walking backward. "I've done my part. I got you here. It's up to you now, to find out if you're really a hero."

"But what about you?"

"Me?" Dark frowned. "Oh, I already know I'm not!" Then the boy faced forward again and disappeared into the underbrush, almost as if by—

"Magic," Seagryn said to himself. For the first time in his life he could speak the word with a grin. He could perform it! And he was about to. Or so Dark's words implied . . . He took his altershape again, merely for the joy of being able to.

Human hearing could distinguish very little over the roar of the waterfall, but his tugolith ears could strain sounds far more precisely. They heard a column of warriors moving through the forest to the east. Seagryn took his human-form and gazed in that direction for a moment. Then with a wish, he disappeared, using that trick Sheth called "cloaking." Although every instinct urged him to take cover in the bushes, he forced himself to stand upon the cliff face and wait as the marchers approached. Soon they came in sight.

The column carried a war boat—or rather, part of the column did so. Armed warriors in uniforms of glistening black urged a distraught band of purple-clad prisoners to work harder and move faster. This a few of the laborers struggled to do, but their burden was enormous, and none of their masters seemed inclined to help. Seagryn listened to several individual exchanges as the boat advanced toward him, picking out the conversation of the commander amid the sporting of soldiers who had found others to do their work for them. As the group swept by him, he joined himself to it, walking a few feet to the right of the leader. "There," the man said, pointing out the place upstream where they would put the boat back into the water. "But we stay well to the right. Get out too far into that current and we'll be in pieces at the bottom of the falls."

"And these captives?" the man's lieutenant asked quietly.

"Usual practice." The commander shrugged, and the lieutenant nodded and dropped a few steps back to a group of boisterous guards. Seagryn dropped back with him. He wanted to discover what the usual practice might be.

"As usual," he heard the lieutenant mutter. "Spread out around them as they put the craft back in the water. Whoever lets one of them escape I toss over the falls myself."

"Yes, chief," someone mumbled, and Seagryn saw daggers slide out of their sheaths as the men made jokes about the falls turning red. These, then, were Arlian warriors returning home from their success in the east. Seagryn supposed their unfortunate beasts of burden must be captive Haranians. Obviously it was normal practice to dispose of the porters, once the boat was upstream of the falls. Unless he did something to prevent it, Seagryn was about to witness a massacre.

The clot of Arlians broke up, the men slipping out to form a perimeter around the grunting Haranians. Panic seized Seagryn as he dodged to avoid a pair of the bloodthirsty captors. What could he do? Turn tugolith and hope the Arlians would run? But these were seasoned warriors, battle-hardened veterans accustomed to the machinations of wizards. Suppose he did manage to startle the troop, perhaps even trample or horn a few—what then? Wouldn't they quickly turn and regroup against him? The captives would be as surprised by his appearance as the Arlians, and would drop the boat and scatter. Some would surely escape, but it seemed just as likely most would be killed despite his efforts—some in the mêlée, others crushed beneath the war boat. And here in this wilderness, far inside territory evidently under Arlian control, what chance would the scattered individuals have of returning home? Ranoth had wondered if Seagryn could do anything other than turn into a monster. Could he? If so, what?

As the group neared the spot where the boat was to be relaunched, the Arlians closed their circle and drew their swords. In that same instant, the boat and its porters disappeared.

"Magic!" the commander shouted immediately. "There's a shaper among us!" The circle of Arlians recoiled backward, but before it broke, their commander shouted, "Hold your ground! They're cloaked, not gone, and a shaper can't do more than one thing at a time! Shaper!" he addressed Seagryn. "I don't know who you are nor why you've interfered, but we have these cowards surrounded! Depart and leave us in peace!"

Within the cloak the Haranian captives exchanged looks of bewilderment. Seagryn had suddenly appeared before them, holding up his hands for silence until he had the eyes of all, then gesturing to them to put the boat down quietly. They saw him scowl at the commander's words, then obeyed as once again he gestured downward. Although they tried to be quiet, their burden touched ground with a heavy thud.

"They've put the boat down!" the lieutenant shouted.

"Hold your ground!" the commander called again, a tremor of fear creeping into his voice. "Shaper! What do you want with us?"

Gesturing again for silence, Seagryn paced around the perimeter of the circle and found the widest gap between Arlians. He then directed the amazed Haranians to slip through it. Those nearest stepped through without problem, but when the warrior he stood next to shouted, "I hear them walking past me!" Seagryn punched the man in the face in frustration. As the Arlian hit the ground the rest of the Haranians panicked and started sprinting through the gap, and the commander yelled, "There! There! Cut them down!"

Arlian swords whizzed dangerously near Seagryn's face, then slashed back again even closer. He ducked out of the way, crawled between two pairs of legs, and bounced back to his feet to check on the fleeing captives. His cloak was holding!

When he looked back around, however, four Arlian swords were pointed at his head and chest, and the commander's eyes bored into his own. "So," he thought to himself, "I've sent the cloak with them and uncovered myself. You learn as you go . . ."

"Who are you?" the Arlian leader demanded.

Seagryn started to respond truthfully, then stopped himself. "You—you don't remember me? I was carrying back in the back, close to the—"

"He's no Haranian," the lieutenant interrupted. "You can tell by his clothes and his voice!"

"Right." The commander nodded, his eyes not leaving Seagryn's. "You are . . . the shaper?"

Seagryn realized he now held the attention of every Arlian, while the former captives scampered into the forest far down the riverline. He'd done it! He'd rescued the Haranians without bloodshed, proving he was indeed a powershaper! Of course, there was the problem of these four swords—

"Speak, man! Are you the shaper or not!"

"Why should I answer? If I say I'm not, you'll slaughter me. But if I am, your tiny swords are ridiculous. What do *you* think, commander? Do you dare to attack me and find out for yourself?''

The Arlian commander watched him nervously. "That—sounds like—a shaper's reply—''

"Then have your people put up their weapons and move away,'' Seagryn suggested. He found he was enjoying this far more than he could have imagined.

The warriors looked hopefully at their leader, but he shook his head and they held their ground. "It's—a bluff, I believe. I know all the shapers and you're not one of them!''

Seagryn shrugged, and smiled wryly.

The boat had become visible again at the same moment as had Seagryn. The commander flicked his eyes that way. "The rest of you! Turn over the vessel and get it into the water! We're taking this one with us!''

Seagryn's smile widened as he watched the Arlians scramble to obey, for he knew now what he was going to do. And Dark hadn't even told him! The boat was soon righted. After some grunting and shoving, they floated it into the river. The commander waved his sword and gestured for Seagryn to climb in.

"If you're sure," he said, walking to the vessel and following ten Arlians aboard. These all had their swords pointed at him uneasily. Seagryn took a place in the center of the boat and waited patiently until the rest of the black-clad warriors had jumped in. "Tie his hands," the commander instructed, and someone stooped to do so. Seagryn smiled throughout the operation . . . waiting.

The boat was launched. As they poled it away from the shore, Seagryn watched the riverbank recede, gauging where the current might be the strongest. "Stay out of the middle!" the commander shouted, evidently feeling they'd gotten too far out. As if that were his cue, Seagryn turned into a tugolith.

First the Arlians shouted in alarm at this beast's sudden and terrible appearance among them. These quickly turned into screams of terror as the boat broke in half under the huge animal's weight. The two pieces instantly filled with water and were embraced by the main current of the river, which hurtled them toward the falls. Half the Arlians had fallen into the water already, while the rest clung vainly to the pieces of the broken vessel and invoked the powers to save them. Seagryn, too, was in the water, discovering to his surprise the buoyancy of his great body and it's inability to do anything but bob like a cork.

"What a time to discover that tugoliths can't swim!" he

thought to himself, just before going over the falls. He didn't fear for his life as he plummeted down through the flood, but it did occur to him that Dark had never mentioned what injuries might befall him on the way to his destiny . . .

Chapter Twelve

✹✹✹✹

INTERVIEWS

"G_{RAB} his hand! There . . . right. Now pull!"

Seagryn felt himself being lifted out of the water, then dropped upon the shore. Someone landed heavily on his chest and started to pump his ribs. "Oww!" he managed to choke past the water that clogged his throat, and he found enough strength to roll onto his side and to pitch off his over-eager savior. "That hurt!" he gurgled, and several voices around him cheered.

"Don't be angry," Dark advised in his ear. "They're just glad you survived."

Seagryn coughed to clear his lungs and tried to sit up. "Who?" he gasped.

"The Haranians you rescued up above. They're very appreciative, you understand." Seagryn got his eyes open and saw Dark standing above him, hands propped on his hips. "Seems like I'm always pulling you out of the mud. There's a weed hanging from your ear."

Seagryn reached up with one hand, found no weed, and reached up with the other. As he pulled the soggy growth free and peered at it, he asked, "How did I survive? I thought my altershape couldn't swim."

"It can't, but it does float marvelously. You went all the way under, then bobbed up, and then I suppose you passed out, for you took your human-form again. As I understand it, wizards lose their altershape when unconscious."

"So then how did I—"

"There were already a number of these fine Haranian warriors in the water, waiting for you. They were so grateful that you'd saved them, they were more than willing to rescue you when I explained what was about to take place."

"They believed you?"

"Of course." Dark frowned, looking offended. "I'll have you know Dark the prophet is honored in Haranamous!"

"That's Nebalath's doing," one of the Haranians explained, and when Seagryn looked over at the man he extended his hand. "Captain Yost. I pulled you out."

Seagryn shook the hand, mumbling a quiet, "Thanks."

"They do have one request to make of you," Dark went on. "In your appreciation of their help."

"Yes?" Seagryn coughed, still trying to clear his lungs of the water he'd swallowed.

"We want you to accompany us to the capital to meet King Haran," Yost explained. "You see, we've lost our shaper and are badly in need of your magical assistance."

Seagryn looked around at Dark. "Did you plan this?"

Dark rolled his eyes in disbelief. "Surely you know me better by this time."

Seagryn looked back at Yost and smiled weakly. "I'll—I'll be happy to travel with you . . ."

To be wanted again for something made a tremendous difference in Seagryn's disposition. He walked through the woods with a new confidence—or rather, with his old confidence restored. He was respected again, and his gifts were being recognized—albeit these were very different gifts from those he'd exercised in Lamath. And it was all so much more enjoyable! These people laughed! Not that his fellow believers hadn't laughed also—it just seemed that this laughter flowed more freely, was more genuine, less bound by the chains of propriety. Of course Haranian jests occasionally ranged into subject matter that made Seagryn blush, but he did his best to hide his embarrassment and laugh along with the rest. He was a powershaper now, not a priest. What a relief it was to walk with a group and not have a dozen people pretending piety for his benefit.

He no longer pretended any piety himself. The One who is not named—the Power, Dark's mother had called it—had abandoned him. Why should he continue to serve such an inconsistent being? Amyryth had called him a spiritual. Perhaps he had been, but he was determined to be one no longer. As Seagryn stalked through the forest east of Tunyial Falls, he discarded an old identity and donned an entirely new one. He'd become Seagryn the shaper—and he could be every bit as arrogant as Sheth!

Dark glanced up at him, read his expression, and cleared his throat. "You know," he began, "you really haven't done all that much yet . . ."

"What?" Seagryn frowned. "What do you mean by that?"

"Oh—just that you may have a higher opinion of your shaper powers than may be accurate."

Seagryn snorted. "What brought that on? Am I about to make a fool of myself in the court of Haran, and you're trying to prepare me for it?"

"You—want to know what's about to—"

"No." Seagryn grunted and walked faster. Dark had to run to catch up. Once he did, Seagryn growled, "The things I've been through have prepared me for anything, Dark! I'm ready to be honored, and I'm ready to be laughed at. It's all the same, because I realize, now, that I'm the only person who cares anything about me."

"That's not true, you know," Dark said, but Seagryn chose to ignore him as he continued.

"I've learned through these past weeks that you can't trust anyone and I intend to live that way from now on. I've committed myself to a dangerous task and I must be constantly on guard. Where are you going?" he added, craning his neck, for Dark had started dropping behind.

The boy shrugged and explained, "I have to live with myself already. I don't need another pompous know-it-all in my life."

Seagryn frowned. "You've just proved my point." Then he turned back to trudge onward, looking neither to the left nor right. The soon-to-be powershaper of Haran could hardly wait to assume his duties.

They hiked for two days before the heavy forest thinned and they started seeing farms and herds of gentle moosers. Soon after, they reached a tributary that fed into the Great River far to the east of the battlefield where Yost and his small brigade had been captured. Realizing they could cut days off their journey by traveling on the water, they hired the services of a raft. But Yost sat pensively on its southwest corner, studying the western bank for signs of Arlians. "They might already be in the capital by this time," he worried aloud.

"Not if Jarnel has his way," Seagryn said offhandedly. When Dark whirled around to shoot him a horrified look, he realized what he'd given away. Yost, too, turned to look at him.

"What do you mean by that, shaper?" he asked evenly.

"Only—that—given his choice, Jarnel would probably already be camping at the sea!" Out of the corner of his eye Seagryn saw Dark breathe again, but Yost wasn't so easily put off.

"I understand." The captain nodded, turning his head to look back at the far shore. "Is it—true what they say about the Conspiracy?" he asked.

"What Conspiracy?" Seagryn and Dark said in unison, then they looked at one another in dismay.

Yost never turned around. "Well. If there should be such a group, I only hope it's found a way to stem the tide of this evil Pyralu. It seems a certainty we can't."

Seagryn looked at Dark, and the boy shrugged and nodded. There was, indeed, a need . . .

The subject didn't come up again throughout the remainder of the raft journey, nor did they encounter Arlian warriors anywhere along the way. It seemed Jarnel had managed to find a way to hold his people in check—but for how long? As they floated toward the river gate and called for it to be opened to admit them, a host of guards scrambled out from behind it, their weapons ready. "I'm Yost!" the captain cried, and someone among the guards recognized him and called out, "It is, indeed!" The rusted iron gate cranked open, and they floated into the heart of the city of Haranamous.

Even before they docked on the palace island, Yost was shouting his report to his superiors on the shore. Within minutes, Dark and Seagryn were warmly welcomed into the most magnificent castle Seagryn had ever seen—and he'd been inside the greatest houses of Lamath.

"What is this place?" he whispered to Dark, and the boy made a point of whispering back.

"You're entering the Imperial House of Haranamous." Then the boy looked up at the battlements soaring high above them and shivered. "The place gives me gooseflesh."

"Why? It's magnificent!" Seagryn said enthusiastically.

"Yes," Dark said. "It's also alive—and mean. But don't tell it I said so!"

"What?"

"You'll see," the prophet whispered uneasily as they stepped through the main entrance. Then they were being separated and led up different rampways.

"Where are you taking me?" Seagryn asked his guide.

The man nodded courteously and replied, "New clothing. This gown you have on seems . . . overused?"

Seagryn glanced down and sniffed. He smelled considerably better than he had as a tugolith, but agreed it was time for a change. Once inside the room, he hesitated momentarily as the servant tried to take his old gown from him. He had been a rather prudish cleric, after all, and didn't like anyone seeing him naked . . . even a servant. As he thought about it, however, he realized how foolishly he was acting. He was a powershaper now and surely needed to dress the part. A few moments later, as he sank deep into a freshly drawn bath, his priestly past seemed less than a dream.

It was Yost, also freshly bathed and dashingly arrayed in a new purple uniform, who came to fetch him. "The king awaits us." Yost smiled broadly as Seagryn stepped out into the hallway to join the captain. "You look much refreshed!"

Seagryn glanced down at the gaudy vestments they'd garbed him in, and shrugged self-consciously. "I suppose I'll grow accustomed to it." They started up the well-lit corridor. Seagryn had been provided with new sandals, and they clacked loudly on the marble floor. Soon they stepped out into a large garden and began to climb a vast circular staircase. It opened onto a throne room, and Seagryn got his first real glimpse of the power of Haran. The wealth that surrounded him dazzled his Lamathian eyes.

"Welcome, welcome," the crowned man upon the throne called to him. This was obviously the king, but he seemed at first glance to be less than pleased by Seagryn's presence. He fingered his chin nervously, and glanced around at those in attendance upon him. "This is he? This is the new shaper?"

"Your Majesty," Yost began, bowing deeply. "This is the shaper who cloaked us from Arlian eyes, saving my brigade and myself from certain death. He also took the shape of a magnificent animal while in the Arlian boat, causing it to break apart and dump all aboard over the Tunyial Falls. We've witnessed these things with our own eyes, and have the testimony of Dark the prophet that this is, indeed, a new shaper in the land. Your Majesty, I request that you welcome him warmly."

"I did that, Yost." The king frowned, and Yost glanced up at the man in alarm.

"He's only being polite," an advisor muttered in the king's ear, and Haran nodded impatiently.

"I know, I know." He looked at Seagryn. "So. You're a shaper."

Seagryn glanced around the room for Dark, but didn't see him. Where had the boy been taken? "I am," he announced. Was that too arrogant? Had he spoken the words too proudly?

"I see." Haran nodded. "Well, I have need of a shaper, as I suppose you know. Nebalath is up there somewhere," he gestured to the ceiling, "playing with himself as usual. Or maybe he's not there. He bounces around these days, and it's hard to keep a finger on exactly where the old mudgecurdle might be. What does it matter?" Haran shrugged broadly. He stood and stepped down off the raised dais, continuing, "He won't help us, in any case. Says Dark's promised this House won't be taken—" he spun around sharply and stabbed an angry finger in Seagryn's direction "—but he's got no promise from the boy that this land won't be!" Haran dropped his finger and returned to pacing, strolling to Seagryn's right. The new shaper followed him with his eyes. "And then there's Chaom," the king muttered. "My chief of staff, but is he ever here? Does he ever report to me? No! And why?" Haran squared around to face Seagryn, a savage sneer on his face. "Because he loses! Again and again, he loses! And then he runs off to—I don't know, somewhere—to conspire against me!"

"Your Majesty, don't you think you—" the advisor began, but Haran cut him off sharply.

"Close your mouth!" he bellowed, and his advisor seemed to be blown backward a few paces by the words. Haran turned back to Seagryn and gave a crooked little grin, his blue eyes never blinking. "They think I'm telling you too much," he explained, "but if you're a shaper, then you already know everything, right? Especially if you've been traveling with that brown-nosing prophet—right?"

Haran chuckled contemptuously, and Seagryn tried to recall if he'd met anyone more uncouth. Then he remembered Sheth.

"Well, don't you?" Haran demanded. His unblinking gaze required some response.

"No, I don't know everything—"

"Liar!" the king shouted, and he turned his back and walked back to the throne. He grabbed its arms and vaulted into it, then looked back at Seagryn and sighed. "I suppose you're in it, too."

Seagryn felt a knotting in his stomach. "In what, your Majesty?"

"Never mind. Have you seen Nebalath yet?"

"Wha—no . . ." Seagryn responded, surprised by the sudden shift of subject.

"Take him up to see the wizard—if you can pry the coot away from his game. And, shaper?"

"Yes, your Majesty?" Seagryn frowned at the king.

"The Arlian army was right behind you on the river. I do hope for your sake you're good, since you'll be toe-to-toe with Sheth tomorrow. Well!" Haran snapped. "I said take him on!"

"Yes, your Majesty," Yost said quickly, bowing low and grabbing Seagryn by the arm. The new shaper of Haranamous was hustled quickly back to the spiral staircase and urged up it. Once out of earshot, Seagryn looked at Yost and raised his eyebrows in surprise.

"Don't look at me." The warrior shrugged. "That was my first audience with him too!" The captain snickered, then they were up onto the next level, where Yost checked signals with the posted guards to discover the whereabouts of Nebalath's apartments. The guards rolled their eyes sympathetically and pointed the way, and Yost grinned at Seagryn again as they entered the indicated doors.

At the far end of an extremely cluttered room, a thin-faced man sat behind a Drax board. Dark sat on a stool beside him. Both were looking at the doorway expectantly. "This is the one," the red-eyed wizard muttered. Seagryn couldn't tell whether that was a question or a statement.

"Dark," he said brightly. "Is this where they brought you?"

"The boy stays with me when he's here," Nebalath explained. "Which isn't often enough, and he never tells me enough—"

"Ask the walls," Dark grumbled, looking back down at the board.

"Don't act your age, lad," the wizard whispered loudly. "This House has its own ways of extracting vengeance—"

"Which is *exactly* why I stay inside it as little as is necessary."

Nebalath glanced up at the wall and seemed to pause for a moment. Then he cackled merrily, and turned to look at Seagryn. "Did you get that?"

Seagryn blinked. "Get what?"

The strange wizard looked up at the ceiling. "He doesn't hear you. How can we be certain he's a shaper if he can't hear you?"

"Why not take my word for it," Dark said, staring down at the Drax board.

Seagryn looked at Yost, whose expression was, if anything, more perplexed than his own.

"Warrior?" Nebalath called.

"Yes, my—Lord?" Yost said.

"We're all quite out of our minds in here. Unless you wish to be too, please go. I'll take care of your young wizard." At this Nebalath seemed to smile at Seagryn. It appeared the old man could be charming when he so chose.

Yost smiled encouragingly at Seagryn, but his own great personal relief was apparent. "Until tomorrow, then," he said and bowed out of the room.

"And close the door!" Nebalath shouted. Yost replied with a heavy slam. Seagryn turned back to the wizard and began to walk tentatively into the room. "That's right, come join us," Nebalath called. But when Seagryn reached the table and started to take the empty stool, he snapped "Not there, that's the House's chair. Sit over there." Nebalath pointed to one pile among a number of piles of books, and Seagryn went to sit down on it, shooting Dark a confused look.

"I told you." Dark shrugged. "The House is alive."

"Alive?" Seagryn winced.

"Of course it's alive," Nebalath muttered, moving one of his pieces and pegging it. "Has been ever since chubby little Nobalog roamed these halls. He needed some company—evidently this place was as full of fools then as it is now!" Seagryn wisely kept his mouth closed, waiting. In a moment the powershaper continued. "What I don't understand is why you can't hear it. All wizards can hear it!"

"You haven't taught him the language," Dark argued without passion. "Teach Seagryn the language and he'll understand too."

Nebalath turned around to Seagryn and grinned at him. "Teach him? How can you teach someone who already knows it all?"

That stung, and Seagryn shot Dark a frown before protesting, "Those are the boy's words, not mine! I know very little about this powershaper business and, in fact, I asked Sheth to give me lessons—"

"Ha!" Nebalath hooted, then suddenly stopped and tilted his head toward the wall. After listening a moment he hooted again and looked back at Seagryn. "You actually asked the bear to teach you something? It's a wonder he didn't bite your head off!"

Seagryn smiled politely, trying a bit of class in the face of what he perceived to be mockery. "I think he tried."

"Ha-ha!" Nebalath hooted again and looked back at the board, listened a moment, then frowned. "You just took my column!" he protested, and with a curse he reached out to move another piece across the board, then pegged it with a jab.

Dark looked at Seagryn. "The Imperial House is winning," he explained.

"As usual," the elder wizard grumbled.

Seagryn glanced around the room, feeling most uncomfortable. When at last he'd built his courage, he said "There is something I'd like to ask you, Nebalath."

"And what is that," the wizard mumbled, eyes still on his Drax set.

"Would you be willing to teach me?"

The old shaper seemed to rise from the board and then off his stool in stages, turning slowly around to gaze into Seagryn's eyes. How bloodshot was that gaze! "You want me to teach you?"

Seagryn cleared his throat. "Why—yes. Sir."

"Sir!" Nebalath whooped, doubling over with merriment as he looked to the walls again. "Sir, he calls me!" When his mirth died somewhat, Nebalath leaned forward until his forehead almost touched Seagryn's. "Why, I would be honored to teach you, exactly as I was taught!" He said it with such sincerity Seagryn found he had to grin. Then the wizard leaned his head upon his chest, angled it to the right—and disappeared.

The snap of air rushing together to fill the void knocked Seagryn off his pile of books. He came up off the floor rather angry, searching the room for some sight of the vanishing wizard. "Did that *mean* something?" he demanded of Dark.

"Two things," the boy prophet said wearily. "First, he was self-taught, and you'll have to be too. Apparently all power-shapers are. And second—I thought you weren't going to trust anyone anymore?"

Seagryn scowled down at the boy, then turned around to walk out of the room. "Seagryn?" Dark called, and his plaintive tone stopped the angry shaper at the door.

"Yes?"

"Can I sleep in your room? This place truly terrifies me!"

Seagryn looked at the floor, his face burning with embarrassment. He needed sleep. Tomorrow he had to cover an entire army and he realized he hadn't a clue as to how to go about it. He needed Dark as much as the boy needed him. "Come on," he growled. Together they found their way back down to Seagryn's room, and both slept the sleep of exhausted campers returned from a month in the woods.

Chapter Thirteen

❈❈❈❈

SHAPER'S APPRENTICE

THE Imperial House of Haranamous had stood upon this confluence of rivers forever—or at least for two thousand years, which is much closer to forever than any man had ever come. For a little less than a thousand of those years it had watched and listened to the people who moved within its bowels. Brought to life by Nobalog, a wizard of great power and even greater mischief, it had been privy to the councils of the giants of history, listened to the hatchings of unnumbered plots, witnessed the collapse of the old One Land, and kept up a running commentary upon it all with a long line of powershapers who were heirs to Nobalog by ability, if not by blood. The House had talked to a lot of wizards—at least one in every generation—and it had certain standards. This Seagryn didn't measure up to any of them.

—He can't be much of a shaper, snorted the Imperial House of Haranamous.

"The boy says to give him time," Nebalath muttered to the battlements. The House's current companion stood on top of its roof, peering westward into the still dark sky while day dawned over his back.

—He cannot even understand this House! the House continued.

"Not many do immediately, remember? Saramech did, you told me. And Arkalapt—and of course Sheth."

—Sheth! the House said with pleasure. —Now there's a shaper!

Nebalath snorted derisively.

—Not the match of you or Nobalog, but a mighty shaper, nonetheless.

"Nobalog's dead, remember? Happened about nine centuries ago?"

—But you're so much like him! the House chortled.

"I've seen the portraits," Nebalath muttered. "He was fat and bald, and I'm neither."

—Appearance isn't everything, the Imperial House sniffed.
—You may believe what this House tells you. You are just like him! Excepting, of course, that you can't play Drax.

"You've been practicing that game a thousand years! How am I supposed to—"

—This new so-called wizard is behind you upon the stair, the Imperial House interrupted.

Nebalath turned around slowly and looked at Seagryn. The younger man stood on the top step, holding onto the railing as he surveyed the horizon.

"Seems to stretch out forever, does it?" Nebalath asked without really asking. "Perhaps humbles you a little?"

Seagryn frowned at him, then stepped onto the roof proper and walked to a low place in the wall. He gazed down at the river, and Nebalath strolled over to join him.

"A little humility is an advantage for a shaper," Nebalath murmured. "Especially on the morning of his first battle."

"I've battled before," Seagryn responded, still looking down.

"Skirmished. Squished a few Marwandians between your enormous toes."

Now Seagryn looked at him. "How did you know!"

"No great feat of shaping, if that's what you guess. I just asked the boy."

Seagryn gazed away again, looked toward the mountains barely visible in the north. "And he told you, did he? He never tells me anything."

"Probably because you're always asking about the future. Being older, I'm much more interested in the past, and that Dark seems happy to discuss. He's still asleep."

"Are you asking me?"

"No need. The House told me." Seagryn had been leaning against the wall. Now he dropped his hands to his sides and looked down at it. "It's all right. The House doesn't mind."

—A presumptuous statement, grumbled the Imperial House.
—Did you bother to ask?

Nebalath paid no attention to this comment, continuing, "Let me see if I can guess what you're thinking."

"Why bother, when you have a prophet to tell you the past and future and a palace to fill you in on the rest?"

Nebalath chuckled. "That's a good question. Perhaps because I care what happens today?"

"If you truly cared, you'd be fighting the shaper battle instead of me." Seagryn had unconsciously reached out to grip the low wall again.

Nebalath noticed the young man's knuckles turning white. Fear? Doubtless. "That isn't necessarily true, you know. You could reason that I feel you're much more likely to succeed than I."

Now Seagryn turned around to stare at him. "How? When, as you say, I'm fighting my first real battle and know nothing of how to go about it?"

"Perhaps simply because you know nothing about it. Sheth won't be prepared for that."

"I've already faced Sheth once. Based on that experience I wouldn't wager on my chances today."

—Never wager on chance, the Imperial House advised. —Wager only on those things that can be controlled. Drax, preferably.

"But that's your advantage over him." Nebalath shrugged. "He'll disregard your abilities and pay too little attention. If he battled me, he would concentrate, and we'd struggle to our usual stalemate. Sheth and I have locked wills so many times we each know exactly what the other will do in any situation."

"But what do I do?" Seagryn demanded. "I've never even seen a shaper battle—I don't know what the possibilities are! And you're no help, since you refuse to teach me."

"How can I teach you to shape?" Nebalath said, shrugging dramatically. "No one taught me. No shaper ever teaches another."

Seagryn just nodded, and stared out over the city. The slanting sunlight painted it in stark contrasts of black and pink. Nebalath watched him, then turned to look out at the rosy landscape himself. It gave him an idea. "You could throw a blush," he murmured.

"A what?" Seagryn asked and suddenly felt so stupid at asking such a ridiculous question that he had to grip the wall to keep from doubling over in embarrassment.

Nebalath understood the emotion precisely—for he had caused

it. "A blush." He shrugged. "What you're feeling." Then he released it, and Seagryn stared straight ahead in shock.

—Cease! shouted the Imperial House. —You have no idea the pain your little demonstration has caused!

"Relax," Nebalath told the wall. "It's not as if I'm inside you."

—Makes no difference! shrieked the House. —Do you enjoy having your hair pulled?

"It felt as if you were inside me," Seagryn muttered, assuming Nebalath's comment was for him.

The veteran shaper didn't bother to correct him. "I suppose it does," he muttered, nodding. "Never felt it myself, since no one's ever done it to me, but I understand it shatters the self-confidence—"

Seagryn still gripped the wall. "Horribly!" he managed to gasp.

"Can you imagine what it might do to an army, when every soldier suddenly feels he's been caught with his pants down, and that every other warrior around is staring at his exposed backside?"

—You're teaching, the Imperial House archly observed.

"Have you done that to the Army of Arl?"

Nebalath leaned his elbows on the wall and looked down at the river. "I try, occasionally. But Sheth counters it with a cloud of false confidence. He has enough of that to share with a hundred armies."

—'No shaper ever teaches another,' the House mocked, obviously irritated at being ignored.

"But these are—emotions!" Seagryn argued with suppressed excitement. "I thought magic was spells and incantations!"

"Tell me," Nebalath demanded. "Have you used one incantation since you found your altershape? Even just one?"

"Why—no—"

"You've heard about such from your Lamathian priests. But what do they know about magic, other than that they refuse to have anything to do with it? Shaping is manipulation of powers or persons by an act of the will. Nothing more, nothing less—manipulation of emotions, of perceptions, of objects, of outcomes, whatever. Everyone shapes, to some degree—even Ranoth. Perhaps especially Ranoth." Nebalath chuckled, more to himself than to Seagryn. "But some of us are better at it than others. Why that is, I don't know, nor do I care. But I do know this—"

—Perhaps you should write a scholarly treatise to place within the library? the House suggested snidely.

"If these fortress walls will let me finish, I'll tell it to you and be done," Nebalath growled. "The essential gift of the true shaper is imagination. Free yours, Seagryn, and use it—else whatever you do won't be shaping at all—just imitation. And that," the thin-faced sorcerer shouted down at the battlement, "is why shapers *cannot teach other shapers to shape*!" Nebalath looked back up at Seagryn, who gazed at him in wonder. "Now," the older man said in as kindly a tone as his naturally gruff voice would permit, "if you'll go on down to the throne room, you'll find General Chaom and Dark waiting for you."

Seagryn blinked. "The castle told you that?"

—Why don't you learn to listen for yourself!

"Currently, the Imperial House is only concerned with abusing us both. I try to be tolerant, realizing that old age makes some beings cranky."

—This House shall talk with the hills when your bones are dust!

"Yes, and they'll probably ignore you too," Nebalath snapped, then turned back to Seagryn. "No, that I learned from Dark last night. He—he *does* tell me the future too, when I ask."

Seagryn nodded absently, still reviewing Nebalath's advice and challenge. Then he glanced down at his hands, and self-consciously patted the wall before turning to walk back to the stairs. There he stopped. "Thank you," he muttered, and he descended again into the Imperial House.

"There now, you see?" Nebalath said. "He even patted you."

—This House is not a horse.

"Some days," the wizard sighed, "there's just no pleasing you."

New ideas unfolded through Seagryn's mind as he left the rooftop and hurried down the spiral staircase to the throne room. Each thought opened onto a dozen new thoughts and all came so fast he had no time to judge their value. His heart danced with terror and thrill. The freedom he'd felt since the skirmish at Tunyial Falls had been tempered by Nebalath's words into a sense of opportunity. Today he had the chance to make history— no, he reminded himself, the assurance from Dark that he would make history—and some guarantee of survival, at least until he could win Elaryl back. He'd lost so much in recent weeks he had nothing to lose today. He hungered for a personal triumph and sensed it within his grasp. He struggled to free his imagination . . .

"Here he is," King Haran grumbled as Seagryn stepped into the huge second-floor room. "We searched, but couldn't find you. I thought you'd run away."

"I—was on the roof. Talking to Nebalath."

"Humph." Haran grunted and rolled his eyes around to look at the man standing on his right. Seagryn recognized the round-faced General Chaom immediately. "The wizards have been talking," the king grunted. "Can normal people ever profit when wizards visit in private?"

"I've no idea, your Majesty," Chaom said quietly. He studied Seagryn's face, sending a signal even as he pretended not to recognize it. "Are you certain this is a shaper?"

"He says he is. Dark says he is. Captain Yost says he's seen the fellow turn himself into a great horned beast—for whatever good that is."

"Yes, my Lord, I've spoken with Yost. What is your name?" Chaom asked loudly.

Seagryn was tempted to respond, "You've forgotten me so quickly?" but instead murmured, "Seagryn."

Chaom smiled slightly, then nodded. "While you two shapers talked, did either of you happen to take note of our military predicament?" Seagryn frowned. "I assume you did not. As you were saying, your Majesty, normal people can benefit occasionally from the conversations of shapers, but only if we can first get their attention."

"I can readily understand that." The king nodded. "Since I've had a bit of trouble lately getting yours."

"I've been fighting a war, my Lord."

"Spare me the details of your days in the field," King Haran mumbled wearily. "I know far more about them than you might hope. My concern at the moment is this column of war boats. Can you and this wizard spare the time from your private concerns to defend this city?"

"Your Majesty, we will do our best." Chaom nodded and bowed. Seagryn noticed, when the general straightened up, how much taller he was than the king. There had been too much going on in that meeting of the Conspiracy for Seagryn to take much note of Chaom. He realized now how big this warrior was. Haran stood on the throne's dais. Chaom stood on the floor beside it, yet the top of his head was level with the king's. Chaom turned to Seagryn. "Shall we go plan our defense?" Without waiting for a response, Chaom turned to leave the room through a door behind the throne. Seagryn nodded to the king, who raised a gray eyebrow, then followed the warrior out.

Chaom stood waiting on the other side of the door, a hand to his lips, indicating Seagryn could not yet speak freely. The general threw a huge arm around Seagryn's shoulders and escorted him quickly down a corridor and into another rather sizable room, decorated with tapestry maps and gilded weapons. "The Chamber of War," Chaom explained, then plunged briskly into his subject. "Nebalath said you would come, but I've rarely had reason to trust the man. Here's our situation." Chaom grabbed a short spear off the wall as he pulled Seagryn toward one of the tapestries. He pointed to a city made of golden stitches, each obviously sewed into the map with loving care. "We're here—the City of Haran."

"Did the king name the city after himself or is he named for the city?"

"The capital always bears the name of the dynasty in power. Try not to interrupt; we've little time to prepare." Seagryn felt his face flush, but Chaom didn't see it as he ran his pointer along a heavy blue line of tightly woven threads and continued, "This is the river. Here's Tunyial Falls. Here's the tributary Yost brought you and Dark down. And here—" Chaom tapped the line of the river a finger's breadth to the east of Haranamous "—is the armada of Jarnel—more than a hundred war boats of the kind Yost said you demolished, each one crewed by thirty oarsmen and capable of bearing a hundred warriors. They're escorted by an armored cavalry of a thousand men on either side of the river. There's nothing to stop their advance save the remains of my army, currently about four thousand strong but likely to shrink again as soon as the pyralu standard is sighted. We'll not stop them through a direct confrontation. Our only hope is in subterfuge. Now this is what I want of you."

Chaom proceeded then to outline a plan of action Seagryn never heard. His mind had moved onto the blue and green weave of the map, and—following Nebalath's lead—his imagination roamed through the tiny trees and rolled down the bright blue waters to a glorious victory. Seagryn had an idea.

"—in that way. Can you do it?"

Seagryn came out of the map and looked at Chaom. "Do what?"

The warrior scowled. "I thought you were listening. I want you to cloak my force here, on the south side of the Rangsfield

Sluice, so that we can shower arrows on each craft as it shoots through. Now. Can you *do* that.''

"Why?'' Seagryn asked.

"To defend the capital from an overwhelming attack, that's why!'' Chaom exploded, stepping toward Seagryn to glower down at him. "I thought you were a shaper! Is this the best you can provide?''

Seagryn felt threatened. Old mental mechanisms engaged, and he responded with an intensity that must have surprised the general. "What's the point of it? To try to whittle down this army before it arrives? You won't, of course. And what happens when the supporting cavalry on the southern bank circles behind you and begins cutting your people down?''

"You're cloaking them, remember?'' Chaom grumbled without conviction. He knew the plan was flawed, but could think of nothing better.

"As Sheth will be cloaking the flotilla, correct?''

"Correct.'' The general nodded. "Do you have a suggestion?''

Seagryn looked up at Chaom and raised his eyebrows in mock surprise. "You would listen to the suggestion of an apprentice powershaper?''

Chaom looked back up at the map. "I'd not intended to convey any lack of confidence in your ability.'' Then he glanced downward, and turned back to gaze honestly at Seagryn. "I'd not intended to, but I did. Sorry—we warriors tend to be a straightforward lot. I'm ready to hear your ideas.''

Along with his apology, Chaom had given Seagryn something else—responsibility. Indeed, warriors were straightforward—and if Seagryn was to work well with this one, he would have to provide more than criticism. Chaom needed working plans . . .

A confident grin lifted the corners of Seagryn's mouth as he opened his imagination to the possibilities.

Chapter Fourteen

✕✕✕✕✕

BATTLE IN THE SLUICE

JARNEL was not surprised to find that the army of Arl had moved from the spot where he'd left it. Neither was he surprised that his own tent had been left standing in place, nor that a band of Merritt's choice warriors waited inside it to arrest him. It did startle him to find a pair of his own advisors among Merritt's conspirators, and it troubled him to recall how easily he'd been duped into trusting them. He'd not come to be an Arlian prince by birthright or chance—he, too, had struggled to rise within the ranks and he remembered acts of duplicity he had committed to advance his career. He'd thought Merritt had underestimated him. But he in turn had underestimated—forgotten, really—the motivating power of stifled ambition.

"When did they march?" he asked as they took his weapons from him.

"Two days ago, Lord Jarnel," one of his former advisors answered quietly. "Lord Merritt felt we could wait no longer, and publicly accused you of the double crime of abandoning your command and consorting with the enemy. Announcing that you'd confessed to being a member of the Conspiracy, he demanded that any warriors still loyal to you defend you in your absence. I'm afraid those numbered only a handful, and they soon saw the wisdom of yielding to Merritt's command."

"You were one of them, of course?" Jarnel smiled.

"I'm—afraid I was not."

130

Jarnel nodded. "The king has been notified of my removal, I take it?"

"We dispatched a boat immediately with the news. Of course, by the time he is actually informed the flotilla will already occupy the Port of Haran."

"You expect it to happen that easily, do you?" Jarnel chuckled.

"Everyone knows you could have taken their capital weeks ago, Lord Jarnel. I'm afraid your leadership has been questioned by many of your warriors for some time."

"Well, who can blame them?" Jarnel chuckled again. "Look whom I've had as advisors!"

"We counselled attack!" his other advisor broke in angrily, and Jarnel nodded in sad agreement.

"You did indeed. And now it's launched. You haven't by chance seen Sheth about?"

"He may already have joined the flotilla."

"Or he may not. So Merritt attacks the capital of Haran without assurance of a wizard. Marvelous strategy." Jarnel grinned without humor. "Your advice again?"

"A war boat awaits us," the first advisor said without expression. "The flotilla is guarded on either side of the river by cavalry and moves slowly to keep pace with its—"

"I know the plans." Jarnel nodded. "You might recall that I had something to do with forming them."

"We've been instructed to catch up with the attacking force. Shall we go?"

Jarnel shrugged and stepped out of the tent. Several of the waiting warriors now moved quickly to strike it, and moments later they were aboard their craft and launched.

Each war boat had fifteen oars to a side. While not all oars on this vessel were manned, most were. "Care to row?" his former advisor asked Jarnel. The Prince of the Army threw back his head and laughed heartily, then ducked into the boat's small cabin and found a chair. He needed to think. He had every expectation Merritt's attack would succeed, and that he and Chaom would be rowing back to Arl together, chained side by side. However, in the unlikely event that it failed, he intended to be prepared. He'd also not become Prince of the Army of Arl by simply waiting for events to take their course . . .

The journey of the past few days had been physically and emotionally grueling. He slept in his chair, nodding off to the rhythmic creaking of the oars. They glided swiftly down the river. When he awoke, Jarnel watched with interest as the Haranian farmlands shot past. While he'd not seen these particular farms before, it suddenly struck him how very much like Arlian farms they looked. He managed to convince himself that these people would have little difficulty accommodating to Arlian rule. He could do nothing to prevent it now, in any case, and began to wonder why he'd tried. The pull of the oars and the war boat's heartbeat rocked him to sleep once again. When he awoke this time, Sheth sat in a chair facing him.

"Did you rest well?" The wizard smirked.

"Yes." Jarnel nodded. "I dreamed of a world where you were not and found it most refreshing."

"I'm not surprised you don't care for this one—having lost your command. Looks like Merritt will be asked to join the Conspiracy in your place. He's apparently quite well qualified."

"What Conspiracy?" Jarnel grumbled, clasping his hands behind his head and gazing out the window at Haranamous. "It no longer exists."

"If it pleases you to believe so, fine." Sheth shrugged. "Certainly it's no longer committed to your high ideals. Then again, I wonder if it ever was? Perhaps that was just a bit of—self-deception?"

Jarnel stared out at the river. He could bear this reversal of his personal and professional fortunes much more easily if he didn't have to endure this insufferable powershaper. "Are you cloaking us?" he asked after a moment.

"I am." The shaper nodded. "Though I don't know why I bother, since my old friend Nebalath has retired."

"There's the new one who—"

"We've had an encounter already." Sheth snickered, and Jarnel felt his last hopes draining out the bottom of the boat. Very well, he told himself. Time to accept the inevitable.

The sun went down, but they kept on moving. Two hours into the night they reached the tail of the flotilla, moored along the northern bank. They tied up there also, and debarked to camp on the sand. Jarnel had slept so much during the afternoon he had difficulty resting now. He kept his mind occupied with thoughts of powershapers, wondering just how many of these boats a monstrous animal could trample to pieces before being subdued by an aroused army?

It didn't happen. He awoke the next morning psychologically

prepared to witness the destruction of Haran—and of his own career. By midmorning the fleet had reached the narrowing of the river called the Rangsfield Sluice.

As the Great River had carved its way through the countryside eons before, it had been slowed by a strata of very hard rock. It widened out and struggled on through, carving multiple channels through the hard wall, none of them very deep. When people began to navigate the river, they'd been forced to walk around these white-water rapids, and a village had grown up on the more gentle southern bank. Now called Rangsfield, the town had grown rich through its trade with those users of the waterway who were forced to carry their boats through its streets. When, at the height of the One Land, the rulers of the empire had seen the value of building a canal around the rapids, the people of Rangsfield had opposed it bitterly. In a bid to keep at least a part of their business, the population had worked together to dig a sluice on the southerly side of the rocky impasse. Boat traffic could thus pass downriver toward Haran without stopping, although the trip past Rangsfield was a rather wild ride. Traffic bound upriver still had to be carried around, much as was done up at Tunyial Falls, or else was pulled up the sluice by mooser teams. The empire had forgotten them by then, and the town had continued to prosper. The Rangsfield Sluice formed the last physical barrier between the Arlian fleet and the walls of Haran. Jarnel had always assumed Chaom would make this his last line of defense before the city walls themselves. His only question lay in how the Sluice would be defended.

The war boat in which he traveled had been moved toward the front of the flotilla. Jarnel thought he knew why—Merritt wanted him close enough to witness the victory at first hand. Sheth was elsewhere—in a safe place, no doubt. Jarnel had never known the wizard to jeopardize his own safety for the good—or bad—of Arl. It really didn't matter where a wizard stood, in any case. Success in shaper battle depended solely upon a wizard's ability to anticipate and neutralize his rival shaper's acts. If Haran lacked a shaper, Sheth's presence merely insured that Merritt's triumph would be more bloody than necessary. When the first five war boats shot down the Rangsfield Sluice unhindered, Jarnel concluded that Haran was, indeed, wizardless. He mumbled a somber good-bye to a promising nation.

Then the first of the war boats hit some invisible barrier, and the vessels following close behind veered away from the center of the river only to strike that phantom wall themselves. When these warcraft began bursting into flame, Jarnel quickly altered his predictions. There was to be a battle in the Sluice after all.

It had taken only a morning, but the whole of the city of Haran participated in the effort. Every skiff, barge, ferry, yawl, rowboat, and masted yacht that floated along the banks of the city's canals had been commandeered, along with enough oarsmen to row them upriver toward Rangsfield. Those not rowing worked to fashion lengths of chain or rope to bind the assorted craft together once they reached their destination. Few in this odd marine force knew exactly what Seagryn had proposed to Chaom. If they had known, some would certainly have objected. But the vast majority of Haranians had such a fear of the Pyralu's tail poised to strike at the heart of their land that they would have deemed acceptable any sacrifice that might deflect its vengeful sting. And although it had been a struggle, Seagryn's arguments had finally convinced Chaom this was the way. Now he needed only to make good his promises—

He stood on the bow of the king's war boat, which had been anchored in the center of the river. Behind him, Haranian sailors linked other boats to its sides, then still other boats to these. They assumed they built a kind of bridge to move ground forces swiftly from one side of the river to the other, to meet the brunt of the Arlian attack. Seagryn didn't take the time to explain that wasn't its purpose at all. Instead he gazed upriver, penetrating the cloak of invisibility Sheth had woven by his will around the Arlian fleet. He knew they came by boat—Dark had told him that much on their own journey down this river to Haran. As they passed through the Sluice the Arlian war boats would move too swiftly to be controlled. If he could bottle a number of them up here below Rangsfield, perhaps those not yet through the upper gate would turn back. While he was no student of military affairs, there had been martial material in the libraries of Lamath, and he had read it. Besides, any fool could see that to surprise and encircle the enemy would increase one's chances for success. Hadn't the Arlian commander at the Tunyial Falls used the same principles?

But that man had failed, Seagryn recalled. The fellow hadn't counted on the presence of a shaper. As he watched, using that ability to penetrate cloaks he'd discovered in his first encounter with Sheth, Seagryn had time to doubt himself thoroughly. What business did he have standing here on a strange king's war boat, preparing to battle wits with the legendary bear? He was a cleric, for Power's sake!

The thought scooted briefly through his mind that this was exactly the case—that he stood here because the Power had ordained it. He tolerated the notion only for a moment before shoving it safely back down whence it came. Seagryn was a shaper now, and an important one. While he didn't know exactly how to go about it, he certainly didn't intend to be distracted by thoughts of some nameless Power in whom he was no longer sure he believed. And Seagryn discovered to his delight that doubting that One seemed to eclipse some of his own self-doubts. He would remember that and think about it when he had the time. Right now he needed to concentrate on seeing what no merely human eye could see . . .

"There," he muttered. He'd penetrated Sheth's cloak to see the first Arlian war boat. Immediately he turned his shaping energies back to cloaking this wooden wall in the middle of the stream, and the war boat disappeared. He took comfort in the fact that as long as Sheth cloaked the Arlian flotilla, his rival couldn't see the response Seagryn had prepared.

"There what?" asked Chaom, who stood behind him supervising the building of the wall while keeping his ears tuned to Seagryn's comments.

"I've spotted them. No, you won't be able to," he added as Chaom shaded his eyes reflexively and gazed upriver. "Nor can I any longer, since I've just begun cloaking this bridge. Is it finished?"

"All but the last few craft—" Chaom mumbled as he looked to their left and right.

"Then let's start the fires and get off of it."

The general nodded, then snapped a crisp order that shocked the sailors standing around them. "Move off the ships to the riverbank, setting fire to each vessel as you abandon it. Go on, move!" Chaom then scrambled over the port gunwale, and Seagryn quickly followed. By the time they reached the southern bank, fire had engulfed the vessels in the center of the line, and thick smoke billowed skyward. "How can they not be *seeing* this!" Chaom gasped as he gazed up at it.

"I do not know," Seagryn answered quietly. It was an honest response. He truly didn't.

Nor did he understand how invisible Arlian war boats could be darting through the Sluice this very minute en route to the barrier. But while they couldn't be seen, everyone on the shore heard as the first boat crashed into the burning firewall. Chaom didn't hesitate. "Fill the air with arrows!" he commanded, and the archers who lined the southern shore obeyed. A second heavy crunch was followed by a third and fourth. Seagryn saw where the wooden boundary bowed; but while he heard the shocked cries of Arlian sailors and soon thereafter the screams of the early wounded, he still could see nothing of the Arlian ships— not even the imprint of their weight in the water.

"Then cloaking is a shaping of perceptions," he murmured to himself in fascination. All about him, men bellowed and warred, but Seagryn was lost in the marvel of his own magic and neither saw nor heard them.

He waited, relaxed now that the battle had begun, for the proper moment to drop his own cloak and reveal the firebridge to the Arlian flotilla. He waited, too, for Sheth to make a move, and had time to wonder aloud, "What's wrong with the man? Can't he see what's happening to his people?"

As if in answer to Seagryn's challenge, the fleet of Arl appeared, and bowmen who had confidently arched arrow after arrow into the empty space before them now recoiled at the awesome number of ships and warriors they faced. Seconds later Seagryn unveiled the wall of fire to the Arlians, and those sailors not busily fighting fires or jumping into the river gasped with an astonishment at least as great as that of their opponents on the shore.

More than a dozen Arlian war boats had passed down the Sluice into the trap. Although their crews now fought to turn them, still others could not be prevented from following. One boat had managed to avoid the Sluice gate, only to founder on the rapids the trough had been built to bypass. Those aboard the boats already within the trap had few options available to them, and none of these were good. They could fight their shipboard fires and be shot down, they could answer with arrows of their own and be burned, or they could jump into the river and swim into the arms of their enemies. Most seemed to be choosing this last choice, but Seagryn's next act made this far less appealing. With a coldness that horrified that part of himself which only stood and watched, Seagryn set the river itself on fire.

It didn't really burn, of course. He'd just used his imagination. Nevertheless, to those on the banks and on shipboard as well, flames leaped up off the water, and those preparing to jump backed away in horror, only to be spitted on Haranian arrows.

And where was Sheth? What was he doing to protect his nation's army? A few moments later Seagryn saw. The Arlians began leaping out again, this time into the apparent flames. Sheth had cloaked his illusion. Seagryn immediately removed it, and glanced around for new inspiration.

As he did, an Arlian warrior nearly severed his head. While he'd watched the battle in the river, the Haranian position on the southern bank had been overrun by Arlian cavalry. A sword slashed toward Seagryn's neck, but bounced instead off his scaly forequarters, and his black-clad attacker quickly scrambled away in horror. Tempted to destroy these ground troops single-hornedly, Seagryn resisted and turned his attention back to the water and himself back into a man. Let General Chaom worry about defending their flank. Seagryn needed to cover the entire army.

Despite his inexperience, he now surveyed the action with the eye of a veteran. No one needed to tell him he had an aptitude for this—he'd recognized it quickly. And as he watched an Arlian sailor swim boldly for the shore, a new idea came to mind.

Seagryn willed—and shaped. And the Arlian, gasping in shock, stopped swimming and stared at a shoreline that suddenly appeared to be a mile away. Seagryn watched, and it appeared as if the man simply gave up. He rolled over, and disappeared under the current to be swept away toward the blazing boats. The thought came to Seagryn's mind unbidden—who was this man's family, and what were they doing this afternoon? Picnicking on Lake Arl, and wondering about their loved one?

As quickly as he'd set it in place, Seagryn withdrew the illusion. He stared now at the carnage before him and gasped at his own terrible power. Everywhere upon the illuminated river floated bodies of Arlian sailors—many of them bristling with arrows. He gazed to his right and watched the vain battle of one crew against the fire that engulfed them, trapped as they were against the line of burning boats by the swift-flowing current. He looked left and saw the rest of the Arlian fleet fighting that same current to move back upriver and away from the deadly Sluice trap, the rows of tiny oars churning the water like the legs of upended centipedes. Then he glanced behind him, and saw wounded and dying sprawled all around him. "War," he muttered. He heard the hosts of Haran cheer their victory, and mumbled to himself, "I did this." Dark had proved right once again. Seagryn was a hero. But the boy hadn't warned him his heroism would make him sick to his stomach.

Chapter Fifteen

❈❈❈❈

ROOFTALK

UDA found her father sitting on the low wall of the Hovel, overlooking the troubled land of Haranamous. He stared southward, but his mind, she knew, roamed the forests of the north in search of Ognadzu. He'd been like this ever since they'd returned from the mansion in the Marwilds, and she was worried about him. He'd not slept well these past few days, if at all. If he fell asleep here, he could easily pitch forward into empty space and dream his way down to death.

She approached him carefully, not wanting to startle him and cause a fall. Despite her best efforts, he suddenly jerked around, saying, "What?"

Uda grabbed hold of his gown to steady him. "Sorry, Father. Don't you want to come in now? The sun will soon be setting . . ." As she spoke she was reaching out to pull his feet back up over the wall to the safe side. He let her.

"Your mother home?" he asked distantly.

"Ah—no," Uda answered. "We don't expect her, remember? Battle between here and Pleclypsa, a bad time to travel?"

"Yes," Paumer mumbled. "Wonder if it's been fought yet. Wonder who won."

"If it has been, we know who won," the girl said as she stood her father up. "Didn't Sheth tell you he was going?"

"Yes." Paumer nodded with little apparent interest. "But you'd be surprised how frequently battles turn out differently from what you expect." He turned his eyes to gaze down at his

139

daughter, then reached out to stroke her glossy hair. "And how life does," he added.

"You need to eat," Uda said. Her father was sick—in his mind, if not his body—and the responsibility for nursing him back to health rested squarely upon her capable shoulders. "Come on inside."

But Paumer lingered on the terrace, now looking westward. Uda followed his gaze. The sun had dropped out of sight behind one of the jagged spires of the volcano's cone. In silhouette, its edges seemed sharper than ever. "Beautiful, isn't it," she gushed artificially.

Paumer grunted. "You see beauty. I see a splinter of rock." He turned away from the sight. "Nothing is beautiful to me anymore," he began, then his eyes caught Uda's and he softened his statement with a quiet, "except you, Uda." Paumer reached out to her again and brushed a strand of hair from her face. "What a fool that younger Paumer was to give you such a guttural name," he murmured. "But you, by wearing it, have turned it into a thing of beauty."

The girl didn't know how to respond to all of this. She knew her father loved her—had always known it. But Paumer had never proclaimed it so fervently as in these days since her brother's flight—nor had she ever heard him speak it in such defeated tones. It made Uda wish her mother *would* come home, and that was a rare feeling indeed. Paumer gazed at her. Was he waiting for some response? She didn't know what to say! Fortunately, they were interrupted. Once again, a powershaper popped into their presence upon the terrace.

"Sheth!" Paumer gasped, for her father recovered from the shock first. "What is it?"

Uda could scarcely believe what she was seeing. While she'd only met this man a few days before, she'd known his reputation all her life. He was the invincible bear, the arrogant one, the most powerful being alive. Yet he stared at the two of them in terror, his hair matted down over his eyes, his once-grand garments dripping pools of water onto the mosaic tile. As startled as they were at the sight of him, Sheth seemed even more so. His teeth chattered together, and it took a moment for him to stammer out, "This new wizard! He ambushed me on the river! He—" Sheth swallowed before continuing "—he has—skills!"

Uda looked to her father, awaiting his reaction. He couldn't know the reassurance she found in the confident smile that curled his lips. Paumer casually ran a hand through his silver hair and muttered, "Well, now. Does this render our little plan unnecessary?" He was in complete control.

"Of course not!" Sheth shouted. "It's now more important than ever! We've fixed an irrevocable compact between ourselves, have we not?"

"We have," Paumer answered, nodding graciously.

"Then you must do as we've agreed!"

"I shall send the messengers tonight," the merchant promised. "But tell me—do I also need to dispatch congratulations to King Haran and send a letter of condolence to your Lord Merritt? My watchers inform me he's replaced your poor Jarnel."

Sheth's expression turned vengeful. "Send what you like to Haran. I suppose your courier will find him celebrating. But you needn't send anything to Merritt. He drowned just a moment ago."

Paumer hesitated in deference to the drowned man's memory, but quickly moved on with business. "Then am I to suppose Jarnel has regained his lost command?"

"Someone back behind the Sluice gave the order to turn the war boats around," Sheth muttered. "It may have been Jarnel."

"That's tidy." Paumer nodded, pinching the bridge of his nose in thought. Then he glanced at Uda, seeming to remember her presence. "What shall we decide then, daughter? A meeting of the Grand Council here at the Hovel, in, say—four days' time?"

"Will Dark be joining us?" Uda asked brightly.

Paumer frowned, then sighed and looked at Sheth. "I daresay he knows of it already."

"I'll kill him when I have the chance," Sheth said solemnly. "His knowledge caused my humiliation! Here. In four days." Then the powershaper departed with a sharp crack.

Uda grabbed her father's arm immediately and jerked it hard enough to make him yelp. "Please, Father! You can't let that happen! You just can't!"

"Let what happen?" Paumer asked evasively, but she could tell by his eyes he knew.

"You can't let Sheth murder Dark!"

Paumer stared at his daughter, then pretended to laugh. "You think I could stop Sheth from doing anything?"

"You'd better stop him from doing this or—"

Paumer gazed at her coolly. "Or what, little girl. What threat do you intend to make?"

"Or you'll wake up one morning and I'll be gone, too." Uda spun around and dashed into the well-illuminated palace. She didn't need to look around to know the expression she'd left on her father's face. But he needed to know that she *would* have her way. Dark belonged to her.

The victory celebration of the Haranian court shocked poor Seagryn to his core. Never had he seen such behavior, never had he even imagined such! Distilled spirits flowed in such abundance he could scarcely breathe the redolent air without becoming intoxicated himself. Shamelessly exposed flesh bludgeoned his eyes, no matter which way he turned his head. The strident hymns of victory grated upon his ears, and the festive garments they'd wrapped about him reeked of a cloying perfume. Worst of all, this was being done in his honor—he was the hero of Haranamous. The motionless bodies of passed-out drunks reminded him of the dead, and the shrieks of lust called to mind the death screams of burning Arlian warriors. They'd been people, just like any people anywhere. Now they were people he had killed.

As Dark had promised, Seagryn had covered himself with glory—and it stank. He had to get out, to get this scent of musky excess out of his nostrils. He struggled through knots of tipsy celebrants, dodging their fawning hands and plowing his way toward the staircase that would lead him out of this fetid throne room and up to the clean air of the roof. "Excuse—no—please— pardon—not now—" he muttered, fighting onward. He heard the drunken king call out for him to come back and be kissed again, but he ignored the summons—he'd almost made it to the railing. Leaping a pair of lovers passionately entwined on the lowest step, he darted up the staircase to freedom.

—He's on his way, the Imperial House of Haranamous said.

Seagryn stopped walking and looked around. Despite the din, he'd heard that!

—He's stopped now. He is staring at these walls—

"Are you talking to Nebalath?" he asked the masonry.

—What's this? Is the dull-witted shaper finally hearing?

"House!" Seagryn called as someone raced down the stairs past him to plunge headlong into the party. "Do you hear me talking to you?"

—This House has been addressed by many wizards in its time. In all honesty you seem exceptionally slow.

"Where is Nebalath!" Seagryn demanded.

—Continue to the roof. Your friends await you. And be it known, the House added, —this House shall not temper its observations merely because you are now aware of its comments. Many powershapers have trodden those stairs. Most were far superior to yourself.

Seagryn didn't bother to respond. He raced on up the stairway and bolted out onto the roof.

"Here he is." Nebalath gestured.

Dark shrugged and said, "I know."

"So you do. Welcome, Seagryn the shaper! They're shouting your praises in the streets—" Nebalath jerked his head back toward the battlements, and Seagryn walked to the low wall and looked over it. Against the backdrop of the nighttime sky, the city glowed a flickering gold. Bonfires blazed everywhere, and the sounds of laughter and music floated toward them across the murky waters of the river.

"They celebrate you, Seagryn," Nebalath said kindly, but Seagryn's gaze had dropped down to the river itself, watching for any flotsam of the battle to drift by. Then he looked suddenly at Dark.

"Was this in my best interests?" he asked quietly.

"What do you want, Seagryn?" the young prophet snapped savagely. "You're a hero! Your actions have changed the destinies of Haranamous and Arl! I thought you wanted to be important!"

"I was a lad once, too," Seagryn responded. "I suppose then I did view such murderous activity as heroic—"

"Be reasonable!" the boy barked with obvious exasperation. "How can you become a hero to any group without at the same time becoming a villain to its enemies! I don't understand you, you—"

"I do," Nebalath broke in, and Dark never finished his sentence, for Seagryn had turned to face the older wizard. "I've felt as you do now. What right have we to wash a thousand futures down to the sea?" Seagryn nodded. "And what right have they to ask us to?" Nebalath added soberly, gesturing out at the joyous city around them. "Then again, they would say they have every right. To them, we wizards are merely a resource. We have this power to protect them, you see, and having it requires that we use it. But how do we have it, that's what I'd like to know. Why should we be so—lucky? I've asked the boy, but he can only manage to babble religious platitudes—"

"Just because something is trite doesn't make it untrue,"

Dark muttered. He was in a foul mood tonight. His tone of voice made that quite clear.

"I want information I can use, boy. That isn't. What do you think, Seagryn? Whence comes this gift of ours and why?"

—Why ask him? This shaper is obviously a mental plodder.

Seagryn ignored the House and considered Nebalath's question. He didn't choose to think of the Power—in fact, he tried hard not to. When the unwanted thought came anyway, he shoved that explanation aside. "Fate? Our destiny?" He shrugged.

"Meaningless words," Nebalath grumbled. "As bad as the boy's religious garbage."

"Then where do you say it comes from, wizard?" Dark demanded. Seagryn wondered why the boy was so angry tonight . . .

"I think we manufacture it," Nebalath muttered, gazing at the paved rooftop. Then his eyes shot up to lock triumphantly with Seagryn's. "I think we each dream it up for ourselves!"

Seagryn shook his head. "Not I. I knew nothing about shaping—apart from the fact it was evil."

"There, you see?" Nebalath grinned. "You did know something after all!" Nebalath tapped the side of his head. "And your dreams freed you to become a monster—the monster you believe yourself to be!"

Dark looked at Seagryn, seeming worried at how the shaper might react. Seagryn saw the look, and it surprised and pleased him. The boy had evidently not yet remembered this moment of his future, for he apparently expected Seagryn to be shocked or angered. But the former priest had lived with his curse for many days now, long enough to examine his misfortune from every angle. This particular idea had come early on, and Seagryn had already come to grips with its truth.

For it was true. He did conceive of himself as a bumbling monster, crushing people beneath the weight of his talent and trampling over events that disturbed or threatened him. Yes, he was a monster. But his public humiliation had somehow made that bearable—punished it—balanced it out. At the moment he was very conscious of Nebalath's cruel little smile, and—like a tugolith—he crushed it.

"And what is *your* altershape Nebalath? I don't believe I've ever heard you say?"

The older wizard's mouth dropped open as the Imperial House suddenly snickered through its roof supports. Dark, surprised again and delighted to be so, turned to look at Nebalath and suddenly hooted aloud in understanding. "Don't say it!" Nebalath trumpeted, and he pointed a warning finger at the prophet. "Don't you dare reveal it!" Then the shaken powershaper fled the rooftop, leaving Seagryn to stare after him in amazement.

"What is his altershape?" Seagryn gasped, amazed by the impact of his remark.

"I think we'd better let you discover that for yourself. Certainly I don't plan to tell you. And incidentally, Paumer has doubtless dispatched his courier by this time to invite us both to the next meeting of the Conspiracy. Shall we leave now and save the messenger the trip?" Dark looked toward the staircase. "I don't sleep well under roofs that talk and I certainly don't want to be anywhere near Nebalath tonight."

"You didn't know this was going to happen?" Seagryn smiled, genuinely pleased.

Dark shrugged. "Oh, I guess I did. I just hadn't—noticed it. Other things on my mind. Shall we go?"

The party continued unabated. Only the Imperial House noted their departure. It was pleased.

Chapter Sixteen

※※※※

DESPONDENT DREAM

THEY fled the golden city with mutual eagerness. Once past the mansions that seemed to line its perimeter, however, Dark slowed down. When Seagryn wanted to know why, the boy only frowned and shook his head. Something was soon to happen, evidently, something too critical to Seagryn's future for the boy to reveal. The powershaper accepted the boy's silence with a mixture of resignation and excitement. Only later did he remember this was how he'd always lived his life before meeting Dark in the Marwilds.

They slept the first night in a field, and Seagryn woke up shivering. For the last few days, the late summer had struggled vainly to hold back the attack of fall. On this morning autumn prevailed, its dry coolness invading his robes and taking his poor legs prisoner. He got to his feet quickly, crossing the lapels of his garment tightly across his chest while at the same time trying to blow warmth into his blue-tinted fingers. He was grateful now for the excessive sleeves of this ceremonial robe. It was warm, and his stopped-up nose prevented him from smelling its perfume. He glanced around for Dark and saw the boy tossing on the ground a few yards away, murmuring to some prominent character in his dreams. Seagryn wondered whether the lad's dreams were set in the future or the past. And did he ever have trouble distinguishing between fictional dreams and truthful visions?

"Wake up, Dark. I'm freezing."

"Eh?" The boy came awake and sat upright in the same motion. He, too, wound his arms around his shivering torso. "Did you know it would be this cold this morning?" Seagryn grumbled. Dark didn't look at him. He just stared ahead, then nodded curtly. "Then why didn't you warn me!" Dark still didn't look his way, but he did shrug. Seagryn grew concerned. "Are you all right?" In answer, the boy shivered again.

Seagryn reached down to grip Dark above the elbows and lifted him to his feet. "Come on. We've got to find something to warm you up!"

"You'll find an inn across the field in that direction," Dark chattered, gesturing with a nod of his head. Then he looked at Seagryn. "This time you know me well enough to know I'm telling the truth, so you lead me straight to it." The prophet gritted his teeth together and fought to keep them from chattering. Moments later they were inside the inn, and Seagryn had him bedded down on the floor in a quiet corner by the fireplace.

"I suppose you knew you'd be getting sick?" Seagryn wondered aloud.

"Not sick," Dark chattered. "I'm terrified!" Then the boy turned his face to the wall, and his body shook with shivers and silent sobs.

Seagryn knew nothing to do except withdraw. He spent the rest of the day watching Dark from one of the tables and speaking quietly with the few other travelers who had taken this day to rest. Although they studied his rich gown with curiosity, he didn't reveal to them his identity, nor Dark's. But it was from them he first learned his new title, as they gave him glowing reports of the great battle waged the day before above the Rangsfield Sluice. "Seagryn Bearsbane" they called him, and then quietly confided that this new wizard had personally skinned the fearsome old powershaper, had instantly cured Sheth's furry pelt, and had then presented it to King Haran as a gift. "It now graces the wall of the throne room!" the tellers finished, then broke into a chorus of triumphant guffaws.

Seagryn heard the words soberly. Though he really didn't know all that much about his rival, he could vouch personally for the man's legendary conceit. And since one of Sheth's chief tools was the fear inspired by his loathsome reputation, he would not abide such rumors cheerfully. There would be a price to be paid for this, and doubtless Seagryn would pay it. And yet he couldn't deny the pleasure he took at hearing incognito the simple folk of the countryside singing his praises. Perhaps the slaughter did have value for human freedom—the freedom of Haranian humans, anyway. Perhaps he'd judged his own motives too harshly . . .

Dark moaned, and Seagryn raced over to him. "Are you all right?" he asked quietly.

"No! No!" The boy groaned weakly. "Sleep! I've got to sleep—" Then he rolled to the wall again, and Seagryn drew back.

"He's seen his own death," he thought to himself. Despite the roaring fire, he shivered in sympathy, then withdrew to an empty table to try to plan what to do next. He discovered that wasn't easy and realized again just how much he'd come to depend on the boy.

It was not a good day; and, when he bundled up himself that night a few feet away from Dark, it was with an involuntary prayer that the Power would keep the young prophet safe. When he realized his own inconsistency, the spiritual disciplines he'd been taught from childhood clamored again for his attention. Seagryn shut them off. He was getting good at that.

"Seagryn?" a voice said quietly, and he came awake with a start. It was Dark. "I think we ought to be going."

Daylight had come. Seagryn rubbed the sleep from his eyes and peered worriedly at the lad. "Are you well enough to—"

"Don't ask," the boy said quickly, then added, "What I've seen, you will experience for yourself soon enough." Without another word the pair paid their bill and departed. For the three days of their journey to the Hovel, they barely spoke at all.

Paumer had done a good job of hiding the path up the side of the volcano. He had good reasons for discouraging the visits of surprise guests. Yet Dark led Seagryn unerringly up the trail, ignoring paved walkways that led nowhere, while finding the true way concealed behind the scrub brush. Seagryn marveled at the boy's gift and marveled too at how courageously Dark climbed to his own misfortune. There seemed very little he could say. He felt helpless in the face of Dark's dreaded certainty—whatever it was. He'd experienced this same impotence as a cleric when called upon to give counsel to the dying. It had always proved wiser, then, to just be—and to listen. He would have listened now, but Dark wasn't talking. They climbed to the crater lake in silence, speaking at last only when they reached its shore.

"What do we do now?" Seagryn asked.

"We ring that bell," Dark mumbled, pointing to their left,

and Seagryn nodded and went to turn the huge bell's wheel. Several minutes passed before they saw a barge push off from the dock below the Hovel, and they had plenty of time to gaze at the grand palace while waiting for the craft to reach them. It had been built to blend with the sharp spires of rock that stabbed up toward the sky on either side of it. At the same time it civilized those savage crags, sophisticating them somehow, rather like a tiny general surrounded by burly guards yet completely self-possessed. Four towers of uneven height rose gracefully from the Hovel proper, the roof of each crowned with glazed emerald tiles that glistened in the midday sunshine. The villa's walls were a soothing tan that bespoke restrained good taste. This was an opulent house, but not the least bit gaudy.

"Have you ever seen anything like it?" Seagryn murmured, his voice full of rural wonder.

"Of course." Dark shrugged. "I've seen it before. In my mind—"

"Always first in your mind," Seagryn grumbled. "But tell me—when a future fact first pops into your mind, are you ever surprised then?"

Dark frowned at him. "You could go through the last few days with me and ask a question like that?"

Seagryn felt chastened—again the insensitive monster trampling upon the feelings of the doomed. He tried to contain his question, but found he couldn't. "And the thing that you saw will come—it happens there?"

"Something happens at the Hovel. Several things happen—different things. I'll tell you this much, Seagryn, and only because we're now here. What happens to you, you'll believe is not in your best interests." The boy turned his gaze out to the approaching barge and added bitterly, "And, of course—what else? You'll blame me."

"Welcome! You're welcome to my house!" Paumer lied effusively as the grim-faced pair stepped off the barge and onto the Hovel's docks. "We've been anticipating your arrival for days! Dark, how are things with you, lad? And Seagryn! What spectacular reports we've been hearing of your exploits! Truly you are honored guests, honored guests. And I didn't even need to provide you with a guide to show you the way!"

"That's Dark's talent," Seagryn responded caustically. "He could find his way here in his sleep."

"Ha!" Paumer laughed. "Oh that was a good one, I'll need

to remember that. Well come on, come on. I'm pleased to see you felt no need for baggage. Everything will be provided for you here, anything you want. Seagryn, I simply must have the story of your triumph from your own lips! Do you think after a refreshing bath you could join me for an iced-punch in the upper gardens? The sun has turned hot again today—'' he added, squinting his eyes at the sky.

Seagryn glanced at Dark for some silent advice, but the boy gazed stonily back toward the lake. ''Will—Dark be joining us?'' he asked politely.

Paumer's smile was equally polite. ''Ah—no. My daughter—Uda's her name, about the same age as the boy—she was there at the Grand Council meeting you attended—perhaps you re-member?'' Seagryn nodded slightly. ''Well, Uda has plans for the two of them—exactly what I don't know, but then I rarely know what my children are going to do, ha-ha!'' Paumer looked at Dark, seeking out the lad's gaze. ''That's all right with you, I hope?'' he asked.

Dark turned his head slowly back from the lake to look deeply into Seagryn's eyes. ''That's fine.'' The boy sighed, and Sea-gryn saw such desperation there that he wanted to reach out and hug the lad protectively. Something was about to happen to Dark, something terrifying, and they both were powerless to stop it. The prophet looked down, then back up at Paumer, and said, ''Shall I go on and meet her now?''

For just a moment, Paumer's expression seemed to reveal his true feelings toward Dark—feelings he'd made public when they'd met before under the mountain. But like a tree snapping back upright after bending beneath the force of a gale, Paumer's smile snapped quickly back onto his lips. ''Of course! You two children have a lovely time!''

Dark needed no directions. He'd already started purposefully up the tile steps toward the mansion. He didn't bother looking back.

Chapter Seventeen

✕✕✕✕✕

PICNIC AT THE HOVEL

As the afternoon cooled at the insistence of a breeze from the sea, Paumer led his assembled guests up a flagstoned walk to a meadow that overlooked the Hovel's towers. Once again Seagryn found himself in heady company, nodding to Chaom who had evidently arrived the day earlier, and to Wilker, the foppish representative of the Remnant who seemed capable only to himself. Seagryn hadn't yet seen Garney, that fierce little Doorkeeper who had expelled them all from the cavern. Had the little man been dismissed from the Conspiracy for that act? Or was this just too trivial an enterprise for him to risk leaving his precious door?

Ognadzu was not in evidence either. Seagryn didn't think he would miss the surly stares of Paumer's only son. The shrewd merchant's daughter was certainly present, however, dressed in a scandalous costume of sheer aqua lace, and she seemed to be wearing poor Dark every bit as much as she was wearing the gown. The girl had clamped her arm so tightly around Dark's waist Seagryn wondered why the prophet wasn't grimacing in pain. After a moment of astonished watching, however, he concluded the boy was too embarrassed to do anything other than blush.

With each step, Uda licked her trembling captive upon the cheek, the ear, or the back of the neck, while her free hand roamed brazenly across his upper body. Dark shot a glance back over his shoulder at Seagryn. That haunted expression remained fixed upon the boy's features, and Seagryn suddenly realized that this girl would play some role in the young prophet's destruction. For the moment, maintaining Dark's full attention seemed to be her consuming passion. She grabbed him under the chin and jerked his head back to face hers, then gazed soulfully into his eyes.

While Seagryn found this public spectacle shocking in the extreme, he still couldn't keep from smiling, nor could he prevent his thoughts from turning once again to Elaryl, especially since her father walked only a few paces behind him.

He had wondered if the two representatives of Lamath would be here when he and Dark arrived. They'd had much further to travel to get here from the City of Lamath—indeed, they'd barely had time to get home from that infamous meeting inside the Remnant before receiving the summons to come again. Seagryn saw clearly now why on occasion Ranoth had been mysteriously absent from his priestly duties in the capital city. Talarath, too, had sometimes been gone, and Seagryn and Elaryl had taken advantage of these infrequent absences to spend long hours in conversation, a practice Talarath sought to discourage when he was present. The dour-faced elder had never liked him, Seagryn reflected. Of all the people in Lamath, probably no one had been more pleased by Seagryn's spectacular fall from grace than Elaryl's father.

And yet this afternoon, when Seagryn had met Ranoth and Talarath sitting under a gazebo in Paumer's elaborately laid-out upper garden, old Talarath had been smiling. He'd even given a passing imitation of a warm greeting. Why, Seagryn wondered to himself? It was obvious that Paumer had been talking with the two elders before he and Dark had arrived. Had they been discussing him? These were all treacherous conspirators, Seagryn reminded himself. And Dark's warning, albeit cryptic, had been clear. Something sinister was being planned, something not in Seagryn's best interests.

As the column trooped up to encircle a sumptuous feast spread upon a damask-covered picnic table, Seagryn sought out Dark's eyes once again, hoping for a signal of some kind. He saw nothing. The boy prophet no longer fought off Uda's free-roaming hands. He'd given up. And he stared sullenly back at Seagryn as if it were the wizard's fault he found himself in this predicament, instead of the other way around. The thought struck Seagryn with the force of a physical blow to the stomach—"I can trust *no* one here—not even Dark!"

"Uda, let the boy *alone*?" Paumer pleaded, and the raven-haired girl shrugged and reached out to toy with her golden flatware. Paumer sighed quietly and glanced around the table. "We're not all here, of course—Garney is missing, as is Jarnel. He, I understand, is busy leading a very surprised fleet home to Arl. And—Ognadzu, my son, is—off in the north on an assignment for me . . ."

Seagryn happened to be watching the girl as her father said this and he saw her roll her eyes in surprise. Indeed, Paumer had not said the words as if he'd intended them to be believed. They appeared, instead, a rather obvious plea to his guests not to bring up the subject of his son's absence.

"And as to Sheth, well—who can guess where he might be? He's like a mountain wind, gone one moment and present the next—"

As if by a carefully prearranged signal, Sheth suddenly popped into view, already seated in a vacant chair. "Hello." He smiled graciously. "Am I too late?"

"Sheth! Welcome!" Paumer oozed. Seagryn had grown accustomed to Paumer's artificial greetings, but there seemed to be an extra measure of falseness in this one. Too late he looked back at the daughter's face, to see if her expression registered any shock at Sheth's abrupt appearance. She was busy squeezing Dark's hand as she peered at the lad, trying to get him to look at her. Dark just stared down into his gold plate. Seagryn looked back at Sheth—and met the powershaper's eyes, gazing intently at him.

"I must congratulate you upon your startling victory at Rangsfield," Sheth said. "You may have noticed—your tactics took me quite by surprise."

Seagryn paused a moment before responding. "I understand that's how shaper battles are usually won."

"You've been talking to Nebalath!" Sheth smiled. "I miss him. Tell me, how is the old fellow?"

Seagryn glanced around the table. "Ask Chaom," he said, picking up his napkin and sliding it out of its ornate ring. "He's seen the man since I have."

"That's not exactly true, Seagryn," Chaom put in as he speared a slab of meat on his knife and dropped it onto his plate. "In fact no one has seen him since the night of your party. Many of us thought you'd gone off together . . ." The warrior left his sentence open-ended for Seagryn to provide more information if he so chose, but Seagryn made a great show of diving into his meal, and the subject was allowed to die.

A wind kicked up quite suddenly, rustling the grass and flapping the tablecloth, reminding them all that winter had sent fall ahead to announce its coming and would not be denied. Seagryn noticed then that the grass of this high meadow had already yellowed. Wasn't choosing to picnic after summer's end just one more example of this Conspiracy's arrogance, as if even the weather could be required to bow to its wishes? He chanced a glance up from his plate and saw that the other diners seemed as uncomfortable as he. Still, no one mentioned the wind or the chill. The picnic continued with a forced gaiety, and Seagryn had to admit that he'd rarely tasted a meal more delicious.

"While this is *very* pleasant," Paumer lied after most of his guests were nearly finished, "we do have important matters to discuss. Most critical, surely, is what we as the Grand Council intend to do to avoid the approaching world calamity—"

"What calamity?" Chaom interrupted.

"Why—the—the problem we've been facing for months! The impending conquest of the other fragments by Arl—"

"I thought that's what you meant." Chaom nodded. "But I'm afraid I don't understand your continuing concern. We've maintained a balance of power between Arl and its neighbors for some time. With Seagryn's arrival, it appears that balance has been restored once again."

"With one victory he's redressed the imbalance?" Sheth grinned. "You'll pardon me for saying this, Seagryn, but I'm not certain our next encounter will prove so one-sided. And if it is, there's every possibility you will be the wizard humiliated—or worse."

Seagryn had just taken a bite. Stunned by this attack, he clenched his teeth a moment, then forced his jaws into motion and methodically chewed and swallowed. He refused to look at his rival or to take any public notice of the taunt.

"There is a way of knowing." Ranoth shrugged. "Let's just ask the boy."

"No," Paumer protested, "rather let us—"

"Be quiet for once, Paumer!" Ranoth snapped. "I, for one, would like to hear what he says. Dark? Who wins the next encounter? Dark?" Ranoth said again, for the lad still eyed his plate as if it were about to eat off him instead of the other way around. It was piled high with food—Uda had served him huge portions of every dish passed—but he had yet to touch it. Nor did he seem willing to partake of this conversation.

"There, you see?" Paumer smiled. "The boy does not choose to—"

"Dark!" Ranoth scolded. "You've pushed your way into our presence again and again! Now that you've been invited, do you suddenly refuse to speak?"

"What difference would it make if I did?" the boy mumbled.

"It could make a great deal of difference. You could help us choose wisely—"

"Choose what?" Dark barked, suddenly coming to life and meeting Ranoth's eyes. "Your choices are already made, as everyone at this table save Seagryn and Chaom know already! Of course Sheth and Seagryn will battle again—they're shapers, aren't they? And isn't it the nature of wizards to struggle? But that will make no difference to your careful scheme, which Sheth himself formulated and Seagryn will have to enact, and which the rest of you have already adopted as your own. And you," Dark continued, turning to look into Seagryn's astonished gaze. "Now that I've revealed my fore-knowledge, I suppose that confirms for you that I cannot be trusted either?" Dark jumped up from his seat and fled down the incline toward the mansion. Uda frowned at her father in obvious frustration, then shot after him.

"Dark! Dark, you'd better get back up here!" Her voice faded as the two of them disappeared into the gardens below.

After a still moment, which Seagryn used to absorb this shock, Chaom spoke up for the two of them. "Now that the children have left us, I think it's time Seagryn and I heard about this plan."

Seagryn nodded and looked at Paumer. The merchant first glanced sidelong at Sheth, then smiled. "It's not a secret, not really. We've just needed to meet like this in order to explain it fully to everyone. Ah—before I share the solution to our problem, let me make clear the need, as I understand it. The fragments of the old One Land—I'm sorry Wilker, but I must speak frankly," he interjected, and Wilker waved at him to continue. "The fragments do not trust one another, for they have no common goal. They are seeking their own interests, not realizing how much more we would all be able to accomplish if we would simply work together!"

"And how much more easily you could enrich yourself," Seagryn thought, but he didn't interrupt.

"But why should we expect our respective fragments to work together? There's no apparent reason for them to do so. What we of the Grand Council must do is provide such a reason. How? By creating a common menace!"

"I thought you had already done that, Paumer," Chaom said, scooting his chair backward in the grass, then leaning back in it and lacing his fingers behind his thick neck. "Isn't your trading concern our common menace?"

Paumer lost his temper. "My house has prevented more wars than you have fought battles, Chaom! Remove the House of Paumer from this society and the economy of every fragment would—"

"Please!" Ranoth shouted, slapping his hand on the table, and Paumer stopped. "I think Chaom was jesting. Go on, Paumer."

"Very well." The merchant sniffed. "As I said, to create a common problem for all fragments that none could solve alone would force them to join together." Paumer warmed again to his subject. "And we have the means at our disposal to create just such a disturbance!"

He paused to smile into the eyes of every person at the table. When he got to Seagryn, the new wizard cleared his throat and asked, "Ah—how?"

Paumer looked triumphantly at Sheth. "Many of you don't appreciate how much of himself our bear friend invests in pioneering new uses of his shaper power. Perhaps one of the reasons you defeated him so easily, Seagryn, was that his mind has been elsewhere in these past few months, creating—a dragon!" Paumer again paused theatrically, but this was not news to most of those assembled, and Seagryn was too much on guard to react visibly.

"What sort of dragon?" he asked.

"A small one," Sheth offered, sounding almost modest for once. "It's a furry little two-headed beast. Not much like the dragons of legend, perhaps, but it does have wings and it can incinerate its enemies." Sheth dimpled handsomely. "I try always to stay on its good side, myself."

Seagryn leaned over the table and frowned down at Talarath, curious to see how the old man was taking all this hideous talk of magic. Strange—was the elder actually smiling again?

"And that, friends, is just a small dragon," Paumer said, picking up where he'd left off. "Imagine the chaos a large dragon might be expected to cause? Why the fragments will be seeking one another's counsel immediately, and we will be ready with a solution!"

"Create the problem, then assume total control while solving it." Chaom nodded. "That sounds like a merchant's way of thinking. I consider it a loathsome suggestion!"

"Why?" Paumer shot back. "Worse than bodies floating down the river through the heart of Haranamous? Haranian bodies, next time? Our purpose is to stop destruction, not cause it! Certainly, by making a large dragon and releasing it, we will cause some suffering along the way, but isn't it worth it? A safer, united One Land justifies any suffering needed to attain it!"

"I doubt, Paumer, if you'll be doing any of the suffering, or you might feel quite differently." Chaom said this with conviction, but without much passion. He spoke the truth! But was he also becoming persuaded of this bizarre plan's value?

Seagryn looked back at Paumer and asked, "Just how would this dragon be made?"

"With your help," Sheth answered, leaning over the table to catch Seagryn's eyes. "You asked me once to teach you. Isn't this a better way than learning through violent confrontation?"

"I—guess so—" Seagryn mumbled. Paumer's mention of bobbing corpses had gotten to him.

"And of what, may I ask, will this dragon be made?" This was Talarath's voice, but not the old man's words. Seagryn realized immediately that the question did not proceed from the discussion, and that Talarath had recited rather than asked it. When he heard Paumer's response, he understood why it had been planted—and why Elaryl's father had smiled as he spoke.

"It will be made out of tugolith! Sheth tells me he made his miniature dragon using a pair of rodents. Think what a dragon could be made from a beast such as—this!" Paumer swept his hand toward the trees at the upper end of the meadow, and all eyes turned that way. When nothing happened, they all looked back at Paumer, whose expression had soured. "Bring it!" he commanded, and they all looked back up at the treeline. There was a crunching and snapping of breaking limbs, then an obviously frightened servant led a tugolith out of the tangle, and the assembled Conspiracy murmured appreciatively.

All seemed stunned by its size and apparent power—all save

Seagryn. He was too familiar with such beasts to show any enthusiasm. And when, as the tugolith was led down the hill toward the table, Sheth mentioned, "Of course, I'll need two of these animals to make it," Seagryn was ready with a response.

"And I suppose I'm the other one."

"What?" The older wizard frowned in supposed confusion.

Seagryn looked toward him. "Me. I'm to be the second tugolith."

"Why—no," Sheth said broadly. "In any case, that was never my intention. Of course, if you wish to volunteer—"

"I do not volunteer! I want nothing to do with this scheme!"

The tugolith had finally reached them. Paumer's attention had been so focused upon the beast's approach he'd heard nothing of Sheth and Seagryn's exchange. He turned to the group and proclaimed with genuine pleasure, "I present to you all—Vilanlitha!"

The tugolith eyed the picnic. "I'm hungry," he said.

"It talks," Chaom gasped, backing around the table to put it between himself and the gigantic animal.

"It does indeed." Paumer grinned.

"I'm hungry," Vilanlitha said again, sniffing the food.

"Quit that," Paumer instructed the beast quietly.

"I can eat this table," the tugolith said.

Paumer snapped, "I told you to quit talking about that!"

The beast looked back at Paumer. "I could eat you." There was no threat in his voice. Vilanlitha simply stated a fact.

Paumer's eyes got very round, then he looked at the group, and saw some very wide eyes watching his. "He's kidding!" he explained hopefully, reaching up to pat the beast's forequarter. "He likes to joke!"

"What is joke?" Vilanlitha asked, and Paumer realized he was quickly losing his audience. Chaom, Ranoth, and Wilker were all drifting backward down the hill, and Talarath's smile had frozen into a mask upon his face.

Seagryn had still barely looked at the animal. He kept his hard stare fixed upon Sheth. "Isn't that what you meant by needing my help?" he demanded.

"Actually, no," Sheth responded, prudently watching Paumer's animated conversation with the single-minded beast. "I made an honest offer. I will teach you what I know, but I also need your magic. To merge two such monsters into an even more enormous dragon will take a considerable act of shaping. I need your abilities alongside my own. Then of course, there's the other thing.''

''What other thing?'' Seagryn asked, standing and stepping away from the table with Sheth as the tugolith, despite Paumer's impassioned imprecations, began to consume it as well as the food spread on top of it.

''You've understood our need quite clearly. We do need another tugolith, and need you to lure one to us.''

So that was it. Now Seagryn understood it all—or thought he did. ''No,'' he announced, and he started down the hill. Sheth pursued him, and Talarath, who had already begun his escape, turned to meet them and fall into step beside them.

''Why not?'' Sheth asked.

''Better to ask me why I should,'' Seagryn snorted. ''Why should I travel to—wherever these things come from—and bring one back to be slaughtered for your purposes?''

''It won't be slaughtered!'' Sheth smiled earnestly. ''In fact, it will live forever! Or at least much longer than you or I can ever hope to live . . .''

''Well . . . to be tortured, then!''

''It won't be tortured either!'' Sheth grabbed Seagryn by the shoulders to stop him and tried to turn him toward Talarath. Seagryn shook himself free and glowered at this wizard who had caused him so much fear and pain.

''Don't you ever grab me like that again!'' he shouted.

Sheth raised his hands apologetically and said, ''Fine, fine. I just wanted you to hear what Talarath has to tell you.'' Then he stepped away and nodded at the elder, who now received the full force of Seagryn's glare.

The old man cleared his throat. This was evidently something difficult for him to say. ''We—Ranoth—Ranoth and I have agreed that this will ultimately prove a good thing for Lamath. Even Dark says as much, and you can't deny the boy can see the future. So—do this for the Grand Council, Seagryn, and you will be received back into the full fellowship of the Lamathian clergy. Perhaps more importantly, you can be wedded to Elaryl the day you return from the north with another one of these monstrous creatures.''

''Elaryl? I can marry Elaryl?'' Until this moment Seagryn had assumed only the worst. After all, hadn't Dark told him this request would not be in his best interests? It took only the mention of his dear lady's name for him to realize that this definitely was in his interests! "All right," he said quietly, struggling to stifle his shouts of joy. "I'll do it."

Chapter Eighteen

※❈❈❈

ARLIAN JUSTICE

It took two weeks for the long column of war boats to row upriver from the Rangsfield Sluice to Arl Lake. Moving the flotilla out of the water and around the Tunyial Falls consumed a full day of that time, and demanded Jarnel's constant attention. With no captives to do the carrying, the Arlian warriors had to lift and port their boats themselves. They'd done that willingly on their way to war, but that had been different. They'd just bid their wives and sweethearts good-bye and were off to make fortunes by looting Haranamous. Instead, they returned home losers. Poor morale made for sloppy effort, and tempers rubbed raw by weeks of warfare sought any excuse to flare. Jarnel reasserted true command over his army that day with a mixture of enraged bellowing, instant discipline, and a surprisingly quick wit. Screaming commands one minute, he was cracking jokes the next, with the net result that his soldiers did what they were told when and where they were supposed to, and the column moved almost magically around the obstacle. Of course his warriors grumbled throughout the ordeal—these were fighting men, after all, who believed complaining was a basic right of every soldier. But they were led once again by a true leader, and they appreciated the fact. Any mention of Merritt's name now drew a chorus of contemptuous snorts.

Hard as the day was, Jarnel enjoyed it. For afterward, when the war boats were again in the water and rowing hard for home, he had nothing to distract his thoughts from the distasteful chore ahead. It would fall to him to report their defeat. And how would he explain this failure to his pyralu of a king?

Despite his high position in government, Jarnel didn't know his ruler well. He wondered if anyone did, for even those advisors who spent their days in the king's presence seemed tentative when attempting to explain the man's policies or report his wishes. That was understandable, for their ruler was a mercurial man who could change position on an issue a dozen times a day and never realize his own inconsistency. That mattered little to the common Arlian; with his single-minded dogmatism and his personal charm, the king could take the most crazed of notions and weave it into a plausible position. Nor did the populace seem bothered when, a week later, the poised king vehemently endorsed the opposite view.

Was the king insane? Jarnel would have appreciated being able to take that view. But he'd seen too much—had himself reported too much—to believe it. And that left only one other option—the man was evil. Whether that evil proceeded out of a terrible childhood or a magical spell or—as the clerics of Lamath contended—some truly malevolent personal force that struggled against some balancing good to manipulate the human will, it made little difference to Jarnel. That much evil with this much political control could not be allowed to grow.

But what could he do? He'd tried his best. He thought it ironic how well he'd served the hopes of his co-conspirators by losing this army to Merritt. Arl had been prevented from striking down its neighbors one more year. But would that stop the king? Of course not. His paranoia was so great he would certainly try again next year and the next and the next. For the moment, he would have to satisfy himself with cutting Jarnel's body into pieces. And in the long view, what did it matter? If the Grand Council had truly become the organization Sheth described it to be, that would certainly prove no better option. ''Better,'' Jarnel mumbled to himself as the boats came in sight of the mouth of Arl Lake, ''to spend my last few minutes with my grandchildren.''

The cobbled streets of the City of Arl climbed the hills that ringed the eastern edge of the lake like the stairway of some giant or like the even rows of some titanic amphitheater. Decent, hardworking people lived along these orderly avenues—shopkeepers and traders, mostly, sharp-minded businessmen who knew how to take the hides and carcasses of the herdsmen to the north and trade them for the grains and fibers of the farmers to the east and end up with most of the profits from the exchange. They were a proud people, meticulously clean in both their laundry and their ledgers. They were Jarnel's people, and he loved them; it hurt him to think how disappointed they would be with the news of defeat.

When the first boats curled out from the river onto the lake and made the big turn into the docks, a cry of triumph rose up from those houses that lined the hills. Arlians rushed into the streets or out onto their roofs to watch the aquatic procession and cheer. Jarnel quickly picked out his own tiled rooftop. In spite of his despair, a smile twitched across his lips when he made out the tiny figures of Cleroklan and his little brother clinging to the chimney and waving madly. This was home. He had at least brought most of his warriors home.

He'd already made his decision. He would go home first, greet his wife and children, and spend the rest of the afternoon—or until they came to fetch him—down on his knees between the two lads, playing the game of their choice. But as his boat glided into its berth, he saw it wasn't to be. Karmelad, a pinched-faced advisor to the king, awaited him on the pier. Sighing bitterly, Jarnel climbed out of the craft and nodded to Karmelad and the welcoming party. "I'm afraid I have bad news to report—" he began, but Karmelad cut him off with a quick jerk of his hand.

"Sheth's already been here," the advisor said quietly. "Just pretend you won, and come with me quickly." The man turned and scurried off the landing platform, and the surprised Jarnel followed him. Sheth had appeared here to admit his failure? That was *most* unexpected.

Karmelad led him into a fishing shed guarded by a squad of warriors who all wore smaller versions of Jarnel's own ceremonial headgear. These were the king's own guards—was the king himself waiting inside? He was known to do stranger things—

No. There was only a small table, still wet with fish blood. There were two rough chairs, one of which Karmelad already occupied. Jarnel sat. "Now," the advisor demanded, "explain why you refused to wait for Sheth to arrive and cover you? Do you suddenly see yourself as a wizard?"

Jarnel nodded. This was more understandable. "First of all, Sheth was there, and the opposing wizard outshaped him."

Karmelad's expression didn't change. "You mean, of course, Nebalath."

"I mean the opposing wizard. Our intelligence sources told

us Nebalath no longer was protecting Haranamous, and certainly this wizard did not shape in any style I found recognizable.''

''Are you saying the failure was Sheth's and not yours?''

''Sheth's and Merritt's.'' Jarnel nodded.

Karmelad frowned. ''What's Merritt got to do with it?''

Jarnel stared. ''Did you not get Merritt's message?''

''What message?''

''And did Sheth say nothing of Merritt's—''

''Sheth appeared to the king in private, delivered his diatribe against your failure, and disappeared. I know nothing more than that—nor do I want to know,'' Karmelad added quickly, preventing Jarnel from interrupting. ''You say Sheth is lying, and of course we thought so. Now listen! Go home, Jarnel, and speak to no one. We will come for you if we need you.'' The advisor jumped up from the table, rubbing his hands on his gown to cleanse them of the sticky blood. ''Remember—I said no one. We've not yet decided whether we won this war or lost it. Don't give your opinion to *anyone*.'' Karmelad stepped out, and a moment later Jarnel felt the whole pier shake as the armed guard tramped off it.

''Home,'' he muttered to himself. The word made his heart dance with excitement. He bolted out of the shack and started up the nearest street. Would the little one be able to say his name yet? In the face of such inherently important questions, affairs of the Arlian state seemed trivial indeed.

They all heard the characteristic tramping first. Then came the knock upon the door—quite polite, really—followed by the ritual summons. ''Jarnel of Arl, your king has need.''

He kissed his wife, and they exchanged the silent look of good-bye they'd perfected through his long years of warfare. ''They did at least give you the afternoon,'' she said sadly. He loved her strength, but felt genuinely sorrowful in that moment that his life had forced her to develop it. He kissed her again and went outside. A contingent of the palace guard awaited him, their heads covered by those glossy black pyralu masks that shielded their identities while terrifying anyone foolish enough to be watching. These could all be very good friends from years past—in fact, probably several were. But their king had needs, and one of those needs was secrecy. Jarnel shrugged it off. After all, in battle he wore the same disgusting headgear.

He turned with the troop and they marched as a unit twenty

paces down the street before Jarnel's suspicions were confirmed. Someone threw a bag over his head, and his hands were bound behind him. "Yes," Jarnel thought to himself, "the king does have needs . . ."

He was guided down one of the steep cross streets that ran from the lakeshore to the crest of the hill, then back to his left along one of the long, curving avenues identical to his own. He didn't bother with trying to guess where he was being taken. It didn't matter. Without a sound, the guards all suddenly stopped marching, and Jarnel ran into the two ahead of him. He was grabbed by both arms and ushered through a door—into a cobbler shop he guessed, by sniffing the rich smells of leather and tanning solutions. That didn't surprise him. Most activities of the king's guards were concealed behind some kind of shop. He had, however, expected to be taken into a butcher's shop instead, and the thought that he might be skinned rather than slaughtered outright caused an involuntary shudder to rustle through his body.

He was propelled through the shop, felt curtains brushing his shoulders, then was set down. After a momentary pause, the covering was pulled off his head. He blinked his eyes against the torchlight, then looked up at his interrogator. That nose, so thin it suggested the man had worn a vice on it throughout his formative years, certainly fit the rest of the squinting face that frowned back. "Karmelad." Jarnel nodded. "You do get around—"

"I've seen the king," the advisor announced flatly, making it appear their conversation had not been interrupted by a full afternoon. "He has decided that you've won. An official King's Account of your stirring victory will be reported in the public square each midday for the next ten days. Your lieutenants are being informed of this decision, and the same general warning is being issued to all—disputing the King's Account shall be considered a treasonous activity and will be dealt with appropriately."

Jarnel heard all of this quietly. "Then I'm a hero," he muttered when Karmelad finished.

"You should be very glad the king chose to make you one," the advisor said, "since you failed to make one of yourself."

"I am. When do I see him to give him the true report?"

"You will not see him. I'm empowered to carry to him any account you wish to give, but before you speak, I wonder if such is really necessary?"

"Surely he would want to know the—"

"There is a second reason why you're here, Jarnel. Would you be so kind as to be silent and let me tell it to you?"

Jarnel didn't mean to stare, but this was such a startling shift in policy he couldn't help it. Always in the past the king had hungered to hear every detail of every battle from Jarnel's own mouth. What had happened?

Karmelad nodded appreciatively at his silence. "Good. The situation is this—the king has discovered that Sheth is a member of the legendary Conspiracy that is sworn to topple all rightful rulers and place merchant puppets in their places. Sheth has made an attempt to assassinate the king—"

"What?" Jarnel frowned.

"When he appeared in the king's bedchamber, Sheth attempted to murder your ruler. As a result the king is now in hiding, and doubtless will remain so until the threat—"

"If Sheth really intended to kill the king then certainly he—"

"You need no details!" Karmelad snapped, his eyes flashing. Then he calmed, and his voice resumed its droning, official tone. "Despite how you've failed him, the king considers you the only man qualified to hunt down this treasonous power-shaper and put him to death. Your warriors are being selected for you. You will depart immediately. Your wife will be informed that your skills were needed elsewhere and will represent you at the victory ceremonies. She will also receive a hero's reward from her grateful sovereign. And if you have no questions, I have one to ask of you—"

Karmelad's expression made it quite clear—Jarnel was not to ask questions, but to answer them. "Yes?" the general grunted.

"Why did you mention Merritt's name today?"

Jarnel absorbed the question slowly, turning it carefully in his mind. It appeared they knew nothing of his absence from the army and of Merritt's mutiny. Of course, they might know the whole story, and were just interested in learning what part of it he might be willing to tell them. Or Merritt could conceivably have been reporting directly to Karmelad—he could have been the advisor's plant, perhaps, in the Arlian Army, completely unknown to the king. While he'd played it well, this game of confidences and assumptions had always revolted Jarnel, and suddenly the relative freedom of leading a pack of bear hunters through the Marwilds sounded enormously appealing. So—how to answer it? Simply, he decided. "Oh. He drowned during our glorious victory at the Rangsfield Sluice."

Karmelad nodded thoughtfully. "Just between us, Jarnel, I never understood why you allowed that man anywhere near you. I would certainly never have trusted him—too much of a nose for intrigue." The advisor's own beak bobbed as he nodded to one of the guards, and the bag was once more shoved down over Jarnel's head. Thus attired, the Prince of the Army of Arl stumbled blindly out of the cobbler shop to assume his new command.

Chapter Nineteen

❈❈❈❈❈

MEGASIN'S CAVE

"**I**T isn't all *that* cold," Seagryn told himself through chattering teeth. He pulled his fur-lined cloak a little tighter around his shoulders and urged his shaggy-maned horse to move on.

It had been a week now since he had ridden out of the Paumer palace at the foot of the Central Gate upon Kerl's broad back, and Seagryn had come to know the animal quite well—"from the bottom up," he joked aloud, but the horse had made no comment. That wasn't surprising. Kerl had a personality as gray as his fetlocks. If the horse had a sense of humor, Seagryn had yet to find it. But Kerl's stolid demeanor did not affect his work, and his stoutheartedness had impressed his rider. Few people in this world could be trusted to behave so responsibly day in and day out. Seagryn had always valued those who seemed committed to that ethic and had tried to live that way himself. But unlike Seagryn, whose good intentions were so often thwarted by misfortune or the inconsistencies of others, Kerl made dedication to duty his obsession. Whatever the weather—and they'd endured two dreary days in the rain—or their food situation—Seagryn certainly had no grain to feed the animal, and there wasn't enough time during their stops for Kerl to forage much—the heavily muscled horse plowed ahead at the same, inexorable pace. And although the lonely traveler on his back delivered endless rambling monologues to his tangled mane, Kerl had never once complained. Seagryn was beginning to love this animal. "You're a lot more dependable than people," he sniffed as he ducked under a branch that threatened to scrape him from his saddle. As he spoke he scowled at a mental image of Dark.

He had tried to be fair with the boy, to listen to him with understanding. Uda's infatuation had placed a tremendous burden on Dark. After all, despite his gift, he was only a lad. And to be honest, his fault wasn't so much that of irresponsibility as it was of cloudy judgment and lack of self-discipline. Seagryn had tried to hide his frustrations, but, as Amyryth had avowed, nothing that would eventually be known could be hidden from Dark. The boy had brought it upon himself. Seagryn had reacted with inordinate kindness and a very forgiving spirit, but Dark's enraged response had made it clear the prophet felt *he* was the betrayed party. Even after *that* exchange Seagryn hadn't exactly been angry. But he realized at last that their partnership had ended when the time came to depart the Hovel; then Dark had crisply informed Seagryn that he would be searching out tugoliths alone. Understandably so! How could the boy accompany anyone anywhere with a pubescent tart draped permanently about his neck?

"Women, Kerl. Be grateful you only have to carry them from place to place and then can be rid of them!" The horse said nothing. "Probably knew that was a lie, anyway," Seagryn thought to himself. He could imagine nothing more pleasing than the thought of Elaryl riding here before him through the orange-tinted autumn woods. He would do anything for Elaryl, Seagryn told himself—after all, that was why he was here—

Seagryn had traveled down the mountain with Ranoth and Talarath, hoping to mine from their conversation a few precious nuggets about his beloved. Yet despite their promise to restore him to favor in Lamath if he succeeded, the two elders had showed little interest in reestablishing any relationship with him. They'd talked mostly to one another, tolerating Seagryn's questions and comments but plainly regarding them as interruptions. At the foot of the volcano they'd parted company, Seagryn turning westward and the two clerics traveling back to the sea to rejoin the Paumer House ship that had brought them to this meeting. Before leaving, they'd reaffirmed once more their promise, but Seagryn had seen in their eyes that neither man cared for him. If he succeeded—and Dark had promised he would—he would still remain tainted—a magic user among the pure.

"And how will Elaryl view me, Kerl? Will she smile politely every night at bedtime, struggling to stifle her revulsion?"

Kerl didn't answer. He just kept stamping forward. The forest around them changed color, growing greener as they climbed from the deciduous growth to the unchanging pines. Seagryn noticed and felt deprived. Fall had always been a time to sprawl across the library window seats and watch as the world danced gracefully by outside. The cold bite in the autumn air tuned his mind to its peak, letting ideas crackle through it like the wind slicing through the colorful leaves. It was not a time to travel, yet he traveled—and not to a place of warmth and stimulation, either, but to some frozen wasteland in the far northwest, where giant beasts with the minds of toddlers bashed their horns together in the snow.

"Elaryl," Seagryn mumbled aloud. "It's for Elaryl." But he'd used that thought too often. This time it didn't thaw a single frozen bone. "Hold up here, Kerl," he muttered, and the faithful horse didn't move another step. Seagryn gingerly lifted his right leg up and pivoted around to glide it over the horse's back, taking care not to let the raw spot on the inside of his thigh brush the saddle. He slipped to the ground, leaning against Kerl for just a moment to let his feet remember what it felt like to stand. Then he pulled his cloak tighter still and stalked away through the trees, dodging pine needles. He wished he could see something ahead of them other than forest.

Horses' hooves suddenly pounded the forest floor. He whirled around, half-expecting to see that Kerl's equine mind had finally snapped and that the crazed animal was determined to trample him into mush. But Kerl stood where Seagryn had left him, gazing back dully.

The hoofbeats still came, and a horse at last broke through the pines very close by. "Help me! Seagryn! Help me!" its rider shouted. There was only time for that much before the roan animal shot through the brush on the other side of the glade, carrying the youthful prophet away with it.

"Dark!" Seagryn shouted after the boy, but he did nothing else. He was so shocked that he didn't know quite what to do.

Other horses, perhaps a dozen, burst into the clearing, their riders all dressed in the red-and-blue livery of Paumer. Obviously in pursuit of the fleeing prophet, none of them took any notice of Seagryn, driving their animals straight past him and back again into the forest.

"Dark!" Seagryn said again, to no one but himself. Then he

started to chase the riders on foot. "Kerl!" he cried, and he skidded to a stop on the pine needles and turned to race back to his dispassionate steed. Another thought occurred, and he skidded again, this time winding up on his bottom right under the horse's nose. "What am I doing?" he pleaded with Kerl. "You're not as fast as those animals! As a tugolith, I am!" Kerl said nothing, preferring to watch. Seagryn bounded to his feet and changed his shape, then bolted into the forest after Dark's pursuers.

While the riders left behind them trees bruised but unbowed, only firewood remained where Seagryn passed. One slim sapling, still quivering with relief at having survived the cavalry charge, felt the full impact of a tugolith horn with a full-grown tugolith behind it. The slender tree split right down to its roots. Branches splintered, pine needles flew, and great chunks were gouged from the leafpack wherever Seagryn's feet hit the ground. His passage was so noisy that he thought the sound alone might scare the riders off Dark's trail. It didn't. But the tumult almost prevented him from hearing Dark's cry.

"Seagryn! Seagryn, up here!"

He didn't try to stop dead this time. Instead he rounded a rather sizable elm, one of the few in this section of the forest, and trotted back toward the spot where he'd heard that second call. He saw nothing.

"Up here, Seagryn! Look up!"

Seagryn did look up and saw Dark crouching on a branch not far above him. "How did you get up there?"

"I flew!" the boy groused. "Now would you please get under me and let me get down on your forehead? I can guarantee those riders are turning around this very instant!"

Seagryn did as the lad instructed, blinking in pain as Dark's jump from the tree landed the boy in the middle of one of his eyes. "Careful please," he grumbled, but the prophet was too hysterical to take much notice.

"That way! That way! Go that way!" Dark shouted. He probably pointed, too, but from where he perched behind Seagryn's horn the powershaper could see nothing of his gesture.

"What way?" Seagryn demanded. "If you're going to give orders, be explicit!"

"Right! To the right!"

Seagryn waited no longer. He shot off toward his right, shouting, "Hold on tight—this might be rough going!"

"I couldn't be *more* certain of that," Dark mumbled.

Before the full import of the prophet's words could register upon him Seagryn felt the ground give way beneath his feet. They tumbled headlong into a black chasm.

"If you knew this was coming, I'll kill you!" Seagryn shouted as they bounced off the walls on the way down. They landed in a remarkably soft pile of soil.

Dark spat dirt from his mouth several times before replying. "Of course I knew it was coming, and you won't. You'll be too busy dealing with her."

"With whom?" Seagryn asked, surprised to hear his human voice and not the bass croaking of his altershape. Without realizing it, he'd taken his human-form again.

"You remember me mentioning a megasin's cave, and asking me what a megasin was? Well, Seagryn, you're about to find out."

"Seagryn? Is that your name?"

The powershaper whirled in the darkness to face the voice, which was very female and very close by. Whoever she was, she smelled wonderful. But why couldn't he see her? He looked up at the hole they'd fallen through and gasped in astonishment as it closed itself in. "How—"

"It's my window. Surely a lady can open her own shutters when she chooses? And close them?" He heard the smile behind her words, and it terrified him.

"Dark! Dark, are you there?"

"Oh I'm here all right," the boy muttered.

"Who is she? What is she? What do I do now?"

"You're the wizard. Why don't *you* think of something for a change?"

Seagryn did. A silver ball of light suddenly danced above their heads; then, just as suddenly, Seagryn doused it. But it had been enough—

"You've seen me," the woman's voice pouted, only now Seagryn knew this was no woman. What it was he couldn't guess, but he felt certain that they sat in the dirt in the presence of something both gigantic and exceedingly old—and she didn't wear her age well at all.

"Run!" Seagryn wailed, and his legs churned soft soil out behind him as he struggled to his feet and sprinted blindly forward. Did a corridor open before him? Or had he just been incredibly lucky in his choice of direction? No matter. "This way!" he shouted to Dark, uncertain if the lad followed, but feeling absolutely no inclination to stop and check. He ran faster and faster, it seemed, although he knew that really wasn't so. It just seemed so fast, far too fast, since his mind kept reminding him he was apt to crash headlong into rock at any moment.

And he did. But this wasn't rock. It was soft, and furry, and it smelled so very—

"I didn't want you to see me like that," the megasin chided seductively as she enfolded him in her powerful grip and crushed him to her hirsute—whatever.

"Help!" Seagryn yelled. "Dark! Are you there?"

"I'm right here . . ." the prophet muttered again. Seagryn didn't stop to wonder how the boy could have beat him here and not be winded.

"You mudgecurdle! If we ever get out of this place I swear I'm going to swallow you whole!" Then Seagryn fiercely took his altershape, angry at himself that he hadn't done so immediately. This female monster should already have been splattered against the walls of her own dungeon! Instantly he broke free of her embrace, uttered a most tugolithic bellow, and charged her. He hit her, too . . . or thought he did. He couldn't tell, since she seemed to become totally pliable when he touched her. He rumbled right on through her and ran into the wall beyond.

That rock, too, was pliable, for a moment, at least—long enough for him to imbed his horn into it, right up to his flaring nostrils. Then it turned hard again, and was solid rock. He knew the awful truth even before trying to pull himself free—he was stuck.

"Mmmm!" the megasin purred appreciatively from behind him. Evidently she'd pulled herself together, for she was now grabbing hold of his hindquarters. "You are some hunk of beast!"

"Dark!" the trapped tugolith croaked. "Tell me! What do I do!"

"Why should I help a creature who's threatened to eat me?"

"Help me!" Seagryn pleaded, and his plaintive tone must have touched the boy's heart at last, for Dark quietly suggested, "Your human shape has no horn. Try changing back and see if you don't come free."

"Oh, no!" the megasin protested. "*Keep* this shape, you magic user! I like it!"

Seagryn needed no further encouragement. With a flick of his imagination, he turned human again, gasping in relief when he came free of both the wall and the megasin's grip. He whirled around to face the creature, and once again a ball of light blossomed into brilliance above their heads.

"Oww!" she whined. "Would you please put that thing out?"

"Not unless you promise to quit grabbing me!" Seagryn demanded.

"Oh, all right," she muttered. Then she looked up at him and blinked her eyes flirtatiously. "I look better now, don't I?"

He had to admit her appearance had improved over that first horrifying vision. Even so, he doubted if he would quickly grow accustomed to a dozen totally colorless eyes staring at him in the hungry way these did. He swallowed hard, hoping to push the contents of his stomach back down where they belonged. He then wished the light away, thinking as he did so that there were advantages to the darkness . . .

"Now you know how I feel," Dark grumbled.

"How you feel about what?" the megasin asked.

"Seagryn understands. Don't you, Seagryn?"

"About what?"

"About Uda!"

Oh yes, Seagryn remembered. The boy had compared his experience with Uda to being in a megasin's cave. "Who are you?" he asked the creature, hoping conversation might distract her from whatever horrible fate she was contemplating for them.

"Who am I?"

"Yes. What is your name?"

"Name . . ." the megasin pondered, evidently trying to make sense of the idea.

"You don't have a name?"

"I don't know," she answered warmly. "I can recall someone asking me that, but I can't remember what we decided."

"Someone . . . who? Who have you known? Who have you talked to in the past?"

"My companions," the megasin said rather sadly. "I've had a number of companions. But they all died. They were all humans, of course. Like you. You people die rather quickly, did you know that?" There seemed to be honest concern in the creature's voice.

"I wonder how long you have lived?" When she didn't answer immediately Seagryn realized she had no real way of reckoning time.

He was going to ask another question when she said, "More rock rumbles than you could ever count, magic user."

"Rock rumbles?"

"When the earth grinds against itself and then shifts—or when the rock's hot blood climbs up the cracks to spit at the sky."

These images filled Seagryn with awe, and he contemplated them in the silence. In a moment Dark took it upon himself to explain, "She means earthquakes and volcanoes—"

"I know what she means."

"I knew that," Dark snapped back, but he sounded embarrassed.

"I've had many companions in that time," the megasin offered, "many who've fallen into my—that is, who've stepped through my shutters. Some of them have been good companions. Of course," she added, "some were not so good." Her voice took on a wistful quality. "But all of them—all—eventually died. Their remains have been accepted into the rock all around you. You may have noticed that rock does as I ask."

Seagryn had indeed noticed and was fascinated. He found her perspective and her history enthralling and thought he could spend an agreeable afternoon just listening to her. But he had a task to perform and a love to regain. From her description, becoming companion to a megasin was a rather permanent appointment. "Did any of these companions attempt to—escape?"

The megasin laughed so gaily Seagryn found himself smiling, despite his fears. "Why concern yourself with the trivial, when I have so much to tell you? Relax! Sit down! Aren't you starving?" Strong hands pressed Seagryn backward and down, and he landed again in the soft dirt beside Dark.

"Sit here while I fetch you something to eat," the megasin said warmly, and Seagryn listened carefully for the sounds of her moving away. After a moment he leaned toward Dark. "Just one question. Do we get out of here?"

"Yes," the boy said firmly.

For a moment that was sufficient, and Seagryn sat gazing at the blackness in front of his face. But soon it wasn't enough, and he leaned toward Dark again. "Make that two questions. How do we get out?"

Dark seemed to answer most unwillingly. "I—don't know."

Seagryn mulled that over for a moment. "You don't know?"

"Right."

"You honestly don't know?" Seagryn tried to keep the panic out of his voice.

"It's really very embarrassing," said the boy prophet. "I mean, I've always known everything. But—as I've told you—I had prevented myself from looking into my own courtship—if you could call it that. And when that began to draw too near to avoid, so too did periods of darkness.''

''Darkness?''

''Times when I wouldn't know what would happen—exactly.''

''Like right now.''

''Like right now,'' the boy agreed. ''Believe me, if you think you're frustrated by it, imagine how I feel! It's as if I can't remember a thing!''

''For you,'' the megasin said from behind them, and both Seagryn and Dark grunted in surprise.

Seagryn twisted around, and tried to stare in the female beast's direction. ''I thought you went the other way!''

''Oh, I did. And I came back this way. I told you before, magic user, the rock does whatever I ask.''

''Then you—you make corridors, and close them behind you?''

''Exactly! Oh, how quick you are! Probably because you're a magic user. I've never had a magic user for a companion before!'' She seemed genuinely enthusiastic. Seagryn felt much less so. ''Here's your food,'' the megasin offered, and she placed in their hands something warm that smelled tempting. ''Eat! Eat!'' she trilled. ''You'll find it wonderful!''

Seagryn was about to wonder aloud exactly what had been placed before them when Dark muttered, ''Seagryn—don't ask.'' He didn't. He just started eating. But he wondered as he chewed if Dark's warning hadn't been worse than knowing. With each new bite his imagination made the source of this food more hideous . . .

Chapter Twenty

※※※※

POWER'S PROMISE

WHEN Seagryn awoke in the blackness he knew exactly where he was. He also knew with great certainty that many days had passed, and that, through them all, he'd not dreamed once. He jumped to his feet and filled this black hole with light. He'd been imprisoned in a bubble hollowed out of the rock—a cage of stone. He scanned the seamless wall, turning in a slow circle. He saw no apparent exit, nor any ventilation. And yet he breathed—

He looked down at his feet in time to see Dark sit up, rub his eyes, and look around. "I suppose that explains my periods of darkness," the boy said flatly.

"What does."

"Did you dream?"

Seagryn grunted. "No."

"Nor did I. And I always dream."

"That food," Seagryn said. "The megasin poisoned us, then shut us up inside this tomb. She'll keep us here until she's ready to consume us." He said this matter-of-factly, without passion. He dared not loose the feelings of terror that suddenly seemed to claw at his back and neck. He had no idea what he might do then.

"Perhaps that's it." Dark nodded. "Then again, maybe she already has."

"Has what?"

"Oh, I just doubt if she'll consume us in the same way we ate her drugged stew."

"What other way is there?"

Dark shrugged. Was he unwilling to confront his own fears? Seagryn wondered. Or had he already seen some terrible future reality and now tried to shield Seagryn from it? "Speak up, Dark. You meant something by that."

Dark hung his head, then shrugged again and explained, "She could eat us emotionally . . ."

"How would she do that?" Seagryn asked harshly. He had some suspicions himself, but found those thoughts far too horrible to voice.

"I think she's stolen our dreams," Dark said. "Seagryn, I always dream! I don't know how she's done it, but I'm afraid she's touched our sleeping minds and experienced our dreams for herself. And that's especially frightening for me—"

"Why should it be any worse for you, lad?" Seagryn shuddered. "The thought of someone prying into my—"

"Because my dreams foretell the future."

"Oh." Understanding Dark's deeper concern now, Seagryn pondered a moment. "Do you think she knows that?"

Dark squinted his eyes in concentration. When his eyelids fluttered open again, Seagryn no longer saw the confident prophet of legend, but a frightened boy. In exercising his gift, Dark had carried burdens no other mortal could even comprehend. But never before had he felt the simple terror of the unknown.

"I—I thought I'd just hidden this all from myself," the distraught prophet whispered. "But—I truly don't know!" Dark's eyes pleaded. "Seagryn! How can you people endure not knowing!"

An interesting question, Seagryn thought, but not one he had time to pursue. They needed to get out of this place. Evidently that responsibility was his. "You've told me already I'd get my Elaryl back."

"I—I did?" Dark pleaded, grabbing Seagryn's sleeve.

"Self-doubt," the wizard said. He could recognize that easily enough, for he'd felt it often. "Yes, you did. Which means we do get out of here. The question is when. Do you remember that?"

"I—don't remember anything!"

"Relax, Dark," Seagryn said with a calmness he didn't feel. "It will all come back to you." Or so he hoped—

No. He *believed*, and the implications of that belief struck him now like a blow to the forehead. For regardless of how he accounted for his own magical abilities, he had always considered Dark's prophetic gift to be exactly that—a gift. And if it was a gift, then there had to be a giver, and who could bestow such ability other than the Power, that One they never named, to whom he'd committed all his adult life?

In that One he believed. He couldn't help it. He simply did. Was that belief itself a gift? "I've been viewing it lately as almost a curse," he muttered.

"What?" Dark implored, and Seagryn looked down at the boy with an enormous sense of compassion.

"Don't worry, lad," he comforted. "We're going to get out of this."

Dark nodded, and his anxious expression seemed to soften. "When?" he asked.

"That I don't know."

"I'm hungry," Dark muttered. As if in answer the rock around them began to rumble.

"She heard you," Seagryn whispered. A moment later one wall of the stone prison disappeared.

"Awk!" the megasin shouted. "Light again! Put it out! Put it *out*!"

"Why?" Seagryn asked. "We people like light."

The monster closed up the wall again, but evidently with only a thin layer of rock, for they could easily hear her voice through it. "You people also like to breathe, I understand?"

The air in the cave had suddenly grown quite stale, and Dark looked at Seagryn with deep concern. "Ah—you think you should put out the fire?"

Seagryn panted, and glanced up at his magical fireball. "Might as well—it's already sputtering." The light blinked out, and Seagryn called, "You can come back now, if you wish. The light is gone."

"Very good," the beguiling voice said from behind him. Her enticing scent permeated the cave, and he felt her hands—all sixteen or so of them—resting upon his shoulders. He didn't shrug them off, nor try to struggle out of her grasp this time. He just let the light blossom above them again.

"No!" the megasin screamed, and once more they found themselves entombed with her outside. "Don't do that!" the creature roared. "Put it out—and leave it out—or I shall have to punish you!"

Seagryn watched Dark's eyes. The boy looked up at him. "Ah—Seagryn?"

"What will you do to us?" the wizard called out. He smiled at his partner reassuringly.

"You—can't guess?" Dark asked, already beginning to choke.

"I think you know," the creature threatened.

"Suppose you suffocate us. Who then will be your companions?" Seagryn still smiled at Dark, who watched him intently. They heard nothing for several minutes, but it did seem that the air quality had improved slightly. Seagryn felt proud of himself.

When next the megasin spoke she had traded her seductive soprano for the flint-hard sound of metal sawing rock. "You think you may tease me, magic user?" The sound alone was enough to drive both of them quivering onto their faces. When Seagryn didn't respond, the monster wailed, "Answer me!" in the voice of a howling wind, and the cage of stone trembled at her wrath.

"Better talk or she'll crush us for sure!" Dark shouted.

"It's gone! The light's gone! It's all gone!" Seagryn cried as he plunged them again into darkness. The tremor stopped. The rock surrounding them fell silent.

Then somewhere above them they heard girlish laughter, and the megasin said, "This is fun!"

Fun? Seagryn marveled to himself, but he dared not speak his thought aloud.

He didn't need to. Dark did so for him. "What do you mean?" the boy prophet asked, his voice quavering.

"Few challenges remain for one as old as myself. But the two of you certainly challenge me!" The megasin laughed and crowed, "One who uses magic and the other who dreams tomorrow. Who could want companions more interesting than these?"

"She knows," Seagryn quietly said to Dark.

"She does," the boy answered in the blackness. "Trouble is—I don't."

"Yet we know we escape the woman eventually."

"I'll have to depend upon you for that, Seagryn. Power knows, I can no longer depend on me."

They refused all food, and struggled together to resist all sleep as well. There were lapses—times they both slumped against the wall, unable any longer to keep their eyes open in the dark—and they woke from each of these to the sounds of wicked laughter that seemed to gush from the rock like spring water. They naturally grew weaker as time fled. Gradually, deprived as they were of sleep and rest and deprived of their dreams when they did sleep, they began losing track of who they were and how they'd come to be here, wandering the bizarre passageways of delirium. At last they had to eat again, and they slept—

"Who is the Power?" the megasin demanded, and Seagryn woke. Disoriented in the pitch-black room, he seemed to float momentarily on the granite.

"What?"

"The Power," the megasin said. "Who is it?"

"How—" Seagryn began, faltered, then rubbed his throbbing head and tried again. "How do you know about the Power?"

"Because you know this Power," the monster replied. Her remarks seemed strangely subdued.

"Not anymore," Seagryn grumbled quietly, wanting to fall back again into sleep. "Why don't you ask young Dark there. He's more in touch than I."

"Yet it's you who come to be shaped by it," the megasin told him, and now Seagryn awoke fully and sat up to look toward the voice.

"Shaped by it?"

"That's what you will call it," the monster said petulantly, and Seagryn didn't know what to say.

"And—how do you know?" he asked finally.

"Your young friend's dreams. They tell me. I've seen much— but I can't control it. His sleeping thoughts seem to bounce from time to time, until I lose myself in a labyrinth of will-be some-days. But in one of these futures, I hear you claim to be shaped by a Power, and it's then that you give me your promise."

"What promise?"

"You think I would tell you your own mind?" the megasin snarled. Then she departed and apparently left them alone. When, despite his struggle against it, sleep claimed Seagryn again, he dreamed that he married Elaryl. When he awoke this time he felt refreshed. He also came awake knowing exactly what he had to do and how to do it.

And yet it wasn't easy. He'd done it all his life—all the life that he could remember—but it had never been easy in the best of times. And now the necessary spiritual muscles were atrophied by disuse. Weeds of doubt had overgrown the familiar tracks in his mind and spirit; an icy wall of anger had blocked all contact. Worst of all, he felt himself buried under a dunghill of shame, a pile he knew he would have to tunnel through alone before experiencing any sense at all of the Power's shaping presence.

Then there was this place—this black gloom so thick with ancient evil it clung like a sticky residue to every granite surface. The megasin had been here a very long time, Seagryn felt absolutely certain. Within these galleries she had trapped thousands of generations of suffering people, for no greater sin than that they'd stumbled through her shutter when she was companionless. Her loneliness made that no less cruel, and her reverence for their dead remains did not ennoble her to him at all—it only made her appear more pitiful. That pattern of injustice would likely continue, whether he and Dark made their way back up to the bright world above or not. He found no hope in this darkness, only thousands of years of constant, helpless despair. How could he think something *he* might do would change it?

"Simple," he growled up into the blackness that crushed downward into his open eyes. "I don't do it." And Seagryn let go.

Although he lay flat on his back on a very solid surface, Seagryn felt that at that moment he was falling. He seemed to drop backward into an infinite pit, falling forever as the factions of fear and faith warred for control of his psyche. He had started it now; he was adrift, and recalled anew the oddness of the sensation, remembering the many times he'd done this before and how strange it was to watch that battle so dispassionately. With that awareness came the anchoring force, the net of certainty which reminded him that he did indeed believe, that there was indeed a Power. With that, he fell once more into that Power's presence.

Why did he always forget how quickly shame metamorphosed into elation? Awe seized his spirit by the throat and sought to throttle it, but warmth and acceptance and the sense of belonging quickly diluted that killing awe into love. He had tried all his life to express the nature of this moment, but had never found words potent enough to carry the images. Yet, as he relived it once again, he felt such clarity of vision he was astonished all over again that anyone could fail to understand. "So obvious! So evident! So clear!" he thought he cried out, though he never could be certain while in this state if the words actually formed upon his lips. It didn't matter. He spoke only to himself. Eternity filled this moment and linked it to all the other times he'd fallen at last to this sweet weakness. Then he was awake, aware, and very much a being shaped by the Power, somewhere in a cavern in the earth. He was aware, too, of the megasin's presence.

"What's happening?" the feminine voice demanded.

"I'm being shaped," Seagryn answered. "By the Power."

"And who or what is this Power that dares invade my darkness and enthrall my companion!"

"Could the rock that melts or freezes at your will describe you to a curious stone from Lamath or a wandering gem from Pleclypsa? I am shaped by the Power. It's wonderful. And now that Power will open up a stairway to the surface, and Dark and I will climb it and be gone. Dark?"

"I'm here," the boy answered alertly. Had his gift returned? There would be time soon to talk and find out. But first there was to be a miracle. Seagryn tilted his head back and looked up.

When the shutter had closed above them—days ago? weeks?— it had sealed itself slowly, a wound in the earth healing up. This stairway, however, showed no sign of its coming. They heard no rumbling in the rock, no groaning of boulders forcing themselves to split. There was darkness where Seagryn looked, then there was light, and a moment thereafter they smelled the frosty scent of new snow and felt a few flakes of dislodged powder drifting down to drop upon their cheeks. Winter sunlight streamed down from above, highlighting each carefully carved stair. They could go. Seagryn looked at Dark, and the boy bolted upward.

"The promise!" the megasin screamed from behind him, and Seagryn jumped, surprised by the ancient beast's pitiful tone of voice. He started to turn around and look at her.

"Don't look!" she pleaded, and hurried on. "Just give me the Power's promise!"

The Power's promise. Now he understood. As Seagryn watched Dark climb carefully up the last few steps and jump joyfully out into the freshly fallen snow, he leaned back again upon the force that shaped him, believing there were words he was meant to say. As he expected, as had happened so many times before in his experience, the words were there in his mind and he spoke them. "It's not *my* promise at all, old megasin. But I can tell you the *Power's* promise. You see the stairway, so you know the Power must be. And if you will seek that Power, you will find at last a deathless companion.'' He started to go, but she stopped him again.

"Where?'' she demanded.

The words came clearly again. "It's not a where that you seek—it's a who. Look inside yourself, old megasin. I must go.''

He thought he heard a whimper behind him—was the megasin mourning his leaving? Then he heard for certain the sealing of stone, and knew she'd walled herself off from this stairway and its light. As he climbed out of the megasin's pit only one thought obscured Seagryn's joy. He wondered if old Kerl had found fodder and shelter. For some reason, all living things seemed far more worthy of cherishing.

Chapter Twenty-one

※※※※

HORN BASHING

From the black of the megasin's endless catacomb Seagryn stepped into the dazzling brilliance of midday sunshine on powdery snow. He stood on the top step and closed his eyes, grinning in triumph as he waited for them to adjust. When he opened them again the gap in the earth had closed beneath him, and his feet were buried in an icy drift. Alarmed, he jumped free, tossing a fluffy plume up toward his face. He brushed the frozen powder from his cheeks and really noticed, for the first time, how very hairy his face had become in the weeks since he'd been driven out of Lamath. Weeks? Or had it been months, perhaps years? He glanced at Dark, ready to ask the boy's opinion, and noticed that the young prophet huddled, shivering, against a snow-covered rock. He ran to him, dancing the last few steps when he realized he could make quicker progress that way. He knelt beside the boy and hugged him protectively. "Are you all right?"

"I'm freezing," Dark chattered through clenched teeth.

"We've got to get you to some shelter," Seagryn muttered, oblivious to the sharp wind that cut through his own robes as well.

"There is none," Dark advised, speaking only with great effort.

"You *know* that? Your gift has returned!"

Dark shook his head. "I remember. From before. I saw this

185

before." He ducked his head and turned his face to the rock, wincing in pain.

Seagryn looked down at his own body with some confusion, then back at Dark. Was it really this cold? Why was he not feeling it? He stood up and walked several steps away from the rock, then turned to face the wind. He couldn't understand it. To him this was just a fresh, bracing breeze after a stifling imprisonment. He glanced around at the soft white carpet that covered everything and felt the urge to dance in it. He didn't understand. It made no sense.

"You're a tugolith, remember?" the boy called out. "I understand they love the snow!"

"But then—why didn't I feel this way before?" Seagryn called back, but Dark had again hid his face against the rock.

Seagryn looked down at himself and reached to finger the heavy gown the servants of Paumer had clothed him in before sending him northward. "In my tugolith skin I wouldn't need this," he muttered quietly, then shrugged out of it and began to doff the clothing beneath it as well. Nearly nude, he carried the pile of garments to Dark and began to wrap the boy in them. He'd never given much thought to the fact that his clothes did not change when he changed shape. That was simply the way things were, the way the magic worked. Although he did remember once when his garments had torn off of him, the day he had—

No, that had been a dream, a dream of his ruined wedding and Elaryl's rejection of him. But his memory of the dream was as real as if it had been an actual event, and was no less disturbing. He shivered slightly, then glanced down at his human flesh and saw it was turning a strange shade of blue.

"You'd better change," Dark murmured, his eyes aglow with appreciation for the added layers of cloth.

Seagryn nodded. He stepped a few feet away, then imagined himself once again in tugolith shape. But something was different when he took that form this time. For some reason he felt more alive within it than he ever had before—as if all the times in the past his tugolith body had been sick, but now had finally regained its health. And he had to wonder—was it the cold, or his renewed affiliation with the Power? He rolled his huge eyes at the drifts piled around him, and decided it didn't matter. He had to dance!

And dance he did, around in circles, up onto his hind legs, on the tops of huge boulders, and between the boles of mighty trees that trembled when he brushed them and sent marvelous showers of saved-up snow down onto his broad gray back. Dark, after at first laughing, ran for his life and hid in a granite crevice. When Seagryn had thoroughly plowed up this once virgin meadow, rendering it a muddy mess, the prophet finally crawled out of his refuge and shouted, "Can we go now?"

There was certainly no more reason to stay. Seagryn stretched out his forelegs in a moderately clean patch of snow and Dark climbed up behind his horn. Then the boy and his tugolith started north.

"How long were we down there?" Seagryn rumbled, glancing down at the ground below his scaly lip.

"I don't know," Dark said. "Days, maybe. Perhaps a couple of weeks. Enough, I hope, to convince that woman I'm gone for good."

"What woman?" Seagryn asked, plodding forward. He was thinking of the wonderful model Kerl had provided for him, and how ironic it was that he was now the carrier instead of the carried.

"Uda, of course," Dark snorted. "What other woman would I be talking about!"

"Oh, her," Seagryn muttered, nodding slightly and thereby bouncing the boy around upon his perch. "I don't quite consider her a woman."

"She considers herself one." Dark gasped in obvious dismay. "I thought I'd never get out of her grasp!"

"Ridiculous." Seagryn snorted, turning his head to rub his chin joyfully in a high drift. "You knew exactly when you would get away."

"Well, yes, that's true," Dark agreed. "It's just that I thought the time would never arrive! And you can't imagine what I had to put up with before it finally did."

"I thought you were rather enjoying it, there toward the end of my stay?"

Dark cleared his throat. "Well," he muttered in obvious embarrassment, "such a heated relationship does have its stimulating moments. But it gets so boring after a while! I felt so stifled! I cannot understand why you're so eager to complete this task and go back and get married. Women have only one purpose in mind, and that's to insure you spend every waking moment paying attention to what they think. I can't believe I purposely hid that whole encounter from myself for so long, thinking it would spoil something wonderful! Talk about your fate worse than death . . .''

''Um-hmm,'' Seagryn grunted, looking about at the scenery. He didn't recognize where they were at all. The topography of this area matched nothing in his experience. The mountains they walked between appeared higher and sharper than any he'd ever seen, and the trees seemed to be shorter, tougher cousins of the evergreens in the Marwilds. ''Do you know where we are?''

''In the north, of course,'' Dark growled, then returned to the recitation of his miseries. ''As you say, I knew I'd get free from her, but it seemed forever before the day arrived. They kept asking me if you'd be successful; of course, I told them yes—''

''I will?'' Seagryn said, pricking up his huge ears.

''I've told you that before. So they—''

''No, you haven't!''

''Yes I have. I just haven't told you how you'll do it. Anyway, they decided they would take the whole entourage up to Lamath to be there to welcome you back. On the way, they left me unwatched long enough for me to escape unnoticed. Of course, I knew exactly where you'd be and how you would come to my aid, so I started riding across country to you as fast as possible, with Uda and her guards right on my tail. She rode with them for several hours, and the things she called me and the threats she made! I'll tell you this, my mother still doesn't know I know those words! It took most of a morning to—''

''Where in the north, exactly?''

Dark sighed. ''Are you not interested in this story?''

''I'm more interested in knowing where we are and how we got here. This looks nothing like the woods we were in when we fell through the megasin's shutter.''

''It's not. She moved us. Or you did.''

''I did?''

''Of course, with all your running away. She just opened the rock in front of you and you ran through it. And who knows how far she carried us while we slept or how long it took her to do it?''

''Then it could have been only a few days after all—we've come to the snow rather than the snow coming to us.''

''However or wherever, I'm just glad to get away from her. What a terrible experience!''

''She is a monster.'' Seagryn nodded in agreement.

"And so was that megasin," Dark murmured with conviction, which confused Seagryn at first. Then he understood.

"You mean Uda again," he said, and Dark nodded. Seagryn frowned a tugolith frown, but said no more. He just kept plowing northward through the snow. Old Kerl had set a high standard . . .

The weather was kinder to Dark than it might have been. The sun shone the rest of that day, keeping him moderately warm under his many layers. By the time they stopped for the night, they both were hungry, but they'd seen nothing in these frozen wastes that looked edible, so they bedded down together beneath a stand of scrubby trees and tried to ignore the noisy growling of their stomachs. "Tomorrow. We'll eat tomorrow," Dark announced.

"Your gift is back!" Seagryn said with an enormous grin.

"No, nothing new," the boy answered, shaking his head. "It's still just memories of previous visions."

"At least the beast didn't steal them from you."

"She may have." Dark shrugged, snuggling closer to Seagryn's scale-covered but nevertheless warm skin. "Who can say what the old megasin knows now about our future—or where she might appear again?"

"Do you know that she will?" Seagryn asked.

"No. In fact," Dark added before dropping off to sleep, "I know as little right now about what's to come as at any time I can remember in my life. Strange—the feeling is really rather peaceful . . ."

Seagryn was still mulling over the young prophet's words when he heard the slow, heavy breathing of a lad asleep. It didn't come so easily for him this night. He rolled his giant head back and gazed up at the stars in the refreshingly frozen sky. He was just too excited about finding out how he would accomplish his task to be able to rest . . .

They woke to the noise of tree trunks being whacked together like twigs. Dark had been snuggled under Seagryn's warm flank, and now he rolled free and kept on rolling through the snow until he was well away from the altered wizard's enormous hooves. For Seagryn awoke leaping into the air. He landed squarely upon his feet, trained his cone-shaped ears in the direction of the noise, and started sniffing.

"What is it?" Dark asked anxiously.

"It smells like—me," Seagryn answered.

"That bad?" the boy prophet wondered aloud, his forehead creased with concern. Seagryn rolled an eyeball around to look at him, but the lad seemed unaware of his own insult. Seagryn sniffed that odor again, and had to admit it.

"Yes," he acknowledged. "That bad."

Dark looked up at his huge companion. "Tugoliths, then. I guess we've found them." At the moment he didn't appear too thrilled by their discovery.

"You want me to go on alone?"

"No!" Dark shouted. "You're not leaving me out here in these frozen wastes by myself! At least not while I remember so little about what's to come!"

"Fine. Then let's go," Seagryn muttered, and he lowered his chin to the ground to let the prophet scale his cheeks. Moments later they stood on a glacial bluff, overlooking a vast valley that glistened with the purest white Seagryn had ever seen. But the drama unfolding directly below them stole his attention from the awesome setting. They witnessed a battle between titans.

Two tugoliths rushed together at full speed, and their horns clacked with the noise of one log smashing into another. Both animals were knocked backward by the force of the blow, but one seemed more stunned than the other. Noting his advantage, the more alert tugolith charged again, and this time his horn made a very different sound as it slid off the horn of his rival and stabbed deeply into that unfortunate animal's flesh. The wounded tugolith screamed in pain and reeled backward to sit on its hindquarters. Fresh blood stained the white landscape crimson, spoiling forever this vista in Seagryn's memory. He closed his eyes against the next blow, unwilling to see any creature so wantonly slaughtered.

But the blow didn't come. Seagryn opened his eyes again.

"Go away," the victorious tugolith ordered firmly, sounding exactly like a schoolboy commanding a bully to leave the playground. In the wake of the bloody beating just administered this almost polite request seemed a little ludicrous, and Seagryn rolled his eyes up to look up at Dark, expecting the boy to agree. Instead he saw the young prophet's fascinated smile. Once more he forced himself to recall that Dark was little more than a schoolboy himself.

"Where?" the beaten tugolith whined.

"To your wheel, punt," the victor instructed. "If it will take you . . ."

"My wheel is dead," the loser rumbled.

The winner turned to look back over his enormous shoulders, and Seagryn noticed then the circle of nine tugoliths that stood behind him, horns pointing outward. Looking back, the victor called out, "We grieve for you. Now go away."

With much grunting the defeated tugolith struggled onto his four legs again and turned to move off slowly. He walked sideways, however, glancing back at his conqueror as if half-expecting another sharp prick to the flanks from that wicked-tipped bone that had battered him to the ice.

Seagryn still watched his departure when Dark murmured a quiet, "Oh, dear."

Seagryn glanced quickly back to the herd to find every horn on every forehead of the ten remaining tugoliths now pointed upward toward them. He looked down at the circle—for they still held to that formation—and muttered a strangled, "Hello?"

The tugoliths all eyed him for a minute before their leader spoke. "You can't get down," he observed sensibly. With that the members of the circle—the wheel?—turned their backsides to Seagryn and Dark and wandered off across the endless ice.

"Looks like you made a good first impression," Dark muttered sardonically. Seagryn thought about tipping his horn forward and dropping the boy headfirst into the valley, but resisted the temptation.

The tugolith leader had been right. There was no way off this glacial cliff other than to turn around and go back. It took them most of the morning to find a kind of rampway down, and by that time both the tugolith wheel and the bloodied loser were beyond the reach of Seagryn's sensitive nose.

"Nothing," he grumbled, giving his head a shake in frustration.

"Could I remind you just once more that I'm sitting up here and that, every time you do that, you threaten to toss me off?"

"Might do you good to experience a little suffering," Seagryn grumbled, sympathizing with the plight of the tugolith who'd been driven away. "Might make you more sensitive to the plight of those less fortunate."

"I can't imagine anyone less fortunate than myself at the moment," the prophet on his forehead responded. "I'm starving. If your sense of smell is so keen, why don't you use it to find us some food?"

"I've been trying," Seagryn said pensively. "I suppose you didn't notice . . ."

"Notice what?"

"That every one of those beasts we saw today appeared emaciated."

Dark paused for a moment, remembering. "They looked fat enough to me."

"How would you know?" Seagryn muttered, then caught himself before adding, "You're not a tugolith."

"I know this. I know you find one of these beasties and lure it homeward. But I do wish you'd get on with it. I'm cold, I'm tired, and I haven't eaten in the-megasin-knows-how-long!"

"Oh, I forgot," Seagryn said with a touch of cruelty. "You're in a rush to get back and rejoin Uda." He shouldn't have said it, he realized. He rarely let that caustic aspect of his personality have any access to his tongue. But it was out—and Dark seemed to freeze in place upon his head.

They said nothing else to one another for many minutes as Seagryn worked his way down a steep slope made treacherous by patches of glass-slick ice. He had time to think about it, and time to feel regret. For of the virtues Seagryn believed himself to possess, the two he cherished most were his loyalty to friends and a basic kindness. "I'm sorry," he said when they finally reached the flat snow plain.

"I know." As usual, the boy reacted flippantly.

"How do you know!" Seagryn demanded.

"Quite simple." The lad sighed. "My gift is back."

Chapter Twenty-two

✕✕✕✕✕

BEING THE WISER

"Just like that? It's back?" Seagryn asked.

"Unfortunately." Dark sighed, sounding as if he really meant it.

"You think so?"

"You remember what I told you last night before we went to sleep, how peaceful I felt? I liked that feeling, Seagryn. I liked it a lot."

The boy had experienced suffering, Seagryn remembered. True suffering of a kind he could only imagine. He felt genuinely sorrowful—for he was, most certainly, a loyal friend.

"One advantage, of course," the boy chirped suddenly. "I know where we can get some food. To your right, Seagryn, and move those hooves!"

It was not very long before they reached a stretch of the snow that seemed oddly pockmarked. Seagryn would have rambled on through it if Dark hadn't suddenly ordered, "Stop."

"Stop? I thought you were hungry?"

"I am hungry. So are you, but don't let it cloud your judgment. Investigate these holes."

A tugolith frown curled Seagryn's scaly lips downward. "I think I liked you better when you were a little more dependent."

"Strange that you should say that," Dark muttered. "I was thinking the same thing myself. But you really should examine these little potholes, Seagryn. They're the reason those tugoliths we saw this morning are starving. Ah—you were right about that, by the way. At the time I didn't know.''

Still frowning, Seagryn shuffled to one of the holes in the ice and sniffed at it. "Something lives here," he observed very quietly. "Something warm and furry."

"You can tell it has fur just by sniffing?"

"Quiet—it's stirring around—" They both hushed then, waiting. Nothing happened.

"It'll come," Dark said firmly.

"Quiet—"

"You'll see."

"I said hush!"

"But you still won't be expecting—"

Out of the hole popped a shaggy little head topped by two quite terrified yellow eyes. They hushed and stared at it, and the little animal responded by staring back at them. After a motionless moment, Seagryn took a tentative step toward the little creature. With a sudden hiss, it swelled its body up to the size of a small dog, and Seagryn, although forty times its size, nevertheless bolted backward. The balloonlike creature didn't budge, nor did its eyes lose their expression of utter horror.

"What is it?" Seagryn asked, expecting the animal to disappear down its hole at the sound of his voice. It didn't.

Dark was silent for a moment as he remembered a bit of the future in order to answer the present question. "The tugoliths call them lesefs, but they never tell you why."

"It's clearly terrified of us! Why doesn't it run away?"

"It can't. It's stuck." Seagryn took a step or two closer to get a better look, but Dark warned him off again. "Whatever you do don't step on it."

"Why not?"

"Its body fluids evidently cause terrible boils on a tugolith's feet. Look, I know you're rather inappropriately clothed, but our dinner is on the other side of these legions of shaggy balloon creatures and you can't get across in tugolith-form. You don't seem to feel the cold anyway, so would you mind setting me down and changing shape for just a few moments? I think you'll be glad you did."

Seagryn took the boy's word for it and assumed his human-form. They quickly threaded their way through the lesef burrows and he modestly resumed his larger guise.

"You see those high cliffs over there?" Dark said confidently.

"Those are the tugoliths' regular feeding grounds. I have it on good authority that the food is excellent."

"Whose authority?" Seagryn asked.

"My own. Words I speak in just a few hours."

And as usual, the boy prophet proved to be correct. The crevices of the cliffs were filled with round objects, well out of reach of most predators but easily harvested by the tip of a tugolith's horn. Seagryn flipped down a dozen or so while Dark busily cracked them open. They were eggs, laid in the cracks by some species of cold-dwelling bird and then abandoned. They proved to have a delicate, salty flavor, and Seagryn soon went back to flip down more. The cliffs held an abundant supply.

"The tugoliths haven't been able to get to them," Dark explained between mouthfuls. "That's why there's so many to harvest."

"Why not?" Seagryn asked.

"You really don't want me to tell you. You'd rather figure it out for yourself. And you will."

"Humph," the wizard snorted. "If you don't blurt it out first."

"Oh, I won't do that," the boy said seriously.

"You're certain of that, I suppose?"

"Very certain. I'll not be with you."

Seagryn stopped eating and looked at Dark. "What?"

Dark didn't look back. Instead he studied a half-eaten egg, turning and twisting it before his face as if he held a gemstone. "My gift is back. And now I know what will be, and where I'll go. You don't need me here, and I'd probably freeze to death if I tried to stay. I'm not a tugolith, Seagryn, and you—at least in part—*are*." The boy carefully placed the egg between his legs, and now looked up into his enormous friend's eyes. "Whether I could stay and survive the cold or not, the fact is I won't. Destiny again, right? My duty's clear, and I'm off to get it done. Oh, and I will be there for your arrival in Lamath, so don't worry about me." Suddenly the boy's eyes fell away, and he seemed to gaze inward again for a moment before saying, "I'm starting to miss the megasin. It was dark and fearful down there, but I can't recall a more restful holiday in my life . . ."

Seagryn's appetite had disappeared. He was already feeling lonely again, and Dark hadn't even left yet. "Can—can you stay the rest of the afternoon?" he asked.

Dark thought a moment. "Well I would, but—some of your fellows are starving . . ."

The boy pointed his finger back the way they'd come, and Seagryn thought again of the wan, solitary tugolith he'd seen bloodied today. Dark hopped to his feet, made a futile attempt to hug Seagryn's enormous neck, then started away, walking southeast along the line of the egg-filled cliffs. After a few steps he stopped and grinned back over his shoulder. "By the way, if you decide to take your normal shape again in human company, I hope you'll remember you haven't got any pants on. Thanks again for the extra layers!" Then Dark waved, and headed onward.

As the lad disappeared behind the icy wall Seagryn pondered his own mixed feelings. Dark was right. This was no place to be a person. And certainly the tugoliths would have a much easier time accepting him if he could devote his entire attention to them without needing to worry about keeping a boy prophet from freezing. Nevertheless, the ancient feelings of betrayal and abandonment that had abbreviated his childhood and given a melancholy cast to his adult life had returned again to nibble at his confidence. Dark was his friend—perhaps his only friend—and there was something inherently unjust in having a friend he really couldn't be comfortable being with. For that was another feeling that had pushed its way into the front of his consciousness—he felt much freer to act when his choices weren't being watched by someone who already knew their consequences. "And Dark certainly must know I feel that way," he mumbled aloud. Once again he found himself grieving for a boy who knew far too much. Dark's gift certainly didn't seem to benefit Dark that much. "Then again," Seagryn mumbled, "I guess these gifts are given for the sake of others and not for ourselves." The next thought followed naturally, and Seagryn heard himself saying, "So whom, exactly, is my gift supposed to benefit?"

He'd addressed this question to no one, but a mental image of starving tugoliths came immediately to mind. It startled him. After all, he'd come here, not to help these animals, but to lure one to—a different destiny. Then again, when he'd embarked upon this quest he'd had only his own self-interest in mind. After his experience in the megasin's cave . . .

"Obviously I need to rethink some of this," he announced aloud. But whatever he did depended upon his forming some kind of relationship with the massive inhabitants of this region, and he decided he'd better get to it.

It took him only a few moments to scamper through the lesef holes again and resume his bulky altershape. Then he was off in search of companionship, and he found his tugolith senses well-equipped for that task. Here among the snowdrifts, where there were relatively few scents upon the wind, he could smell things that had to be great distances away. His hearing, too, was far sharper than that of his human ears. It wasn't long before he heard the tramp of heavy feet and scented the pungent aroma of his adopted species. He turned his own gait in that direction and began making very large tracks.

Did the group smell him coming? They stopped, evidently, for, after a while, he no longer heard their movement, and the odor became richer. At last he topped a small ice ridge, and there they were, waiting for him. They'd formed themselves in the same kind of circle he and Dark had seen earlier—and all ten horns pointed directly at him.

He hesitated upon first sight of them, but only for a moment. When he started forward, one of the group broke free from the circle and advanced toward him. The rest of the beasts closed ranks as this leader called out, "Where is your wheel?"

Seagryn had expected him to say, "Go away." He had prepared a speech to make in response. But this question surprised him. "What?" he answered. Ten pairs of tugolith eyebrows raised in response, then immediately knitted in contempt. He suddenly felt very foolish.

"You have no wheel?" the lead tugolith asked suspiciously.

"I—don't even know what a wheel is. I mean, I do know, of course. I just don't know what *you* mean by it."

The tugoliths stared at him.

"What I'm saying is, you obviously aren't talking about a wagon wheel, or anything like that."

Still they stared.

"Perhaps—by a 'wheel,' you mean what group do I belong to? As you yourselves are formed into a group? Do you make up a wheel?"

The lead tugolith had an unmistakable frown upon his face, and it occurred to Seagryn he'd seen just such an expression on the weathered visage of old Talarath many times before. "You talk too much," the animal said politely.

"I—I'm sorry. I just don't know how best to—communicate . . ." His words faded out, for the tugoliths were no longer listening to him. The entire circle—wheel?—was mumbling to one another.

Suddenly one young female spoke up. "He's the Wiser." Her words caused an enormous stir.

"He's no Wiser."

"He's a punt."

"He can't talk."

"He talks too *much*."

"He has no wheel!" This last had come from the lead tugolith, and it seemed to put a period on the discussion. When the leader looked back at him, Seagryn was in the midst of marveling at how he could know the relative age and gender of each member of the wheel. There were no obvious physical differences, yet he simply *knew*, and that amazed him. "You have no wheel," the leader observed again.

"You could let me join yours," Seagryn suggested. He was quite unprepared for the response. The leader reeled backward onto his hindquarters, much as the loser in today's battle had when beaten backward by a mighty bash of a horn. The members of the circle began to dance in agitation, particularly the females. The young males snarled with barely fettered rage, and two even turned to rush together and clack horns in the center of the wheel before returning to their places in the circle to dance in frustration. The whole group seemed to churn with shock and embarrassment—all, that is, except that young female who'd said something about a Wiser. The snarls and growls startled Seagryn, and the clashing horns made him tremble a bit inwardly. But to be honest, the gaze in this young female's eyes worried him more. It appeared—almost human.

The head tugolith finally got back to his four feet, and sputtered out, "You have no pair!"

"No what?" Seagryn asked. He'd already created a furor. He supposed it didn't matter now if he caused even greater confusion. He needed to know these creatures, and he couldn't think of a better way to go about it than this.

"Pair!" the old male roared, his huge eyes bulging.

"He smells of food," the young female said loudly, and suddenly the stamping and muttering was replaced by a chorus of sniffing. Then the wheel stood silent again, all horns once again pointing toward him.

"He does," the lead tugolith agreed with evident consternation. It appeared he wanted time to mull this over.

"How did you get food?" Predictably, this was the young female again. Seagryn directed his response to her.

"I walked to it."

"There are lesef holes."

"I walked through the lesef holes and got it. That's what I've come to tell you. I can lead you to the food."

He'd tried to make his sentences clear and declarative this time, and the female seemed to understand. But Seagryn had evidently breached tugolith etiquette again by talking to her. A young male standing beside her growled, "Berillitha! Don't talk!" He punctuated his command with a forceful prick of his horn to her flank, causing Berillitha to yelp and Seagryn to frown.

"Are you her mate?" he asked the male sharply, prepared to debate the female's right to an opinion. He realized a moment later he shouldn't have bothered.

"She is my sister!" the youthful male screamed in fury. Then he charged. There was no mistaking his intent. He wanted to split Seagryn's skull.

While he'd never been attacked by a tugolith, Seagryn had battled scores of playground bullies. Dodging to one side, he watched the tugolith race on past him, a slave to its own tremendous momentum. Seagryn glanced around to insure no other beast was charging, then turned to face his angry assailant.

Berillitha's brother made a long turn, slipping slightly in the snow, then started back again, looking more vengeful than before. Seagryn waited until the last moment, then leaped aside again. The male rumbled into the midst of the wheel this time, scattering the others before managing to get himself righted once more. He didn't hesitate to charge again.

How could he handle this situation to cause the least damage, Seagryn wondered. He didn't want to hurt the beast—he wanted to join these creatures, after all. Should he fight as a tugolith? Change shapes and fight as a man? He could use his magic that way, of course. Then again, he'd also lose his chance to identi—

Crack! He'd thought too long and acted too little, and this creature he fought could learn. This time as Seagryn jumped to the side, the tugolith changed course to meet him. For the first time his horn felt the impact of a tugolith blow struck in anger, and Seagryn not only went back onto his hindquarters, he continued on over them, somersaulting backward in the snow. He scrambled immediately to his feet, but not quickly enough. The tugolith jabbed his tusk savagely into Seagryn's exposed flank, and the wizard now understood for himself why young Berillitha had yelped. The horn piercing his side felt like a dagger thrust between the ribs. Fortunately he'd been rolling away from the attack, and the wound did not go deep.

Seagryn bounded forward, then lost his footing on the ice and slid down onto his belly. He spun around on it so that he faced backward. Once again he proved lucky; though his body was out of control, his horn was still between himself and the next charge, and he was able to angle his head to parry the brother's attack. This one hurt less than those previous, but it propelled him backward across the ice, and Seagryn decided he'd had enough. He turned human just long enough to explode a fireball in the young tugolith's face and dive sideways into a snowdrift. When he shot back out of it a moment later, again in his tugolith-form, the entire wheel encircled him, their armored jaws gaping down to the ice in astonishment.

"I told you," Berillitha said triumphantly. "He's the Wiser."

The lead tugolith took a hesitant step forward and asked Seagryn quietly, "Are you the Wiser?"

Of course he had no idea what that meant. But it sounded a lot like wizard, and Seagryn could willingly admit he was that. If being the Wiser could save him from any further punctures from that young monster's horn, Seagryn determined he could certainly learn to play the rôle. "I am," he said clearly. He hoped he sounded convincing.

He evidently did. The lead tugolith looked around at the other members of the wheel, then said with great solemnity, "This is the Wiser." They all nodded—and stared.

"Now then," Seagryn thought to himself. "Just what does a Wiser *do*?"

Chapter Twenty-three

❈❈❈❈

BOUNCING LESEFS

"**Y**OU are the Wiser," the leader of the wheel intoned expectantly. Then he stepped back into his place in the circle, and waited.

Seagryn turned slowly about, examining each member of the wheel in turn. He hoped this looked wise. He also hoped he might see in one of these faces how he was expected to behave. When he got to young Berillitha, he stopped. An idea had come.

"You were the one who recognized me," he said boldly, and he paused to give her a chance to respond.

"Yes," she said at last. Just that. Nothing more.

"I see."

While he puzzled over what to do next, she responded to that comment too. "We can all see."

Seagryn looked at her. "Yes." He hoped she might elaborate, but apparently she'd spoken her whole mind on the matter and that was that. Now what?

It dawned on Seagryn that perhaps none of these tugoliths had ever seen a Wiser before. Was it possible that none of them knew how he was to act either? He had, after all, committed some grievous social blunders, yet now they seemed to be hanging upon his every word. He decided it was worth a try. "Do you have names?" he asked in a voice full of authority.

"Yes," several of them answered him, and he waited expectantly. Nothing. Seagryn was discovering these were extremely literal-minded beasts.

"Tell me your names."

They did as he asked, but since they all spoke at once it did him little good. He turned around to face the old leader and said, "Your name again?"

"Yashilitha," the leader said, and Seagryn nodded curtly and turned to the wrinkled female standing beside him. She spoke her name in turn, and Seagryn continued on around the wheel this way until he faced Yashilitha again. He'd made a great show of looking interested in each name as it was said, but the only one he recalled besides those of the leader and Berillitha was that of Gadolitha, the hot-tempered brother who had buried his horn tip in Seagryn's hide. The young male seemed docile at the moment, but did a smirk of disbelief play around his black-ridged lips? Seagryn would remember Gadolitha—and watch him closely.

They followed his instructions without question. A Wiser was evidently a leader of some sort, so Seagryn decided to express his leadership. "You are hungry," he said, and the entire wheel stamped and shuffled in agreement. "We will go to the food." He started toward the edge of the wheel, expecting them to part and let him through. They didn't. Had he guessed wrongly? Were they not going to follow him after all?

Seagryn gazed into the faces of a pair of tugoliths who looked back at him blankly. "Let me pass," he instructed, hiding his concern. They stepped aside. "Seagryn," he mumbled to himself, "these are *very* literal beasts. Follow me!" he called loudly, and he started back through the frozen landscape in the direction from which he'd come. After a moment, he glanced surreptitiously behind to see if anyone had obeyed him and saw that indeed they had. He was being followed by the whole wheel, walking two by two. Seagryn faced forward, feeling justly proud of himself. Not only had he made contact with these enormous beasts, but they were even willing to follow him!

By the time they reached the line of lesef holes late in the afternoon, however, Seagryn's high spirits had been lowered considerably. You wouldn't know it to look at them, he thought to himself, but tugoliths were terrible whiners. Not long after the beginning of their march he began to hear criticism of his leadership issuing from behind. One beast expressed displeasure at his poor choice of pathways through the ice, and another responded—was that Gadolitha's snide voice?—"A Wiser should know better." When it became apparent where they were bound, the complaints grew sharper and came with more frequency.

"We are going to the cliffs."

"We can't get through the holes."

"We will burn our toes."

"The Wiser is not wise." Gadolitha again? Seagryn wanted to look around and check but refused to reveal that he even heard their comments.

"I'm tired."

"Let's rest."

"I don't like to burn my toes."

"We should stick the Wiser."

That had been Gadolitha; Seagryn was certain of it. He whirled around suddenly and glowered back at the startled column. "Now listen! No one is going to stick me! We are going to food! No one's toes will be burned!"

"The lesefs will burn our toes," a wheel member interrupted, and Seagryn was about to shout her down when he realized this was Berillitha who had spoken and he stopped himself.

He pondered his next move a moment, then commanded "Berillitha! Come and walk with me."

He knew immediately he'd done it again. Yashilitha fell choking to his knees, and Gadolitha rolled his eyes twice and stared at Seagryn, aghast. Berillitha's expression could not be seen, for she'd buried her head in a nearby snowdrift. The other female members of the wheel were hooting softly in either laughter or shame. But what could he do now, besides carry through with what he'd begun? He needed Berillitha's advice. If his asking for it humiliated her somehow, it couldn't be helped—that certainly hadn't been his attention. "I am the Wiser," he reminded them all sternly, and the hooting faded away. "Berillitha, come here!"

The wheel stared at him silently. It was Berillitha who eased the tension. She pulled her face out of the drift, walked to the head of the line with great dignity, and waited there, facing forward, for his command. "Follow me," he shouted again and with great relief saw the wheel start walking once more. Berillitha matched her pace to his, saying nothing. "Now," he said in a moment. "How do the lesefs burn your toes."

Berillitha glanced at him as if amazed that he wouldn't already know, but she did answer. "We step in their holes. They fill up. They pop. Their juice burns our toes." She took a deep breath after this, as if she'd just delivered a speech of major proportions.

"Can't you go around their holes?"

"There are many lesefs."

"I understand. But aren't burned toes better than starving?"

"Burned toes stay burned. Bad burns turn black. Whole wheels died." Again Berillitha labored for her breath. This walking and talking at the same time was not an easy task for her.

"The burns are that bad—" Seagryn said to himself, letting his sentence trail off.

"Yes. I am your mate."

Berillitha's statement took Seagryn very much by surprise. He responded with very natural shock. "What?" he blurted out.

"We have paired," Berillitha observed, glancing down at the way they walked together.

"Ah—wait. You don't understand. I—I can't be—paired to you! I—I just wanted some information!"

"Yes," Berillitha responded, but he had the keen impression she still didn't comprehend when she repeated, "We are paired."

"Ah—Berillitha—listen to me. Please! I—I'm not like you. I'm not like the rest of your—wheel. In fact, I'm not even a tugolith!"

"Yes."

"No! I'm different!"

"Yes. You are the Wiser."

"But listen, I . . ." He struggled to find the words to explain.

"I can hear," she said encouragingly.

He glanced up and saw they were very near the lines of lesef holes and within sight of the food-laden cliffs beyond. "We will speak of this later!" he announced nervously, and the young female nodded in agreement. His head reeling from the enormity of his *faux pas*, Seagryn struggled to turn his attention to the task at hand. He approached the lesef warrens, and suddenly thousands of yellow fur balls popped out of the ground to eye him with terror and suspicion. Now he really felt up against it, for Seagryn had absolutely no plan for circumventing the furry yellow barrier. When he turned to look back over his shoulder he saw the wheel had formed up behind him and now silently watched his every move. What was he to do?

He couldn't just stand here looking back at the lesefs. He decided to walk toward them. As if they were one beast, the thousands of little heads dipped perceptibly lower in their dens. He took another step and they ducked deeper, but still watched him carefully. He was close enough now to see—there was indeed no clear path through the perforated ground for a tugolithsized being. He could do nothing in his altershape. Then it occurred to him that if he revealed himself in human-form, perhaps Berillitha would get a much clearer picture of what he'd been trying to tell her and persist no longer in this notion that they were paired! He changed.

He heard the gasp behind him; while he'd briefly taken his human-form during his battle with Gadolitha, most of the wheel had been watching the explosion of light and not him. Now he felt their eyes upon his back, but he hadn't time to look. He was already tiptoeing through the potholes, watching yellow balls on every side ducking out of his way. Once on the far side, he dashed to the cliffs, took his altershape and gouged out a dozen eggs with his horn, then turned back into a man and scooped them up in his arms to carry them back through the lesefs to his astonished followers. He distributed the eggs among the wheel, then again turned himself into a tugolith.

"There," he announced, a bit breathlessly. "Eat."

They all obeyed. With a single bite, each tugolith disposed of the egg before it, then all turned to gaze at Seagryn again. It didn't take him long to catch the unspoken meaning of their stares. "More?" he said. "You want more." They nodded.

Seagryn made another trip. And another. But by the time he weaved his way back through the lesef traps for the fourth time, he was feeling rather put upon and decided another means of doing this had to be found. He had to get the tugoliths through the warrens so they could harvest the cliff eggs for themselves. As he deposited this helping before his bored diners he announced his intention. "I can't do this for you anymore. Now you must follow me through."

"Through?" Yashilitha frowned, and the whole group seemed to frown in confusion with him.

"Through the—the lesef holes," Seagryn tried to explain, but the frowns remained fixed upon faces.

"How?" Gadolitha demanded sharply, and the others all shuffled in agreement with his question. They were like children, these tugoliths! Seagryn's patience felt sorely tired.

"We must find a way together—" he began, but again Gadolitha demanded:

"How!"

"Patience, Gadolitha," Seagryn said without feeling any himself. "It may take us some time to—"

"A Wiser would know."

This was more than he could stand. "I *am* a Wiser, Gadolitha!

I've led you to food and I've fed you! Now it's time for you to use some of your good sense and help me to find a way to—''

"You don't know," Gadolitha snorted and he turned his hind-quarters in Seagryn's face and started away.

"Come back here!" Seagryn demanded.

Gadolitha only paused long enough to toss an insult. "You are not a Wiser," he said contemptuously. "You are a people!"

"Come back!" Seagryn demanded, truly frustrated by this huge beast's stubbornness. He turned to run back to the line of lesef's and shouted from there, "Come back! I'll help you get through!" But Gadolitha's action and Seagryn's lack of a plan had seriously undermined any influence the wizard had possessed. Several others were turning away to watch Gadolitha, and even Berillitha now wore a doubtful expression. "You mean you're all going to give up that easily?" he shouted. The wheel responded by turning away.

It had been a difficult day. He'd been abandoned, attacked, punctured, exalted, criticized, and apparently wed. He could not stand being ignored, too. He took his pique out on the nearest thing handy—which happened to be a terrified lesef that stared up at him from his feet. He grabbed up the furry animal in both hands, snarled with contempt as it ballooned to three times its normal size, then suddenly drop-kicked it high into the air over Gadolitha's head. It took off with a squeal, and Seagryn was immediately astonished at his own insensitivity. But when he saw it hit the ice on the far side of the departing wheel and bounce up almost as high into the sky beyond them, he realized he really couldn't have hurt the little animal very much. Apparently they were made to absorb such shocks. Besides, he'd discovered booting it had felt quite satisfying—so much so he wanted to do it again. He grabbed up another lesef and kicked this one in the same direction, and when it bounced over the heads of the retreating tugoliths they stopped and looked back at him in panic. These were, after all, the little beasts that had caused their toes such pain in the past. Was the Wiser punishing them now for their disloyalty by raining the fiery creatures on their heads?

Seagryn was puzzled by why the little animals didn't explode when they hit the ice, but he decided that was easily explainable. Crushed within the walls of their burrows by heavy tugolith feet, they had to burst—there was no other place for the air inside their inflated skins to go. But out here there was no need—they could bounce on along for some distance; yet once at rest, they could quickly find their tiny feet and scamper back into their holes—

"A path—I can clear you all a path!" Seagryn shouted to the tugoliths who now stared back at him. "Come! Come on! Berillitha! Come here!" As he called to them he was grabbing up swelled lesefs and punting them in every direction. He soon stopped kicking them, finding it much easier just to grab two or three at a time by their shaggy hair and toss them to one side or the other. After a very little time he'd managed to clear a strip through the yellow fur balls at least a tugolith wide, and took his altershape to demonstrate to Berillitha where to step. "Come on!" he instructed. "Come before they all scramble back!"

Berillitha obeyed. And once beyond the torn-up earth, she galloped quickly to the cliffs and began scooping down eggs and devouring them as quickly as her great horn would permit. It was her example that led the others to make the passage, and soon the entire wheel—Gadolitha included—was feasting contentedly as a result of Seagryn's diligent game of kickball. As for the lesefs, they seemed none the worse for their brief evictions from their dwellings. They were all safely back in place before Seagryn caught his breath.

Chapter Twenty-four

❊❊❊❊❊

THE GREAT WHEEL

"**W**E must go," Yashilitha said the next morning.

"Go?" Seagryn frowned as he blinked his eyes to wake up. "Where are you going?"

"We must go."

"You said that," Seagryn nodded.

"*We,*" Yashilitha affirmed, stamping the frozen ground for emphasis.

"Oh, you mean I'm to go too?" Seagryn said, now understanding. He wasn't certain the news pleased him. "Ah— where?"

Yashilitha appeared confused by the question. "Where?"

"Yes—to what place?"

"The Great Wheel."

Seagryn nodded thoughtfully. "Is it far from here?"

"Very far."

"I see," Seagryn muttered.

"We all can see," Yashilitha said with a puzzled frown. He apparently failed to understand the Wiser's purpose in constantly bringing up the subject of vision.

"Why must we go, if it's far?" Seagryn asked.

"You are the Wiser," Yashilitha said flatly.

"Yes?" But the wheel leader would say more. "I se— I understand. I think . . ." Seagryn added to himself.

"Of course you think. You are the Wiser." Yashilitha turned toward the cliffs, reared his head back, and began to pry his

208

breakfast from the cracks above. As Seagryn watched, he noticed the snowflakes that had started flipping gracefully down from the sky to recarpet the ground with white shag. He also noticed that Berillitha stood only a few steps behind him, watching him without expression. He wished he could pretend he hadn't seen her, but that wasn't possible.

"Good morning." He nodded.

Berillitha wasted no time. "I am your pair," she said quietly.

Seagryn glanced back at Yashilitha to see if he was listening. He appeared to be far more interested in his meal, and Seagryn looked back around at Berillitha. "You—saw yesterday that—I am not like you."

"You are the Wiser." She shrugged.

Apparently that was a convenient explanation for anything odd he might do, but now he found it annoying. "Yes, but I didn't *know* I was until you said so," he grumbled.

Berillitha frowned. "The Wiser did not know?"

"The Wiser knows very little of anything at the moment." He missed Dark's flawless foresight. Why couldn't the lad have shared a few more hints about Seagryn's time with these beasts before disappearing to the south? Seagryn had already done the one task Dark had projected for him—he'd saved these creatures from starving. But there'd been nothing about a lengthy trek to any Great Wheel, and *certainly* nothing about bashing horns with an overprotective sibling and then being paired to the sister!

"Are you hungry?" Berillitha asked, and he glanced up to see great compassion reflected in her expression. She raised her eyes to the cliff face in a silent invitation to partake. When he shook his head she nodded, and waited peacefully for him to decide what to do. She was a kind beast, he thought to himself. She'd certainly make some other tugolith a very fine wife someday—

"We must go," Yashilitha said again, swallowing the last of a great mouthful of eggs. The whole wheel turned to face Seagryn expectantly.

He looked back at them. "Am—I supposed to say something now?"

All but Berillitha looked back at him blankly. It was she who explained. "We will burn our toes."

"Ah." He nodded. They had to cross the lesef strip once again. He sighed wearily, took his human shape, and bent to the task.

As they traveled northwest across the new layer of powder in a column of pairs, Seagryn mulled over his situation. He didn't need to be doing this—not really. What he should be doing was heading south, taking one of these tugoliths back to Lamath to trade for his restoration and his bride. One of the loners would do best—that one he'd seen driven away yesterday by another wheel might appreciate being wanted by somebody for something. Perhaps they would meet him or another lone tugolith on their trek. Perhaps they would meet such at the Great Wheel. What was the Great Wheel? He turned to Berillitha, who walked faithfully beside him, and asked her.

She didn't stare at him for asking such a ridiculous question, for which he felt most grateful. She simply answered, "It is the center."

"Um. Of what."

"Of all the wheels."

"Um. Are there many wheels?" he asked, but this question proved too difficult for her to comprehend. He decided that tugoliths had little occasion to count. "What do wheels do at the Great Wheel?"

"Think and pair," she said without hesitation.

"Oh." That again. Were they going to the Great Wheel to—formalize their relationship? Seagryn shivered at the thought. "Perhaps—perhaps you'll meet a nice male there you can mate with," he suggested hopefully.

"I am paired to you," she said quietly, her eyes on the ground before them.

"Ah—but perhaps—there would be *another* there, someone—more to Gadolitha's liking?"

"Gadolitha is gone."

"What?" Seagryn said, startled, and he looked around at the rest of the column behind them. "What do you mean?"

"Gadolitha is a punt."

"Oh, you needn't call him names on my account—"

Berillitha frowned and labored bravely through his confusing comment. "His name is Gadolitha. He is a punt."

"Since when?"

"Since—?" She struggled with the concept.

"When did he become a—punt?"

She studied him carefully, as if uncertain exactly what he was asking. "You chose me to pair . . ."

Had she answered his question? "What *is* a punt, exactly?"

"Exactly—?"

"What's a punt," he corrected, simplifying his question.

Berillitha tilted her head to one side and blinked, then took a deep breath as if preparing for another major recitation. "A punt has no pair. With no pair a punt has no wheel. A punt is a lone tugolith."

The tragic truth began penetrating the fog of Seagryn's pervasive humanness to speak to the tugolith sense that seemed to accompany his altershape. "But he had a pair until yesterday."

"He was my brother pair."

"Ah." Seagryn nodded sadly. "Then I came, and . . ."

"Gadolitha is a punt," she finished for him.

He had an idea. "What if I could find him for you and bring him back? Could he be restored then?"

Berillitha narrowed her eyes thoughtfully. "We would leave the wheel?"

"I would leave the wheel, go get him, and bring him back. He was with us just a little while ago, he can't have gotten too far away . . ."

"You would leave me?" the female wondered, bewilderment upon her massive features.

"Yes?"

"Then *I* am a punt," she said quietly. She spoke with great dignity, but also with great sorrow.

Seagryn swallowed with difficulty, afraid to ask— "If I leave that makes you a punt, too?"

"Yes."

Seagryn recalled again the expulsion of a punt he and Dark had witnessed and asked, "What happens to punts? Where do they go?"

"All punts die," Berillitha said. "I will die," she added matter-of-factly.

Now Seagryn realized that he'd been the ruin of not just one tugolith's life, but of two. Nothing in the ethics books of the Lamathian library had prepared him to handle this! What was he going to do? For one thing, he would not let this female become a punt by leaving her! Yet the question remained—how was he to resolve this situation?

He was still wondering that three days later when they reached their destination. They crossed through a narrow pass that separated the two most exalted mountain ranges Seagryn had ever seen in his life and stopped on its crest to look down onto an enormous glacial plain, populated by circle after circle of tugoliths. Seagryn had to pause for a moment and scan the horizon from the foot of one perpendicular peak to the foot of the other.

There seemed to be not a spot in that vast expanse not marked off by a wheel of great animals, except for a raised area right in the center. That place was reserved for the Great Wheel itself—the first structure Seagryn had seen since he left the Paumer mansion at the foot of the Central Gate. That thought caused him to grunt, and Berillitha, who waited patiently for him to follow Yashilitha down onto the ice plain, looked over at him. "I was just thinking about a little pass in the south we humans have considered very important," he explained to her, adding, "A tiny place, compared to this."

Indeed, the Great Wheel had been constructed upon an awe-inspiring scale—understandably, since it had been built by giants for giants. Huge stones twice as tall as the length of the largest tugolith pointed up from their places in the ice, and each was paired to another by a traverse stone across its top. These pairs of stones formed a ring as wide in diameter as the crater lake of Paumer's volcanic mountaintop. In the center of it was a high platform. Built of rings of stones, it ascended in concentric circles to a dais large enough for one tugolith to stand upon. At the moment it was empty.

"What's the platform for?" he asked Berillitha quietly, his voice hushed by his sense of awe.

"The Wiser stands in the center." Then she looked at him proudly, and—smiled?

"The Wiser," he mumbled.

Yashilitha was already down in the bowl; he turned around and looked up. "Come down, Wiser. You must speak." Seagryn was given no chance to refuse. The rest of the wheel crowded up behind him, eventually shoving him down the incline and onto the ice plain. Yashilitha turned around and led him regally to the Great Wheel itself and under one of the soaring arches. Moments later he found himself at the foot of the dais, being introduced by the leader of the wheel who had found him.

"This is the Wiser. He came to save my wheel. We have eaten. He came to save all wheels. He will speak." Then Yashilitha climbed carefully down off the platform, and urged Seagryn to go on up. The time had come.

As he climbed the very broad steps Seagryn's memory jumped back through the years to the first time he'd addressed the congregation in the High Hall of Lamath. He'd been terrified that day, too. He'd been tongue-tied. He'd wondered then why anyone would have any interest in what he might have to say, and especially the assembled host of the land of faith. But he'd been well trained and so he'd turned his thoughts to the One they did not name—and words, important words, had come.

When he turned atop the dais to look into the faces of this very unlikely throng, the differences with that former time seemed less important than the similarities. Without conscious thought, Seagryn turned his mind again to the Power who'd freed him from the megasin's cave. The words came:

"You call me the Wiser! Perhaps I am. But if I am wise, it's because I know this! There is One who is still Wiser! There is One who made us all. It is that One who has sent me to you. Hear the Power's words!"

He paused then, and looked around. The sea of monstrous animals gazed up at him in rapt attention. He saw their gaunt faces, then viewed again with awe the massive wheel of stone they or their ancestors had built between these mountains. And—as had happened to him so many times before—the Power's message came through him. He was always a bit surprised by this. His listeners appeared not to be at all.

"You are hungry! Your food is kept from you. Lesefs burn your toes! You cannot cross over their holes. Yet you have made the Great Wheel out of stones!" He looked into the faces of those nearest him, to see if they were understanding him. Some tugoliths frowned, but others—Berillitha, for one—nodded and stamped the ground in agreement. He spoke again:

"We will go to the cliffs of food. We will build a great bridge across the holes of the fur balls. This we can do! And you will not starve!"

Then, as abruptly as the words had come to him, the authority to speak any further disappeared. That was it. The message had been given. And with a slight feeling of embarrassment, Seagryn came down the stairs.

Berillitha waited for him at the bottom. There was no mistaking it now: As nearly as the heavy features of her tugolith face would permit, she was beaming.

He led the long trek back through a snowstorm that intimidated his human mind but caused his tugolith blood to pound with excitement. He danced, and the column of pairs that stretched out endlessly behind him danced to the rhythm he set. Berillitha danced at his side, her eyes sparkling with girlish pleasure. And somehow, when they finally reached the line of lesef holes again three days later, Seagryn felt himself gripped by a strange and powerful grief that the journey had to end at all.

Berillitha caught his shifting mood. She gave him the solace of her somber silence as the wheels formed up again along the line of watching yellow fur. "Well," he said at last and went to work.

He led the great migration through the lesefs the old-fashioned way, and let them eat their fill while he reflected on his future. He couldn't remain a tugolith; he knew that. He had responsibilities in the land of humans, and he needed soon to return to them. But he realized now that he could not trick one of these fine creatures into going with him. He would need to find one who was willing to volunteer. Even at that, Seagryn's conscience wanted to bother him. Was it the Power's doing? Where was the Power in all of this?

When they turned to the task of building the bridge, he felt he *knew*. It mattered little, he decided, what purpose his abilities had served or would serve for the race of men. If he had been gifted for no other reason than to rescue this starving species, that was certainly enough. He used his magic to help cut away portions of the cliff, heating cracks and then letting them cool and freeze until large slabs broke free and tumbled to the ground. The tugoliths used their strength to drag them into place. While there were some toes burned in the process, and thousands of lesefs were permanently evicted from their warrens, there was at last a wide causeway of stone over which the tugoliths could walk, and through which the lesefs couldn't tunnel. It was done.

Many wheels celebrated by trading pairs, which Seagryn learned was the conventional way of arranging for mating. Two wheels would circle together, one inside and one outside, until brother-sister pairs of each wheel faced one another. Then the males would ceremonially bash horns with one another, and trade places. A wheel kept its own females and gave away its males, but always, always in pairs. Then the new pairs would wander off together to find a snowdrift, and what ensued there Seagryn didn't want to know, for it inevitably brought to mind the question of what he was going to do about Berillitha. He had searched among the circles for Gadolitha, Berillitha never leaving his side, but they'd not found him. They'd not found any punts at all. And now that the bridge was completed and his unfinished future in the south again began to dominate his thoughts, the problem became acute.

"Berillitha," he said on the first day free traffic was permitted over the platform, "what am I going to do with you?"

"You are the Wiser." Berillitha smiled. He sometimes found

her confidence in him overwhelming. And he had to face it—
she had many virtues he wished Elaryl possessed.

Then again, Elaryl was beautiful. As a picture of her face
floated into his imagination, Seagryn decided this was the day.
But which beast would he take with him?

A ceremony was necessary, and so the wheels gathered at the
bridge, standing on both sides of it while Seagryn stepped to its
center to address them all.

"You have done it!" he shouted, and he smiled. The throng
shuffled and stamped in agreement and self-approval. "I congratulate you all! Now my work is done. I must go to be with
people. But I must take one of you with me! I offer to one of
you the chance to live long after your wheel is gone! I offer one
of you the chance to be greatly honored by men! Who would
like to do this? Who will go with the Wiser?" He waited for a
response for what seemed to him a very long time. "Well? Who
will go?" Still no one answered his summons. "Is there not one
of you who will go?"

Yashilitha was frowning. Seagryn looked at him and said,
"You didn't understand all that, did you."

Berillitha's father cleared his throat. "I don't understand."

Seagryn tried again. "I want one tugolith to go back with
me."

"One?"

That was it. They did everything in pairs. Once again, Seagryn wished he could make contact with a punt. There had to
be some around somewhere, but where to find one—

"I am one," said a soft voice behind him; when he'd walked
out onto the platform, Berillitha had tentatively followed.

"Oh—Berillitha. No. No, I couldn't ask you to do that."

"You asked one to go. I am one. I will go."

"No, but not you. I—I just can't take you—"

"I am your pair," Berillitha said firmly. "I go."

"But Berillitha—"

"I will horn you."

Seagryn stared at her. Never had she taken this tone before,
and it shocked him. "What?"

"I will go. Or I will horn you." The young female obviously
meant it.

"I see." Seagryn nodded.

"We all can see," Berillitha reminded him quietly.

Later that day they began their journey southward to the land of men. Berillitha danced, but Seagryn found the road very tiresome indeed.

Chapter Twenty-five

❋❋❋❋

ELARYL'S CHOICE

As she stood before the mirror, Elaryl made a great show of studying the two dresses. She first held the magenta fish-satin under her chin, admiring the way it enhanced the natural blush in her cheeks. On the other hand, the rich dark green of the velvet gown seemed to turn her hair into threads of spun gold— and Seagryn had always loved her hair. Which should she wear? She turned slowly around to face the flippant girl who sprawled across her bed. Holding up first one dress, then the other, she asked, "Any opinions?"

She teased, of course. She'd known Uda only a few days, but she'd discovered immediately that Uda had an opinion on everything and felt compelled to share it, whether or not she was asked.

Nor did the girl disappoint now. "The green, I should think. It's both formal and ethereal, and I like that. You haven't seen this man in months and you mustn't let yourself appear too accessible. After all, just because your father wants you to marry him doesn't necessarily mean you have to want to."

"But I do want to marry him," Elaryl mumbled, changing hands again and examining herself once more in the magenta. "What's wrong with this one?"

"Nothing's *wrong* with it. It's—mysterious. Flirtatious too, I think. I don't know. It's warmer, certainly. If you really want to set his heart pounding that frank invitation is what you want."

"A frank invitation?" How gauche! Elaryl frowned at the

217

girl. "Where *do* you get all these ideas, Uda?" Elaryl said disapprovingly. "You can't be any more than sixteen . . ."

"Thirteen," Uda corrected, and she rolled over onto her stomach. "From my mother," she added.

"Your mother lets you talk that way?"

Uda cackled, and looked up at the much older woman. "Why? Will yours *not*?"

Elaryl raised her eyebrows, then looked back down at the dresses. She really wasn't interested in choosing at the moment, nor did she wish to know anything more about the family life of a spoiled adolescent. Still, Elaryl was too polite just to ignore Uda's remark. "In this land we don't think that way," she murmured, trying not to sound prim, but failing, since that's exactly what she was. She felt fully justified in being so.

Uda responded with a chortle far too cynical for one so young. "You may *say* you don't think that way. But there are far too many little Lamathians running around underfoot for me to believe you."

Elaryl stiffened her back and stared coldly at the girl. "Uda, you speak of matters you can't know a thing about. Perhaps it would be better for us to part company until the reception this after—"

"Don't send me away," Uda pleaded, suddenly sitting up. Her reaction startled Elaryl.

"Why—why is it so important to you to stay?"

"I don't have many women friends," Uda confessed quietly. "I'm sorry. I didn't mean to embarrass you."

"Why, I'm not embarrassed," Elaryl said, flushing. "I'm just—don't you talk with your mother? I thought you said that your mother allowed you to—"

"My mother rarely stays home anymore," Uda mumbled. "I don't know why."

Due, perhaps, to the presence in the household of a difficult teen? Elaryl wondered. She didn't say it, however, choosing instead the easier road. She *always* chose the easier road, she thought bitterly. "Very well then. You may stay." And keep your mouth shut, she wanted to add. She didn't, however. She couldn't.

As she gazed at her pretty face in the unromantic glass she beheld with much displeasure a young woman incapable of speaking her true mind. Because she didn't really know it? That's what her father had told her. But Talarath had always believed anyone who didn't agree with him must be utterly mindless.

It wasn't that. Elaryl knew what she thought. And it was often far more sensible than the ridiculous attitudes of the Lamathian leaders she'd known since she was a child. But how could she speak those opinions, how could she make known her views when all any man in authority expected from her was a childish remark, a silly giggle, and a quick exit so that they could turn again to their important work? She was a Lamathian woman— the model Lamathian woman, she supposed, since she lived her life in full view of the public. She'd frequently overheard Lamathian mothers pointing her out to their daughters as they struggled to inculcate the values of the present into yet another generation of believers. It wasn't that Lamathian girls were not required to think great thoughts. It was in fact that they were required not to.

And yet—she couldn't help it. Elaryl looked about her with eyes honed by a lifetime of watching the machinations of the powerful. She'd seen the good, of course—the generous, thoughtful, forgiving acts that had eased the burdens of thousands and seemed to give mute testimony to the watch-care of the One they never named. But she'd witnessed such enlightened leadership one day reversed the next by bumbling stupidity, pettiness, lazy incompetence, and so much self-congratulatory meanness that she sometimes couldn't even bear to look. Her gamine grin protected her in those moments when she'd sooner vomit in disgust—for she could say nothing. And yet she was required to take her appointed place and smile supportively through the worst political shenanigans.

Like this one. But this time she couldn't hide behind her glistening teeth and free her imagination to take her elsewhere. Today she would play a principal role as the land of Lamath welcomed home a sacrilegious magic user. It wasn't enough that she'd been publicly humiliated at the altar when this man she thought she knew suddenly shaped himself into a revolting monster. Now she had to proclaim it had all been a ruse, a masterful illusion designed to gain some advantage over the Marwandian raiders who attacked the regions bordering the Marwilds. How could she make the people believe a notion so manifestly ridiculous?

And how—how could she make herself kiss him? She'd not yet been able to forget the stench of that beast who only moments before had been a lover, binding her foot to his own! She'd told Seagryn her secrets. Had he told her his? No! And yet—

In the many lonely hours since their wedding day, she'd been forced to review his attempted confession over and over again. Had he somehow been trying to warn her that he was not all that he appeared to be—or rather, that he was much more? She wanted to believe that of him. For despite his abominable act of public betrayal, she loved Seagryn. She'd tried not to—oh, how she'd tried!—but without success. And when her father had returned from another of his frequent mysterious meetings, saying Seagryn would be returning home, she'd been unable to repress her shriek of joy.

But that, of course, was before the arrival of the sleazy Paumer and his undisciplined daughter—and the odd boy Uda kept as a pet, who claimed to be Dark the prophet and never smiled. Strange people, all of them, with disturbing attitudes and horrible manners. Especially the boy. He seemed to take pleasure in exposing each person's opinions of the others, then sitting back and watching as more polite people—herself included—struggled to soothe the wounded feelings. He'd heartlessly carved her own emotions twice already, all the while claiming to have become Seagryn's closet confidant. It was he who had predicted the time of Seagryn's arrival and the direction from which he would come. Despite her own skepticism, she'd had to join everyone else in making preparations for the ceremonial greeting and the reception following. She didn't like the boy—he didn't seem *balanced*—and she certainly didn't like the liberties he took with her own and everyone else's future. Unfortunately, he'd proven to know entirely too much about her past experience with Seagryn and had shown no inclination to hide his knowledge. Elaryl had been forced to admit that either he did know Seagryn very well—and that Seagryn had shamelessly babbled about the most intimate details of their relationship!—or else that he was exactly who he said he was and that the future he'd predicted for her would come true.

"Still can't choose?" Uda whined, boredom reflected in her complaint. "Dark's outside. Why don't I call him in? He can look at the events of this evening and tell you what you decided—"

"I'm quite capable of making up my own mind, thank you," Elaryl replied, striving to make her voice as icy as the weather outside the pink-tinted windows.

"You're not still angry at him for telling you what you wanted to know—"

"I did not want to know that."

"But you asked him to tell you where you and—"

"A party game, Uda!" Elaryl scolded. "Light table chatter! I'm not surprised that he doesn't know the difference but I thought perhaps that you might!"

"Dark doesn't ever play games," Uda said, her expression unbearably smug. "He always tells the truth—even when it hurts him."

"I'd like to hurt him," Elaryl grumbled under her breath, not at all intending for the girl to hear it. Uda did, however, and her response was painfully direct.

"You think that he doesn't know that?"

Elaryl felt the color rushing into her cheeks again. She whirled back to the mirror, threw the green gown onto the floor, and held the rose-toned garment under her chin once more. "It's this, I think. Definitely this. If I'm going to spend the rest of the afternoon with crimson cheeks I'm at least going to look ravishing doing so!"

"Suit yourself." Uda laughed sarcastically. "I think it's a mistake, but—"

"Yet another good reason to choose it," Elaryl snarled. She surprised herself—she didn't normally talk this way. But if the girl persisted in such objectionable behavior, she certainly wasn't going to stand here and say—

"Dark?" Uda called, and Elaryl jerked around to see Uda had hopped off the bed and padded over to the door. "Come in here a moment."

"*Don't* bring him into my room! I'm *dressing*!"

But Dark had already poked his head inside, his boyish face as gloomy as ever. Uda looked back at her. "You're not dressing *yet*. Dark, what's she going to wear to the ceremony?"

Dark looked sadly back at Elaryl, seemingly unaffected by her contemptuous scowl. "I'm sure she'd like to make up her mind for herself—wouldn't you, Lady Elaryl?"

He'd spoken so gently, how could she abuse him in return? "I—why, yes, I would."

Dark grabbed Uda by the wrist and dragged her out the door—a rather brave act, Elaryl thought as she watched him, recalling how the girl abused him without provocation. Uda struggled, but Dark proved stronger. He suddenly appeared to remember something and pushed the girl out the door and shot across the room to the bed. He jerked the coverlet off it, calling, "Seagryn's going to need this a little later." Then he rushed back across the room in time to push Uda back out before him. He slammed the door behind them, and Elaryl heard them arguing as they moved down the hallway toward Uda's apartments.

She looked back into the mirror and gazed into her own eyes. "Now what will Seagryn be needing with my coverlet later on?" she asked herself.

Elaryl appeared upon the ceremonial welcome-stand wearing the magenta gown under her white fur cloak. She'd made a choice—and it was her own.

Chapter Twenty-six

✳✳✳✳

HERO AND HUSBAND

As they shuffled forward along the icy road, Seagryn heard the noises of a celebration not far ahead. He heard clearly the babble of many private conversations, and the slogging of feet through mud that might have indicated preparations for battle, had that noise not been tempered by the laughter apparent in so many voices. He glanced worriedly at Berillitha and saw that she too had heard. But why should she be concerned, Seagryn reminded himself. The young female didn't know enough about people to realize that such sounds were not to be expected on a wintry day near the northern boundary of Lamath. Seagryn turned his head to one side and peered into the distance with one huge eye. But tugolith eyes were made for short-range seeing, so he could really tell nothing. So, as he'd done several times already on their journey south, he took his human shape to verify with his better eyes what his better ears had already told him.

He knew then exactly what it was, and why it was happening. He stopped walking. Berillitha halted too, and looked at him expectantly. He changed back—it was just so much easier for him to address her when they stood shoulder to shoulder.

"That is a reviewing stand," he explained carefully, and when she still frowned, he added, "Important people stand on top of it."

Berillitha didn't yet comprehend. All tugoliths were important. All pairs, at least. Seagryn sighed and looked back down

223

the road. It appeared now that even his tugolith vision could make out the wooden scaffold, a dark silhouette against a dismal gray sky. It was cold here, but not as cold as his altershape would have liked; while there had obviously been snow on the ground, it had already thawed into brown mush. This was not the place he would have picked for his own homecoming celebration, but he realized that had never been his choice in any case. "Dark," he murmured. "Dark's there."

"It is day. The dark comes later," Berillitha said patiently. In their travels together she'd apparently not grown weary of stating what seemed to her obvious and then being corrected by him. Indeed, she seemed almost to enjoy it, as if his every comment was a wonderful new mystery and she was determined not to let a single one slip by unsolved.

"No, I mean Dark the prophet. It is his name." Seagryn looked back at her, and saw her smiling serenely. She was, certainly, one of the sweetest persons he had ever known. "But what am I going to do with you here?" he murmured. He shook his immense head, then turned to shuffle forward again, Berillitha following faithfully.

He had tried his best to send her back. He had searched his mind for simple language to explain how unkindly men might treat her. But while she listened with unbroken attention to his every word, nothing he said to discourage her seemed to penetrate her armor-plated skull.

And so, Seagryn had brought a tugolith home, just as he'd promised. But he had no intention of turning her over to the magical mutations of the poisonous Sheth. What Seagryn would do with Berillitha, only time would tell—or rather, Dark would.

Someone ran toward them. Seagryn saw without surprise it was the prophet himself, running with a kind of blanket held before him. Seagryn took his human-form to meet him. "Why the blanket?" he asked.

"For you," Dark grunted as he sprinted the last few steps to throw the coverlet around Seagryn's shoulders. The lad clung to the wizard for support, breathing hard to catch his breath before explaining, "Your father-in-law, your lovely bride, Paumer, Uda, and a host of the faithful are waiting back there to welcome you," he puffed. "You can't very well greet them naked."

"I dreamed this," Seagryn murmured quietly, and the sense of humiliation and rejection recalled from that night was held over him as if he'd just dreamed it again. "I don't want to see these people! Why did you bring them here?'' he demanded savagely.

"Why do I do anything I do?'' Dark shrugged and nodded past Seagryn to Berillitha, who watched this exchange with open-minded curiosity. "So this is she.''

"She who?'' Seagryn snarled.

"The tugolith you brought back.''

"I didn't bring Berillitha back with me; she followed me here against my wishes!''

"Of course.'' Dark nodded.

"She's not for Paumer and Sheth to play with, regardless of how things might appear! I've changed my mind, Dark. I've changed my spirit. I'm the Wiser to these creatures, and the Power has given me responsibility for them!''

Dark was nodding his head agreeably through all of this. When Seagryn slowed down, the boy waved his hand and smiled slightly. "Ah—you don't have to tell me any of this, you realize . . .''

"I do have to tell you—you and all of them down there waiting! I cannot in good conscience keep the agreement as stated! Berillitha will not be a part of any dragon!''

Still Dark nodded, smiling both at Seagryn and at Berillitha. "Of course. Of course,'' he mumbled.

"You do understand me, don't you Dark?'' Seagryn said, and now a hint of pleading had crept into his emphatic self-defense. "Tell me you understand.''

Dark clenched his jaw, wrestling with his own internal dilemma. "I understand you perfectly, friend Seagryn, far better than you'll ever understand me. I understand that you would like to disappear from this place right now and go to live someone else's life in a different age. I'd like that, too. But I also understand that we're soon going to have to turn around and walk down to that reviewing stand and continue on with what awaits us there. If it's any help at all to know that someone else feels as you do, then know it. But you're a hero, Seagryn—they're waiting on you. And heroes are helpless to be anything else. The public won't allow it.''

Dark stepped past Seagryn then and walked toward Berillitha, who regarded his approach calmly. "You are welcome here,'' he told the tugolith. Then he waved at them both and walked back down the road toward the watching crowd.

When the distant figure of Seagryn and his huge companion began moving toward them again, the assembled host began to cheer. Seagryn wrapped the so-called cloak tightly around his shoulders and marched forward, eager now just to have it over. All his life he'd sought such acclaim. But in the last few months, he'd had enough—first from the Haranians for slaughtering their enemies, then from the tugoliths for leading them to food. Now his own people cheered him, but for what? For his participation in a despicable conspiracy.

Of course, they didn't know that. And as he glanced up the line of shouting faces to either side of him, it occurred to Seagryn that they could know. He could reveal the duplicity of their leaders here and now and proclaim Lamath's need for a new, honest Ruling Council. The closer he came to the reviewing stand, the more his conviction grew, and he had almost convinced himself he would do it when he saw Elaryl.

She was smiling . . . at him. And he knew then what Dark had doubtless known back there on the road during his harangue. He would not expose anyone, nor accuse anyone, nor refuse anyone. This was his real life—here, with her—not the adventures of a dashing wizard, nor the noble acts of a Wiser. He was Seagryn, a cleric of Lamath. And he was about to be restored.

Ranoth and Talarath themselves met him at the bottom of the stairway, and they each took an elbow and led him up onto the grandstand to receive the ovation of the well-bundled host. Where they had managed to find such a throng, Seagryn couldn't imagine, until he remembered that he'd chosen to come this direction because there was a logging community located not far away, as well as a rather hardy brotherhood of monastics.

But apart from that first glance, Seagryn didn't look much at the crowd. Elaryl drew his gaze back to her and held it, her bright eyes sparkling with an implicit invitation. He saw no hint of that imperious priestess of the unnamed One who had scorned him in his dream and sent him cowering to the earth. This was Elaryl—of stolen conversations in the library stacks and pecks upon the cheek in the alcoves.

Ranoth made a speech explaining that a great injustice had been done and requesting all Lamath to give attention to the events of this day. Another of the Ruling Council, a teacher Seagryn had known and loved for years, gave a stirring account of Seagryn's academic brilliance and honest spirituality. Then Elaryl stepped up to him, her eyes still locked into his. "I told you I could forgive you anything," she whispered. "It took a while, but—I do.'' Then she turned to face the crowd and, much to Seagryn's surprise, began a speech of her own.

''This man—my hero and my husband!—has been falsely accused! I, myself, even doubted! But he has been engaged in a great act of self-sacrifice with far-reaching consequences, not only for Lamath but for all the fragments of the old One Land. The dreadful acts he appeared to commit were but illusions to entrap those who attack us! As his wife, I plead for his forgiveness before the One we do not name.'' Her words were greeted with the most heartfelt cheers of the day, for Elaryl was truly beautiful and commanded the full attention of male and female alike. When she threw her arms around Seagryn's neck and kissed him passionately there under the open sky, who could deny that she'd spoken the truth, or refuse to receive her message?

Who—except Seagryn! For it was a lie. He kissed her back, certainly, and when they broke away he managed to smile weakly down into the throng, who interpreted that faint grin as they chose and laughed lustily. There was that in it, Seagryn thought. But there was more. Somehow he saw his scruples being trampled under by a stampeding herd of compromises and he felt himself powerless to turn them away. His eyes drifted down to the ground just below the grandstand and met the gaze of a very confused tugolith. Berillitha looked more than just puzzled, however. The young female looked angry.

''Oh, dear,'' he mumbled.

''What?'' Elaryl asked out of the side of her mouth, while managing to maintain undimmed her radiant smile.

''You'll see later on,'' he answered, and she merely nodded, for Talarath had stepped to the front of the platform and the crowd was quieting to listen.

''This man,'' he began hesitantly, ''was in the midst of binding feet with my daughter when he was—called away.'' Talarath cleared his throat before going on. ''That sacrament has not been dissolved—that binding has not been revoked. By the Name we do not speak, I declare them bonded—and I also declare this ceremony at an end!''

The wind had picked up, bringing with it an increased chill, and no one would argue that the event should be extended any longer. Seagryn and Elaryl were hustled to the bottom of the steps. There they were met by a group of monks bearing a litter, completely enclosed in turquoise fish-satin. Elaryl jumped in quickly, but Seagryn paused. Berillitha had been given a wide berth as she'd made her way to the litter, and she now stood beside it, watching Seagryn somberly. He had no words to say.

Elaryl popped her head back out of the curtains and frowned, first at the beast, then back at Seagryn. "What does it want?" she asked.

"To be with me." He spoke quietly, staring into one of the tugolith's troubled eyes.

"Well I'm sorry," Elaryl huffed, and she ducked back inside the litter.

"I'm very much afraid you will be," he muttered under his breath, crawling in after her.

As the litter bearers hoisted them up and marched off through the mushy snow, Berillitha called out. "What is this?"

"Just a little trip, Berillitha. I am safe," he shouted back. Elaryl frowned at him. "It's—she's very protective of me," he explained.

"*She* is?" his wife asked, arching an eyebrow.

"Yes—it's a she," he replied firmly. "I assumed Dark had already told you that." He recognized Elaryl's mood. She was deciding whether or not to be displeased.

"This boy who claims to be Dark—he also says he's now your best friend. Is that true?"

Seagryn reflected quickly over the crowded weeks since last he'd seen Elaryl. He longed to pull her directly into his mind and show her all his experiences without having to recount them one by one. He was different, he knew—and she would wonder why. He wanted to make her understand what all of it had meant to him. But this was no time to begin that tale, so he simply shrugged and said, "Yes."

"He is. Well, I'm sorry to say I've found him difficult to appreciate. His—gift—can be most annoying."

"Indeed it can, my lady. Most annoying."

She smiled at that, appearing a bit relieved. "Although, I must say I prefer him as a friend to that beast out there!"

Seagryn smiled stiffly. "Please speak a little more quietly, my darling. Tugoliths have marvelous ears."

Elaryl's eyebrows pinched together in aggravation. "Afraid of hurting her feelings?" she asked, if anything raising her volume.

"Just . . . cautious," Seagryn answered softly, and he changed the subject. "You've told me what you think of Dark. What about Paumer and his daughter?"

"Oh!" Elaryl groaned. "I've never met a ruder child in my life! She and Dark deserve each other!"

"I rather think he deserves something better," Seagryn mumbled, but Elaryl didn't hear him.

"I don't really know much about her father. He spends most of his time in secretive discussion with the Ruling Council, which seems—odd."

"It does, doesn't it?"

"Still, he's a very charming man . . ."

"Charming, yes." Seagryn nodded. The pace of the litter had slowed, and he wondered why. Then they were moving up a hill, and he and his lady were tilted backward against the seat.

Elaryl turned her head to look at him and grinned playfully. "Now this is nice—don't you think?"

They were able to squeeze in several kisses before they arrived at their destination—several very long kisses. Suddenly they were turned upright again, and the four legs of the litter crunched down into hard snow. Seagryn threw aside the curtain and looked out.

The hillside was beautiful, its slopes decorated with perfectly conical fir trees, their branches all glazed with identical helpings of snow. But the structure that crowned its crest did everything possible to spoil the picture. The misshapen building was flat, blocky, and awkwardly gangling at the same time. Most of it was a squat box of cut rock, but right in the center a spindly tower, constructed in an entirely different architectural style, pointed nakedly at the sky. Perhaps its flaws would not have been so noticeable had the building's stones not been painted turquoise and yellow. A more garish place Seagryn had never seen, and he looked at Elaryl in shock.

She let a hint of a smile turn up one side of her mouth as she nodded toward the litter-bearers. "These are the men of Stator Monastery," she announced to prevent him from sharing his opinion out loud. "And this is the monastery itself—designed, I understand, by its founder."

Seagryn looked back at the building and blinked.

"What is this?" Berillitha asked, and Seagryn looked around to see she had followed them up.

"It's—a dwelling. A place where we live."

Berillitha looked up at this huge blemish and said, "It is ugly."

Seagryn looked back at Elaryl and caught her helpless shrug. "I doubt if anyone could put it more plainly," she said, and she held out her hand for Seagryn to help her from the litter.

Other litters crawled up the hill, bearing Paumer and Ranoth, Talarath and Elaryl's mother, Uda and Dark, and the other dignitaries who had gathered at this place to welcome Seagryn. He would have waited for them, but Elaryl took his hand and led him toward the door. He turned around to call to Berillitha, "I am fine. I will be inside here. Enjoy the snow!" The creature gave him a dubious look but didn't move from where she stood. Elaryl led him inside and down a high-ceilinged hallway to the apartment they would share.

"Ah!" she said as she stepped inside. "Just as I ordered!"

"What did you order?" Seagryn replied as he walked to the lead-lined window and glanced out to insure Berillitha had remained outside. She had.

"A bath!" Elaryl cried, loudly enough to get him to turn around and look at her. She stood beside a large ceramic trough filled with steaming water. Already she had shrugged off her fur, and now she turned her back provocatively and said, "Untie these bows, won't you?"

The magenta gown made her cheeks glow like roses. Seagryn crossed the carpeted room in two strides. When the bowstrings hung loose, Elaryl turned her head back and looked inquiringly into his eyes. "Join me? You already seem dressed for it—" She glanced down his body and he realized then that in his haste he'd let the coverlet Dark had brought him gape open. She glanced immediately back up, and her confident smile relaxed him. "It's all right, Seagryn. Remember? We're joined at the feet . . ."

They slipped down into the water together, and Seagryn wrapped himself in its warmth and her arms. They kissed and the tugolith outside was the last thing on his mind—until the window behind them shattered, and Berillitha thrust her huge head inside it. Elaryl flew out of the water and raced to the doorway, pausing only long enough to grab up the discarded coverlet. Then she was gone, disappearing down the hallway.

Seagryn stared at Berillitha in shock, and the tugolith returned his gaze. Then she smiled. "What are you doing?" she asked.

Chapter Twenty-seven

✸✸✸✸

MAKING NEW PAIRS

When at last he joined the others for dinner, Uda assured him that Elaryl was fine. "I told her all about tugoliths," the girl explained officiously. "I have one of my own, of course—well you've seen him. And I told her what was going to happen to this one and that she didn't need to worry. She said to tell you she's not angry and she'll be down soon—*if* you promise that the beast won't barge in on our supper."

There was no longer any chance to sit down unobtrusively, but Seagryn still took a place at the far end of the table and responded as quietly as he could and still be heard. "The tugolith is safely within the monastery enclosure. I don't think there will be any further problems. She'd just never seen a human dwelling before, and was curious."

Uda nodded as if he'd addressed this directly to her, and said, "Elaryl wasn't all that surprised. How could she be? Dark had already told her it would happen."

Seagryn took note of this, but didn't comment directly. He tasted cooked, human food for the first time in weeks, and found it delicious. He savored it momentarily before looking across the table at Dark. "Then your gift is fully restored?"

Dark nodded, but didn't speak, instead shoving food into his mouth as if this were his last meal. It occurred to Seagryn that the boy would know . . .

"No more blind periods?" he asked.

"No," Dark grunted. "Not for a long time, in any case."

Seagryn took another bite, and glanced down the table to nod at Paumer, Ranoth, and Talarath. Was his father-in-law scowling? It was so hard to tell with the old man. He *always* seemed to look that way.

Talarath finished chewing a bite and swallowed, then peered earnestly at Seagryn and said, "You'll be leaving tomorrow then?"

Seagryn's eyes widened. "I will?" he said. He looked at Dark. "I will?"

"We will," the boy grumbled, took another piece of bread, and halved it before stuffing both pieces into his mouth.

"Is that the best plan?" Seagryn wondered aloud, feeling as helpless as he always did in the face of Dark's certainty. "I've just arrived here in Lamath from a very long journey. I think a day or two of rest—"

"We can't allow that animal out there to destroy this monastery!" Talarath thundered. His fierce frown turned his bushy eyebrows into a continuous line across the bottom of his forehead.

"What Talarath is saying," Paumer stepped in quickly, "is that there is a grave need for haste in all these matters. You and Dark were—delayed—I understand, underground. That was time the Arlian king spent profitably in resting and refitting his army for another attack upon the east. Now that Haranamous is without the services of either Nebalath or—" he smiled "—may I say it? Or Seagryn Bearsbane, the people of that fair land are just as vulnerable to attack as they were last summer. Perhaps more so, since now the Pyralu Army want vengeance as well as spoil. No, Seagryn, I'd say there's little time to rest. Unfortunate, but true. We need to get this tugolith down to Sheth as quickly as possible, so the two of you can get on about making the dragon."

"We? Are you going too?"

"I am." Paumer nodded. "Not that I can do anything to help in its construction, of course, but we all know Sheth, and it *does* seem to be in the best interests of the Grand Council to be well represented on site, as it were."

Seagryn was staring now at Dark, searching the lad's face for some acknowledgment of what they'd talked about today upon the road and for some guidance as to how to handle Paumer's pressure. Dark wouldn't look up. He just kept filling his mouth full. To keep from having to talk? Seagryn wondered.

"There she is," Uda announced, and she nodded toward the

door. Seagryn looked around, saw Elaryl, and jumped up to go to her.

"I'm all right," she said frostily, holding up her hands to keep him from touching her. "I—should have believed what I'd been told," she added, glaring at Dark. The prophet paid her no attention, so she strolled over to take her seat at the table. Seagryn joined her, watching her face earnestly. She glanced up, caught him watching her, and snapped, "I said I'm fine!"

He nodded and returned to his food. He was hungry, still, but it seemed he could no longer taste. He ate with good appetite but little passion.

"Of course," Talarath murmured, clearing his throat before continuing, "your wife will return with us to southern Lamath until you've completed the job."

"What?" Seagryn said, sitting up and staring at his father-in-law.

"It—would be better for both of you," the old man added.

Seagryn saw that now Dark did choose to look at him, but gave him no signal other than a supportive smile. "My dear sir," Seagryn stated with great formality, "what my wife does shall be my concern—and hers. We've just this day been re-united. I do not intend to part with her again tomorrow morning!"

Talarath didn't look at him as he growled, "If the decision rests partly with her, perhaps you should ask my daughter what she intends to do."

Seagryn felt very certain in his dealings with old Talarath and the rest of the Ruling Council. He knew the way their minds worked, and had learned how to counter them. He felt far less secure when it came to predicting Elaryl's wishes. Her father had evidently been working on her already, and the episode with Berillitha this afternoon would not encourage her to want to travel off to the Marwilds with the creature. But he had said she would share in the decision. He had to let her. He looked into her eyes and raised his eyebrows. "What will you do?" he asked.

"I'm really not sure yet. Can we talk about this later? I'm hungry."

So they left weightier matters aside and finished eating. By the time the after-meal sweets had disappeared from the table, Elaryl and Seagryn were laughing and flirting as of old. A trio of the brothers had been scheduled to provide after-dinner entertainment, but their singing was as bad as the decorating tastes of their order's founder; anyway, the couple had already planned other entertainments for the remainder of the evening. They slipped away hand-in-hand, while everyone at the table took pains not to notice their departure.

"This way is shorter," Elaryl whispered, and she dragged Seagryn out through a pair of double doors into the cobblestoned courtyard. It had started snowing again, thick, wet flakes just right for packing into balls, and Elaryl stooped to scoop some up and shoved it into Seagryn's face.

"You—" he gasped. Then he, too, grabbed a handful and pushed it toward Elaryl, laughing as she shrieked and danced away. She wasn't dissuaded by his attack, however. It just called for a strong retaliation, and she skipped to a stone bench layered with snow and flung it into his face with a swoop of her arm. Cackling with delight, Seagryn chased her, grabbing her around the waist and throwing her into a pile of snow that had drifted up against the courtyard wall. Their laughter was cut short by a bellow of rage neither of them had expected.

"You are making new pairs!"

Seagryn was on his feet immediately, facing the charge of a furious tugolith. He'd understood in a moment—all tugoliths birthed their offspring in male/female pairs—and they mated in drifted snow. Berillitha had understood at last what Seagryn had tried so hard to tell her. The tryst in the snowbank made it clear.

"You are paired to me!" Berillitha trumpeted.

"Berillitha, no!" he shouted, but she'd already targeted her horn on Elaryl and had lowered her head to strike.

"I will horn this punt!"

There was no time. Seagryn took his altershape and jumped between them. Berillitha's horn pierced his right forequarter and lodged there. This was a far deeper wound than her brother had inflicted upon him, and Seagryn nearly fainted from the pain. He managed to keep his feet, however, and held his ground on the slippery stones as Berillitha struggled to pull her bloody spike free.

"Not you!" she shouted. "You are my pair! I will horn her!"

"You will horn no one but me," Seagryn gasped. When she did finally manage to back out of his flesh, he squared around to face her and waved his own horn in her face. "And if you try, I will horn you back."

Standing nose to nose with him, Berillitha blinked. "But you are the Wiser," she whined.

"That may be," Seagryn rumbled in his deep tugolith voice, "but I am also a *man*. And as a man I am paired to *her*."

The tugolith looked back at him, watching his eyes. Seagryn was aware that a crowd had gathered at the double doors, and that they were waving at Elaryl to run to them. She started to go, and Berillitha jumped to that side of him. Seagryn leaped to meet her, and their horns bashed together with a bone-jarring *clack*!

"Stay where you are, Elaryl!" Seagryn commanded. He could see Berillitha's eyes follow Elaryl back to the snowdrift.

"I can't horn the Wiser," Berillitha complained, looking for a way around this obstacle.

"You must, if you plan to get to her. But I will horn you back if you try."

Berillitha stopped shuffling and stood motionless before him. "I am a punt," she said quietly. Then she turned her back on him and walked back to the far side of the courtyard. She lowered her head and leaned against the wall. Seagryn could no longer stand to watch. He took his human-form again and walked back to look down at Elaryl, who still cowered in the snowbank. He held out his left hand to her. "It's all right now. Everything is settled. She won't try to harm you anymore."

Elaryl gazed up at him, her expression that of fear mixed with admiration. Then she saw his shoulder, and jumped to her feet. "You're bleeding!"

Where Berillitha had horned him, Seagryn now had a deep wound, but not nearly so deep as it would have been had she stuck him while he was human. He'd really not noticed it much, but now it started burning, so he stooped to grab some snow to pack against it.

"Come on," Elaryl ordered, and she led him inside, ignoring the crowd at the door as she pulled him through to the kitchen. She doused his shoulder with ale, then led him back out into the hallway where everyone seemed to have clustered to share their impressions of the event they'd just witnessed. Elaryl marched past her father to Ranoth, who stood talking with the leader of the order. "We are sleeping in the tower tonight," she announced firmly. This was a statement, not a request, and she didn't wait for permission. She guided Seagryn through the crowd and up the staircase into that spindly yellow and turquoise tower they'd both considered so grotesque.

In the tiny circular room at the top there was a mattress, a candle, and little else—but that was enough. Elaryl sat Seagryn on the bed and undressed him, taking care to keep the material of his garments from touching the wound. Then she pulled back the cover and helped him to lie down. Finally she stripped off her own clothes, blew out the candle, and snuggled in beside him. Despite his wound, they did not immediately sleep.

Later, as they drowsed in one another's arms, Elaryl struggled up onto one elbow and whispered, "Seagryn?"

"Hmm?"

"I'm going with you tomorrow."

"Hmm." He smiled in the blackness and hugged her closer to him.

"On the condition that you do whatever it is my father and Ranoth are asking you to do. I want all of this to be over, Seagryn, so that we can go back home and get back to our lives." Elaryl turned over then, wriggling her long body backward into his, and soon began breathing the slow, deep breaths of sleep.

For Seagryn that did not come so easily. He lay in the darkness, thinking about the beast he'd betrayed, who now mourned against the courtyard wall below them. Just before he slept, he thought he heard a quiet, mournful hooting—then weariness finally wrapped her cloak around him, and Seagryn sought forgiveness in his dreams.

Somewhere toward dawn he awoke, very thirsty and very sore in the shoulder. Then he remembered the hooting, and listened for it. He sat up with alarm. What if Berillitha had gone?

There were three windows in the tower, and he went to each until he found the one looking down upon the courtyard. There she was, still leaning against the wall, her back covered with a coating of white from the night's snowfall. But Berillitha wasn't asleep. She'd turned her head up to look at this window as she watched and waited for her Wiser's return.

Chapter Twenty-eight

❋❋❋❋

BEHIND THE MASK

"**Y**OU may relax, Talarath," Paumer said as he pulled on his leather gloves and laced his fingers together to fit them down tightly. "It can't be a dangerous journey. We have the best of gear to preserve us warmly through the worst of blizzards. We have the finest of horses, and they're well rested now. We have the boy to see our future and help us avoid trouble. What can happen?"

Talarath snorted contemptuously. "Marwandian raiders, first and foremost! Can you guarantee you'll not be hacked to death by the first band of rogues that happens across your path?"

"The boy could." Paumer shrugged.

"But will he? All I've ever gotten from this so-called prophet is shifty eyes and slurred speech!"

"Talarath, friend." Paumer smiled warmly. "Surely you realize you terrify the child. He's very forthcoming with information when asked and he's assured me that our journey will be successful and the dragon will be made."

"Will you all arrive safely? Will my Elaryl make the trip in comfort? These are the matters that concern me!"

"She'll be traveling under the protection of her husband, Talarath, who is after all a wizard . . ."

"You seek to set my mind at ease by reminding me of that?" Elaryl's father snarled. "That's precisely the cause of my concern!"

Seagryn overheard all this as he saddled the horse assigned

to him, but he felt no need to involve himself in the confrontation. Talarath was Talarath and would ever be so. Elaryl had promised to go with him, and, during breakfast, he'd received Dark's quiet verification that indeed she would. He had to smile at Paumer's simplistic assessment of Dark's ability to avoid danger. In fact, the prophet had intimated they would find trouble in the Marwilds, but he'd offered no details and Seagryn had not sought any. It was better not to know.

As he led his mount out of the stable, his eyes fell across something that made him stop and turn around. He thought he recognized the dull gray haunches sticking out of a stall in the back. "Kerl?" he said, stepping around to see if he was right. "Kerl!" he exclaimed when he found to his delight that he was.

The horse glanced at him disinterestedly, then turned back to face the bare wall of his stall. Kerl obviously wasn't the type to get sentimental over shared experience. Seagryn regarded the horse he'd already saddled, a spirited roan stallion that looked as if it might gallop all the way to Pleclypsa, if given its head. Just looking at the horse made Seagryn feel weary, and he stepped out of the stable and called out to Paumer, "If you have no objection, I'd like to change horses."

Paumer probably didn't, but this interruption gave him an excuse to break away from the troublesome cleric, so he frowned and came down the hill toward Seagryn.

"You're dissatisfied? That horse is one of the finest in all my stables—"

"But there's another mount in here I've ridden before." Seagryn chuckled, ducking back inside with Paumer behind him. He pointed at Kerl. This time the stolid gray didn't even bother to look. "Your people at the base of the North Mouth gave me that animal to ride up here."

"That's one of my horses?" The merchant winced. Then he frowned thoughtfully. "Those who pursued young Dark at my daughter's bequest did say they'd found a mount from our stables near where he disappeared—but I'd hardly call this a horse! No wonder it took you so long to get here!"

"Oh, Kerl's a little slow, but he's steady. And to someone as weary of travel as I, he's the horse of my dreams. You don't mind?"

"I—I'm a bit embarrassed he even belongs to me. But . . . if you're sure . . ." He glanced sadly around at the other horse and patted its powerful flank.

"Why don't you let *Uda* ride that roan? I'm certain she'd enjoy it—"

They departed soon thereafter, although Seagryn nearly had to pry Elaryl loose from her weeping father. As he lifted her onto her saddle, the sight of her tear-streaked cheeks caused a lump to come up in his own throat, but he managed to get it swallowed and climbed onto the passive Kerl. Then they were off—Paumer, Dark, and Elaryl riding abreast of one another, Seagryn behind—and Uda unhappily in the lead, swearing loudly at the red stallion as she fought it all the way down the hill.

Berillitha waited patiently until the line of horses passed by her, then turned to follow Kerl. Seagryn wondered if the tugolith's presence might alarm the horse, but Kerl didn't even seem to notice. Berillitha, however, had taken note of Kerl.

"Why do you ride?" she asked Seagryn.

"Where we go is a long walk for a man."

"Don't be a man."

"I'm not a tugolith, Berillitha," he said firmly. "You know that by now."

"You were," she said, and she conveyed such grief that the lump came back up in his throat. His guilt prompted it. He was the source of her grief. And that burden was so unbearable he thought he might do anything to absolve himself of it. But how? The deed was done. And if absolution wasn't possible, he would do the next best thing—remove his guilt by removing its source. Now, he couldn't wait to get her into Sheth's den and get to work. The sooner she was part of a dragon, the sooner he would be free of Berillitha's sorrowful stares.

The first day's ride was easy—for Kerl, anyway. Uda's horse had almost given out by noon, and they'd been delayed briefly, but Kerl just plowed through the snow as if it were meadow grass, keeping all his observations to himself. They made camp near a stream that had not yet completely frozen over—and a marvelous camp it was. The finest fish-satin tents of the most airtight construction were furled and staked down with the minimum of effort. Paumer knew how to travel.

Even so, he sniffed apologetically at the accommodations and promised, "We'll be back under a roof tomorrow. I have a mansion less than a day's journey to the south—if I can just remember how to get to it . . ."

They found it by nightfall the next day, but due to Dark's memory of the future, not to Paumer's of the past. "Well I've only been there once," the merchant snapped when he thought he heard complaint in Elaryl's voice. They all enjoyed their warm beds, and arose well-rested and in much better moods. They each received fresh mounts as well, although Seagryn hated parting from his stalwart friend. "If you'll leave him here I'll *give* you the horse!" Paumer pleaded finally. "You can pick him up whenever you return!" With that bargain struck, Seagryn bade the old gray good-bye. He hoped to be riding him back north to Lamath very soon, but Dark would neither confirm nor deny that possibility. Dark was very quiet these days—and very tense. That was cause for concern.

And yet, four days into their journey, they'd still not encountered even a minor crisis. Weary as he was of his seemingly endless travels in this fragmented land, Seagryn nevertheless had even begun to enjoy this trip. The longer they were all together, the better acquainted they became, and Seagryn found himself revising upward his opinions of Paumer and his daughter. The merchant could tell a story with extraordinary charm, and Uda had the quickest wit he'd ever seen in a girl her age. She also had an annoying habit of interrupting him as he explained things, to interpret what he was saying to Elaryl. But she did seem to have a gift for that, and occasionally it proved to be helpful. Then too, he had noticed that her attitudes toward Dark had matured. She still treated him as her chattel, but she now directed far more genuine affection toward the prophet than she had during that first week up at the Hovel.

But by far the most enjoyable aspect of the journey was the chance to ride quietly with his wife and catch up on all the days they'd spent apart. At times, he paid no attention at all to what she was saying, caring only to hear the lovely sound of her voice and to watch her lips move as she spoke. And when the wind blew colder and she complained that she was about to shiver right out of her saddle, he tied her horse behind his and set her before him; thus they could drape their cloaks about them to hide their hands from the others and talk in intimate whispers.

The more time Seagryn spent with Elaryl, the less Berillitha talked. She kept pace with the group easily, her eyes always on Seagryn, waiting and watching for any instruction he might condescend to give. Whether she became accustomed to his ignoring her or just had an infinite supply of patience, he couldn't tell. Seagryn was grateful, however, that she left him alone, for then he could ignore his burden as well.

He became so used to her silence that he grunted in surprise when she suddenly came up behind him and said, "Wiser—"

"Hunh? What?" He turned in his saddle to look back at her.

"There are horses all around us," she said flatly. "People too."

"Riders? All around us?" He craned his neck about, trying to see, but they rode through an area of dense thickets. Even though the leaves were off the bushes, their many thin branches obscured the view. "How do you know?"

"I hear them." She frowned. "Don't you?"

"No," Seagryn whispered, controlling his growing sense of alarm. He would keep this news from the others until he could plan a good response—though of course, Dark already knew. This was the danger the prophet had seen. Seagryn looked over at Dark and saw the boy staring back at him, expressionless. "Where did they come from?" he asked Berillitha quietly.

"They have been behind us."

"What? How long!"

"Since you awoke."

"Why didn't you tell me sooner?" he demanded.

"They have been behind us," she repeated.

"But now they're—"

He didn't finish his sentence—there was no need. The whole party instantly became aware of their danger. A moment before they'd been riding peacefully through the snowy woods. Now the were surrounded by a hundred black-clad riders, all wearing the glossy heads of the hideous pyralu. These warriors were armed with short bows, all drawn, and with arrows in place. The sight stole Seagryn's breath away.

Paumer gasped in horror. To be captured by the King of Arl had been his nightmare ever since that ruler had begun expanding his borders. The merchant had always taken precautions to avoid even chance encounters with armed Arlians, but he'd relied too heavily on his own interpretation of Dark's prophecy. He stared at the lad now, aghast, his eyes and mouth wide with shock at this betrayal. Elaryl jerked around to clutch at Seagryn. After firing her own look of contempt at the passive Dark, Uda looked at the wizard too.

"Wiser? Shall I horn them?" Berillitha asked loudly, and Seagryn hastened to hush her.

"Quiet!" he whispered. "Don't speak!"

But before he finished the phrase, a voice came from behind one of the black masks. "If you are a wizard consider carefully before you act. Remember that you are surrounded. Should you cloak yourself and these others, we will fire our arrows where we last saw you and kill some of you, at least. If you take yourself elsewhere by some act of will, good riddance, but we shall deal harshly with those you abandon, in vengeance for losing you. Indeed, we Arlians have much to avenge upon wizards, so, if you are one, please reveal it so that we may single you out for special attention.'' The voice was cultured but hard-edged. They'd been captured by an intelligent man trained in the use of violence—and Seagryn found that frightening. Far more so was his mental image of Elaryl's arrow-pierced body. Dark had warned of danger, yet seemed also to predict success. Seagryn chose the way of subterfuge—he had, after all, been a cleric much longer than he'd been a wizard, and he knew well what magic could be woven of words alone.

"The tugolith said 'wiser,' not 'wizard,'" Seagryn announced loudly, looking at no particular warrior, but scanning the eye-slits of those directly in front of him. "It is the title she knows me by.'' No one answered, and the silence following his statement became most uncomfortable. When Seagryn could stand it no longer, he filled it himself. "What is your business with us? May we proceed on our way?''

"What is your business here?'' one of the masks demanded.

"We are—on our way south,'' Seagryn offered—a bit lamely, he recognized.

"And your business there?''

"Is—business.'' Seagryn shrugged. "We are—merchants. We're looking for goods to carry to Lamath and—elsewhere.'' He glanced sidelong at Paumer, wanting the man to exercise some of his fabled shrewdness. But Paumer stared down at his saddle, hopelessness shaping his face into an ugly caricature of itself.

"And what do you intend to trade for such goods—*should* you find anything of value in these Marwilds?''

"We—we—''

"You appear to have nothing with you for that purpose. Where are your pack animals? Where are the results of your success to this point? In whose name do you trade? These lands belong to the King of Arl, and only those traders who have licensed their name with our king have been permitted to work these regions. I assume you have stamped papers with you, indicating you have sought and received such permissions?''

Now Seagryn actually turned his head to peer at Paumer, and found the man still staring downward. The merchant had clearly known the facts of trade in this area already, and realized this alibi had doomed them. A web of words could indeed weave magic—Seagryn had just chosen the wrong words.

"We await your permissions."

"That is—I didn't know that—"

The articulate warrior cut him off short. "You are in violation of restrictions on travel in this region. You will accompany us."

The line of masked riders parted directly in front of them, backing their mounts out to open a hole in the ring and to form wings on either side of their captives. Someone waved the small party forward, and Seagryn spurred his horse's flanks. Seagryn didn't turn around, but he felt certain there were arrows aimed at his back. He would need to do something to free them eventually, but this didn't seem the right time or place to try. None of these warriors appeared to think him a shaper. He saw no reason to reveal it until necessary.

"Where are we going?" Berillitha asked.

Seagryn winced. If she suggested he take his altershape or perhaps said his name, and they recognized it from the battle of the Sluice . . . "Be quiet, Berillitha."

"Do you fear these black things?" she asked.

Seagryn saw masks twisting around to look at him again. "These are men, Berillitha. Please do not talk."

"They don't look like men."

"Berillitha—"

"They look like bugs."

"Berillitha, *please*—" He made his voice as threatening as possible, but she still said:

"We squash bugs."

"Shut your mouth!" This was not Seagryn, but Elaryl, and Berillitha grunted in aggravation. Seagryn gripped his reins and took a deep breath, uncertain what he might have to do in the next moment. Remembering Nebalath's advice, he scanned his imagination for new options. Unfortunately, he didn't feel very creative.

And then he remembered. "Power—?" he murmured, and he waited, expecting that gush of supernatural presence he'd felt in the megasin's cave to swirl around and through him once again. It didn't. "Power?" he repeated. Still he felt nothing, and panic clawed at his chest.

However, Berillitha had stopped talking. And while Seagryn had certainly not felt the intervention of the Power—had it come, just the same? Had Berillitha felt it, perhaps, and been silenced? Or was it just—reality?

The warriors on the point of each wing directed them through the stark woods, until they saw before them a clearing and a rock the size of a small mountain. The side facing them had been hollowed out by some natural force into a kind of gray-green canopy. As they came closer, Seagryn saw the tents of an encampment snuggled up against its inner wall, sheltered from the winter's worst. They were motioned into the camp and told to dismount. By the time they were off their horses, they'd each been surrounded by masked riders and were quickly escorted to the largest tent and thrust inside its black flaps. A half-dozen warriors sat around a table, evidently discussing some campaign. It amazed Seagryn to see that, even in this intimate setting, they did not remove their masks. How could these people ever be certain with whom they were dealing?

The moment they stepped inside, the meeting adjourned, and the conferees walked back to look at them. One of them pointed soundlessly to the table and gestured for them to sit. As they moved to obey, this masked superior waved his lieutenants out of the tent and waited until all were gone before coming back to sit himself. Seagryn couldn't help but feel pleased—he liked these odds much better. Now if he could just decide what to do—

"Why are you here, Paumer," the man behind the pyralu mask growled harshly, and Seagryn straightened up in his seat. He knew that voice!

Paumer did too, and a smile blossomed across his worried features. "Jarnel! Jarnel is that you?"

"Whisper!" Jarnel demanded, and Paumer covered his mouth and repeated his question in a whisper.

"Jarnel!"

"It is imperative that you not reveal my name. This is a secret assignment—so secret the king will not allow us to acknowledge that we know one another's identities. It's a ridiculous notion, of course, since anyone present might be an external spy—from Lamath perhaps," he added to Seagryn, then he turned his eye-slits to focus on Uda. "Or perhaps from your land of Harana-mous? But that's meaningless to him, since he suspects all of his subjects of treachery, and those in his army especially."

"Perhaps he should," Paumer whispered, evidently intending it as a joke. Jarnel jerked around to look at him, and Paumer put his hand over his mouth again. The eyes behind the mask did not smile.

"Why are you here?" Jarnel repeated quietly.

"We're on our way to—"

"I'm certain I know where you're all bound. What I asked is the reason why. Seagryn—that is your name, is it not?"

"It is." Seagryn nodded. He didn't catch the sarcastic edge in Jarnel's voice, and so was unprepared for the savagery of the general's response.

"Do you really think I would forget! Do you think me such a fool that I don't know by smell the enemy who burned or drowned a half of my command? Oh, I know you well, Seagryn. Your name is known well in all of Arl and is enthusiastically cursed whenever it's spoken. Hear me, all of you—I know you're all traveling to the cave of the bear, and that you're certain to find it for no other reason than that you have young Dark here along with you. But why? Give me some good reason why I should let you go on and why I should not follow you myself in order to pinpoint that evil traitor's location and to destroy him?"

"Destroy him? Your own wizard?" Paumer frowned.

"Our own wizard abandoned us in battle, leaving us at the mercy of this brutal young cleric! Can you tell me, Paumer, why I should appreciate the efforts of *any* wizard?"

Seagryn rose to his own self-defense. "Your people attacked Haranamous—" he began, but Jarnel cut him off.

"Very stupidly, I might add. Tactically, we deserved all the damage we received. Please understand, Seagryn, that I do not blame you for the outcome of that battle. I blame Sheth. But neither can I bring myself to like you, as you would readily understand if the rôles had been reversed and those had been Lamathian bodies floating in the river." Jarnel turned his masked face back to Paumer. "I'm waiting."

The merchant glanced across the table at Seagryn, realized that the wizard was not going to be the one to explain, then launched into a full description of the most recent meeting of the Grand Council and of the plans launched there. Jarnel listened to it all in silence. It became apparent to Seagryn midway through the tale that the merchant was having trouble talking to a mask. It gave him no visual response at all. Still, he was the most effective salesman alive. By the time Paumer finished, Seagryn, at least, was more convinced than he'd ever been.

Jarnel sat quietly a moment, reflecting before he spoke. "You people don't know Sheth as I do," he finally growled. "The man does nothing for the good of anyone—not even—" here he shook his head in dismay "—not even for himself. I don't know." They all waited, watching him. But Seagryn saw a relaxed confidence on Paumer's face that in turn relaxed him. The merchant seemed to know he'd made a sale . . .

"Perhaps killing Sheth would be the better solution," Paumer offered sardonically. "Then you could also kill young Seagryn, lead your war boats to vengeance and victory in Haranamous, and conquer the rest of the One Land soon thereafter! What joy, to be able to watch as your secretive king puts black masks on the whole world in order to prevent any possible conspiracy against him!"

Jarnel gave no indication that he'd heard this. He just sat quietly, deep in thought. Then he sighed heavily. "I don't expect any of this to work as you *say* you have it planned, Paumer. How can it, when someone so inherently evil plays such a prominent role in this beast's construction? Dark, sitting there staring at me with his troubled eyes—he knows what's to come. But we can't let him tell us, for that would do us ill. Am I correct in that, lad?"

Seagryn looked at Dark. The boy nodded his head slightly, then looked away.

"And yet the alternative—" Jarnel tapped the side of his mask "—is too hideous to contemplate. Go ahead. Go find him, and get it done. And Seagryn—" he added. "I do hope that Power your people talk about exists and is doing something to counter all this." He sighed. "Certainly I've done all I can do."

They all sat there, waiting for something more to be said. When Jarnel just gazed at the table top, Paumer finally asked, "Do you mean we can just walk out of here, and these warriors who nearly killed us will let us ride away without a question?"

"Certainly. Easiest thing in the world." Jarnel shrugged.

"Why so easy?"

Jarnel turned his eye-slits toward the merchant. "Simple. I just tell them you're still more secret representatives of the King of Arl. Who would know the difference?"

Chapter Twenty-nine

※※※※

WITHIN THE DEN

THEY might have wandered for years in the Marwilds and never found Sheth's hideaway had the wizard himself not come out to meet them and lead them to it. "What's wrong with your sense of direction, boy," he sneered at Dark moments after suddenly revealing himself in the middle of their tent. "Did you lose your gift along with your innocence?"

"Sheth!" Paumer gasped. "There you are! We've been hunting for you for a week!" The merchant said this with relief, then his tone turned petulant. "Where have you been!"

"Running errands." The wizard chuckled, flashing his dimples at Uda and turning to gaze hungrily at a still-shaken Elaryl. "And who is this?" he asked, grinning lewdly. He took obvious pleasure in her discomfort, then turned his gaze slowly to Seagryn to see what rage he might have stirred up there.

Seagryn met his eyes evenly. "Elaryl, this is the wizard known as Sheth. The woman is Elaryl—my wife." He would not be intimidated by this tasteless punt—and yes, he thought to himself, that's exactly what Sheth was—a punt. Let him find his own mate! Seagryn withstood the temptation to take his altershape and ram his horn through the grinning shaper's rib cage. Sheth snickered, and turned back to Paumer.

"It took you long enough to get here," he snorted. "I expected you long before this."

"It took Seagryn a bit longer than we anticipated."

"Oh? Why is that? Was the Bearsbane not up to the task?"

Sheth turned back to Seagryn and added, "I understand there's a rhyme in the local inns of Haranamous that says you've already tacked my skin to old Haran's wall . . ."

Seagryn didn't look away. You couldn't with Sheth. The man designed his every remark as a test of resolve. The competition never ceased. "I'm not responsible for what peasants sing in taverns at the end of a frightening war," Seagryn replied smoothly. "I am partly responsible for their feeling the freedom to sing."

Sheth stared at him a moment, then sneered and looked back again at Paumer. "Surprising how easily a cheap victory can make a man forget the mud in his ears and nose . . ."

Paumer's patience suddenly snapped. "Would you two please stop this posturing and let us pack and move on? This tent is doubtless the best made anywhere in the world, but my old bones are frozen through, just the same! I need to find a truly warm spot before nightfall or I shall prove very difficult to live with, I can assure you all of that!"

"He means it, too," Uda added, both in defense of her father and to get a little attention directed back her way. "Dark," she ordered imperiously, once all eyes had turned her way, "start putting the robes in the bag and let's get on with it."

"Hop to it, boy!" Sheth mocked. "You don't want to feel Uda's vengeance!"

Dark said nothing. He just started following the instructions of his mistress, his face bearing that same empty expression it had carried all the way from the Lamathian monastery. And while it grieved Seagryn to see him so, it also prompted him to stir around and do the necessary packing to move them on. Elaryl and Paumer joined in while Sheth slipped outside to wait. Soon thereafter, they had packed their bags and were ready to load their horses.

Sheth stood looking across the animals, keeping them between himself and Berillitha. "So this is your offering?" he asked as Seagryn walked up to throw a pair of bags across the rump of his mount.

Seagryn's throat constricted—guilt or grief? It didn't matter. The outcome would be the same in either case. "This is Berillitha," he muttered quietly.

"Oh-ho!" Sheth crowed. "He has a name, does he?"

"Of course she does. Don't you?"

"It's a she." Sheth nodded. "The other tugolith will doubtless be pleased."

"Not necessarily," Seagryn said, tying tent stakes to his horse's saddle. "He may be a punt who did not care to be paired."

"Punt?" Sheth smirked. "You sound like an expert on these stinking beasts. When this is all over, why don't you go collect a few more and keep them as pets?"

Seagryn wasn't ruffled. "They are loving, caring persons," he responded. Then he looked directly at Sheth. "Far more human than some people I know."

"Who is this man?" Berillitha asked quietly.

"This is Sheth," Seagryn answered. He tried to think of something to add, but hesitated. He'd still not been able to bring himself to explain their purpose to Berillitha and found he wasn't ready even yet. Sheth, watching with too much awareness and too little sensitivity, just laughed.

"Is he going with us?" the tugolith asked.

"Yes—he's going to lead us to his place."

"I really don't need to, you realize," Sheth said casually. Then he pointed to Seagryn's horse. "Nor is there much point in tying those bags onto your animal. You see," he added, "you're right here at it."

"Where?" Seagryn frowned and looked around. They had camped last night by a stream that burst from a nearby rock with unexpected warmth; but other than that, he saw no distinguishing features in the landscape—just bare trees interspersed with snow-laden evergreens, and a white-shrouded hill slanting up away from the source of the hot spring.

"Right there." Sheth pointed to the stream. "Aren't you all packed yet?" he shouted harshly, and the others looked up from what they were doing to frown at him. "Watch!" he called, and he walked a few paces above the mouth of the spring and plunged down into the snow.

"Isn't that *freezing*—?" Uda called, but she broke off her question with a shout that expressed the surprise they all suddenly felt. "He's disappeared!"

"He's down inside!" Seagryn called back, and he ran to the hole in the snow and knelt beside it. "There's an opening underneath!" He looked up at Dark, who walked wearily toward him carrying a load of baggage. "It's like the megasin's window! Did you know this was here?"

"What do you think?" Dark grunted, dropping the bags.

"Why didn't you tell us?"

"Why should I?" Dark mumbled, abruptly jumping through

the window himself and disappearing from view. Seagryn leaned over the dark hole and heard the boy calling up to him, "Would you mind dropping those things down to me?"

"Those are my clothes!" Uda protested. "Where is he taking them?"

"I think we've reached our destination," Seagryn answered as he shoved the baggage through the hole.

"Here?" Paumer frowned.

Seagryn looked across the brook at Paumer, shrugged, and went back to fetch the rest of the gear.

"Where are you going?" Berillitha asked as she watched Seagryn unpack the horse he'd so recently been loading.

"Ah—under the ground. I—I want you to stay right here—with the horses. I'll be back."

The tugolith shuffled her feet to indicate she'd heard and agreed, and Seagryn carried a load back to the window and thrust it down and through the hole. Someone on the other side grabbed it. In moments, there was nothing left to go through but the people. He looked at Elaryl. "Ready?" he asked.

"Will you go in first?" she said, her eyes anxious.

"I'll be right below to catch you."

By the time Elaryl was ready Uda had gathered her courage and dropped through. Paumer had followed. Seagryn looked back at Berillitha. "Wait here!" he called again, then he stepped to the hole and jumped in.

The drop into the dark was frightening but brief. It took a moment for his eyes to adjust to the darkness; before they did, he heard Elaryl plunging through from above him and reached blindly upward to grab her and break her fall. Dark waited nearby with robes for both of them and he immediately wrapped them up and led them down the corridor. "Fire's down here," he explained; as their eyes adjusted, they could see its flicker on the walls. They walked beside the warm stream about twenty feet before the cavern widened and they could see the fire to their left. This was under that snow-covered slope, Seagryn realized. The deeper they went, the higher the ceiling became, so they could soon stand up all the way. "So this is the bear's lair," Seagryn muttered, looking around, but he had no interest in exploring it at the moment. Elaryl rushed to the fire and huddled beside it with Paumer and Uda. Seagryn and Dark soon joined them, and the five travelers' teeth chattered in chorus as they waited for the blaze to warm them. Sheth sat on the far side of the fire pit, his eyes fixed on the flames. He seemed to be very far away . . .

After a while, Seagryn thawed enough to begin asking questions, and his first was about the fire. "Why didn't we see the smoke outside?"

"Hmmm?" Sheth said, looking up at last. "Why? Is that important?"

"Just—curious." Seagryn shrugged.

"Uhm." The other shaper nodded, his eyes sliding back to the flames. He seemed mesmerized by them, but he answered anyway. "I have three fires that I keep burning all the time. The smoke goes up—and goes out. I don't know why, exactly. The cave was like that when I found it."

"Then there are—shafts, out to the air?"

"We've been in a ventilated cave before, haven't we?" Dark asked meaningfully, and Seagryn looked over at him. The boy raised his eyes upward, and ran his gaze back and forth along the ceiling, perpendicular to the line of the stream. Seagryn followed his gaze upward, and understood immediately. The cave through which the stream ran was a natural fissure, the kind made by the normal shifting of the earth. But this wider section where they sat had been carved from the rock in a very familiar way.

"The megasin!" Seagryn gasped. This gallery had the exact shape and dimensions of those chambers in which the megasin had housed them—and in which they'd been able to breathe. "You think she—"

"There may be more than one." Dark shrugged. Then he smiled sweetly at Sheth, who frowned across the flames at him.

"What are you talking about?" the shaper demanded.

"I thought you intended to make the dragon within your den," Dark said quickly. "Where is the other tugolith? And how do you expect to get Seagryn's tugolith inside here?"

Sheth gazed at him. "You know how . . ." he grumbled after a moment.

"You don't know what I know. Nor does Seagryn. And if you intend to work together I think you ought to—"

"What you think is meaningless, boy," Sheth snarled. "I've not forgotten it was *you* who caused my humiliation at the Rangsfield Sluice, and you must know already I never will!"

"Father—" Uda said, looking at Paumer with worry, and the merchant cleared his throat to intervene. Sheth hushed him with a fierce wave.

"Relax, Paumer," he muttered before continuing to Dark. "You may thank your young lady for your life—she wrung a promise from her father and he one from me. But I suggest you keep well out of my way. And that includes keeping your prophecies to yourself!"

Seagryn waited for the tension to settle, then asked "But what about the tugolith? And what about the horses? They need to be stabled and—"

"I'll get the second beast inside, you needn't worry yourself about that. As for the horses—you may as well go and slaughter them now. Their meat will keep well in this cold. We're certain to need it, since it appears you've brought no other provisions with you, and making a dragon takes time."

Seagryn felt grateful now that he'd let Paumer persuade him to leave Kerl behind. He glanced over at Elaryl and saw a sick look spread across her face as she said, "You mean we're going to eat the horses?"

"Why not?" Sheth shrugged. "They're very filling. Although," he added with a sinister chuckle, "raw Marwandian is much more tasty!"

Elaryl stared. "People?" she asked.

The bear laughed as he rose from the fire and disappeared into the black bowels of the cave. Elaryl seemed to be choking. As Seagryn scooted closer to her to comfort her, she looked around at him with big eyes. "He doesn't mean that—does he?" When Seagryn could do nothing but shrug, his wife groaned in utter dismay. "Seagryn! What have you gotten me into!"

He had no ready answer—only that dreadful sense of guilt that seemed to deepen with every new event. It prompted him now to wonder if he would ever be free of it. Once again he sought some other source to put it off on, someone else to blame. Although it wasn't her purpose, Uda provided him some relief.

"Yes, Father!" the girl snarled accusingly at Paumer. "What have you gotten us into?"

"Why, I'm as—as—as astonished as all of you!" he sputtered. "The man is—is a shaper, of all things! A powerful personage in this world! Since he's unmarried, I'd not assumed that he lived in palatial luxury—it's women that tend to push for such, wouldn't you agree, Seagryn?" Seagryn raised his eyebrows, but fortunately Paumer's question proved to be rhetorical. "Even so, I'd not expected living conditions quite so—grotesque. And this horrifying reference to raw Marwan-

ians? Certainly that's just a fiction he maintains to preserve his
ublic image?''

"Certainly!" Uda sniffed. "After all, why should he trouble
imself to go looking for bear hunters when he has us here
nytime he gets hungry!"

"Uda!" Paumer snapped.

But the girl went right on. "And you've handed us over to
im! Have you no better sense than to trust such a—"

"Silence!" Paumer commanded. "You sound just like your
1other!" The comment evidently stung her, for this time Uda
rudgingly obeyed. "Besides," he grumbled, looking at Dark,
'I thought your prophetic swain here could prove his worth by
eeping us out of any such difficulties!"

"One would certainly think so!" Uda said in the same dis-
lainful tone of voice, only now she directed her vitriol at her
'outhful prophet. "Why didn't you warn us what we were get-
ing into? Didn't you know?"

Dark calmly met her gaze. "What have you gotten into?" he
isked.

"This!" she screamed, standing up and baring one of her
:hivering shoulders.

"Oh. Goose-flesh." Dark nodded. "Terrible tragedy. I really
)ught to have prepared you better—such a burden."

"And this!" she shouted again, gesturing about her at the
)rimitive cave, the walls of which seemed to reflect back little
)f the fire's illumination.

"Ah." Dark nodded, still unbothered. "And have you inves-
:igated this place, to know that it's so terrible? Couldn't it be
:hat Sheth has carved a gorgeous dining room from the rock
somewhere back there, and we're just sitting in his courtyard,
so to speak?"

Uda frowned. "Are we?"

Dark chuckled, and Seagryn looked up in surprise. He'd not
heard the lad laugh since—since— "Actually, no," the prophet
explained. "At least, I never see it, if he does. But this is a
rather extensive dwelling, and I assume it meets the needs
of our host. As to my not having told you what it would be
like . . . Did you ever really ask me?"

Paumer snorted. "We assumed you could be trusted to steer
us away from unpleasant—"

"You assumed. Seagryn didn't. Did you, Seagryn?"

Now they all looked back at Seagryn again, and somehow—
how did this happen?—the group blame rolled inexorably back

onto his shoulders. He was a powershaper, he knew about Dark's abilities and might have explained them more fully to the others in the party, he was an adult and the prophet was, after all, still just a boy. He was guilty.

Seagryn met Elaryl's eyes. Even she wore an expression of cool distaste upon her pretty features as she waited for him to respond. There seemed to be only one other source to blame, and Seagryn did so. "It's neither my fault not Dark's. The Power gave Dark his gift and me mine, and probably Sheth his, though to what good end I surely don't know. That's the cause of all this. Why don't you blame the Power?"

"Why don't you come eat dinner instead?" Sheth called from down the corridor. Apart from Dark, they looked at one another with trepidation. The boy, however, had no qualms about eating. He jumped to his feet, and smiled at the rest of the group.

Trusting Dark, Seagryn stood and reached down to help Elaryl up. They followed Dark down the tunnel—for that was really what this place was. A closer look at the walls confirmed Seagryn's belief that it had been carved by the megasin, or something like her. Recently? He shivered at the thought, and Elaryl glanced back at him in worry. "It's nothing." He smiled confidently.

"I don't know how you can say that," she muttered, adding to herself, "I should have listened to my father."

Yet as they turned the corner and saw the second of Sheth's fires, their spirits lifted considerably. This room was as dark as the cavern they'd left, but it smelled wonderful. Next to the fire Sheth had placed two small tables, and on the tables sat a dozen golden serving bowls, each filled with steaming food. Sheth took a gold plate and offered it to Elaryl. "You'll not think it rude of me to request that you serve yourself?" he asked with mocking politeness.

"Where did this come from?" Uda asked, having come up behind them with her father.

"Oh—this?" Sheth said, gesturing at the imported feast. "Call it a gift from the King of Arl. It did come from his kitchens—although he appeared to be nowhere around . . ."

"Oh, yes," Paumer offered, brightening. "I remember now Jarnel once telling me that the king had gone into hiding because you kept appearing unannounced in his bedroom!"

Sheth dimpled wickedly, then his forehead creased in a slight frown. "Jarnel?" he asked. "Where did you last see the dear prince?"

"In these woods. He took us captive over a week ago."

"Took you captive?" Sheth said, grimacing over at Seagryn, who was at that moment filling his plate. "Weren't you veiling these poor people?"

Seagryn felt glad of the darkness, for he knew he was blushing. "It never occurred to me."

"What's the use of having shaper powers if you don't use them?" Sheth exploded, but in derision rather than anger. "You're a fool, Seagryn, did you know that?" He looked at Elaryl and asked, "Did you realize this husband of yours had left you exposed to all the dangers of the forest?"

"There was no danger we didn't know already was coming," Seagryn protested, angry at feeling the need to defend himself, but unable to keep from doing so.

"Oh, yes! Your little fortune-teller. But did he not suggest that you might have avoided such by using simple shaper's caution?"

"He did not, because I didn't ask. That can't be a surprise to you, surely? You, who've told him to keep his mouth shut? Besides, we learned some information during our encounter with Jarnel that you might find useful."

"And that is . . ."

"That the King of Arl has instructed his warriors to assassinate you on sight." Seagryn said it forcefully, expecting Sheth to be shaken.

The wizard only laughed. "This is valuable information, Seagryn? That's been the king's intention ever since he became king. He's had raiding parties scouting the Marwilds for my den for years. In fact, I sometimes wonder if half of the supposed Marwandian bear-baiters aren't really Arlian warriors under my dear king's specific instructions to kill or entrap me." Sheth looked at Paumer. "Surely you knew that? Why else would I associate myself with your little Conspiracy?"

Seagryn looked at Paumer, but the merchant's expression revealed nothing other than his appreciation of the cuisine. "Wonderful food, Sheth," the merchant replied after a moment, as if the wizard had just asked his opinion of the meal. "And it's encouraging to know you were only jesting when you talked of eating horse meat or Marwandians!"

"Yes," the wizard responded—almost wearily, Seagryn thought. Then he disappeared.

"Now where's he gone?" Paumer frowned.

"Perhaps he'd not gone anywhere," Seagryn said. "Perhaps

he's just cloaking himself to get away from us—or to watch and listen while we settle into his dwelling.''

''Or perhaps,'' Dark offered from his place by the fire, ''he's gone to get the other tugolith and bring her inside.''

''Is that in fact where he is?'' Paumer asked.

''I just said perhaps,'' the prophet responded. He never took his eyes off his plate.

Investigation revealed that the system of natural caves and megasin channels was indeed extensive—nothing to compare with the underground city of the Remnant, but certainly more than enough space for an individual. Seagryn found his way blocked repeatedly by wooden walls constructed across the openings of new channels, each with a door set into the center of them. All the doors were locked. Sheth was a secretive individual in the world outside; why would he be any less so within his den? Seagryn wasn't certain whether the walls and locks were designed to keep people like himself in, or creatures— potentially dangerous creatures?—out. He did decide, however, that at least one of these channels must lead to the outside and that Sheth intended to bring Berillitha into the den that way. The locks were strong and couldn't be forced. But Seagryn noted with some encouragement that the wooden barriers could easily be torn loose from their moorings in the rock wall if one leaned upon them in tugolith shape. And he wondered—where was the other tugolith?

By the time Sheth reappeared, Seagryn had found Vilanlitha's pen. It was on the far side of the cavern from where they'd eaten, past that first fire where they'd dried themselves, across the brook and on beyond a third fire. He found another wooden barrier closing off a channel, which he decided must be backed by yet another wall, enclosing a room. He knew from the powerful scent that a tugolith was near, and he guessed the beast was housed beyond this room.

''You've smelled your way to it, I see,'' Sheth said behind him, causing Seagryn to jump and spin around. ''Easy, I would suppose, to track your own stinking kind?''

''Did you try to lead Berillitha inside? I imagined you might need my help—''

''I didn't try to move her, I moved her. She's back beyond that wall,'' Sheth said, pointing across the corridor to a barrier opposite this one. ''Listen carefully. You mustn't suppose that because you bested me in that Rangsfield encounter your control over the powers is the equal of mine. I told you once, Seagryn—

I'm the foremost shaper of this age, with abilities that would astonish and threaten you were I to reveal them. I won't. I prefer to hide them until needed. You may find this remarkable, but I speak this way for your benefit, to insure you don't thrust yourself between me and my goal. That would be very foolish—and very costly to you personally. I need your assistance, true—that's why you're here. But it must be as an assistant and when I request it. Do you understand?''

"I do. But there are some things which you need to—''

"There's nothing I need to hear from you, Seagryn Bearsbane, other than an expressed willingness to aid me in my effort. You could say no, of course—but then I'd kill you. You see?'' Sheth smiled suddenly, incredibly. "You have no choice. So you don't have to feel so responsible for it all! You Lamathians—always bearing such responsibility for everything! Forget it.'' Sheth's face grew fierce as he finished with great gravity, "But do what I say, Seagryn—or you will be responsible for some hideous results.

"Now," Sheth went on, much more brightly. "Why don't you go back to where I left you and comfort your pretty wife? I'm afraid some of the day's events may have alarmed her.''

Seagryn did as he was instructed, amazed at himself for acquiescing so meekly. Then he realized that wasn't so amazing after all. Sheth had relieved him of a great burden of guilt. The bear was right. Seagryn didn't have to feel so responsible anymore. He could blame it all on Sheth.

Chapter Thirty

※※※※

THE DRAGON FORGE

Seagryn and Elaryl made an uneasy peace with their surroundings. They slept on the cavern floor near the second fire, as did Paumer and his daughter and the increasingly withdrawn Dark. They had all requested separate rooms since there seemed to be an abundance of them, but Sheth had responded angrily that this was no public house. "Those rooms are *filled*!" he shouted. And, of course, they'd all backed down.

Sheth slept—elsewhere. None of them knew where, although Seagryn speculated it might be in a bubble in the rock, open to the larger cavern only enough to provide ventilation, and accessible to Sheth alone through his magical ability to shift himself from one place to another. Sheth could feel secure in such a place, Seagryn reasoned—and perhaps nowhere else. Seagryn had never known a man more self-protective.

Sheth did open those other rooms to them eventually, when he chose to. As he had said, they were filled. Some contained treasure, a huge hoard that would please any ruler, to which Sheth added on a regular basis. He'd not returned the gold service to the kitchens of Arl just because the food was gone. Seagryn saw that the plates, unwashed of course, had been deposited here upon the pile. "I'm the world's most excellent thief," Sheth had cackled as Seagryn toured the room. Yet he apparently found no joy in it. Too easy, perhaps, when one could simply be and begone whenever and wherever one chose?

Other rooms contained an evil-smelling collection of herbs,

roots, and animal parts that Seagryn had no wish to investigate further. He was intrigued, however, by Sheth's library. "I own the best collection in the old One Land," the wizard boasted, and Seagryn believed it. Why not, when Sheth could add cherished volumes to it with the same ease that he increased the height of his treasure trove?

And then there was the room of the mouse-dragon.

"Careful," Sheth instructed as they stepped inside. "It may be a tiny beast, but it could kill if you offend it."

"Kill me? How?" Seagryn asked.

"Perhaps you'd like a demonstration?" Sheth smiled, his mustache spreading wide. He disappeared with that acrid *snap!* that never failed to shock. Seagryn growled in frustration and not a little fear, for here he was in the room with a potentially lethal creature and he didn't even know what to worry about. He stood by the door, looking across the room at the mouse-dragon's cage. It was hard to see, so he stepped a little closer, enough to see the tiny beast squatting on its floor, devouring the leg of an unfortunate toad. The creature had two heads, and one of these stopped eating and raised upon its lengthy neck to look curiously at Seagryn. Its face was mouselike, even to the whiskers, but gone was the pink nose, replaced by a scaly green appendage that drooped over teeth too long for any normal rodent. Its eyes, too, had been altered. They looked at him with much more intelligence and far less fear than any mouse he'd ever faced. Of course, the most dramatic changes in the creature was in its long, snakelike necks—one for each head—and its batlike wings, which it currently tucked down close to the tiny ridge along its back. Oddest of all was its color, for the body of the creature was piebald, mixing patches of white fur with areas covered by greenish gray scales. Small as it was, Seagryn considered it horrifying, and froze in place to await Sheth's return.

"Couldn't find a cat," the wizard suddenly was saying behind him, and Seagryn sighed with relief and stepped aside. "But I guess this squirrel will do." Sheth walked to the mouse-dragon's cage, opened its door and tossed the pitiful squirrel inside.

The squirrel had no interest at all in the winged creature, only in getting free, and it threw its weight against the wires in terror, tipping the cage over onto its side. Wild with fear, the squirrel scrambled past the confused dragon as it made a quick circuit of their tiny prison, then made the trip again. In the process, it raked the mouse-dragon with its claws, and suddenly both of the little beast's mouths were spitting in fury.

"Ha! Now watch—" Sheth announced.

The two necks stiffened; then the two heads angled down so that all four of the beast's eyes focused on the squirrel—or tried to, at least, for the squirrel was still in motion, and it was several minutes before it drained out all its terror and had to pause for a rest. It never moved again. In that pause, the mouse-dragon managed at last to concentrate its gaze upon the squirrel, and suddenly the panting animal burst into flames.

Seagryn stared. He couldn't restrain his astonishment that a man of such power as Sheth would actually go hunt down a squirrel to demonstrate the lethal abilities of a tiny monster. Sheth misinterpreted his look.

"You see!" The wizard chuckled. "You don't want to let both heads look at you at the same time—at least not in anger. I don't know, obviously, but I expect it would be fatal to a human, too."

"And—you—made this creature?"

"I did." Sheth smiled proudly and walked to a lectern in the corner of the room. "Here are my notes on how I did it. I don't know how much is actually necessary and how much is waste time, but it works. Exhausting, too—we'll want to sleep for days afterward."

"We . . ." Seagryn murmured, looking at the notes Sheth had pressed into his hands and thinking involuntarily of Berillitha.

"We'll work together up to a point." Sheth nodded. "The final making is a solitary process—an art—and I need no one's help for that. But I'll need your shaper abilities to help hold the tugoliths in place and to bind them together in a single magic net. I could do that myself with the two mice—who needs magical netting when you can hold the raw materials in your two hands? But I can't exactly do that with our two giants, can I? So I need your assistance in accomplishing that. I could probably also use your help in confusing the two creatures as they struggle."

"You could use any two creatures, could you not?" Seagryn said quietly, struggling to restrain his outrage at himself for even being a part of such a hideous endeavor.

"I guess so. Theoretically, I suppose we could make a human twi-beast, given the raw material—"

"Or two pyralu? Could you make a pyralu dragon?"

Sheth took a hard look at Seagryn, then whooped in laughter. "What a vicious imagination you have!" he cackled. "You may make a worthwhile powershaper yet!"

"It would be a horrible monster, wouldn't it? Worth banding together to war against, terrifying in every aspect?"

Sheth grew suspicious. "It would. Get to your point."

"Why must we make a tugolith dragon when we could make one far more heinous out of a pair of pyralu?"

Sheth thought on this for a moment, then a slight grin flitted across his lips. "Only one good reason I can think of."

"And that is?" Seagryn asked, trying to hide his hope.

"We don't have two pyralu. And I, for one, am not inclined to go searching for any! Are you?" He chucked. "Or are you just going priestly on me again as you battle with your moral dilemma? I warn you, Seagryn. Stew yourself in ethical concerns all you like, but if you try to interfere, you'll quickly discover that there really is a fate worse than death." Sheth let one side of his face dimple, then turned back to watch the mouse-dragon.

Seagryn glanced toward the cage but quickly looked away—the tiny, bat-winged beast now devoured portions of the squirrel. "Cooking its food seems to increase its appetite," Sheth said enthusiastically. There was no mistaking his admiration of his own bizarre handiwork.

Seagryn had to get out of the room. As he made his way to the door, Sheth called out, "Get some rest. We'll net the two together tomorrow."

Seagryn did not sleep easily that night. He dreamed he was a tugolith who shrank to the size of a squirrel, and then was torn apart and gobbled down by the two snapping heads of the mouse-dragon. When Sheth woke him the next—morning? Who could tell inside this sunless hell?—he was almost appreciative.

"Since you're the expert on these tugoliths," Sheth began, "tell me what we might expect when we introduce the two monsters to one another."

"They've not met?" Seagryn asked.

"Not yet. I didn't want to give them the opportunity to conspire together."

How very like Sheth to be worried about such, Seagryn thought. And how very unlike the tugoliths he'd known. Then again, he did not know Vilanlitha, Paumer's pet. Had that beast spent enough time in the Hovel to absorb some of Paumer's devious outlook? Seagryn's own experience had proved these animals were most susceptible to human influence. Would a domesticated tugolith differ greatly from those he'd encountered in the icy north? "I'm not certain how they'll react to one another. These are communicative beings, Sheth—persons. Paumer would know his own tugolith better than I.''

"It belongs to Uda. We'll enlist her help. But first we need to practice casting the net,'' Sheth decreed, and they spent the rest of the morning involved in that task. Seagryn found the process so fascinating he was almost able to forget why he was learning to do it. But the time came at last for him to fetch Berillitha into the long gallery where the dragon would be made, and all the old feelings returned.

"Why are we here?" she asked calmly as Seagryn watched Uda walk out of sight around the other end of the tunnel. He chose not to answer.

"Quiet. You'll see soon enough."

"You are the Wiser," Berillitha said, and she closed her vast mouth and waited.

"You are Uda," Vilanlitha said sagely. Though the girl didn't realize it, this was a major achievement. It had been many days since he had seen his mistress, and tugoliths had difficulty recognizing human faces. They all looked so much alike.

"Yes, I'm Uda," the girl grumbled as she led the beast down a corridor toward the cavern Sheth called the dragon forge. She was irritated at the wizard. He ordered her about as if she were a servant!

"Where am I going?" Vilanlitha asked. He really didn't sound all that interested, which was fortunate, Uda thought. She didn't want to be the one to explain to this huge monster that he was about to be turned into something different.

"Down a tunnel." Uda had spent enough time with her tugolith to understand how to talk to him. The simpler you kept it, the less the creatures bothered you with questions.

"Am I going to be a dragon?"

Uda gulped and almost stopped walking. She didn't—just a slight hesitation in her step, then she was right back up to speed—but she was wondering, now, how to answer. "Ah—I—how do you—"

"I want to be a dragon," Vilanlitha offered, probably not realizing how much his announcement relieved his diminutive mistress.

"You—you do?"

"I do!" He smiled.

"Oh. Who told you?"

"The man who brought me here."

"Sheth?"

"Of course." Vilanlitha snorted.

"Sorry," Uda said quickly. "Didn't mean to offend. So he talked to you about it?"

"I said so," Vilanlitha replied pointedly. He was not a stupid beast, as Uda had frequently reminded members of the palace staff when they'd trembled in fear before him. She chided herself for treating him so.

"Why do you want to be a dragon?" she asked.

Vilanlitha got a far-away look in his enormous eye—from where she walked Uda could only see this one—and murmured, "I can go anywhere. I can eat anyone. No wheel can keep me out!"

"What?" Uda asked, but they'd just turned the corner into the dragon forge and Vilanlitha had spotted Berillitha. His whole body stiffened.

Seagryn had a hand on Berillitha's forequarter, and felt her doing the same. "You'd better get out of the way, Uda," he called. "I've never seen lone tugoliths meet, and I'm not certain what will—"

The two creatures launched themselves at one another.

Uda needed no further counsel. She scrambled quickly and efficiently to safety first, then sprinted back down the cavern the way she'd come.

The two animals did not seek to cross horns initially, as Seagryn had come to expect. Instead they drove their points for one another's eyes, and only by dodging aside at the last moment did Berillitha avoid being blinded. She didn't avoid being struck, however, and her scream of pain echoed down the corridor.

"Berillitha!" Seagryn shouted. While not completely unexpected, this was happening far too fast to control.

"Good!" shouted Sheth, who stood well out of the way. "Oh, Seagryn, this couldn't be better!"

But Seagryn didn't hear. He chased after Berillitha, screaming for her to dodge, to duck, to dive out of the way, for Vilanlitha raced hard upon her heels, endeavoring to drive his horn between her legs and cut them from under her. "Berillitha! Berillitha! Turn!"

"Don't interfere, Seagryn!" Sheth shouted fiercely before breaking back into his beaming smile. "This is excellent! Far better than I had expected!"

Whether she'd heard Seagryn's shouts or not, Berillitha did turn at the very last moment, which proved to be the critical instant to divert Vilanlitha's jab. The male tugolith had left his feet and, as she whirled unexpectedly and reared up on her hind legs, he sprawled harmlessly before her. Seagryn had never seen her do this, and he gaped in surprise. Then Berillitha dropped her full weight across the male's back, and Vilanlitha's groan echoed through the cavern every bit as horribly as had her scream.

"Get off him!" Uda cried, watching from a safe haven at the far end of the tunnel. "Can't you see you're crushing him to death?"

But Berillitha did not get off. As Seagryn ran up beside them with Sheth right behind, she raised her head triumphantly and called out, "Be a tugolith, Wiser! Kill this punt!"

As Seagryn stared up at her he felt Sheth grab him by the sleeve and say, "The net, together. Ready? Now!" And, just as they had rehearsed it throughout the morning, Seagryn found himself working in concert with this man he loathed. The "net" was invisible, woven by their combined imaginations out of the powers that pervaded the old One Land. And it was effective, enclosing and trapping the two tugoliths, binding them together in a seamless, unbreakable web.

Berillitha perceived it first, and Seagryn thought his heart would rip apart when she looked at him in puzzlement and asked, "Why?" He knew what she meant. Why could she not move? But her word cut into him much more deeply. Why was he doing this to her? Why, when he'd told himself and Dark he would not? He looked back up at her, and saw the growing alarm in her huge eyes. "Wiser?" she called. "Why?" She sounded exactly like a frightened child.

"Now that was easy enough," Sheth called out loudly, and the others began to come out of their places of safety.

"You did it already?" Elaryl asked.

"Well done!" Paumer shouted merrily, skipping a bit as he bounded out of hiding. "You two shapers work well together!"

Vilanlitha groaned in agony, and Uda scrambled back up the corridor to stroke his flank and appeal his case. "Sheth! Seagryn!" she shouted angrily. "Couldn't you wait until she got off him? She's crushing him! Can't you see that?"

But all Seagryn could see were Berillitha's eyes. They wore that same expression of betrayal he'd seen the night he and Elaryl had rolled in the snow. "Why is this happening?" she asked quietly. She'd controlled the panic in her voice now, but he could hear it there still. He knew she deserved an answer.

"Yes!" Vilanlitha wailed, echoing much more loudly, "Why is this happening?"

"You wanted to be a dragon, didn't you?" Uda shrugged at him matter-of-factly. "This is how you become one."

"I don't *choose* to be close to this punt!" Vilanlitha cried, and now he, too, sounded like a frightened toddler. "She is not my pair!"

Sheth snorted, amused by their childish whining. "She is now," he called out. "And you'd better get used to her, for she will be forever." Then he turned around and sauntered away, Paumer hurrying after him.

Elaryl slipped up beside Seagryn and glided her arm through his. "Come on," she murmured in his ear as she tried to pull him away. "You can't help it. You did only what you were required to do . . ."

Seagryn resisted her tugging. "No," he responded quietly. "I didn't have to do this at all. I chose to."

"Wiser?" Berillitha called softly. "I am sorry I fought. Can I get down?" Seagryn gazed up at her, not knowing what to say. "Please?" she added.

She spoke so pitifully that Seagryn's eyes, already wet, spilled tears onto his cheeks. It was the only answer he could make. No words could have passed the enormous knot in his throat.

"You're forgetting," Elaryl whispered in his ear. "I asked you to do this—remember?"

Seagryn looked around at his wife's face and saw her motherly expression in place upon it. And although he didn't want to go, he no longer felt the emotional strength to resist her pull. As she led him down the dark tunnel, he looked back over his shoulder, watching and listening as Berillitha said repeatedly, "Please can I get down? Please? Please . . . ?"

He lay that night clutching Elaryl to him, so tightly that at one point she jabbed him with her elbow to get him to let her breathe. He loved her—there was no denying that. But Seagryn had to find some justice in all of this somewhere, and merely loving his wife did nothing for the cause of justice. Action—he needed to take action. And yet again, as he watched the constantly burning fire cast its flickering light on the smooth-cut ceiling above, the questions bubbled back up for his attention: Was this in the Power's purpose? Did the Power need a monumental weapon forged, a scourge with which to punish a disobedient civilization for failing to take the One seriously? Or was this all a perversion of the positive human impulse to unite for the common good which had been pushed, somehow, beyond the margin of acceptability, beyond the edge of honesty, beyond the good into the realm of organized evil? "Justice," he whispered at the ceiling, and Elaryl rolled over and mumbled "Hmm?" before snuggling back into the warmth of his arms and returning to her dreams.

He looked down at her face, and found it so beautiful that he postponed his quest for justice until later. He had decided what he must do, but it took him another week to move from decision into action. He waited as long as he could, clutching Elaryl to him at every available moment . . .

"I discovered with the rodents that if they're looped together long enough they stop thinking of themselves as two individuals. Then you can begin to make them believe they are one. Pain seems to accomplish that best. Inside the net, when one creature experiences pain and struggles against it, the other is jerked about and suffers as well. When one shrieks the other does too, if only to stem the ringing in its own ears. We shall punish them equally, making them both hate us, giving them a common purpose—our destruction. But, of course, they're bound together and immobile, so we also heighten their shared sense of frustration. I should think the real key will be mental, however. These are language-using beasts—which, by the way, means the finished dragon will probably speak! But it also means we can use our words to confound them, confuse them, and ultimately to convince them—convince it—that it is a single beast with a single purpose . . ."

"And that is?" Paumer asked expectantly.

"To destroy mankind wherever it might be found," Sheth finished, gloating.

They planned this morning for the horrible conditioning they would begin tomorrow upon the netted beasts. Seagryn sat slumped against a wall upon the cavern floor. His mind was on his own plan for Berillitha's escape. He could put it off no longer.

Paumer chuckled at Sheth's expression, and shook his head. "I can easily understand why you savor this so. Your hatred of your fellow beings is of legendary proportions."

"Now you're sounding like the priest here," Sheth said with undisguised contempt as he gestured down at Seagryn.

Paumer laughed again, enjoying the philosophical debate while apparently giving no thought to the incredible sufferings his actions here would dump upon the rest of humanity. "No, I'm not that. I'm a people-*lover*, Sheth. It's my hope your plan will finally bind us back together into one—"

"You don't love people, merchant!" Sheth interrupted with a savage glee. "You love nothing but *wealth*!"

Paumer's smiled tightened, but didn't entirely die. "No, now that's where you're wrong. You see I . . ."

The discussion continued, but Seagryn didn't listen. He'd already heard enough to force his hand.

"Tomorrow we begin, then," Sheth affirmed. Then he bent down to shout in Seagryn's ear, "Is that quite all right with you, wherever you are?"

"Tomorrow." Seagryn nodded. But by tomorrow, he and the tugoliths would be gone.

He forced a smile through his dinner with Elaryl—a tough piece of fried horse-flesh, since Sheth had now lost himself in his art and refused anymore to go meal-hunting. He watched her carefully, aware that she watched him the same way. Had he raised her suspicions with his smile? Were any of the others aware of his intentions? Did he wear his evening's purpose upon his face, proclaiming to all who might look there that he was going to free the tugoliths tonight? Most critically—was he going mad? For this was a maddening place, an endless night broken up by day-long intermissions in one's sleep, during which unconscionable things were planned by powerful people living like savages—and where even more horrendous things were done. Were they *all* mad, to congregate here together under the hill for the purpose of forging a scourge for mankind? And lest he forget while calling the roll of the irresponsibles—where was the Power in all these acts? Within this dungeon, the simple faith of Dark's mother seemed more childish than the pleadings of captive tugoliths—far more childish. And he wondered again— was this all in the Power's purpose? If so, what Kind of Power did Lamath serve?

There was no more time for reflection. Once Elaryl slept soundly, he forced himself to get up. One last longing gaze, then he tiptoed away through the cavern. The fires burned as brightly now as they did throughout the period they called day, and Seagryn felt totally exposed. He passed by the second fire in the natural cavern and followed the warm brook upstream to the dragon forge. He slipped inside it carefully, hoping the beasts would not make a stir when he woke them.

Berillitha wasn't asleep. "Wiser?"

"Quiet, please. I've come to set you free."

Her next question startled him. "Why?"

"Why? Because—it's right. It's—just."

"Just what?"

"Justice."

"Oh," Berillitha said. "What's justice?"

"Later. Can you quietly wake Vilanlitha?"

"I don't know." Berillitha frowned. "He has an ugly temper."

"Try to wake him quietly."

"I don't want to," the tugolith told him honestly. "I don't like him."

"Wake him anyway. I've come to set you free."

"I told you not to interfere with me, Seagryn!" Sheth shouted from behind, and Seagryn whirled around in time to see a ball of fire shooting toward his head. He dodged to one side, hid himself within a magic cloak, and quickly came to grips with this new reality. The worst had happened. He'd been caught, and he'd seen enough of Sheth's power demonstrated to realize he'd never win a face-to-face encounter. Only one thing was important now, and that was to free Berillitha.

It would be an easy thing to cut the net—just a flick of the mental image that had set it in place, and its fabric would tear. But he would have to show himself to do it, and Sheth could probably counter him if it wasn't timed just—

Sheth penetrated his cloak and spotted him. This was in itself an act of shaping, meaning the other wizard's power wasn't focused at this moment on preserving the net. Seagryn showed himself, and willed the web to tear—

With a roar and a grunt, Berillitha and Vilanlitha came unstuck and tumbled free and a moment later both came charging down the tunnels. "This way!" Seagryn shouted as he leaped aside to let Berillitha fly past him toward one of the wooden walls that blocked the end of the passageway. "Stop them now!" he taunted Sheth, who instantly turned and looked at that same wall. Suddenly Berillitha swerved to avoid it, rushing around a corner and out of sight. Sheth had thrown some illusion, but Seagryn didn't wait around to discover what. He turned tugolith and chased after the charging female.

She had rushed into the main cavern and now charged around inside it just as Seagryn had watched the squirrel circle aimlessly through the mouse-dragon's cage. Paumer and Dark dodged aside on one side of the fire, then Berillitha was rumbling around to the other side and Elaryl and Uda were diving toward the walls. As Sheth appeared in the center of the cavern, Seagryn charged the only wooden barrier in this room.

It splintered on his impact, and his tugolith voice shouted, "Berillitha! Through here!" As he pulled up alongside it, she rumbled past him into a room Sheth had never showed him, and he watched with satisfaction as she demolished its contents on her way to destroying another barrier that blocked its far side. Seagryn saw nothing beyond this one but darkness. "I hope that's the right direction," he said, more to himself than to her. Then he suddenly felt a terrible burning cold surrounding him and freezing him into place. "So this," he murmured, "is what the net feels like."

Elaryl rushed up to him and grabbed him around the foreleg. He peered down into her stricken face as he heard Paumer shout, "The female! She's getting away!"

He couldn't see Sheth, for the powershaper was behind him. He heard him, however. "No matter," the wizard announced calmly. "Vilanlitha's still here, and we have Seagryn. We'll start the process tomorrow—just as we'd planned."

Chapter Thirty-one

✻✻✻

SACRIFICES

"**W**HAT harm will it do to *ask* him?" Uda argued.

Elaryl frowned, and glanced through the fire at Dark. The boy sat cross-legged against the far wall, his gaze focused on the heart of the blaze. He propped his elbows on his knees and his chin in his cupped hands and just sat there, staring. She quickly looked away. "What's he *doing*?" she asked Uda.

The younger girl turned to look across the cavern with knowing eyes. She'd spent enough time with Dark now that she thought she understood him. "He's waiting."

"For what?"

"For you, probably. He knows we're over here discussing whether or not to talk to him, and he's waiting."

Elaryl shook her head. "He's—such a—pardon me, Uda, but he's so odd! He's just sat there for days! He never talks—he never smiles. He did nothing to help Seagryn escape, and they're supposed to be friends. Why should he want to help him now?"

"Because he does." Uda shrugged. "Look, it's really very simple. He knows what he will do, because it's as if he's already done it. He lives in the future, you could say. Seagryn didn't ask for help. Dark knew he wouldn't. Seagryn's trapped now. Dark knew he would be—"

"He told you that?"

"No, he never tells me anything," Uda grumbled.

"Then how do you know he knew?" Elaryl asked skeptically.

"By his eyes. They never show surprise. Believe me, he al-

270

ready knows what will happen to Seagryn. And what's the harm in asking?''

Elaryl pulled down the hem of her skirt. She'd never in her life worn such rags. She would never forgive herself for ignoring her father's warnings and coming along on this hellish adventure. He had known! But that was the trouble. Her father had always known what was best for her and had always forced her to do it. If he'd only allowed her a little freedom in deciding for herself what was best for her before all of this began—

"Go ahead, Elaryl. Ask him now, before my father and that terrible bear-person web Seagryn and Vilanlitha together."

Elaryl looked again at Dark, and saw he was now staring at her. This was just a little boy, he had no right to be so all-knowing! She put her head in her hands and rubbed her forehead as she thought about Seagryn.

He didn't seem to be bothered by his situation. In the few hours he'd been awake since Sheth had netted him, he'd raved like a madman about the value of self-sacrifice and the justice he'd done. But this wasn't justice, was it? To trade a lifetime of promise for the freedom of a very large, very stupid piglike creature? From what he'd told her about tugoliths during their journey, the poor beast couldn't even return to her family. She would die probably, lost somewhere in these Marwilds, and what would be the point? If she could just talk to the creature, make her understand what was at stake and—

"Why don't you go ahead?"

Elaryl whirled around to stare up at Dark. "Why did you creep up on me like that!" she demanded.

"He didn't creep up," said Uda. "I waved at him to come over here."

"Go ahead," Dark said again. "Do it."

"Do what?" Elaryl snapped. She did not like this boy. He was just too pushy. But then, so was Uda. And so was her father, for that matter. That was one thing she appreciated about Seagryn—he didn't push, he didn't prod, he didn't try to order her around. And in the next few days they were going to turn him into a dragon—

"Go talk to Berillitha. She's close by, you know. She didn't go far."

Elaryl frowned at him. "How do you know that?"

Dark blushed, and looked at Uda, who answered for him. "He's Dark, remember?"

Elaryl looked at her fingernails. They were broken from her constant chewing of them. "What—would I say to her?"

"What you think."

"She'll probably eat me."

"No," Dark said firmly. "She won't eat you."

"You can guarantee that?" Dark nodded. "Where is she?"

"Just beyond that last wooden wall Seagryn broke down."

"Why? She couldn't find her way out?"

"She didn't try. He didn't tell her to, and she won't do anything he doesn't directly command."

Elaryl looked at Uda. "Why are you doing this?"

The girl shrugged. "I have my reasons."

Elaryl thought she knew. "You just want to spite your father."

Uda shook her head. "That's not true. The dragon will be made in any case, so I'm not spoiling my father's scheme. I just can't bear to see such a valuable resource as a powershaper go to waste. If I can play some role in preventing Seagryn's destruction now, I figure perhaps he can be of help to me someday."

Elaryl nodded absently. She'd not really intended her question to be answered. She realized she was just stalling. Dark and Uda waited for her response. "Do I just—walk out there and call her name?"

Dark stepped aside as he answered, "That would be a good start . . ."

Elaryl got up off her rock, looked back and forth between her two child advisors, then walked toward the cavern where Seagryn stood frozen in magic. He was asleep again—she'd gathered from some comment Sheth had made that the net had that effect, but Seagryn told her he'd been feeling too guilty to sleep lately and that now he was free to catch up. She walked by him, trying to ignore his tugolith odor as she passed on through the demolished rooms.

She saw nothing but blackness beyond the last shattered wall, and she hesitated. She was no heroine! What if Sheth should be watching her this very moment? She remembered how her childhood friends had dreamed aloud of questing for dangers. She'd not been interested in any of that boyish foolishness. She'd never wanted adventure—just to be joined at the feet to some wonderful husband who would love her and take care of her and let her do what she liked. As she stared around this dark cavern, a step away from utter darkness, she marveled again at how the One they never named could have so miscast her. But in her hesitant survey, she looked back over her shoulder, and there was Seagryn, asleep standing up in the form of a beast, a peaceful smile on his great dumb face. It was that expression that drove her out into the dark.

"Why didn't I bring a torch," she muttered. "I'll have to go back and get one."

"Will the Wiser come soon?" a voice said behind her, and Elaryl whirled to face the sound, her heart pounding, her breath coming in short gasps.

"What?" she managed at last to force out.

"Why does the Wiser wait?"

"Berillitha?" Elaryl whispered. Dark was right. She hadn't gone far at all! "That is you, isn't it?"

"I am Berillitha," the tugolith said sadly. She couldn't be seen, but evidently she'd wedged herself in between the tunnel wall and the one part of the wooden barrier still standing. "You are the Wiser's pair."

"I—yes," Elaryl whispered. This was too close to the bear's lair! She felt certain Sheth stood somewhere nearby, listening to every word—

"Why do you leave him?" the tugolith asked.

Was she being scolded? Elaryl wondered. "When? You mean now? I came to look for you!"

"I would never leave my pair," Berillitha announced.

This time Elaryl heard with certainty the chiding tone, and it made her angry, for she realized suddenly why the tugolith had waited here in the darkness instead of escaping. Berillitha still felt paired to Seagryn. Absurd as it was, that still stirred Elaryl's jealousy. "If he's your pair, why didn't you do what he told you to do?"

The beast was silent a moment, then asked, "What did the Wiser say?"

"He told you to—"

Elaryl stopped herself. This had all just become very clear to her. She was, after all, the true pair to the "Wiser." This tugolith knew that. Could she not also give instructions for the Wiser? For example, to tell this great hunk of flesh to get herself back into the cavern and volunteer to become a dragon? She could. She certainly could.

But she didn't. "He told you to run away," Elaryl said flatly. "That was his purpose in freeing you. Are you too stupid to see that? Are you going to waste his sacrifice by just standing there?"

There was another long pause. Elaryl assumed the beast was

filtering all those words, and reminded herself that she needed to calm down and speak slowly and simply.

"The Wiser—set me free?"

"Yes."

"He—sends me away?"

Elaryl again said, "Yes," but a bit more compassionately this time. She heard something odd in the huge female's rumbling voice. Was it—a whimper?

"I am truly a punt," Berillitha said quietly, and then moaned—a very slight, high-pitched moan for a creature so big, more like the whine of a pup. Elaryl put her hand over her mouth and waited. The back of her throat began to ache, and it surprised her. Was she really ready to weep in empathy with her enormous rival? "I hoped he would come. . . ." Berillitha explained, and again gave a keening wail. And Elaryl's question was answered for her. Yes, she would weep.

"He—he can't come." She sniffed.

"Why?" Berillitha asked, through what Elaryl could only assume were tugolith sobs.

"He's—trapped," Elaryl said, wiping her nose on her sleeve. Oh, how she hated crying! "The way you were, before he freed you." That brought a very different reaction from Berillitha, one that scared her so she jumped back against the far wall of the tunnel.

"The net that freezes and burns?" Berillitha roared.

"Yes!" Elaryl answered quickly in a loud whisper. "Quiet! Sheth will find us!"

"I'll horn him!" Berillitha trumpeted, and the tunnel shook from the sudden shuffling of her enormous feet.

"No! No! That won't work, don't you see? You can't horn a wizard; and besides, if you did Seagryn would stay like that forever!"

"Wizard?" Berillitha grunted. She sounded puzzled. "This evil punt is a Wiser?"

Elaryl understood. "I said wizard. Different thing. Listen to me," she said, and she waited until she was certain the animal was listening. "We both—" she took a deep breath and said it "—love Seagryn. I know of only one way to free him from that net." She paused.

"What is the one way," the tugolith intoned. Berillitha was not in the mood to waste time.

And yet Elaryl found it very difficult to go on. How could she ask this of anyone? She was about to ask this animal to sacrifice her life for—

"What is the one way!" Berillitha roared.

"Right, right, I'll tell you—" Elaryl whispered quickly. "We must go back into the light. We must find the evil—punt. And then you must . . ."

"I must be bound again. To that whiner punt. By the net that burns," Berillitha finished for her. "We go," she snorted, and the tugolith started back into the cavern.

"Wait!" Elaryl stopped her. "There's much more. They will—change you, Berillitha. They will make the two of you together into a—a dragon." She could see Berillitha's head now, dimly. She thought she saw one vast eye blink in confusion.

"What is a dragon?" the creature asked simply.

"It's—an enormous—monster, that flies—and— oh, I don't know." A bit belatedly she added, "I'm sorry."

The tugolith grunted. "Why?"

"Because—it's a terrible thing to be."

"Oh," Berillitha answered. Then she said, "No. A terrible thing to be is a punt. A terrible thing to be is out of the wheel. A terrible thing to be is watching your pair hurt. These things I understand." Once again the huge beast started to walk back into the dim light of the cavern, but stopped. "I have a question."

Elaryl could hardly answer. Her eyes swam with sorrow at the enormity of the tugolith's sacrifice. "Yes?" she choked out.

"Will I remember?"

Elaryl blinked. "What?"

"When I am a dragon."

"You mean, will you remember that you were once a—I . . . I don't know . . ."

Berillitha snorted thoughtfully. "I hope I do not remember." Then she shuffled back into the lighted section of the cavern, a very thankful Elaryl following behind.

Chapter Thirty-two

❈❈❈❈

THE BETTER HEAD

Seagryn slept a lot, and he dreamed. He dreamed of Bourne, of his mother and father, of school examinations and school pranks, of Elaryl—and of tugoliths. He smelled tugoliths in his sleep and for some reason felt more in common with dream tugoliths than he did with dream humans. He dreamed things about tugoliths he had never learned—much more of the way they thought, of their poetry—of their jokes! And he would sometimes wake up laughing . . . and discover again where he was, and remember what awaited him.

Elaryl was always there, now, waiting for him to waken, watching over him. And the time seemed to be stretching out—"He hasn't netted me to Vilanlitha yet?" he always asked, and Elaryl's reply was always the same.

"Don't rush him. Perhaps he'll forget how." Then she talked of other things, reminiscing with him about their courtship, fretting about his not eating. For although Seagryn could talk, and thus could surely eat if he'd wished to, he found he did not.

"I'm not hungry," he said and tried to shrug; but he couldn't move a muscle other than those in his face.

He felt remarkably content. Oh, he'd spent hours thinking how he might rescue himself and Elaryl from this predicament and carry her off to Lamath to live happily forever after, but he knew that wasn't going to happen. He'd tried some shaping, early on, and discovered it was impossible. Of course, he'd finally realized, for he was in his altershape, and no powershaper could do more than one thing at a time. He'd hoped that might mean his being netted would prevent Sheth from any shaping as well, but remembered that Sheth had fought him with wizardry while the two tugoliths remained fixed to one another. This, then, was a spell. Thus the priests of Lamath had been correct, and weird old Nebalath had, for his own reasons, lied. Seagryn assumed only Sheth himself could undo it—and he would not until he was ready.

Sometimes Seagryn woke to find Sheth grinning up at him, but the sorcerer never said anything. He only waited until Seagryn was fully awake, then went away laughing. And the time passed . . .

One person he greatly missed was Dark, and he asked about him frequently. "He's gone," Elaryl finally told him, but there was something in her voice that made him question that. He knew Paumer wasn't gone, for he heard the merchant's sugary voice on occasion, and he doubted Uda would leave without her father. And Uda surely wouldn't have allowed the youthful prophet to leave without her, would she?

He was dreaming of the Great Wheel, only now it stood in the middle of the city of Lamath, and all the assembled tugoliths wore clerical robes of ceremonial green. He was addressing them on the nature of the Power when a strange sense of gloom blew through the vast city square, and all the beasts turned their rumps to him and looked at the darkening clouds far to the south. And then he heard the scream—

"What was that!" Seagryn shouted, fully awake and terribly alarmed.

"It's nothing, go back to sleep!" Elaryl pleaded, but her expression seemed false and her reassurance too facile. When another shriek echoed through the bear's den she winced in surrender and turned away.

Seagryn had never heard a scream like that in his life, and it caused a tremor in his frozen intestines. That scream conveyed volumes of pain—inexpressible pain, the kind that comes with such intensity it instantly builds a sharp-edged monument to itself within the memory. It trumpeted rage, an anger freed by hatred to vent itself upon any available object—in this case any listener's ears. And it wailed with despair, the kind of desperation that remains to torment the sufferer with hope in the midst of an utterly hopeless situation.

Seagryn understood immediately, but he asked Elaryl anyway. "What is that?" He expected—and got—that hesitant look he realized now hid the truth and had been hiding the truth for days.

"It's—Vilanlitha. Isn't it horrible? Oh, Seagryn, I can't stand the thought of the same thing happening to you!"

"But it won't now. Will it?"

Elaryl gazed at him, her sweet expression beginning to sour as she saw her lies exposed. "No," she said defensively—or angrily. Why was she angry at him?

Another shriek grated through both of them like fingernails upon slate, and Seagryn found himself screaming back in sympathy. Elaryl clapped her hands over her ears and ran from him, stopping to look back once before dashing on out of the chamber. He'd seen her cheeks in that brief instant—they glistened wet in the ever-burning firelight. Then she was gone.

The tormented beast answered from the dragon forge, and Seagryn understood now how it could say so much with one scream. It gave vent to its feelings with two voices, powered by a pair of lungs each the size of a house. In horrible pain and horrible sorrow, the new-made dragon called to him, and Seagryn struggled to break loose of his net, even as he trumpeted his response.

"You can't do it by yourself!" someone behind him shouted, and he almost didn't hear it for the screams.

"Shut up! Would you shut him up?"

"You can't! But you do know how to let go!"

That had been Dark's voice! Seagryn stopped screaming and listened, but all he heard was a heavy thump and someone's answering grunt. "Dark!" he shouted, but the prophet's voice had been silenced.

Still, it had been enough. Had the boy known from the beginning of their friendship that it would be? Had he silently harbored that assurance throughout all their intervening conversations? It was enough, for Dark was right. Seagryn knew how to release himself to the power of the One he now named. "I don't know why I labor so, when I know better," he told the Power, and—as he'd done in the megasin's cave—he surrendered himself to that Power's shaping.

Peace came first, stilling his rage and funnelling it into resolve. Elation always came along with that, for any commitment to action empowered by that One brought with it tremendous potency. Seagryn could do what needed to be done, not by his own wisdom or strength, but by and through the Power. It didn't bear description. There was no time to think about it, nor to relish the feeling. Seagryn moved, the net broke free, and he sprinted down the corridors of the bear's den toward the source of the horrible screaming.

"Sheth!" someone behind him—probably Paumer—was warning as he sprinted into the dragon forge. "Seagryn's free!"

Seagryn saw the delight on Sheth's face just before the wizard whirled in alarm to look at him. Delight in his own creation? Or delight in the tormenting of it? For there was no question that Sheth had been tormenting the great dragon—which filled the entire tunnel. Seagryn stared at the twi-beast in shock, but had the presence of mind to distract Sheth first with a twist of his imagination. He'd set fire to the wizard's sandals—it proved to be simple but effective. As Sheth danced and cursed and Paumer came running into the dragon forge behind him, Seagryn gazed up into the frozen features of the two-headed dragon—and saw instantly which head had once been his pair.

"Berillitha," he said to the head on his left, and its eyes seemed to narrow in confusion.

"Do you address me?" that head wondered, perplexed.

The other head roared with frustration, "I am not a Berillitha! I am Vicia-Heinox!"

"No, I am," the once-Berillitha head said.

"That's what I said!" the other head screamed.

"And I agree."

They continued, but Seagryn listened no more. Sheth had doused his sandals and disappeared. Seagryn felt it best to do the same, and that left Paumer in the middle of the room shouting, "Sheth! Seagryn! Where are you both?"

Seagryn ran to a wall and crouched beside it, scanning the room for some sign of Sheth. He didn't think to try to penetrate, however, and obviously Sheth had, for he suddenly appeared two feet in front of Seagryn and took his bear shape, then slashed Seagryn across the face with a mighty swipe of his claw.

Seagryn took it across his horn instead of his nose; while it knocked his snout aside, it did no damage. He immediately dipped his head and horned upward, but Sheth was gone again, and Seagryn cloaked himself and ran to the other side of the tunnel as quietly as he could. His mind was swirling. What to do next?

Again Sheth was on him. This time flames engulfed his head and he nearly panicked. Instead, he jumped forward, grabbing Sheth with both arms and shoving his burning hair into his rival wizard's face. Sheth screamed and jumped backward, and Seagryn wished for water and found it flooding him. Thoroughly scorched, he ran a side-winding route through the dragon forge, looking for something he might use as a weapon. He'd not fought enough shaper battles to have a storehouse of stock responses. Human weapons he thought he understood.

He found he suddenly had gained another adversary. The mouse-dragon was loose, and it flew, squeaking fiercely, at his face. This terrified him more than Sheth's attacks, for suddenly he saw before him that bloody squirrel, and realized both mouselike heads were focused on his!

Seagryn ducked and disappeared at the same time, not certain that would help his cause at all. To his delight it did—the diminutive dragon shot right over his head. Seagryn leaped up and raced for the much larger dragon. In its attack, the twi-beast's tiny predecessor had given him a critical idea. He heard footsteps behind him and imagined Sheth wearing on his two feet that special double-footed shoe he and Elaryl had donned on the day of their wedding. A moment later he heard a heavy clump behind him, and Sheth's voice swearing in frustration. By that time he was already climbing the side of Vicia-Heinox.

He found it was easy to scale a dragon if he used the dragon's scales. He made his way quickly up a foreleg and onto the saddle between the twi-beast's humped back where its two necks joined its body. Then he stood up, dodged a ball of fire flung from below, and decided that the better head—the one who had been Berillitha—was atop the neck to his right. He climbed it.

This was not so easy. Although he was still cloaked, Sheth could see him clearly and kept tossing magical projectiles of all descriptions at him. Besides, each neck was spined with vicious, razor-edged scales. He was glad he climbed this dragon while it was still frozen by the net—he could imagine a far more treacherous climb if the twi-beast were mobile.

"What's that on my neck!" the better head shouted.

"I don't feel anything on my neck," the other replied.

"I do, too," the Berillitha head argued. "Can I look at my neck and see?"

"I see nothing," the other said petulantly. "Sometimes I think I am crazy," it added.

"And sometimes I know I am!" snarled its pair.

"You're right," Seagryn announced as he climbed onto the better head. "I mean about something being on you! I'm Seagryn, and I'm on you, and I'm going to release your net!"

He did. He had to dodge another fireball to do so, however,

this one thrown from ten feet in front of him. Immediately after tearing through the net Seagryn gasped in admiration at his adversary's daring. Sheth had grabbed hold of the mouse-dragon's legs and let the tiny twi-beast bear him all the way up to the cavern's roof. To Seagryn's great fortune, the little creature didn't have the necessary strength in his wings to keep both itself and Sheth aloft, and one of its heads darted down to nip Sheth on the arm. Seagryn heard the wizard yell as he fell, but he didn't watch. His eyes were studying the roof.

"Don't do it, Seagryn!" he heard Paumer shout from far below, and he wondered how the merchant knew already what he was contemplating. "It's not trained yet! Think of what you'll be releasing upon the world!"

Of course, he thought to himself. Dark must have told Paumer what would eventually happen—or perhaps he told Uda, and she told her father in confidence? It didn't matter. He had a task to perform, and he bent down to a dragon ear to begin it.

"Vicia-Heinox," he said, "you have power you may not yet realize."

"What?" the better head said. "Something is whispering in my ear—"

"I don't hear anything," the other head said doubtfully.

"Then by all means, allow me to shout!" Seagryn shouted.

"Ah! I do hear it."

"I told myself I did," the better head pouted.

"You must focus all your eyes upon the rock above you," Seagryn instructed with great authority. "Do it. Do it right now, before the one who hurt you recovers!"

That got the dragon's attention, and it raised both of its heads upward in response to his command.

"Now. You see the rock above you?"

"I see," both heads said in unison.

"Just—wish it out of existence!" he shouted.

"What?" the better head asked.

"I don't understand," the other said.

"I know I don't! Voice, could you explain?"

This had once been two tugoliths, Seagryn reminded himself. He needed to talk slowly and simply. "Don't you wish you could see the sky?"

Again, he struck a nerve. "Yes!" both heads said together, and they turned their eyes to the roof. There was a rumbling inside the cave, and a chunk of its roof suddenly turned to powder and drifted to the floor.

Sunlight! Bright blue sky! Some snow dropped into the cavern also, but what Seagryn longed for most was the sight of daylight. When he saw it he shouted for joy. "Fly!" he cried. "Fly through it!"

For the first time in history the twi-beast flew. They shot through the hole and straight up toward the clouds, with Seagryn fighting to keep from being shaken loose by his own giddy laughter. He rode upward, higher still, passing through a layer of fog, back out into the blue, then forward, gliding out past the cloud cover over an endless carpet of evergreens. Seagryn belatedly realized his own danger and he glanced down in concern. His breath caught in his throat, and he would have been hard-pressed to say if it was fear or wonder that choked him.

He flew above the old One Land and saw not a single border drawn anywhere upon the green and white map below. Winter still clung tenaciously to the land it had possessed so briefly, but the sun on Seagryn's back told him that spring's youthful energy would soon prevail. It had been too long since Seagryn had felt the sun, and he reveled in the promise of its warmth upon his back!

But this would be a different spring from any the One Land had ever experienced. As the dragon began to test his wings, screeching with a terrible excitement, Seagryn at last had a moment to reflect on the warning Paumer had shouted. The merchant had been right.

He rode upon the better head of a monster—not upon Berillitha's head, he realized, for Berillitha was gone. He could recognize some of her nature in this head's sensible eyes—it seemed a far different personality from that reflected in that other face across the way. But that was the point—this was no longer Berillitha at all, it was Vicia-Heinox, and he—yes, Seagryn felt compelled to view this twi-beast as a he—would be a terrible addition to the many ills of the world.

And yet—perhaps by its very horror the dragon would perform its intended function and unify the fragments once again. To that end, Vicia-Heinox needed to be recognized as wild—not *trained*. Paumer's training would have resulted in a dragon totally loyal to the red-and-blue, which would make the world subservient to its greedy master. And who could say what such a beast might become, under the watch and care of the evil Sheth . . .

So the twi-beast was free, to find its own destiny, and to shape the world as it would. Had this been the Power's purpose all along? Was this why he had been gifted—and Dark, and even Sheth? Seagryn still wondered. But since he didn't know, he decided to sit well back on this better head and enjoy what would certainly be the ride of his life. For, in the end, while he couldn't be certain this was right, it did feel a lot like justice.

Chapter Thirty-three

✖✖✖✖✖

BACK ON KERL

"**Y**OU'RE sure he's coming?" Elaryl pleaded again.

As he had the last five times she'd asked him that question, Dark ignored her. He just gazed quietly at that spot on the far side of the snow-covered meadow where he'd remembered Seagryn would appear and waited.

"But how did he get down?" she begged again.

Dark sighed. "Elaryl—dear lady—he's coming. When he arrives, I'll depart from this place and leave you with him, and you can ask him all the questions about his dragon ride you wish to ask. He'll describe it at length, in marvelous detail. So why should I spoil it?"

"What's taking him so long!" she demanded, stamping her foot in the melting snow and splattering slush up onto Dark's gown. "Sorry . . ."

"As I told you before—he's riding on Kerl. You remember Kerl? Isn't that enough to answer your—"

He didn't finish the sentence, for Elaryl had left his side. She sprinted with shrieks of unfettered joy across the clearing toward the rider of a stolid gray horse that had just that instant walked out of the woods. Dark watched without surprise as Seagryn tumbled from Kerl's back in excitement, then picked himself up out of the snow and ran to grab Elaryl around the legs and lift her above him. Then he turned to look elsewhere as they kissed. After what he thought was a proper interval, he turned back around and walked toward them.

"I knew you would meet me somewhere!" Seagryn was shouting. "I knew if I just kept Kerl plodding onward, we would meet you somewhere along the way!"

"But how did you get *down*?" Elaryl demanded gleefully, squeezing his head tightly to her breast. When he managed to get his head free, Seagryn laughed aloud and told her.

"I talked it into landing! That wasn't easy of course—the two heads were bickering with one another all the time we were aloft, and whenever I managed to get one head listening to me the other just seemed to take offense. It was the beast's first flight, of course, and it was none too steady on its wings, so I suggested it—he—" Seagryn corrected himself a bit sadly. "—should land for a moment and try to get the movements of its—his—wings coordinated. That was almost a disaster in itself, since the dragon had never landed before, either! When he touched the ground, his heads were arguing over what to do next, and he didn't start moving his feet, so we turned heads-over-tail along through the snow for a moment before finally skidding to a stop—"

"And you weren't *killed*?" Elaryl demanded—rather unnecessarily given the circumstances, Dark noted, but he didn't interrupt.

"I took my tugolith shape and bounced away." Seagryn grinned at her. "I got a few bumps and bruises, of course, but that body can surely withstand injury!"

"Which bodes ill for the eventual destruction of the twi-beast, who was made from such," Dark thought to himself, but still he didn't interrupt. It was too happy a moment for this couple he loved.

"I immediately cloaked myself and ran away, not certain *what* the dragon might do to me if he caught me on the ground. I got as far away as I could as quickly as I could, and was deep into the trees when I heard a screech and saw the thing take to the air again. He was flying much better this time—" Seagryn said this reflectively, turning his eyes to the sky as if he saw the vision again. Elaryl kissed him hard to bring him back to the present, and he laughed and finished his tale.

"I had no idea where I was—Elaryl, you can't tell anything about this world down here when you're up in the sky! It—it looks like—a toy!"

"The Power's toy?" Dark mused. "Sorry," he added in his mind, in case that One might be listening in . . .

"As it turned out, I wasn't far from that last Paumer House

mansion we stayed in, and I knew old Kerl here was waiting in the stable. I cloaked myself and went in and spent the night. The next morning I got Kerl and we started this way! What about you? How did you get out of the bear's den?''

"Oh, there's not much left of the bear's den I'm afraid," Elaryl said with mock sadness. "Much of it collapsed inward. After Sheth screamed curses at you for a few moments, he disappeared. Paumer was furious, and he and his daughter had a terrible shouting match in the rubble. Poor Dark here had been knocked unconscious. By the time I got him awake again, Uda and her father were already packing up to leave. We had no horses of course, and Paumer is still terrified about meeting more Arlian soldiers, so we had a long debate over what to do next. We finally decided to sleep there one more night and start walking the next day—but Dark woke me up in the middle of the night and said we had to leave right then to come and meet you here!'' Elaryl's beautiful smile spread all across her face. "I didn't argue!" She grabbed him tightly again, and Dark waited patiently for the question he knew would come next.

"Where are they now?" Seagryn asked him.

"They're several hours behind us.'' He shrugged, then added, "They'll be very angry when they arrive.''

"Then we won't be here!''

"You won't, no.''

Seagryn frowned. "Meaning you will?''

"Meaning I will.'' Dark nodded, and Seagryn looked at him with concern. "And no, you can't change my mind—because—it's not mine to change. As you know.'' He smiled a brave smile then, and gestured northward. "Go on. Get on Kerl's back and ride—he's carried you both before. Cloak yourselves. Go back to Lamath—and live!''

Seagryn studied Dark's face, wondering, pondering—choosing. But Dark already knew what the powershaper would decide. He wouldn't ask. Seagryn knew better. Instead, he released Elaryl just long enough to grab the boy and hug him, hard. Then he stepped back, nodded, and murmured, "Well. Then this is it.''

"Yes," Dark said emphatically. "This is it. Good-bye Seagryn. Good-bye Elaryl.'' He leaned around them and waved at the horse. "Good-bye Kerl,'' he shouted.

Kerl, of course, said nothing.

The three of them laughed, hugged once more, and broke apart. Seagryn put his arm around his wife and led her back to the gray horse that still stood rooted in the place where he had tumbled off.

"I can't believe it's over," Dark heard Elaryl murmuring in relief, and he quickly turned his back lest they should see his expression—and know better.

"Let them believe it for a little while, at least," he whispered quietly to the Power. He wished he could, but Dark already saw a screaming dragon circling in the air above a city on fire, and . . .

"But why think of that now?" he asked himself as he set off briskly through the melting snow to meet Paumer and his furious lady. He would have to face Uda today and he might as well get it over with.

GLOSSARY

altershape—The animal shape taken by a wizard when he or she so chooses. The animal-form taken reveals something of the wizard's personality or desires.

Amyryth—The affectionate mother of Dark the Prophet—his "s'mother."

Arl—A warlike state located in the mountainous region southwest of the Central Gate. Its capital sits upon a promontory in the Arl Lake.

Bearsbane—A title given to anyone who has slain a bear.

Berillitha—A female tugolith met by Seagryn in the far north.

Chaom—Leading warrior of the army of Haranamous and chief military advisor to Haran. He is a large, careful man not given to revealing his feelings.

clawsp—A glossy purple-shelled flying social insect that loves sugar and exudes a substance harmful to human flesh whenever aroused.

Dark the prophet—An adolescent with a gift of foreknowledge so exact that his name is already legend. Other than that he's a normal youth.

Drax—A three-sided table game played throughout the old One Land, usually with wagers on the outcome.

Elaryl—Blond bride of Seagryn and daughter to Talarath. She is well-meaning, naïve, and a bit prudish, in addition to being very lovely.

Gadolitha—Berillitha's twin brother. A protective, somewhat bad-tempered tugolith.

Garney—The small, self-important Keeper of the Outer Portal for the old One Land, or Remnant. He is single-minded in his sense of duty.

Haran—King of the land of Haranamous, which bears a part of his name.

Haranamous—A coastal state rich in culture and farmland located south of the Central Gate and bordered by Pleclypsa and—unfortunately—by Arl.

Imperial House of Haranamous—The royal palace of the dynasty of Haran, brought to life centuries earlier by the wizard Nobalog.

Jarnel—Prince of the Army of Arl and a representative to the "Conspiracy" from that warlike state.

Karmelad—Secretive advisor to the paranoid King of Arl.

Kerl—A stolid, stalwart, gray horse who comes to mean much to Seagryn.

Lamath—"Land of faith," the large coastal land located north of the Central Gate ruled as a theocracy by the Council of Elders.

lesefs—Small, shaggy animals that live in burrows in the snow. They balloon up when excited or alarmed. Their blood is caustic to other animals.

Marwand—A non-state composed of bands of fierce, independent warriors battling Arl or raiding into Lamath. It has no borders but roughly occupies the Marwilds.

Marwilds—A vast, sparsely settled forest land to the west of the Central Gate occupied primarily by Marwandian raiders and wizards.

megasin—An ancient power who can shape rock with her will and who craves human companionship.

Merritt—Conspiring second-in-command to Jarnel.

moosers—Hooved herd animals domesticated to provide meat and milk.

mudgecurdle—A furry creature looking just like a rabbit but ejecting a horrible stench when startled. Also an epithet meaning traitor.

Nebalath—A thin-faced wizard of some years who has long been the covering powershaper for the land of Haranamous, and is a friend to the Imperial House.

Nobalog—A long-dead wizard who brought the Imperial House to life and taught it to converse with wizards.

Ognadzu—Hostile son of Paumer, recently made a representative to the "Conspiracy" from Pleclypsa by his father.

Paumer—The most successful merchant in all the fragments of the old One Land, he is an organizer of the "Conspiracy" and a representative to it from Pleclypsa.

Pleclypsa—A warm, sunny land to the south of Haranamous, bordered on three sides by the sea and populated by merchant-types.

powershaper—Anyone gifted with the ability to shape the powers, but classically only one who, among other talents, can change into an altershape.

pyralu—Enormous, deadly insect taken as the symbol of the Army of Arl.

Quirl mod Kit—Leader of a band of Marwandian raiders living in the Marwilds on the edge of Lamath.

Rangsfield Sluice—A man-made feature of the Great River built by inhabitants of the village of Rangsfield to preserve their economic stability.

Ranoth—Wise, diminutive leader of the Council of Elders, the ruling body of the land of Lamath.

the Remnant—Name of the underground kingdom which maintains the ancient dynasty of the old One Land.

Ritaven—A pleasant village on the eastern edge of the Marwilds.

Seagryn—A cleric of the land of Lamath with a formidable personal problem.

Sheth—The foremost wizard of his time. He is secretive, charming when he chooses to be, irresponsible for all his great talent, and occasionally cannibalistic. His altershape is a huge black bear.

Talarath—Tall, dour member of the Council of Elders of the land of Lamath, and father to Elaryl. A difficult man to please.

tugoliths—Enormous horned creatures from the far north who can carry on human conversation at the level of toddlers; called "northbeasts" by the Marwandians.

Tunyial Falls—Vast waterfall that interrupts the navigability of the Great River between Arl Lake and the sea.

twi-beast—The name bestowed by Sheth upon the two-headed dragons he manufactures.

Uda—Youthful daughter of Paumer, she is bright, ambitious, and manipulative. She is also infatuated with Dark the prophet.

Vilanlitha—An arrogant punt, or lone tugolith, given by Paumer to his daughter Uda.

Wilker—Foppish, posturing bureaucrat within the Remnant. He bears the title of Undersecretary for Provincial Affairs and as such is a member of the "Conspiracy."

Yashilitha—An older tugolith, father of Berillitha and Gadolitha and head of their wheel.

Yost—A captain in the army of Haranamous.

✖✖✖✖

About the Author

Robert Don Hughes was born in Ventura, California, the son of a Baptist pastor. He grew up in Long Beach, and was educated in Redlands, Riverside, and Mill Valley, gaining degrees in theater arts and divinity. That education continued and he finished a Ph.D. in Missions, Religions, and Philosophy in Louisville, Kentucky.

He has been a pastor, a playwright, a teacher, a filmmaker, and a missionary, and considers all those roles fulfilling. Besides the *Pelmen the Powershaper* trilogy he has published several books of short plays, and presently teaches communication and mass media. His two passions are writing and football—not necessarily in that order, especially in October. He is married to Gail, a beautiful South Alabama woman who loves rainbows, and fills his life with them. They lived in Africa for several years where he did missionary work. They now live in Louisville, Kentucky, with their daughter Bronwynn, who was born in Africa.

Most of all, Bob likes people. The infinite variety of personalities and opinions makes life interesting. The sharing of faith makes it worthwhile.